DEVIL'S LILY

NIGHTSHADES
BOOK 1

ROSELYN ASH

SASHA LEONE

1

ELIRA

"No, Elira." My bodyguard, Dren, plants himself in front of me, arms spread wide as if he's trying to contain a wild animal. Which, honestly? Not far off. My heart's pounding a desperate drum of *freedom-freedom-freedom.*

I roll my eyes, mustering every ounce of princess-y disdain I can manage. Time for plan B—or as I like to call it, the old switcheroo. I spin on my heel, the picture of dejected obedience, shoulders slumped just enough to be convincing. *That's right. I'm going back to my room. Good obedient Elira.*

Three, two, one...

The second I sense Dren's guard dropping, I whirl back around and duck under his arms, darting past him like a rabbit escaping a cage. The marble floors of our mansion-slash-prison are cold under my feet as I sprint away, my red curls a wild corona around my face.

"*Elira!*" Dren's voice cracks with that edge of panic I've heard too many times before. But I don't listen. I'm done listening to what I'm supposed to and not supposed to do. At least for today.

Because it's my twenty-first birthday, for crying out loud. I'm an adult now, not the helpless girl I was ten years ago. If I can't taste freedom today, then when?

You're the princess, El. You need to be kept safe from our enemies. My brother, Roan's voice echoes in my head like it always does when I'm about to rebel against our father's dictatorship. But this time, I don't listen to it either. It wasn't my fault what happened all those years ago, so why should I keep paying for it?

I make it halfway down the hall before it dawns on me—wait... no footsteps? Skidding to a stop, I glance back to see Dren standing where I left him, arms crossed, face set in an expression that screams *I'm too old for this shit*. The sight makes me grin; he looks so done with my antics.

"Well?" I call back, pushing my red curls out of my face. "Are you coming with me or not?"

"Your father is going to kill us both," he mutters under his breath, but he starts walking towards me anyway.

"Probably," I agree cheerfully, already heading for the sweeping staircase that leads to my *atë*'s office. "But think how boring your day would've been otherwise!"

I bounce down the steps, sliding a little on the polished marble, the thrill of rebellion making me giddy. Yet, as I near the office, the excitement gives way to a tightening knot in my stomach.

"What?!" *Atë*'s voice booms through the door as we approach, and I walk faster, pressing my ear to the wood to catch the voice replying in low Albanian. It's Gjon, his second-in-command.

"Unfortunately, Leonotti was at the harbor when our shipment arrived, and he had his men check through the container to make sure we weren't smuggling people in. That's when he came across the weapons."

"That son of a bitch." A violent thud follows *Atë*'s curse, and I can almost see his fist hitting his desk. I shift against the frame, eager to hear every detail, and my gaze accidentally meets Dren's disapproving frown. I glance away wordlessly. I know I shouldn't be listening to this, but I'm so tired of being kept in the dark.

"He's refused my request for a meeting. He's not going to give in, Afrim. We need to do something drastic and—" Gjon trails off, and my interest piques. I lean closer, ear practically glued to the door now. Is he whispering? Why can't I—

The door suddenly yanks open, and I stumble forward with a very un-princess-like yelp. My hands flail out, trying to catch myself, but Gjon's iron grip clamps onto my wrist, hauling me upright before I can hit the floor. Ugh, not that I'm grateful; I'd rather face-plant than let him touch me.

Before I can complain, he's dragging me deeper into the office, sneering down at me, "Eavesdropping, *princess*?"

The way he says it makes my skin crawl. When Roan calls me that, it's wrapped in affection and love, so I don't mind it. But Gjon's tone is just pure mockery, and I hate it. I flatten my lips, raising my chin in that arrogant way I've noticed pisses people off, and stare down my nose at him.

"No. I simply wanted to talk to my *atë*. But you yanked the door open before I could knock. Why did you do that? What if I got hurt?" I frown in censure, satisfaction blooming as his eyes darken ominously.

"Let her go, Gjon," *Atë* says wearily. His green eyes meet mine, exhaustion etched in every line of his face. "What is it, Elira?"

Gjon releases me with a contemptuous scoff, and I shake my arm, fighting the urge to scrub at the skin where he touched me as I walk towards my *atë's* desk. The dark circles under his eyes make my heart clench. "Did you get enough sleep last night? What about your—"

"*Elira*." His sharp tone cuts me off before I can ask about his medication. His gaze flicks pointedly to our little audience.

"Gjon and I were in the middle of an important meeting. What's this about?"

Oh... He doesn't remember.

I blink back the sudden sting of tears, cursing myself for caring so much. Even Roan, who's currently somewhere in Long Island, remembered to send me a text. But my own father... who's *right here*? I inhale sharply and steel myself. "Today's my birthday. I want to go outside."

Behind me, Gjon practically chokes like I've just cursed out the gods. If I weren't fighting back tears, I might have enjoyed it more. But *let him choke.*

Atë's eyes narrow, but I don't miss the flash of contrition in them. "Happy birthday, angel," he finally says, and despite him forgetting, my heart lifts at the endearment. He studies my face with a little furrow between his brows before his gaze shifts over my head. "Take the jeep, Dren. Have Anton and three other men go with you."

Wait. What? I blink. Did he just...? *No freaking way*. Freedom—actual, beyond-the-compound freedom—just handed to me? A wide grin stretches across my face, and before I can stop myself, I'm circling the desk to throw my arms around him. "Thank you, thank you, thank you!"

He pats my back awkwardly, like he doesn't quite know what to do with the affection I'm throwing at him. When I pull away, something warm flickers in his eyes, but his gaze once again moves behind me, and the moment passes. That's just how he is. My father's not one to show affection or say sweet words, especially not in front of others. Because, in his world, any display of emotion might make him appear weak.

I don't really mind, though. I know he loves me, even if that love has become suffocating as I've grown older. His overbearing protectiveness and his reluctance to let me out of our compound—it's all rooted in love, twisted as it may be. Honestly, it's a miracle he even agreed to let me go out this easily today. I was ready to fight him, to manipulate him with my tears if I had to. But here we are—*he's actually saying yes*, and I'm so not about to question it.

I skip out of his office before he can change his mind and practically float up the stairs with anticipation rushing through my veins. In my room, I make a beeline for my closet and dive right in, pushing aside clothes like a treasure hunter searching for gold. Five years. It's been five freaking years since I've been beyond our compound's walls. Last time, I was sixteen on Roan's twenty-first birthday, when we snuck out for what was supposed to be a night of harmless fun. Instead, some idiot catcalled me, Roan broke his nose, and suddenly I was back to being Rapunzel in her tower.

Atë was so angry when he found out that he tightened the security around me even more, which is so unfair. Roan was the one who got into the fight, yet he didn't lose his outside privileges like I did—not that I had those privileges to start with. But after that, sneaking out became impossible.

Now, a taste of real freedom is finally within reach! Well, freedom with a five-man security detail, but hey, I'll take what I can get.

At last, I settle on a pair of black skinny jeans, a sleek camisole, and a leather jacket that screams badass. The finishing touch: the black leather boots Roan got me for Christmas, still spotless from only being worn around the house. *Time for you to see the real world, babies.*

I twirl in front of my full-length mirror, admiring the girl staring back. She looks dangerous, ready for anything. *Free.* One last glance, then I'm out of my walk-in closet, bouncing outside my bedroom where Dren is waiting for me by the door.

His usual stern expression softens just a fraction when he sees my barely contained joy. "That happy?"

A vigorous nod is all I can manage. Then with a giddy laugh, I dash outside and, unable to help myself, do a spontaneous little dance. A quick twirl, a few goofy steps—just because I can—before hopping into the back of one of the Range Rovers. My phone is already in hand, fingers flying to text Roan.

ME:

Guess who just got permission to live it up OUTSIDE on her twenty-first birthday? This girl!

I drop my phone face down onto the seat as I lean back and glance out the window during the long drive up to the tall gates of our compound. Roan's currently in Long Island on our paternal uncle's territory to learn how to better expand our hold here in Queens. I miss him so much it aches.

After the playground accident ten years ago—the one that cost Mama her life and made me a prisoner in my own home—my uncle and father had a huge falling out. Then two years later, we all moved out here, even though I always hear *Atë* murmuring about the Italians blocking his way, making everything hard for him.

But right now, none of that matters.

The gates slowly part, and my heart leaps into my throat. My face almost smashes against the window as the outside world unfolds before me. Our pristine, suburban neighborhood comes into view, looking bigger, brighter than I remember. The houses sit farther back from the road, each spaced out with pretty little gardens. A few even have gates, though none as imposing as ours. None as much of a prison. This... this is what freedom looks like. *Wow!*

"Where to, birthday girl?" Dren asks from the passenger side, his voice light but not fooling anyone with how tense he looks.

"Nowhere. Everywhere." I grin at him, my mind racing with possibilities. "I want to see it all—downtown Flushing where

I've read everything seems to happen at once, Forest Hills, Astoria. Heck, let's leave Queens in the dust and hit Manhattan or Brooklyn!"

I'm finally outside, and knowing my father, this might be my one shot for the next five years, so I'm set on exploring every inch of this city and beyond. A bitter laugh suddenly bubbles up. Funny how my name literally means freedom, but I've never been free.

Anton and Dren share a look, clearly thinking I've lost my mind. Typical. With an exaggerated eye roll, I say, "Park the car."

Dren's head whips around, his eyes wide like I've just asked him to hijack a plane. Actually, he'd probably freak out less about that. "What?"

A second eye roll threatens to surface, but I stifle it. They need to get it together. I'm serious about this, damn it. "You heard me. Park the car, Anton. I want to drive."

Anton's gaze meets mine in the rearview mirror, and for a moment, I think he's about to tell me no. But then he pulls over, and I try not to bounce in excitement as I slip into the driver's seat. Victory! I make a point to ignore the identical blacked-out Range Rover slowing down behind us. The rest of my entourage are there. But whatever. Let them follow. I'm *outside*. And now I'm *driving*.

The seat, mirrors—everything needs adjusting, of course. I huff under my breath about ridiculously tall men as I fiddle with every lever, button, and knob, shifting things until they feel just right.

Then comes the best part. I twist the key, and as the engine purrs to life, so does something wild inside me. Slowly, I pull away from the curb, wiggling and giggling in my seat like a crackhead. Roan would get a kick out of this. *I love him so much.*

A silent thank you goes out to him for all those secret driving lessons in the compound. If it were left up to *Atë*, I'd be completely clueless about half the stuff I know. But Roan refused to let our father's rules hold me back. He taught me how to drive, how to fight, how to hotwire a car, shoot a gun—*yeah, don't tell anyone that part*—and basically a lot of other things that would make *Atë* lose his mind to find out about. Roan's not just my brother, he's my best friend. My partner in crime.

Damn, I wish he were here.

But there's no time to dwell. I shake myself off before my excitement can fade and press down on the gas, laughing maniacally when Dren's hand shoots up to the handlebar above his window, white-knuckled. Behind me, Anton starts muttering what sounds suspiciously like a prayer.

Their sheer terror only feeds the adrenaline surging through me, and I slam the pedal down harder as we hit a stretch of open road with no traffic.

I don't know these streets, since I've only ever driven around our compound, so I let instinct guide me for the first hour, zipping through street after street until they blur together. I'm pretty sure I've turned us around a few times, but who's keeping track? Every new road is an adventure.

Eventually, I slow down to take in the bustling sidewalks and the various buildings clustered together. So many people, all going about their lives. Free to go wherever they want. *Must be nice.*

"You wanted to go to Flushing? Welcome to Flushing," Anton says dryly from the backseat.

I drink in the streets with fresh eyes. So *this* is Flushing. I glance at the blend of modern and older historic buildings, glass-frosted malls, and the mishmash of commercial buildings. It's chaotic, alive, and it hits me all at once. My heart swells. *I love it.*

Rolling down the window at a red light, I stick my head out, letting the city air—exhaust fumes, cigarette smoke, and who knows what else—fill my lungs. "Everybody, it's my birthday!"

"For Christ's sake, Elira," Dren groans like I'm giving him an ulcer, but whatever. Somebody on the street yells at me to shut the fuck up, another flips me off, while everyone else simply keeps moving, heads down, too caught up in their own worlds to care about some crazy redhead yelling about her birthday. My grin threatens to split my face as I bounce in my seat. Best. Day. Ever.

I take a few more turns until we find ourselves in a quieter neighborhood. The energy shifts immediately. Anton goes rigid behind me, and from my peripheral, I catch Dren's hand sliding into his jacket, where I know his gun is. I frown at him, then promptly put it out of my mind as I observe the street. The buildings here are newer, and with that understated elegance that screams money—or rather whispers, 'we're rich but pretending not to be'.

My stomach lets out an angry growl, reminding me it's been way too long since breakfast, and I glance at the dashboard. 12:18 PM.

Oh no. I'm starving, but this looks like a residential area. Not exactly brimming with places to—wait. *There.* Just up ahead, a brownstone building catches my eye. Four stories tall, with deep blue awnings over the glass windows, pretty black railings, and most importantly, the unmistakable sign of a restaurant.

Mughetto's. Next to the name is a picture of a pretty flower with numerous white bell-shaped bulbs drooping down from its green stem: *lily of the valley.* I smirk, feeling way too proud of myself for recognizing it, all thanks to that random botanical book I flipped through in the library when I was bored a few months ago. Who knew it would actually come in handy!

I slow down, scanning for a parking spot, but after a

minute, I just give up and pull right in front of the restaurant. Twisting the key in the ignition, I shut off the engine.

"Elira, no. Let's go somewhere else," Dren says, his voice edged with warning. "Start the car. Now."

I give him a long look, then glance back at Anton, who also seems fidgety. What's with these two?

"No," I say firmly. "You can't tell me no today, Dren. *Atë* gave his permission for this excursion, so unless you have a good reason, if I want to eat some pizza or pasta at this lily-of-the-valley restaurant, that's exactly what I'm going to do."

I wait, but he only grinds his jaw in silence. So, with a decisive nod, I pop open my door and step out. A chorus of doors follows as my security team reluctantly falls in line.

"Elira, please you have to—" Dren's protest dies when I push open the restaurant's glass door. Chin up, I strut right in to the sound of cursing behind me. Part of me wants to know what has him so spooked, but a bigger part is tired of always being told what to do, where to go, how to live. He can't just say 'you can't go in there' without giving me a real reason—and I doubt he has one that would stop me today.

The interior is stunning—just as gorgeous as the outside promised. Gleaming hardwood floors, soft brown walls adorned with more lily of the valley paintings, and immaculate wooden tables paired with cushioned chairs. Classy. Elegant. My stomach rumbles in approval.

However, it's also empty.

Well, almost.

I go still as my gaze meets those of about eight or so muscular men sitting around a large table at the back. *Oh.* Their surprise mirrors my own, and as one, they rise to their feet.

All except one.

The man still seated raises one strong masculine hand, fingers crooked in what must be some sort of silent command.

Instantly, the others sit back down, though they remain tense, eyes pinned on me like predators watching prey. But do I feel like prey? Hardly. *I feel more like the one on the hunt.*

Because I can't tear my gaze off *him*, the one obviously in charge. My throat dries up, and I almost swallow my tongue. Sweet Mary, Joseph, and baby Jesus. That's a face that's broken many hearts—and probably a few bones too.

Hair black as midnight is cropped close to his nape and ruthlessly smoothed back from his temples, leaving nothing to distract from that carved-from-stone face. Total Greek god vibes. Chiseled jawline, sharp nose, full lips that should come with a warning label, and eyes—dark, intense, dripping with sin. He's the full package. And though he's currently sitting, I can tell he's tall. The navy suit shirt he's wearing, minus the jacket, stretches across the muscular frame of his broad chest and thick arms like it was created specifically for him. His tie is neatly knotted, but the sleeves of his shirt are rolled up, revealing a smattering of tattoos climbing up from his wrist. Yeah, he's a walking contradiction of polished and raw.

He leans back in his seat, all casual, those dark eyes doing their own assessment of me, and even if I hadn't just seen him command eight men without a single word, the power rolling off him is impossible to miss. It's almost electric—buzzing, alive, filling every inch of space around him.

Actually, now that I think about it, he's the opposite of me in every way. Not that I'm ugly, far from it, but I mean the features. Where I'm pale, he's blessed with tanned skin, and where I barely have any control over my own life, he's clearly the master of his domain and everyone in it. That combined with his devastating handsome looks sets every nerve in my body tingling.

As I watch, he lifts a tumbler of deep brown liquid—whiskey, if I had to guess—at me in a silent cheer before taking a slow sip.

Heat infuses my body, from the tips of my toes to the top of my head, sending my heart into a wild drumbeat as I walk deeper into the restaurant and slide into one of the many empty seats. Behind me, the familiar shuffle of boots signals my guards filing in, surrounding me in their usual protective formation.

My handsome guy's gaze flickers to them, and for a fraction of a second, I catch the briefest flash of something crossing his too-calm face. Annoyance? Recognition? Whatever it is, his expression smooths out so quickly it's almost like I imagined it. Almost.

Ohh, but that tiny crack in his armor... *I love it.*

When his dark, smoldering eyes return to mine, a delicious thrill zips through me.

My twenty-first birthday just got a whole lot more exciting.

2

MAXIMO

The moment she waltzes into my restaurant, time grinds to a fucking halt. I've seen thousands of people walk through that door—criminals, cops, politicians—but never anyone like her.

The tension at my table spikes as my men and I watch this little slip of a woman with fire-engine red hair slide into one of the tables. Her curls tumble down her shoulders in wild spirals, untamed and vibrant like a cascade of flames.

It's not just that she's gorgeous—though she is. Maybe the most beautiful thing I've laid eyes on in my long, jaded life. *And trust me, I've seen plenty*. But no, what really draws me in is the defiant tilt of her chin, the stubborn furrow of her brow. She has an energy that demands attention, even as she seems completely oblivious to it.

I can practically *smell* her innocence from here—sweet and tempting as forbidden fruit. It's in the way she moves, in the openness of her expression. This is someone life hasn't taught a lesson. Not even close. In my line of work, you learn to read people fast—it's how you stay alive. But this girl... her thoughts play out on her face like a fucking book. Her wide-eyed pleasure when she took in my restaurant. The flash of surprise when my men got up. And finally, that spark of curiosity when her gaze landed on me. Everything about her is on full display.

For someone like me, who takes pride in my poker face, who knows the value of keeping your thoughts hidden, her transparency is both fascinating and worrying.

My gaze shifts to the men walking in behind her, and my own jump up again, hands moving to their concealed weapons. I don't recognize the five men who fan out around her in a protective stance, but they're obviously armed and professional. Guards. Expensive ones.

This only deepens my interest in her. Who could she possibly be to have this kind of security detail? And how, in the midst of what must be a dangerous life, has she maintained that childlike innocence that radiates from her?

"Stand down," I order quietly, and my men settle back into their seats. But I don't take my eyes off her for even a second. I twirl my glass of scotch as I study her every move. It should have sent alarms going off in my head. Shit, this is exactly the kind of distraction that gets people killed in my world. Instead, it just makes me want to look longer.

"Dante. Go ask her what she wants."

My second frowns at me—he's not used to playing waiter—but he knows better than to question me. As he starts to move, I add in soft Italian, "Hey. *Sii gentile.*" Be nice. His frown deepens, and I understand why. *Nice* is the last thing we are, the last thing we stand for. But something in me doesn't want to spook her, doesn't want to see that innocence shatter. *Yet.*

He gives me a reluctant nod, then continues on to her table.

The girl stiffens as Dante approaches, and her guards shift on instinct behind her. They're itching to move, but they know better than to do anything. The girl might not know where she's stumbled into or who I am, but I see the recognition dawn on her guards' faces. *Foolish things*. They should have stopped her from coming into my territory. Some lousy guards they are.

Dante stops in front of her table and says something. He must actually be following my order to *be* nice, because her face slowly lights up and her hands move animatedly while she answers. My chest expands, filling with an odd satisfaction, as I study her pretty face and the play of emotions on it.

Fascinating.

A few seconds later, Dante walks back to me, looking a little dazed, and my lips curl up in the corners. He's always so composed. Nothing ever rattles him. Until now, apparently. "Today's her twenty-first birthday," he reports. "She was taking a tour of the town when she saw our restaurant and decided to stop here to get a bite to eat."

Twenty-one. She's practically a baby. But fuck if that's going to stop me. She's a legal adult in front of the law, and that's all that matters—as Romero would say.

One of my men makes a choking sound. "A bite to eat?"

The others shift uncomfortably, and for damn good reason. Because *Mughetto* has never been a functioning restaurant—it's a front for our 'business', just like my office on Main Street, and everyone in town knows to stay the fuck away.

Everyone except this red-haired angel who just wandered into the devil's den, completely unaware.

Anyone with half a brain would feel the danger the second they step inside—see it in my men's icy glares and the not-so-subtle bulges of guns under their suits. But not her. She's looking around like she just strolled into fucking Disneyland.

As I watch her tuck a stray curl behind her ear, her face glowing with excitement at being here of all places, I make a decision that surprises even me.

"Which one of you can cook?" I ask, still glued to her, mesmerized by how she impatiently flicks another red curl back. I'm reluctant to take my eyes off her, but when no one answers, I finally turn my focus to my men. "*Well*?"

Silence stretches even more until Santino tentatively raises his hand. I snap my fingers at him. "Perfect. Go tell her the dishes you can cook and let her choose what she'd like."

"B–but… we don't have any ingredients."

"Then we'll get them. Whatever she wants."

Santino rises and shuffles over to her. And then it happens again. My little redhead tilts her head up to meet his gaze, and when she flashes him her smile, it's like the damn sun decides to show off just for her. My breath catches, and my pants tighten around the crotch. Fucking hell.

They speak for a few minutes, and then he comes back with the same dazed expression Dante had earlier. "She wants chicken soup, spaghetti alla carbonara, and calamari."

I eye my heavily tattooed ex-cage fighter with new interest. "You can make all that?"

The tips of his ears go red. "I can. Had to learn how to cook because I needed to monitor my diet while I was an active fighter," he mumbles defensively like I might mock him for this hidden talent.

Instead, I nod. "Good. Give Piero the list of ingredients so he can fetch what you need." After they leave, I turn to my remaining men. "The rest of you, go over there and sing her the birthday song."

They blanch. You'd think I'd just asked them to walk into enemy territory unarmed.

"With all due respect, Maximo, but I sound like a dying cat," Dante protests, and the rest murmur their agreements.

I level them with a hard stare, letting a hint of the danger I'm capable of seep into my voice. "Are you questioning a direct order?"

That gets them moving. They scramble to their feet and make their way to her table. Her guards immediately tense again, but my girl doesn't even flinch. She welcomes them with another breathtaking smile. Then, her eyes find mine across the room, and even from here, I can see the sparkle in them—

bright, beautiful, full of curiosity. Fuck, I can't wait to get close enough to see every fleck of color in them.

I give her a short nod, and she returns it, her smile somehow getting even bigger. That smile shoots right through my heart. Who the hell is this girl? And why am I reacting this way to her?

Then I catch it—her pupils dilating, her breath hitching. I'm not the only one attracted. She wants me too. *Good.*

Her lashes flutter shyly and her cheeks flush red; she breaks eye contact as my men stop awkwardly in front of her like they're about to humiliate themselves—which, let's face it, they are—but I'm enjoying every second of this little show. And it sure isn't the men I'm focused on.

She licks those full, luscious lips in anticipation, and my cock damn near rips through my pants. Dark, wicked urges ride me, making it a battle to keep seated. I want to play with her, please her, spoil her, turn her ass red to match her hair. Hell, I want to watch every emotion play like a reel on that expressive face as I treat her to my brand of ownership.

My men open their mouths, and *dear God...* The sound that follows can hardly be called singing—it's more like a chorus of croaky, off-key voices fumbling for harmony. But then her laughter bursts forth, making it all worthwhile. She throws her head back and releases a rich, throaty laugh that shakes through her. Her hair spills down her back, cascading in waves, exposing that delicate, pale curve of her throat.

Her happiness is so infectious, so unrestrained, I find myself smiling, completely caught up in her energy. I want more, more, more, *more*. More of her laugh. More of that smile. More of the way she lights up the room without even trying. It's intoxicating.

I take my phone out and text Fergio. Time to make some arrangements.

When Dante and the rest of my men finish their tone-deaf

performance and return to the table, they look disgustingly pleased with themselves despite their earlier reluctance. Whatever spell this girl has cast, it's affecting everyone around her after spending just a moment in her presence. *I want to experience her magic firsthand.* But I force myself to wait. Good things come to those who wait, after all—or so they say.

My attention drifts to her again. She's leaning back in her seat now, sighing softly. Her fingers absentmindedly play with the napkin on the table, eyes momentarily distant, as if some thought is running through her mind. Then, with a small shake of her head, she slides her phone out of her purse, and impossibly, her smile just *grows* as her fingers fly over the screen.

That better not be some guy.

My fists tighten as that possessive thought hits me. What the hell? I don't even know her name. Don't know a damn thing about her. Why should I care if she has a man?

Because she's *mine.*

The crazy notion flits through my head, and I don't fight it. I *embrace* it, eyes locked on my smiling little redhead who has no idea what kind of hornet's nest she just poked. The moment she stepped into my territory, she sealed her fate. I *will* have her. Whether it's for a night or a week remains to be determined.

Piero returns, arms full with ingredients, and Santino wastes no time getting to work in the kitchen. Not long after, Fergio arrives, buried under shopping bags. My girl watches him curiously as he drops the bags on the table in front of me.

Leaning in close, Fergio speaks low in my ear. "Your request was so vague, Mr. Leonotti, I wasn't sure what exactly you had in mind, so I brought everything I could think of."

I wave my hand, urging him to show me. Bag after bag, I sift through the goods with a smirk tugging at my lips. "Perfect."

I point at one particular shopping bag, which contains a luxury designer brand bag I assume might mean something to her, and have one of my men take it over as my birthday gift to her.

I watch closely as she tentatively accepts the shopping bag from him and peeks inside. Her brows furrow with a cute little frown, then she casts a glance at me before saying something to my guy and handing the bag back.

Well, that's not gonna fly.

Unsatisfied, I grab another shopping bag. She's clearly used to luxury, if her entourage and the cars she arrived in are any indication. So, what exactly *will* impress her?

As I settle on the sleek box housing a gold necklace, Santino emerges from the kitchen with the first dish. *Chicken soup.*

I tighten my grip on the box.

Let her eat first.

Afterwards, I'll shower her with more birthday gifts. Maybe with a full belly, she'll be more pliant and accepting of them. And once that's out of the way... well, then we can move on to more... pleasurable activities.

One way or another, this birthday girl is leaving with more than just a meal.

3

ELIRA

The expensive Gucci bag sent to me as a birthday gift fades from my mind as I lose myself in each heavenly bite of my meal brought to me by the chef himself—a strong, stocky man covered in tattoos who looks more like he belongs in a fight club than a kitchen. If I saw him in a dark alleyway at night, I'd run the other way screaming at the top of my lungs.

I'll admit, when he first introduced himself all hesitantly as the chef, I was a bit skeptical. But oh, how wrong I was! Each meal he places in front of me is more delicious than the last, and soon I'm practically licking the plates clean, my manners be damned.

This is truly the best birthday ever.

I'm floating on a cloud of pure bliss, high above the mundane world below.

Stopping at this restaurant was a stroke of genius—or was it fate? I don't know why it's empty of patrons when the food is this good, but I've come to like the quiet private atmosphere. It should be eerie, but instead, it feels intimate, special—like I've stumbled into a secret world where scary-looking men sing birthday songs and mysterious strangers send gifts.

Speaking of strangers... I know it's all because of *him*—the darkly handsome man who hasn't taken his eyes off me since I walked in. His gaze feels like a physical touch, making my skin tingle. But I soak up the attention nonetheless, loving every second of it even though I shouldn't. Atë would have a conniption if he knew.

As I twirl the last strands of perfectly cooked spaghetti around my fork, another man starts approaching me. I let out a little sigh, but it's tinged with an undeniable thrill of anticipation—he's holding another gift bag! I pretend to be all nonchalant, but my fingers are already itching to open it. What's it this time? Jewelry? Perfume? A tiara?

When he hands me the bag, I accept it just a bit too eagerly, barely containing my excitement. But then I frown as I peek inside—it's a small, elegant box. I hesitate. Something in my gut tells me its contents will make the designer bag from earlier look like a bargain bin find. Part of me says I should just hand it back without looking. That would be the smart thing to do.

Still, curiosity wins. I snap the lid open and... oh *wow*. The gasp that leaves my lips is completely involuntary. The necklace inside practically *shines,* scattering little sparks of light that make me squint, nearly blinding me with the bling. It's pure gold, delicately crafted with a two-step, almost bead-like design. It's stunning. It's perfect. *I love it.*

And I can't keep it. I really *can't*.

Regret floods through me as I run my fingers over the jewelry one last time. This insanely handsome man offering me expensive gifts is definitely not doing it out of the goodness of his heart. There are strings attached—there always are. And I'm in no position to get tangled up in anyone's strings, no matter how attractive the puppeteer might be.

Besides, there's this aura of danger around him that I didn't notice at first, but the longer I study him, the more I realize I don't want to be tangled with him. Even if part of me—the reckless, hungry part that's been locked away for so many years —desperately wants to know what it would feel like to be consumed by that danger.

With a heavy heart, I snap the lid closed and hand the box back to the waiting man, who accepts it with a resigned sigh and returns to his boss.

The stranger takes the rejection with an intriguing mix of amusement and determination. He runs a powerful hand down his chin as he watches me. Then, to my disbelief, he glances down at the selection of bags on his table, and I slowly shake my head, silently pleading. Surely, he's not going to choose something else?

But he *does*. His lips curl into a mischievous smirk that sends a jolt of electricity through my body as he hands another bag to the poor man who's now become his personal courier.

"We need to leave." Dren's low voice behind me matches the growing unease in my gut. I nod absently, though excitement fizzes through my veins at the thought of what might be in the next bag. Yes, we need to leave. *Soon*. But... *just one more peek*.

The man drops the bag on my table unceremoniously, and I scoop it up. This time when I look inside, I nearly drop it like it's full of live snakes.

No. Way.

Did I see that right?

Hesitating, I force myself to look again, just to confirm my eyes weren't playing tricks on me.

Nope. *It's real*.

Nestled inside is the tiniest scrap of white lace I've ever seen —a thong that's more suggestion than actual underwear, paired with an equally minuscule bra. The little triangle cups are so small *my breasts would spill out of them indecently*. My face flames as I realize that's most likely the point. It's lingerie, after all, designed to reveal, not conceal.

The heat spreads from my face throughout my body, my

heart pounding erratically as that heat concentrates between my thighs. I jolt when I feel an answering trickle of wetness spill into my panties. My eyes widen, and I tense up, feeling as if everyone in the room can suddenly sense exactly what's happening inside me. Oh gosh, can everyone tell? Can they see how this man's audacious game is turning me on? Worse... can *he?*

I leap to my feet so fast my chair skitters back and the bag tumbles to the floor, but thankfully, the contents remain hidden. If Dren or anyone else saw what's inside, I'd combust on the spot.

"Okay, okay, I'm ready to leave now," I babble to my bodyguard, spinning around to give my mysterious stranger my back. But even with my eyes averted, I can *feel* his presence.

Dren's brow furrows as he watches my flustered state, then his gaze moves to a point behind me, and his face transforms into a fierce scowl.

Oh no.

The small hairs on my nape stand up, and goosebumps ripple over my body as a dark, rich, masculine cologne fills my nostrils. My belly does a series of Olympic-worthy gymnastics, and I know without looking back that *he* is behind me. I gulp and slowly turn around. Still, I'm startled by how close he is. Closer than I expected. Too close.

"Leaving so soon, *mia piccola rossa*?"

His voice is deeply masculine and rumbles through me, sending fire skittering across my skin. Italian. Of course he speaks Italian. Because being dangerously handsome wasn't enough. I clap my hands to my burning cheeks, hating how easily my face gives me away while his expression remains so frustratingly unreadable. Does anything faze this man?

Before I can think of something clever to say, he reaches for my hands, and my heart does this ridiculous flutter. I see Dren take a step forward, all protective, but this man, this dangerous, beautiful stranger barely even spares him a glance—like Dren's no threat to him at all.

"I was enjoying your company. Won't you stay for dessert?" he continues, dropping my hands from my face, only to settle on adjusting my leather jacket with a familiarity that makes my head spin.

His closeness is overwhelming, like he's everywhere all at once, and my brain is scrambling to catch up. I try to swallow, but my mouth is dry, my tongue too heavy. Why can't I say anything? Is this what being tongue-tied feels like? Because if so, it sucks.

"You don't want to talk to me, that's fine. Just tell me your name, *bella*."

His question finally triggers my survival instinct as Roan's warning rings through my brain. *"You can't fathom the power someone knowing your name holds over you, El. Never give someone you know you can't trust your name."*

I shake my head, forcing the words past my dry throat. "I–I can't."

With every ounce of willpower I possess, I take a step back. Then another. And suddenly, I'm running, fleeing the restaurant with my father's men hot on my heels. The Range Rover beeps as Dren unlocks it with the key fob behind me, and I throw myself inside, pressing a hand to my galloping heart.

What was that? Never... never have I been so affected by a man before. Crap, he's a very dangerous one, isn't he? The kind of man who could ruin a girl with just a look. The kind who could make her forget every warning she's ever been given.

"Are you okay?" Dren asks, slipping into the passenger seat, while Anton takes the wheel. I nod wordlessly as the car purrs to life and we pull away from the restaurant.

The drive passes in a haze of conflicting emotions. I don't even protest when I realize Anton's taking us back home instead of continuing my tour of the city. Some birthday this turned out to be—I finally get a taste of freedom, only to end up running from the first interesting man I meet.

The moment the car stops, I'm out of there, up the front steps and past the foyer, barely registering the bewildered look from Adriel, our housekeeper, as I make a beeline for my bedroom.

Once inside, I close the door and lock it for good measure. Then I rest my back against the door and slowly slide down to the floor, sinking my hands into my curls as I try to get myself under control. But the sticky wetness between my legs only sends shots of pleasure through me as my thighs rub together, so I quickly get back on my feet.

With a frustrated groan, I kick off my boots and unbutton my jeans, pushing them down my legs. As I shrug off my jacket, I notice a strange heaviness in the pocket. Frowning, I reach inside and pull out a hard, rectangular object.

It's a black flip phone. Definitely not mine. My mind immediately jumps back to the restaurant, to the moment when the stranger adjusted my jacket. *He* must have slipped it in then, that sneaky son of a—

I was so lost in his presence I didn't even notice. But more importantly, how did *Dren* miss that? He's so sharp-sighted, he notices *everything*, down to when I change my nail polish color.

I suck my bottom lip between my teeth as I flip the phone open. No password. Figures. I go straight to the contacts, but there's only one number saved:

M.L.

It doesn't take a genius to figure out who that belongs to.

Pacing my room, I chew my lip raw as I debate what to do. The logical side of me knows I should tell Dren. Have him look into it. But... I don't *want* to.

I can't shake the thrill I felt earlier as the stranger flirted with me from across the room. Because that's what he was doing, wasn't it? I might be sheltered and more innocent than other girls my age, but I'm not completely clueless. I know what flirting looks like—I've just never experienced it firsthand.

How could I? My whole life, I've only been surrounded by my father, my brother, and their men. And those men wouldn't dare look at me the wrong way unless they wanted to face the wrath of *Atë* or Roan. So this is the first time a man has seen me as... well, a woman. Not just someone's daughter or sister.

What's the harm in letting this little flirtation play out for a bit longer?

It's not like anything can actually happen. After today, I'll be locked back inside my gilded cage, and he'll be out there somewhere in the city. Far away. *This is something I can have for myself.*

Besides, if I don't like where our chats are going, I can just tell Dren about the phone and have him handle it. Right?

I nod to myself, decision made. I'll talk to the guy, find out what he wants, maybe flirt with him a little. Then I'll give Dren the phone. It's the perfect plan.

I nod again, more firmly this time, flipping the phone shut and tucking it away in my nightstand drawer. With that settled, I finish peeling off my clothes and head for my ensuite to take a shower.

As the steam fills the bathroom, my mind races with possibilities. What will I say to him? What kind of messages does a man like that send? And... what kind of girl am I for wanting to find out?

The shower might wash away the lingering scent of his cologne, but it does nothing to calm the butterflies in my stomach or the anticipation building in my chest.

For the first time in my life, I'm about to do something *truly* rebellious.

4

MAXIMO

"Maximo, I've sent you the location we traced the phone to." Dante's face twists like he's just bitten into a lemon. I arch an eyebrow, wondering what crawled up his ass this time. He's been pissy ever since I told him about slipping one of our burner phones into my mysterious redhead's pocket yesterday. Guess he doesn't appreciate my innovative tracking methods.

I unlock my phone and thumb through my emails until I spot one from Giorgio, our IT guy. There's a link to an online map, and when I click it, my eyes nearly bug out of my skull.

"What the fuck?" I blink at the location pulsing on the screen, frowning as I try to make sense of it. "Is this some kind of joke?"

Dante shakes his head. "You know Giorgio. The guy's a fucking savant with tech. Had him run the application twice, just to be sure. That's really where she is."

Her location is Malba, a small, rich suburban neighborhood in the northeastern part of Queens, situated on the peninsula between the East River and Powell's Cove. But that's not the problem.

Under normal circumstances, I wouldn't give two shits about some ritzy area like that. But this isn't just any neighborhood—it's the breeding ground for the Albanian rats I've been in a rivalry with for the past few years. In fact, the massive mansion she's in right now belongs to none other than Afrim Përmeti, the goddamn leader of those scumbags.

Just who the fuck is she?

But that doesn't even matter. What matters is that Përmeti's men were in my territory, armed to the teeth, and I fucking let them waltz out of there with their limbs still intact. How did that slip past our radars?

My grip on the phone tightens as rage engulfs me. Was this their plan all along? Dangle a pretty little redhead in front of me as bait to distract me while his men... what? Stand around looking menacing behind her? It doesn't make sense.

"What have our Albanian friends been up to lately?" I ask Dante through gritted teeth.

Afrim's plotting something Is this his idea of payback for the weapons shipment we intercepted? What were they doing yesterday morning while I was busy trying to impress their mole?

Dante's answer only deepens the mystery. "That's the weird part. They've been dead quiet. If not for this new development, I'd think they were still licking their wounds after we hit their shipment. But they can't be that devastated if they're bold enough to send armed men into our territory in broad daylight. I just don't see what their aim was."

I drum my fingers on my desk as I try to think what their end goal might be. It would have made more sense if the girl hadn't run off, face as red as her hair, when I touched her. If she was their mole, shouldn't she have milked the situation for all it was worth?

She could've gotten way more information—or whatever

the hell they wanted—if she stayed, accepted my gifts, and went to a hotel with me... so why run?

The more I think about it, the less it makes sense. Something's off.

"Maybe Afrim finally lost his marbles in his old age," Dante offers with a sardonic grin. "Dementia catching up to him?"

I snort. "If only we were that lucky. What does Giorgio have on the girl?"

Dante shakes his head with regret. "Nothing yet. It's like she doesn't fucking exist. Would've been easier if we'd snagged a picture. He could've run it through his intelligence database."

Frustration gnaws at me, but an idea forms. I shoot out a text to the burner.

ME

I want to see you. Tonight. Come to Mughetto.

Let's see how she responds. If she's really their spy, she'll jump at the chance to work her charm on me. They probably think they have me hook, line, and sinker after yesterday's performance. And fuck me, if it weren't for this new intel, they'd be right.

Hell, even the discovery of her treachery does nothing to abate how hard my cock gets when I think about her and the delicious citrus-vanilla scent that filled my nostrils the second I got into her space. I shift in my seat, trying to adjust myself discreetly. Dante, ever the professional, pretends he doesn't notice, but I catch a glimmer of something in his eyes.

My alarm beeps briefly just as the notification for my conference meeting with my brothers pops up on my computer screen. Christ, it's 9 PM already? Time really flies when split between lust and unraveling a problem that could screw us all.

I dismiss Dante as I fire up the video call. Four faces fill my screen, and despite the circumstances, a small smile tugs at my lips as I take them in.

My brothers—not by blood, but by choice, bound together by the dark shit we survived fifteen years ago. Looking at them now, you'd never guess the nightmares we've lived through.

"Can we make this quick?" Romero grumbles, shuffling a stack of documents around on his desk. "I have a mountain of paperwork to get through before midnight for my court appearance tomorrow."

Ah, Romero. Don of Brooklyn by night, hotshot lawyer by day. You'd think running the entire borough's criminal underworld would be enough for the guy, but nope. He's still got time to take on cases for the city's elite criminals—politicians, CEOs, trust fund brats who've never worked a day in their pampered lives.

Once a lawyer, always a lawyer, I guess, even if he now works for the wrong side of the law. It's almost poetic.

Michael rolls his eyes, arms crossed over his chest as he leans back in his seat. His dirty blonde hair falls over his forehead, and with an exaggerated huff, he blows it out of his face before running a hand over his tattooed scalp. "You're not the only one with a packed schedule, Romero. We've all got shit to handle. But these weekly meetings are why we're the most feared dons in the city—and four of the five New York families, at that. So suck it up."

I'm about to chime in when something catches my eye. I lean closer to my screen, squinting. "Hold up. Is that a fucking piercing?"

Michael Hart is the oddball of our little family, the only one without a conventional legal job so to speak.

I head Leonotti Corporation, overseeing construction, imports, real estate—the works. Rafael's the big shot in hospitality, with chains of resorts, hotels, casinos, and restaurants under his belt. Then there's Romero—the legal eagle. His law firm is one of the best, not just in the city, but probably in the entire Northeast region.

But Michael—well, most simply, he's an IT genius with a Fortune 500 tech company that churns out everything from the nation's go-to social media platforms and addictive video games to cutting-edge cloud storage solutions and mobile phones. Hell, the guy is even developing tablets now. It's like he never sleeps.

His career means his net worth rivals that of Rafael, the richest among us. But here's the kicker—it also means he doesn't have to deal with nearly as much legal red tape as the rest of us. So, when it comes to looking respectable, he gives zero fucks.

His hair is shaved clean on the sides and back, leaving a mop of dirty blonde hair in the middle of his head. And don't even get me started on the ink. After we all got our first tattoo together, he caught the bug bad. Now he's tatted up from head to knuckles, even the damn skin under his hair.

He's the wildest looking and perhaps the most unhinged. And trust me, that's saying a lot.

Michael smirks at me, his icy blue eyes glinting as he also leans closer to his screen, turning the side of his nose just enough to show off the black hoop. "Like what you see, Maxo? I have more in less... public places. Want a peek?" He throws in a wink for good measure.

Crazy motherfucker. "Jesus Christ, no," I mime gagging, earning a chuckle from Romero.

"Enough." Rafael's voice cuts through our banter.

Time for business.

We dive into updates, each of us sharing what's been brewing in our boroughs. And surprise, surprise—looks like I'm not the only one dealing with an infestation of Albanians. They're spreading through the richest, most tucked-away parts of the city, multiplying like the rats they are.

"Why are they leaving Long Island to infiltrate our territories?" Michael asks, casually flicking some lint off his shirt. "I vote we smoke them out, bomb them in their nests. Nothing says 'fuck off' like a few well-placed explosives."

"No," Rafael shoots him down. "We need to handle this carefully."

He's right, much as I hate to admit it. The Albanians got into an alliance with the Bratva a few weeks ago—the singular force strong enough to oppose the *Cosa Nostra*. Their boss in Long Island City even sold off his daughter to the ancient Bratva *Pakhan* to seal the deal.

And it doesn't stop there. Now word on the street is, they're trying to get in good with the Irish too. That would explain their newfound balls to creep out of Long Island and sniff around our turf. Confidence can make you stupid, though.

"If they're truly in talks with the Irish, declaring war on the Albanians could mess with our alliance," Romero adds, tapping his pen against a stack of legal papers. "We have them cornered for now. Given enough time with their backs to the wall, they might give up and fuck off on their own."

"Or they could get desperate and strike first," Michael counters. "I doubt the Irish would care all that much about us wiping out a few pests crossing a boundary in our cities."

But that's the thing. They *haven't* crossed any boundaries. Not really. Moving into our territories and trying to smuggle weapons through our roads isn't enough to justify wiping them out. Not in the eyes of our allies, at least.

"Once they attack, though, all bets are off." A sinister smile crosses Rafael's face. "If they fire the first shot, we'd be well within our rights to retaliate, and nobody can say shit. But until then, we wait. We can't be the one attacking first."

And just like that, the unspoken rule hangs between us. They make the first move, or we sit tight and let the pressure build. Either way, it's only a matter of time before someone snaps.

The conversation moves to other parts of our operations—

like the shipment of high-tech weapons we're importing from China through my company.

"You got it handled?" Rafael asks me.

I nod. "Of course. Everything is going smoothly, and delivery is on track to arrive as scheduled."

"Good." Romero glances at his watch for the millionth time. "I think that wraps things up. See y'all's ugly mugs next week. Same time and pla—"

"Wait!" Michael interjects. "I have something to add. I've been digging into Emily's disappearance, and I think I might be getting close to her trail, and—"

"Don't." Rafael's voice drops into a low growl, his impassive face clenching tightly. "Let it go and stop looking into her."

The silence that follows is thick enough to cut with a knife. Michael's jaw works furiously, clearly chafing at being told what to do. But the fact is, even though we're all bosses in our own right, we wouldn't be where we are—wouldn't have this power—without Rafael. He's our leader, and we owe him our loyalty.

To me, Michael, and Romero, Emilia Rossi is a *sorellina*. Our little sister by choice and shared trauma. But to Rafael, she was something else entirely. Whatever went down between them ten years ago must've been nuclear, because he's banned even mentioning her name. No one talks about her. No one looks for her.

I miss her. I'm sure Michael and Romero do too. Rafael had more time with her back then, while we only had that one brief interlude, playing Michael's first video game, before everything went to hell.

I feel cheated, robbed of her presence. But if Rafael's asking us not to look into her or even mention her name, he has a good reason. The man was fucking obsessed with her, talking about making her his wife and shit. It's hard to believe that it never actually happened.

"Whatever. Goodbye," Michael grits out, and his screen goes black. He left the meeting.

"Well, I have that case to prep for, so..." Romero trails off, giving a half-hearted wave before he too vanishes from the call.

It's just Rafael and me now. I study the man who's probably my best friend, noting the cracks in his usually impenetrable mask. "You're unraveling, man."

"Don't start that shit with me, Maxim." He rubs a tired hand across his eyes. "I heard about the girl in your restaurant yesterday."

I roll my eyes. The *Cosa Nostra* gossip network puts a pair of old ladies at tea to shame, and with Rafael's men everywhere, I'm not even surprised the news has traveled to him. "We're not talking about me."

He chuckles softly. "We are now. What gives?"

For some reason, I hesitate to spill the beans about my latest discovery—that my mysterious woman might be an enemy in disguise. Maybe I just don't want to appear weak in front of him, I'm not sure. I shrug, trying to play it cool. "Nothing. Yet."

"Don't do anything I wouldn't do."

I snort. "That doesn't leave much off the table, does it? Can't think of a single thing you'd balk at."

He smirks, but a shadow lingers behind his eyes. "Just be careful. Women can be... deceitful snakes."

There's a bitter edge to his voice that makes me want to dig deeper, but before I can question it, my phone pings with an incoming message.

My heart does a traitorous somersault when I see my mystery woman has replied. "Hold that thought, Raf. We'll talk about it later. Gotta go now." I quickly exit the meeting window, then turn my full attention to my phone.

MY BURNER:

Why did you slip your phone into my jacket pocket?

She ignored my command to meet up to ask her own question. Ballsy. I smirk as I reply.

ME:

Why would I drop my phone into your pocket? The more logical conclusion would be that you stole it.

Almost immediately, three bobbing dots appear on the screen as she types her response.

MY BURNER:

That literally makes no sense. You gave me more expensive gifts, why would I grab this ancient phone unless someone–you–slipped it into my pocket while I wasn't paying attention?

I chuckle at the sass in her tone, then catch myself. What the fuck am I doing? She's in enemy territory, possibly a mole. I need to pull my head out of my ass and focus.

ME:

Bring my phone back to my restaurant, you little thief.

MY BURNER:

A of all, I didn't steal this phone, so I object to being labeled a thief. B, I can't meet you to return your phone even if I wanted to, so I guess you'll have to let it go.

ME:

Once something is mine, I never let it go, piccola rossa. And why can't you meet me even if you wanted to?

MY BURNER:

What does that mean?

Nevermind, I checked it on thessius. A little redhead, really?

A surge of pride runs through me at the name of Michael's search engine. It means she's using his phone because, for now, Thessius is only available on *Celtros*—his phone brand.

I shoot a text to Michael.

ME:

Hey bigshot, I think I just discovered someone other than the guys and us who uses your phones. That's a total of what, five people now? Very soon, you might even become a household name.

His reply is lightning-fast and predictably irritated.

MICHAEL:

Fuck you. Over seven hundred thousand people and counting have purchased the Celtro A1 and A2 alone.

I grin and send a thumbs up, knowing it will piss him off even more. Then I reply to my mysterious woman.

ME:

Don't try to evade my question. Why can't you meet me?

MY BURNER:

Nosy much? Ugh, fine, I'll tell you so you don't think I'm trying to avoid returning your phone to you because I didn't steal it.

I can't meet you because, well, I actually can't. I'm not allowed to leave.

Her response sends my mind reeling. Not allowed to leave? What the ever-loving fuck does that mean? She left yesterday, didn't she? Before I can release the barrage of questions building up, my door swings open and Dante storms in.

"Maximo, you might want to see this."

5

ELIRA

My teeth sink into my bottom lip as my toes tap out an impatient rhythm on the floor. He's read the message, but the response is MIA. Did I let too much slip? Ugh, I shouldn't have replied to his message, no matter how tempted I was. With a frustrated huff, I toss the phone on the nightstand and burrow under the covers.

I should've gone to sleep an hour ago, but I couldn't stop agonizing over how to reply to his message. He asked me to meet him, and I froze. I mean, how was I supposed to respond to that? And now, even though I finally sent a reply, my pulse still refuses to settle. *He wants to see me again.* The thought sends delicious tingles down my spine and my toes curl involuntarily.

Who knew texting someone I'm not related to could be so... exhilarating! Not just anyone, though—*him*. The hot Italian from the restaurant, the one who tried to lure me close with expensive gifts like I was some prize to be won.

I toss and turn for what feels like hours, my mind a whirlwind of 'what ifs' and 'maybes'. When sleep finally claims me, it's anything but peaceful. My dreams are a chaotic mess, featuring my hot Italian—but not all of him. Just those dark-as-night eyes boring into my soul and that rich, masculine voice commanding me to meet up with him *now*. It's intoxicating and terrifying all at once.

I wake up with a migraine, the kind that threatens to split my skull in two. Just what I need. A groan slips out as I push my unruly mane off my face and drag my feet to the bedroom. After peeing and washing my hands, I splash some cold water on my face, hoping it'll shock me awake—or at least dull the pounding in my head. No such luck. With a sigh, I trudge out of my room like a zombie fresh from the grave.

Dren raises a brow at me as I shuffle past him. Usually, I'm Little Miss Sunshine in the morning, much to his constant annoyance. But right now, it feels like I've had all of an hour's sleep, and I'm in no mood for pleasantries.

I make a beeline for the kitchen, knowing exactly what I need—*Çaji I malit,* my go-to Albanian mountain tea. Thankfully, there's already a pot of hot water in the kettle, a small blessing in this moment, and I waste no time grabbing a tea bag and dropping it into a mug. As I pour the water over it, steam curls up, and I shiver with anticipation as the mouthwatering aroma instantly wafts up to greet me. My muscles relax just smelling it. It's like the tea knows exactly how to soothe me.

Cradling the warm mug between my palms, I stare blearily outside as I wait for the tea to cool a little. I'm the only one in this house who drinks *Çaji I malit,* even though it's one of the star products from Roan's new beverage company. Roan and *Atë* prefer *kafe turkit*— classic Turkish coffee, another gem from his brand—and *raki*, the traditional Albanian alcohol.

Unable to wait any longer, I lift my mug to my lips and gulp greedily. It scalds my tongue and the roof of my mouth, but I don't care. The burn is well worth it.

By the time I drain the mug, my killer migraine has dialed down from nuclear explosion to a vague annoyance at my temples. I'm wide awake now, practically vibrating with energy. I rinse the mug, place it on the counter, and glance around the kitchen, feeling a little more like myself again.

Of course, that's when thoughts of my hot Italian guy sneak back in, and I shake my head at the ridiculous notion that he might be *mine*. Maybe baking some *ballokume*—good ol' Albanian butter cookies—will help clear my head.

And distract me from the overwhelming urge to check the flip phone to see if he's texted back.

I gather ingredients, ready to lose myself in the comfort of baking, but just as I'm about to start mixing, Besart, the cook, walks in with his usual grumpy expression.

"No, Elira. You're not going to take over my kitchen today. Out, little miss."

I pause mid-reach for the flour. "But, Besart—" I clasp my hands together, channeling my best puppy-dog eyes.

He's not having it. "Out," he repeats firmly. "I have to make breakfast for the *shef* and his guests. You can come back and bake your heart out later."

Atë has guests? Frowning, I reluctantly start putting the ingredients back in their places. There have been a lot of men coming and going from the compound these past few weeks, but I hadn't really given it much thought, since I was too focused on finding the courage to ask him about letting me out. Now, though, I can't help but wonder if something's going on.

As I head back to my room, Dren trails behind me, poking at me like always. "What's up with you? You don't usually rush for your tea like an addict chasing a fix," he adds jokingly, and I flip him off without even looking back.

His laughter follows me as I slam the door shut.

My eyes immediately zero in on the flip phone on my nightstand, and I make my way to it. Oh crap, I was too careless. I should have hidden it, at least tucked it away in the drawer. What if someone had come in and seen it?

I snatch it up, silently thanking whatever deity is listening that Roan isn't home. He's the only one who still barges into my room unannounced, the jerk.

With shaking fingers, I tap the phone screen to wake it up. There's a new message waiting, and suddenly my heart's doing the cha-cha, my palm turning into a sweaty mess as I read it.

M.L:

If you want to get out, I can help you.

I swallow hard. My heart is no longer doing just the cha-cha; it's hosting a full-blown rave. *He can help me get out?* My immediate instinct is to say yes, yes, a million times yes. Being cooped up in here is starting to drive me insane. A 21-year-old who's spent 90% of her life locked up like some fragile, overprotected flower. This can't be it—this can't be my life.

When I insisted on pursuing higher education after finishing my homeschooling and passing my GED, *Atë* gave me an ultimatum: either take virtual classes or forget about it. So, of course, I took the stupid online classes. Like I had a choice. With no friends outside my family and zero social skills, what else could I do? At least my brother made sure I picked up some survival skills along the way. Small mercies, right?

But going out on my birthday? *That* was a mistake. I thought I'd do it once and move on, scratch that itch, and be content. But now that I've gotten a taste of what I'm missing, I want more. No… I *need* more.

I read the message again, my fingers hovering over the keypad. Then, finally, I type out a reply.

ME:

How?

His response is almost instant, like he's been waiting for me.

M.L:

You don't expect me to reveal my secrets just like that, do you, rossa? I'll need your full name to execute my plans. If you want my help, that is.

I bite my lip in worry, thoughts spiraling, crashing into each other until my mind is a jumbled mess.

Should I do it? I try to weigh my options. If I tell him my name and he somehow helps me sneak out for the day, he's most likely not doing it out of the goodness of his heart. Sure, he wants his phone back, but he also wants something else. *Me.*

But hell, even the idea of that sexy man wanting me, creating a diversion just to have me, only makes me more tempted. Would it be so bad to spend a day with him? A day with a hot guy that wants me, out in the city, free from the suffocating walls of my gilded cage.

Whatever con there might be must be worth it, surely?

Atë will blow his top, probably triple my security and have people watch me all day and night. But what if it makes him realize he can't cage me forever? That as I get older, I'll only get more creative in my escape attempts? Okay. My mind is made up. *I'm going to take this stranger's deal.*

But first…

ME:

I want your help. I'll tell you my name if I have to, but in exchange, you have to tell me yours.

M.L:

Deal.

I chew my lip, hesitating. Once I send my name to him, there's no going back. An illicit thrill rushes through me as I take the plunge.

ME:

Elira Përmeti. Your turn.

I wait. He reads it. And then... nothing.

Five minutes tick by.

Then ten.

My blood starts to boil, and before I know it, I'm stabbing the screen with furious fingers.

ME:

HELLO? YOUR NAME?

M.L:

You'll find out soon enough, mia rossa.

ME:

Are you seriously going back on our deal?

M.L:

Yes.

Never trust the word of a man you don't know, Elira.

My jaw drops in disbelief as I read his texts over and over again. Somehow, it never occurred to me that he might back out of telling me his name. *That asshole.* Does he even have a plan to get me out of the compound, or was it all just a trick to find out my name? As if he's read my mind, another message comes in.

M.L:

The distraction will be orchestrated in an hour. Be ready. When it happens, lose your guards and leave the house. Come straight to me when you're out.

I let out an exaggerated scoff. Right. A distraction. Because that sounds believable. Who does this guy think he is? Without giving him the satisfaction of a reply, I toss the phone in my nightstand drawer, mentally kicking myself for being such a gullible idiot.

I need a reset.

After a quick shower washes off some of the frustration, I'm dressed in a pair of jeans and a black V-neck top, curls pulled up in a messy bun that screams *I don't care*. Then my hands automatically start filling my small purse with some essentials —credit cards, a few hundred bucks, lip balm. The basics. As I'm zipping it up, thinking about what else I should add, there's a knock on my door.

My heart jumps, but I quickly reel it in. *Calm down, it's just a knock. Nothing's happening. I'm not readying myself in case there is a distraction*, I tell myself as I make my way to the door. I'm just... prepping for another normal, boring day at home, and filling my purse just because.

One of *Atë's* men stands in the doorway with my breakfast tray, and I mutter a quick thanks as I accept it. The food is probably delicious—Besart is a phenomenal cook, after all—but it tastes like ash in my mouth.

After choking down breakfast, I'm still buzzing with so much restless energy and leftover anger that's got nowhere to go, so I storm into the kitchen to bake. As I gather the ingredients for my favorite dessert, *sheqerpare*—those buttery, melt-in-your-mouth shortbread cookies—from the pantry, thoughts of the asshole Italian slowly fade until all that's left in my mind is the familiar routine of caramelizing sugar and water.

Once the mixture starts boiling, I add a slice of lemon to the syrup and lower the heat. Got to let it simmer just right, or else it will crystallize and ruin everything. Next, I turn back to the counter and dig into the dough, kneading it with a vengeance while imagining the Italian's smug face under my fists.

After molding the dough into perfect little rounds, I start

scoring each one with a fork, getting them ready to top with almonds when suddenly—BRRRIIIIINNGG—an ear-splitting screech shatters the air, sending my fork skidding across the dough. The whole compound seems to explode into a frenzy, and I flinch, eyes wide as shouts in panicked Albanian reach my ears.

I shoot a confused look at Dren, who's been silently guarding the doorway like he always does while I bake. He's tense, eyes narrowed like he knows exactly what's happening.

"What–"

"Fire." He cuts me off, his eyes flicking to the window. I follow his gaze to see some men running past with extinguishers. "That was the fire alarm and—"

The rest of his words are swallowed by another deafening alarm, then another, and *another*, until the house feels like it's vibrating from the sound. Dren's practically vibrating himself, all clenched muscles and twitchy glances, clearly itching to burst through the door and jump into the action. I get it—this isn't just one little fire. Multiple alarms mean the fire is in more than one area.

How though? How can the compound suddenly just go up in flames without affecting the main house? That doesn't happen by accident.

The distraction will be orchestrated in an hour. Be ready.

Oh. My. God.

I whip my head towards the digital clock on the wall. 9:46 AM. Only thirty minutes have passed. Could it be the Italian? My gaze darts to Dren who's standing close to the window now to monitor the chaos outside.

Despite my pounding heart, I play it cool, calmly turning off the oven and removing my apron, then rinsing my hands before facing my bodyguard. "I'm going up to my room. Why don't you go check out what's going on? You know I'll be safe up there."

Dren barely blinks, too distracted by whatever is happening outside. So he just gives me a quick nod and stalks out of the kitchen, leaving me alone. Perfect.

As soon as he's gone, I bolt upstairs and yank the nightstand drawer open. The flip phone stares up at me like a loaded gun. I snatch it up.

M.L:

Now. The front gates are unattended.

I gulp. *How does he know that?* Did he actually set fire to my compound, or was it just some elaborate trick with the alarms? How did he even pull it off?

No time for twenty questions, Elira. What are you going to do?

I glance down at my clothes, tuck the phone into my jeans pocket, then pull my hair free from the bun, quickly tying it into a tight ponytail. Red hair stands out too much, so I grab a black hoodie from my closet and tug it over my head. Essentials? Check. Slinging my slim purse over my shoulder, I take a deep breath before carefully cracking the door open just enough to peek through.

The coast is clear. Thank goodness.

I force myself to walk casually down the hallways, descend the stairs, then slip out the back door. The usual patrol guards are nowhere to be seen—off dealing with the fire, no doubt—and though I know the cameras will document me sneaking out, I'll be long gone by the time anyone checks the footage.

My heart pounds fiercely, hands nervously clenched into fists as I head towards the gate. Sure enough, the guard station is deserted, and the huge gates are just standing there, unwatched. I toss one last glance at the house, then push open the small door by the side of the gates and make my escape.

I'm not going to meet that lying asshole, of course. I didn't really trust him before and definitely don't trust him after he went back on our deal. *Why couldn't he just tell me his name?*

But still... this is too good an opportunity to pass up. No guards breathing down my neck, no one keeping tabs on my every move. I can go anywhere I want, do anything I want, completely on my own terms. And when I've had my fill of fun, I'll just sneak back into the compound.

Even if the guards are there by then, they wouldn't deny me entry. And *Atë*... well, I'll deal with his temper when the time comes.

I give myself a quick nod and pick up the pace, adrenaline pumping through my veins as I jog down the pristine street. My phone is already out of my purse to download a taxi service app. Taking one of the cars would've been way more convenient but too risky. Plus, they probably have trackers on them, and I'm not looking to get caught that fast.

Setting up the app is a breeze, and within ten minutes, my driver is pulling up in front of me, a few blocks from the compound. I pull down the hoodie, then shake out my red hair before sliding into the backseat.

"Where to?" the driver—Greg, according to his profile—asks, barely glancing back at me, eyes glazed with the same bored expression he's probably worn for every ride today.

Where to? The world is suddenly wide open, full of possibilities. But I already know where I want to go. My heart does a wild little dance as I answer, "Flushing Meadows Corona Park."

One of the biggest parks in the entirety of New York. I've only ever dreamed about going there. Roan and I tried planning trips there a million times before, but there was always one problem—*me* not being allowed to step foot outside the house. But today, nothing is stopping me.

I can already picture myself blending into the sea of tourists Roan says swarm there from all corners of the world. For once, I'll be just another face in the crowd.

As Greg pulls off the curb, my phone pings with a text.

M.L:

You still remember the way to Mughetto, don't you? Or do you need me to send someone to pick you up?

This asshole. I roll my eyes as I debate how to tell him to go fuck himself in the nicest possible way. I scroll through the emojis until I find the perfect one. With a grin, I hit send and lock my phone.

Leaning back in the seat, I let my head rest against the window, feeling the vibration of the car as it speeds through the city. This is *my* time. My stolen freedom.

Once Dren realizes I'm missing, it's game over. *Atë* will be alerted, and I know it will only be a matter of time before I'm found.

But until then, I'm going to milk every second.

Today, I'm not Elira Përmeti, the sheltered daughter of a powerful man. Today, I'm just a girl, ready to take on the world.

Let the adventure begin.

6

ELIRA

I shove some crumpled bills into Greg's hand before practically springing out of the car. No time to waste. *Freedom's calling*. My feet hit the pavement, and I'm already making my way into the park, feeling the excitement bubbling up with every step. A mouth-watering aroma hits me right away from a concession stand near the entrance, and I can't help but grin as I watch the people queue up in front of it. My nose tries to lead me to the back of the line, but the rest of me screams *nope, I'm not here for snacks*. Not yet, at least. Snacks can wait.

Breezing past the stand, I head deeper into the park. It's so much quieter than I thought it'd be. Guess most people have actual jobs to go to during a weekday morning—sucks to be them, or so I hear.

I inhale deeply, filling my lungs with the fresh, earthy scent from the luscious gardens I pass. Overhead, the birds are singing their little hearts out like they're having the time of their lives, and honestly, *same, guys*.

My eyes bounce from one thing to the next: families lounging on picnic blankets across the green lawns, some kids racing around in an intense game of tag, a woman pushing a stroller, and every now and then, a jogger zips by, their footsteps rhythmic on the cobblestone path.

Perfect. This is everything I've dreamed of.

Now if only I could find the Unisphere. The iconic relic from New York's World Fair has to be around here somewhere, but this sprawling park seems determined to keep its location secret. After wandering aimlessly for what feels like hours, a sinking feeling grows in the pit of my stomach, and I have to admit it: I'm hopelessly lost, aren't I?

Ugh, I can't believe it. First time out solo and already wandering in circles. I don't want to ask for direction, but desperate times...

With a sigh, I reluctantly approach an older woman sitting on a bench, scribbling furiously in a leather-bound journal.

"Excuse me," I begin, plastering on my brightest, most 'help me, I'm lost' smile. "I think I might be lost. Do you know where I can find the Unisphere?"

The woman's head snaps up, her expression morphing from annoyance to outright hostility. Then without a word, she slams her journal shut and storms off with an indignant harrumph. I gape after her retreating form. *What the—?*

Well, that was... unnecessarily aggressive.

Before I can process it, someone chuckles behind me. I whip around to see a man in jogging shorts and a tank top slowing down.

"Typical rude New Yorkers, huh?" he says with a knowing look.

I shrug. "I guess so?" Honestly, I wouldn't know. My New Yorker interaction count is pathetically low, but most people I've met so far have been *way* nicer than Miss Grumpy Journal over there.

The jogger's eyes crinkle with genuine warmth. "Well, allow me to restore your faith in our hospitality. The Unisphere isn't that far from here. Just take a right turn up at the end of this path." He points to where the path forks into two. "Go straight ahead, ignore the first turn, and then take another right. You can't miss it."

His directions sound simple enough. I flash him a grateful smile. "Thank you so much. You just saved my day!"

He gives me a one finger salute and continues his jog. The sun's climbing higher now, and since I don't need to play invisible anymore, I strip off my hoodie and tie it around my waist. Following the jogger's directions, I set off down the path.

'Not far' must mean something different in jogger language, because after ten minutes, I'm still walking. When I round that final turn, though, a massive sculpture stops me in my tracks—an athletic man frozen mid-launch, one foot perched on a tall arch, hurling what looks like a small rocket into the sky. A trail of flames connects his hand to the projectile, while his other hand reaches up towards a swirl of small stars circling the rocket. Epic doesn't even cover it.

At the base of the sculpture, little blue and yellow flowers stretch out like a soft blanket, but as I'm admiring them, something in my peripheral vision steals my attention. So, I turn slightly and lose my breath entirely. *Holy—wow.* My lips part in pure wonder.

Because there it is.

Right down the cobblestone path, framed by big trees on either side, stands *the* Unisphere in all its jaw-dropping glory.

Almost in a trance, my feet carry me towards the massive stainless-steel representation of the earth.

Other visitors are gathered around it, taking pictures while I just stand there, head tilted back in awe. The sleek metal glints in the sunlight, making me squint a little. As I start circling the sphere to admire it from all angles, a sudden hissing sound breaks the spell. Out of nowhere, thick streams of fizzing water shoot skyward around the globe, and I leap back with a startled gasp. *Whoa! Definitely didn't see that coming.*

The water dances in the air, catching the light, and the crowd erupts in delighted cheers, cameras clicking frantically. Fine droplets kiss my skin, but I barely notice. The globe is mesmerizing—majestic. No. *Magical.* Yes, that's the right word. Because this is straight-up magic.

But then, through the streams of water, a tall man on the other side of the sphere grabs my attention. And not just casually—like, *he owns it*. Even from this distance, there's something striking about the way he carries himself. His navy suit hugs his muscular frame perfectly, and as he adjusts his cufflinks, thick strands of shiny dark hair fall over his brows, adding to his commanding presence.

My heart does a stupid little tug, and I have to mentally slap myself. *Get it together, Elira. You're not here to ogle random men.*

But as the stranger begins to circle the sphere, mirroring my own path, I find myself unable to look away. His long, confident strides eat up the distance faster than mine could ever do, and very soon he's rounding the corner and heading right towards me. I hold my breath as he draws near, lifting his gaze to meet mine—

Oh no, no no no.

It's *him*.

7

ELIRA

The infuriatingly handsome Italian from the restaurant. The one who slipped his phone into my pocket and orchestrated my great escape.

"You were supposed to come to me, Elira." His dark eyes run over my body as he comes to a stop in front of me, but I just watch him in stunned silence.

How is he here? Is this... *fate?*

I feel a weird sense of déjà vu, only this time, I'm not so sure fate has my best interests in mind. He's a lying asshole, after all.

His right hand slowly reaches up, and the calloused pad of his thumb brushes my cheekbone, smearing away droplets of water. The touch is feather-light, yet it sends electricity jolting through my body. I jerk back, heart pounding.

What was *that*?

One bushy brow arches upward, but he lets his hand fall without a word. The morning sun glints off his watch, drawing my gaze, and for a second, I'm distracted by the pretty ink curling around his wrist and disappearing under his sleeves.

"How—how did you find me?" I stammer out.

He steps closer, invading my space until his scent overwhelms me, drowning out the refreshing park air and making my head spin. "You were supposed to come to *Mughetto* and bring my phone with you. Why did you run away?"

"I didn't run." I roll my eyes at the notion. Okay, technically I did run from home, but not from *him* specifically. "I just wasn't interested in meeting a man who could so easily go back on his word." The reminder of that sly trick of his stirs up my anger, effectively piercing through the fog of attraction clouding my mind.

His lips curl into a slight smile, and oh dear—is that a dimple appearing on his left cheek? My heart skitters. He has dimples? How did I miss that detail before? Now, all I want is to see him smile fully, just to know how deep they go.

"Still angry about that?" His tone is laced with amusement. "So eager to know my name?"

"You can shove your name where the sun doesn't shine, asshole," I retort in Albanian, enjoying the way his brows pinch together in the middle, though a glint I don't understand appears in his onyx gaze.

"Did you just curse me out in your language, beautiful girl? You did text me a middle finger earlier."

I smirk at the recall. "You'll never know. Now go away. You're ruining my morning." I wave my hand dismissively, trying to shoo him off, but he doesn't budge, neither does he look like he has any plans of moving soon.

"You have something of mine in your possession, Elira. I can't just walk away." The way his tongue rolls over my name makes my stomach flutter. Damn him. And that glint spreads into a brief, amused smile that flashes another hint of that dimple.

With an exasperated huff, I fish the phone from my pocket and slap it against his chest. "Here. Happy now?"

Before I can pull away, his hand flies up, capturing mine and pressing it harder into his chest until I can feel the heat radiating through his clothes. My heart goes haywire and goosebumps pop out all over my body as I try futilely to tug my hand free.

"Is this your first time away from your father's clutches without his men trailing you?"

"That's none of your business, you fucking asshole." I try to snap, but my voice comes out a little too breathless for my liking. "Let me go, or you'll regret it."

His lips curl up in that maddening half-smile again. And there it is—another hint of dimples. "Now, now, no need to show your claws, *gattina*. I merely want to know if you've ever had the chance to explore the beauty of my city without guards breathing down your neck."

His city? The quiet confidence in his voice piques my curiosity. Just who is this guy?

"If you're truly not allowed to go out," he continues, "there must be a lot of things you haven't seen, a lot of things you haven't done." His words curl around me like smoke, warm and inviting. "And I'd like to show you everything."

"Everything?" I find myself whispering, tilting my head back to hold his dark, sinful gaze.

"Everything," he confirms. "How would you like to see my favorite view of the city?" He lets go of my hand and pockets his flip phone, but he has my undivided attention.

His favorite view of the city? "I don't think anything can surpass this view." I wave a hand at the Unisphere—though, if I'm honest, I'd all but forgotten its existence in the last few minutes.

He slowly shakes his head, his words weaving a hypnotic spell. "There are so many things that can, *gattina*. You just have to be willing to see them... and I'll show you."

His offer is pure temptation, and damn it, I want to see what view he thinks could possibly outshine this magnificent sphere.

Geez, my heart has been racing ever since he showed up. I

don't even remember what a normal heartbeat feels like anymore. It's probably unhealthy at this point, and I should be worried, but the feeling is so intoxicating. I'm about to have exactly the kind of adventure I've been craving my entire sheltered life.

"How do I know I can trust you?" I ask, even though I'm already so close to saying yes. *Take me everywhere; show me everything.* Let me devour every experience I can before I have to return home by the end of the day like Cinderella at midnight.

"You don't." He shrugs carelessly. "In fact, you shouldn't trust me, Elira. I'm a very bad man who wants to do very bad things to you."

His eyes drop to my small cleavage, then slowly trail down my body, sending heat all over the spots his dark gaze touches. My nipples bead up, and I wrap my arms over my chest in a useless attempt to cover my body's reaction.

His complete lack of effort to win my trust only draws me in deeper, damn him. "I can hold my own," I finally answer. "Show me this view you think is so great." I raise my chin, trying to look down my nose at him, even though it's nearly impossible when the man towers over me. But I try anyway.

To my surprise, he throws his head back and lets out a hearty laugh that brings his dimples into full glory. My breath hitches at how the carefree expression transforms his face from handsome to downright breathtaking. *Literally*. I actually forget to breathe. Is this what dying from a smile feels like? Because yep, I'm pretty sure I'm on my way out.

I raise my hand to my throat and press down, like that will somehow regulate my frantic pulse, but all it really does is remind me to breathe—slowly, measured. And even then, I'm not sure I'm doing it right.

"Let's go," he says once the laughter fades, stretching his right hand to me. I blink at his outstretched palm, momentarily confused, but before I can figure it out, he chuckles again and simply wraps my much smaller hand in his. A jolt of warmth shoots through me at the contact, and I'm left staring, mesmerized by how perfectly our hands fit together. His tanned hand completely engulfs my pale one, and what is it about that that feels *so* arousing? It *shouldn't* be.

"Come on," he urges, his voice dropping into this husky, low timbre that sends my gaze flying to his, and... oh. The heat in his eyes tells me he's just as affected by this innocent hand-holding as I am. He tightens his grip, and we start walking, side by side.

Every nerve in my body hums with awareness of his warm body next to me, his strong fingers laced through mine, and his intoxicating scent filling my nostrils until he's all I can think about.

As we stroll, an older couple, who seem to be taking a walk around the park stops us. The woman beams as she takes us in. "Hello! What a beautiful couple," she says with a bright and sweet voice. "You remind me of my Arthur and I thirty years ago." Her husband chuckles, raising their joined hands as proof of their bond.

"Oh, no, we're not—" I start to correct her, but the Italian just smiles and thanks her, making me glare at him as we continue walking. "Is every word that comes out of your mouth just a lie?"

"No, not every word. For instance, I *am* going to show you the best view in New York City. But before we do that, maybe we should do something you want first. Because once you see this view... everything else will just pale in comparison."

I let out a snort. "So you're already backing out on your promise to show me the best view? Not even surprised." As I talk, I glance back casually and do a double-take.

A few men are trailing behind us, trying to look casual in their street clothes, and while they might blend in to the average observer, I know a bodyguard when I see one. I've had enough of them tailing me my whole life to recognize the signs. My gaze darts up to my dark-haired *adonis*. Are they guarding him?

"No, *gattina*, not backing out. Ever heard of delayed gratification?"

"Well, I'm not a masochist, so I don't subscribe to that notion," I retort absently as I steal another glance behind us. His laughter rings out again, deeper this time, and I notice something odd—the bodyguards blanch and exchange glances at the sound of his laugh. What? What's so strange about that?

"Well..." He trails off, noticing the direction of my gaze. "It's fine, Elira. They're with me."

"Oh? Are you in danger or something? Why do you have bodyguards?"

"They're not bodyguards. They're just... with me." His answer is cryptic, making me even more confused. I should've connected the dots at that moment. That was my first clue. But I was too caught up in the moment.

"Now, come on," he says, changing the subject. "I hear this place has a lot of different activities that are supposed to be fun."

He glances back and waves at one of the men, who jogs forward, takes out a pamphlet from his suit jacket and hands it to the Italian.

"Are you really not going to tell me your name?" I press when his man melts back into the background. "I'll just refer to you as 'the Italian' in my head if you don't."

His lips quirk up as he unfolds the paper. "That's alright, *gattina*. You can do that—for now. It's not yet time to reveal my name to you."

He hands me the pamphlet. My brow furrows as I read it. It's some kind of park directory with a list of attractions. "What is this?"

"Pick one you want to go to."

"Hmm." I scan the list, my eyes lighting up at one particular entry. "Can we go to the Fantasy Forest Carousel Park?" I blurt out, then bite my lip nervously. "But... it sounds like it might be for kids." The idea of hanging around a bunch of screaming kids isn't exactly appealing, no matter how fun the amusement park sounds.

He raises a brow, but a teasing smile plays at the corner of his mouth. "Fun doesn't have an age limit. If that's where you want to go, we'll go."

He nods to his man—let's call him Bodyguard 1—who whips out a phone and makes a rapid-fire call in Italian.

Still holding my hand, the handsome Italian leads me down a quieter path. We walk in comfortable silence for a few minutes, admiring the surrounding beauty, before the distinct cries of little kids reach my ears.

Oh no. I tense immediately. Maybe this was a mistake. Kids are cute and all—from a distance, preferably where I can't hear their tantrums or deal with sticky hands. No way I'm spending my only day out surrounded by crying children.

We round the corner into chaos. The path ahead is clogged with parents looking one harassed scream away from losing it, dragging whining, fussy kids behind them—all of whom seem to be making a beeline towards us.

The Italian steers me onto the freshly mowed lawn, his men flanking us as we wait for the crowd to disperse. "What's going on?" But nobody answers me.

Agonizing minutes later, when the path finally clears, the Italian steers me back onto it, and we make our way into a deafeningly silent park. I glance around, my jaw dropping as I take in the sight.

The park is empty. Every ride, every stall—vacant. Except for a few very nervous-looking staff members, it's like a ghost town. What the heck just happened? "Umm... I think they might be closed for the day, *Italian,*" I say slowly. "They probably kicked those families out because of that."

I can't help but chuckle a little at the absurdity. Was that a tantrum-triggered evacuation? Only in my luck could a simple day out lead to a deserted amusement park.

"They *are* closed," he answers as the gates close behind us. "But not to us. You wanted to come here, so here we are. I just didn't feel like dealing with an uncontrollable crowd, so they had to leave."

My brain short circuits. did he just... "Wait—you mean *you* had those poor families sent out?" I gape at him in astonishment.

He shrugs, completely unfazed, as if ejecting families from an amusement park is a normal Tuesday activity. With a casual wave, he leads me deeper into the park towards the fantastical rides, ignoring the stiff staff. There are six rides total, two definitely sized for children. But he assures me we'll fit into everything. I follow him, bemused, as we approach the miniature train.

The poor worker manning the ride looks like he's five seconds away from fainting, and when I offer him a small smile to set him at ease, he simply drops his gaze. *That* should've been my second clue—because why do these employees all look like they're about to face the gauntlet if they breathe wrong? But of course, I missed it again, too lost in the moment.

Like a proper gentleman, the Italian helps me into one of the trains. It's ridiculously small, clearly meant for children, and common sense screams that we should sit across from each other for any chance of comfort, but no. He squeezes himself into the space right next to me, squashing us together so tightly that I can feel every inch of his warm body against mine, sending my already erratic heartbeat into overdrive. As if that's not enough, he leans back, draping his arm over my shoulders like he owns the space, like he owns *me*. The casual possessiveness of it leaves me tingling all over. And then, with just a flick of his wrist, he orders the staff to start the ride, like he owns him too.

The train begins to chug along at a slow, almost laughable pace, but when my Italian shoots a glance back at the employee, the speed ramps up fast. And just like that, I forget about the kids this asshole denied their playtime, and the terrified staff hovering in the distance. I'm lost in the thrill, zipping round and round, and I can't help the giggles that bubbles from my chest.

By the time we stumble off the train, I'm lightheaded with laughter, not caring a bit when he steers me towards the next ride—the teacups. Once again, he wedges himself in beside me. "Do you have separation issues or something?" I tease as the ride starts, and he just smirks, brushing a strand of rebellious red curls behind my ears. Of course, they bounce right back, defying him.

But that casual touch sends sizzles of electricity through me, making my gaze drop to his pink, and way too tempting lips. *Why do they have to look so kissable?* Before I can let myself spiral any further, I tear my gaze away, clearing my throat like that's going to help me get a grip. Just in time too, because the ride starts moving, and we spin—slowly, annoyingly tame, considering this is a kids' ride.

The spinning isn't enough to make me dizzy, but *he* sure is.

One by one, we weave through the rides, always close together like it's the most natural thing in the world. And honestly? It feels that way. He can't seem to keep his hand off me for a second—not that I'm complaining. Every casual brush of his fingers against mine, the way he tucks my curls behind my ear, or how his hand rests on my back—it's driving me mad, in the best possible way.

By the time we reach the final ride—the carousel—I'm not just excited; I'm practically floating on cloud nine. *This feels like a date, right?* I can't believe I ended up here with this gorgeous mystery man glued to my side.

He invited himself into what was supposed to be my solo adventure, turned all my plans upside down, yet somehow, everything since has been nothing short of magical. My nerve endings sing from overstimulation, and all we've done is ride some kiddie rides. Though, I don't think the rides have anything to do with it.

"Scared?" he asks as we stand before the circle of brightly painted horses.

"Please." I roll my eyes. "I survived the rollercoaster, didn't I? This is nothing." With my chin held high, I step inside, confidently choosing a horse and swinging myself onto it.

He starts to follow, but then Bodyguard 1 swoops in and whispers something in his ears. I swear I can almost feel the temperature drop as my Italian's eyes turn ice-cold, sending a chill down my spine. When he glances back at me, his gaze softens fractionally.

"Go ahead without me," he says, his voice laced with an unexpected tension.

Before I can protest—because for some bizarre reason, I don't want to ride without him—the carousel jolts to life, and I'm forced to hold on for dear life.

Holy hell, it's fast! Way faster than I expected, especially considering the sleepy pace of the other rides. And it doesn't help that my chosen steed isn't just spinning; it's bobbing up and down like it's trying to launch me into the stratosphere. I don't know when my startled yelps turn to squeals of delight, then full-blown hysterical laughter.

The park blurs around me as the carousel spins round and round at what I'm positive is the speed of light. *Kids go on this? No wonder they're so fearless.* My heart is about to pound out of my chest by the time the ride finally comes to a stop.

Well, the carousel may have stopped, but the world still

spins in a colorful blur. I hop off, but my legs turn to marshmallows under my weight. Just as I feel myself tipping, strong arms wrap around my waist, pulling me snugly against a sturdy chest. I glance up at my Italian—when did he stop being just *the* Italian and become *my* Italian? The realization sends a thrill of warmth through me.

He smiles down at me, his dimples winking. "Enjoyed yourself a little too much, didn't you? Need me to carry you?"

I don't have the strength to give him a biting retort. Seeing that, he chuckles and carefully guides me to a nearby bench. As soon as I sit, a cold drink is pressed into my palm, and I gulp it greedily, enjoying the cool, bubbly fizz tickling down my throat.

"Ahhh," I exhale as the bubbles shoot straight to my brain, waking it up from the haze. Bit by bit, the spinning slows, and the world begins to come back into focus.

"Better?" he asks when I'm done, and I nod.

He takes the can from my hand and downs the last few sips before tossing it into a nearby trash can. My face heats up. Did he just put his lips exactly where mine were? That's... intimate, isn't it? Or am I reading too much into this because I'm so sheltered and have never been on a date before? Wait, is this even a date? Does *he* see this as a date? Why is he still here? He got his phone back, but he's still lingering around, touching me, and staring at me like he wants to devour me whole or something.

If he keeps this up, is he going to take responsibility for my feelings?

"Ready to see the best view?" he asks, giving me his hand once more. It feels like the most natural thing in the world to slip my fingers between his.

He pulls me to my feet, and I can't resist a bit of sass. "Oh, we're finally seeing this view?" His answering chuckle sends a wave of butterflies through my stomach.

As we leave the amusement park and walk back into the main park, I dig out the crumpled pamphlet from my back pocket and scan the list of attractions again. This place is massive—almost like its own little universe. Tucking it away again, I bounce on my toes, curiosity buzzing in my veins.

Where is he taking me?

I expect my Italian to do something dramatic. Maybe lead me out of the park to the highest point in the city where he could show off a sweeping rooftop view. That's totally his style, right? From what I've picked up about him today, he seems to have this whole *I own the city* vibe going on, so it wouldn't surprise me if his favorite spot is somewhere he can literally look down on it all—*his* city, his kingdom.

But he doesn't go where I expect him to.

Instead, he leads me deeper into the park, down a scenic path ending at an imposing, modern building. The sleek, glass-and-concrete exterior catches the light in a way that almost blinds me. I squint up at the sign. *Queens Museum?*

Disbelief spills out of my mouth. "*This* is where the best view in the city is? A museum?" Really? I eye him skeptically, trying to reconcile this choice with the man I thought I was getting to know. He doesn't strike me as the type to get all sentimental over paintings, trying to 'experience the artist's vision' or whatever pretentious thing people say. While there's nothing wrong with that, he just seems too impatient.

His smirk is enigmatic as he leads me through the glass doors. "You don't think it's possible for a museum to house it?"

"I mean..." I trail off with a shrug. We walk into the building with pretty, gleaming brown wood floors and soaring ceilings. But I don't get a chance to take in much before he's whisking me past exhibits and a gift shop—because of course we don't do normal sightseeing—and up a glass staircase that spirals into the second floor.

As we navigate a maze of hallways, I catch glimpses of antique treasures behind a long glass shelf I'm itching to get a closer look at, but we don't stop to look at any of them. My Italian is on a mission, and I just have to keep up.

Finally, we arrive at a set of double glass doors. I'm barely able to read the word *Panorama* on the wall before we're walking in.

"Here it is," he announces, releasing my hand to wave a majestic hand over the glass railings.

I step forward, eyes wide as I lean over. "Whoa."

8

ELIRA

Spread out below us, is a breathtaking miniature version of a city that unmistakably resembles New York, every detail so finely crafted that it looks almost alive. It's enormous, covering the entire length of the floor of the room.

"The panorama of New York City, the best view this city has to offer."

My lips remain parted as I whip my head around, my brain scrambling to take in every inch of it at once. "It's stunning!" I gasp, eyes darting from one tiny landmark to another, trying to spot anything familiar, but unfortunately, I don't.

"The entirety of New York City is here," he says, coming up next to me. "All five boroughs."

Suddenly, my eyes catch something moving. "Look!" I point, breathless, at the tiny plane soaring across the miniature landscape, complete with realistic engine sounds. My eyes follow the plane, mesmerized, as it travels over a section of the panorama and lands on a small runway.

"LaGuardia Airport," he tells me, almost too casually, like it's no big deal that this miniature airport even has moving planes. A moment later, it takes off again, disappearing over another section. *Wow.*

I'm already moving, walking the length of the glass balcony, my fingers gripping the railing as I peer down at this incredible recreation of the city. Every step I take brings a new thrill as he starts pointing out landmarks I actually recognize.

Central Park. Brooklyn Bridge. The Upper East and Upper West side. Midtown Manhattan. The Empire State Building, the Statue of Liberty. And then...

I freeze, staring down at two unmistakable towers. The original Twin Towers, still stand proudly among the rest of the city. My breath catches in my throat. "They haven't been replaced," I murmur.

"The plan is to recreate the new World Trade Center here when the entire complex is complete. They've actually printed out the digital model already, but until the whole thing has been constructed in the real world, they're leaving the towers as they were."

I nod slowly as he explains, unable to tear my eyes away from the sight. It's like a glimpse into a world frozen in time.

He nudges me gently, and we continue walking along the balcony. "There's Queens," he says, pointing towards the borough where we live. But before I can say anything, the lights dim, and an orange tint washes over the landscape. He stops. "Watch the sunset."

I inhale sharply as the golden–orange replica of the setting sun slowly cuts across the miniature city, the lights lending a mystical, magical quality to the masterpiece. The orange glow darkens until the city is pitch black, and then one by one, tiny lights flicker on in some of the miniature buildings, perfectly mimicking nighttime in New York.

Absolutely stunning.

"Do you believe me now?" His voice is close, low, and

suddenly, I feel his hand on my waist. I don't even think about it —I scoot closer, letting myself melt into the moment as we watch the city slowly light up again. "The whole cycle—sunset and sunrise—takes about ninety seconds," he informs me as we start walking again so we can actually get a closer look at Queens.

When we reach it, his hand drops from my waist, and I immediately feel a twinge of loss, as if he's taken a part of me with him. I turn to him, only to see him taking a pack of cigars from his jacket pocket.

I glance around the room, scandalized, but it's just us and his men. Still, I blurt out, "I don't think you're allowed to smoke in here."

His eyes dance with amusement as he places a cigar between his lips. "Are you a stickler for rules, then?" he challenges, returning the pack into his pocket and exchanging it for a lighter.

The tip of the cigar flares orange, and suddenly the air is infused with a rich hypnotic scent. He takes a long drag, then exhales a cloud of fragrant smoke that wraps around me like a cozy fog. "Well?"

But I've forgotten his question, forgotten the panorama, forgotten everything but him. It's like he has cast a spell, and now I can only focus on him. The warmth of his body so close to mine, the mouthwatering scent of his cologne mixed with the cigar. *I had no idea cigars could smell so good.*

Or is it just him?

He notices me staring and, as if reading my mind, offers me the cigar. My mind races with wild thoughts, and I don't know what comes over me, but the tension that's been riding me since I saw him across the room of his restaurant two days ago finally snaps. I can't resist any longer.

Heart pounding a storm, I step into his space, just like he's been stepping into mine all day. Then, before I can second-guess it, I rise up on my toes and press my lips against his, giving him my first kiss.

For a heart-stopping moment, he freezes, and a wave of self-deprecating doubt fills my head. *Oh no, I'm a horrible kisser. Terrible, even. What was I thinking?!*

I start to retreat, cheeks burning with embarrassment, but then—*whoosh*—his arm swoops around me, yanking me close. And suddenly, *gloriously*, he's kissing me back. It's no soft kiss either—it's hungry, hot, and full of this raw need that makes my heart race. Has he been wanting this too? His lips drag across mine, coaxing them open, and when his tongue finally slides inside—*wow*—a jolt of something warm and electric shoots right down to my core. I've never felt anything like it. *Ever.*

I gasp—no, *moan*—because the pleasure is so overwhelming, so unexpected as the intoxicating taste of spicy cigar, mint, and *him* fills my being. My hands, as if acting on instinct, fly to his skull, fingers sinking into the silky strands of his hair, gripping like I never want to let go. Though, I don't even know if I'm doing this right.

He angles his head, his palm moving in slow circles on my back, soothing and reassuring even as his hot tongue explores the depth of my mouth. When he pulls my tongue between his lips and *sucks*—holy crap—dark spots blur my vision, and my knees actually feel weak as more pleasure cascades through me. *Is this normal? Am I going to melt?* Because I feel like I'm losing control, like I'm freefalling into something I'm not sure how to handle.

And then—*oh God, what's that?*—something hard pokes against my belly, startling me. *No way, is that his*—I jolt back, breaking the kiss. My eyes nearly pop out of my head when I spot the very obvious bulge in his trousers, and suddenly, I'm scrambling back, trying to process what just happened.

He lets me go without a word, watching me carefully, and I feel my face heat up. *Of course, I'm blushing. Stupid redhead curse.*

My blush is always so noticeable. But still, he says nothing, just... passes me his cigar again? This time, I don't even think twice about it as I accept it from him. Anything to distract me from the fact that I just realized he—*yeah. He does want me.*

I've never smoked before. I've missed out on so much in my life thanks to my overprotective father who couldn't handle the loss of his wife. But I'm done missing out. I want to experience everything—*all* the things I've been sheltered from my whole life.

Sex. Being reckless. Not worrying about consequences for once. And smoking this cigar, offered to me by this insanely hot man who I've been on a date with all day and just gave my first kiss to.

I place the cigar between my lips, hyper-aware that *his* lips were just here moments ago. Then, I inhale, dragging the rich, spicy smoke into my lungs like I know what I'm doing, and—*oh crap, nope.* My throat clamps up immediately, and my eyes water as I choke and start coughing.

"You're—you're such a bad influence," I rasp through my coughing fit, wiping at my tear-filled eyes as I hand him back his cigar. My lungs are on fire, and I probably look like a complete mess, but weirdly, I feel more alive than I ever have.

Less than a week. That's how long I've known him, but already he's got me running from home, spending hours with him at a children's park he emptied out just for us, kissing him, having all kinds of sexual thoughts, and now even smoking a cigar. *A freaking cigar.*

Atë would have a heart attack if he knew what I've been up to. *He'd lock me in my room for life.*

My Italian rubs his hand soothingly down my back, and like magic, a bottle of cold water is being thrust into my hands. I gratefully unscrew the cap and gulp the cool liquid, which helps calm the burn in my throat a little. But when I try to hand it back, the bottle slips from my fingers, and the room takes a slow, dizzying spin around me.

I tilt towards him, instinctively grabbing his shirt for balance, but something's wrong.

A sudden yawn forces its way out as this heavy, overwhelming drowsiness washes over me. The room spins on a loop like I'm still on the carousel, only this is way more disorienting, and everything is blurring, darkening. What's happening to me? Is this what getting high feels like? But that's impossible, right? One drag shouldn't hit this hard. Am I that much of a lightweight?

"Shh," he murmurs softly, continuing the soothing movements on my back. "Don't fight it. Just go to sleep. I've got you."

Wait—*no*. Warning bells ring through my head at his words, and I groan as the dawning horror hits me.

He drugged me. That bastard!

But it's too late. As my eyelids grow heavy and darkness pulls me under, that's when the third clue clicks into place.

How could I not have seen it? Of course, it simply never occurred to me that I could randomly meet a man in the same line of business as my father at a restaurant I just happened to wander into on my birthday—and first time out of the compound in years.

A man who could easily be one of *Atë's* rivals and possibly even one of the enemies my brother painstakingly warned me about and trained me to escape from.

Stupid. I was so clueless.

And fell right into his arms.

9

MAXIMO

The amber scotch catches the light as I twirl the tumbler between my fingertips, eyes fixed on my sleeping redhead. She looks so tiny, completely swallowed up by the thick blankets, her face peaceful in a way that makes something twist uncomfortably in my chest. My fingers twitch with the urge to move closer, to trace the soft curve of her cheek, but I don't. Instead, I lean back in the chair, forcing myself to stay put. That's not what this is about.

The moment she texted me her name, I knew who she was. Përmeti's mysterious daughter, the precious jewel we've only ever heard about via the rumor mills. A ghost, really. Nobody knew her age or what she looked like. Aside from the closest members of her family and Përmeti's men, I doubt anyone had ever actually seen the girl.

If she truly was not allowed to leave the compound, as she said, then that makes sense.

In fact, I'd nearly convinced myself his daughter had died along with his wife ten years ago, on that beach where his family was attacked. Because that was the last time anyone had reported seeing her. Yet here she is, right in my grasp.

I couldn't let this chance to control Përmeti slip through my fingers. What luck to have found her just when she was itching to escape her cage. Unfortunately for her, she's only traded her father's cage for another: *mine.*

A restless moan breaks the silence, and I place the scotch on the table next to me, steepling my fingers as I watch her fight her way to consciousness. I was hoping she'd remain knocked out until we landed, but oh well, that can't be helped, I suppose.

Her eyes snap open, brows furrowing as she takes in my jet's bedroom—scanning, assessing. When it clicks that she's somewhere unfamiliar, she's up in a flash—feet planted, knees bent, fists raised. So, someone taught the precious princess how to defend herself. *Interesting.*

As her gaze zeroes in on me, those pretty green-brown eyes swirl and harden with anger. But fuck, that only highlights the spattering of golden dots on her nose and underneath her eyes. Freckles. Never thought I'd have a thing for them.

"You bastard, where did you take me?" she growls, remaining in her fighting stance. I wave a hand at her to sit down, which only pisses her off more.

"I guess the legendary redhead temper is not a myth, after all." I comment mildly, testing the waters.

And there it is—the spark. Her fists tighten, her eyes narrowing into pure, murderous slits. Hell, if she could breathe fire, I'd be nothing but charred toast right now. I can't help it; my lips twitch in amusement. *Cute.*

Then, like I flicked a switch, she starts marching towards me, each step packed with intent. Death stare in full effect.

She's a bold little thing, I'll give her that. Part of me wants to let her close the gap, just to see what she thinks she can do.

"Whatever you're thinking, stop. I wouldn't do it if I were you," I say, the warning clear, though I already know that's not going to slow her down. Not with that look in her eye. I sigh, rubbing my temple. "I didn't want to have to play this card so soon. I wanted us to land first and—"

"*Land?*" she cuts in, freezing mid-step before whipping her head towards the window. Her eyes widen, and she practically lunges for the thick gray curtains, yanking them aside. The gasp she lets out is so dramatic it's almost theatrical. "You're smuggling me out of the country?" Pure scandal drips from every whispered word, like I've just committed high treason.

"No, sweetheart, not quite. We're only making a quick stop in Vegas. We'll be back in New York tomorrow." I roll up my sleeve to check the time. "And actually, we're landing soon, so I suggest you sit down unless you're a fan of turbulence."

"Landing soon? In *Las Vegas*?" She spins back to me, eyes blazing again. "How long was I out? What the hell did you give me!?" Her anger is back in full force, and honestly, it's kind of impressive how fast she cycles through emotions.

I wave it off casually. "Just a mild sedative. Nothing sinister." But of course, she's not buying it. If anything, she looks even more pissed. She snaps the curtains back into place and starts marching towards me again just as the plane dips into descent. The sudden tilt sends her lurching forward, and before she can hit the floor, I'm on my feet, cursing as I catch her.

"For fuck's sake, I *told* you to sit down." My hand wraps around her upper arm, and—*fuck*—that instant jolt zings right up my spine as I steer her towards the chair next to mine. Once she's seated, I retake my own seat.

She crumples forward, shoulders hunching in defeat as she buries her face in her hands. "The one time I rebel, I get kidnapped. Roan was right. Oh God, *Atë*." Her head snaps up suddenly, those enchanting eyes burning with desperate urgency. "Does my father know you've kidnapped me? What do you want? Ransom money?"

Money? How mundane.

I scoff, insulted by the worry on her face. "No, Elira. Hurting you isn't the plan. On the contrary." The plane eases onto the runway, and I stand, offering her a hand. She slaps it away with a roll of her eyes as she gets up on her own.

"I'm not setting foot off this plane unless we're back in New York. So you can go tell your pilot to turn back around immediately." Her hands plant themselves on her hips, chin lifted in defiance. "Whatever you want, trust me, my father *will* give it to you. You've won. You don't need this over-the-top charade of flying me out of the country."

"We're still in the country," I point out, and she lets out this adorable, exasperated growl. I swallow my chuckle, pretty sure that won't go down well with her.

"You know what I mean!"

"Look, while I'm sure your father loves you enough to bend to my demands, I doubt he'll give me what I want quite so easily. Besides, I'm not one to ask for permission, so I simply took what I wanted."

"Oh? And that is?" she asks with derision.

I hold her gaze as I answer, "You."

The color drains from her cheeks, and I watch in fascination as emotions war across her expressive face. Surprise, a flicker of something that looks dangerously like pleasure—quickly buried under an avalanche of confused fury. That brief glimpse of pleasure intrigues me. Maybe there's more to her than I thought.

It drags me back to that impulsive kiss she threw my way earlier, a bold move I sure as hell didn't see coming. But the way her lips pressed against mine, the hesitant brush of her tongue, spoke volumes about her inexperience. No practice—just raw, tentative want. It was unexpectedly sweet, and it stoked something in me, something dark and greedy, something that hadn't been part of the plan when I followed her to that park.

"Me?" she finally manages. "What do you mean, *me*? I'm not an object you can just take."

I shrug, walking out of the room, and her footsteps follow me exactly as I expected. Every quick step of hers behind me is practically vibrating with her simmering fury. I lead her down to the cabin's spacious meeting area, my temporary office when I travel, and wave a hand for her to take the leather chair across the table from me.

Her gaze flicks to the desert landscape stretching out beyond the window, then returns suspiciously as I slide the document I had my lawyer draft up at the last minute this morning towards her. She picks it up with a cute furrow between her brows, but as she reads it, they shoot up to her hairline, her eyes wide with disbelief all over them.

God, she's easy to read. It's refreshing after years of dealing with faces carved from stone.

The moment she comprehends what she's reading, she drops the document like it's a ticking time bomb as she glares up at me. "You're crazy if you think I'm going to sign this or marry you."

I glance down at the prenup. "The terms are fair to you." And they are. Thirty percent of my wealth—at least the legal ones—will be hers as soon as we're legally married. She'll also get a black card to shop for all her needs and a car, even though she won't have any reason to use it—but she doesn't know that part yet—and so much more. "Do you want to add anything else? I'm open to negotiate."

"Oh my God, you really *are* crazy." She looks at me like I'm a whole different species. "You *kidnapped* me, psycho. I don't even know your name and you expect me to negotiate *marriage terms* with you? No way in hell. And once my father gets wind of this, you're as good as dead. That is if I don't end you first."

I wait for her tirade to finish before I give a slight bow. "I suppose it wouldn't do for my own bride not to know my name." I lean in just enough to watch her reaction. "Maximo Leonotti, at your service, *dolcezza*."

She inhales sharply, but it's not because I called her 'sweetness'. Recognition floods her face, draining it of color once again as understanding dawns in her eyes. Hmm. "I take it you know me? Or at least you've heard of me?" I ask, watching her carefully.

"There's not a soul alive who hasn't heard of the *Nightshades*." She spits the name out like poison, and I smirk. I can't imagine her father talking to her about business, but she's a smart one, my wife-to-be.

"Knowing who you are doesn't change anything, *Maximo*." My name becomes a curse on her lips. "I'm not going to marry you, not even if you torture me or put a gun to my head."

I sigh sadly. "I was afraid you'd say that." I take out my phone, hesitating before I unlock it because I know this will change the dynamic between us. If she didn't hate me already, this will seal the deal.

Well, it can't be helped. I don't want her affections anyway —just her, and the frustration and anger the knowledge of his precious daughter with me will cause her father. And if a gun to her head won't give me her consent, perhaps a gun to someone else's head will.

Without a word, I pull up my media gallery and hand her the phone. She doesn't need any prompting to play the video. The gasp that escapes her lips says it all. I can't see the screen from this angle, but I know exactly what she's watching; I've replayed it so many times it's burned into my memory.

The scene unfolds with my man on the rooftop of the three-story building next to Përmeti's main house in his gated estate, the one built for his men. But I had a few of mine infiltrate it yesterday while the distraction for my little redhead to run into my arms was in full force.

The video starts with my sniper on his knees, steadying his

rifle against the railing, eye pressed to the scope, watching his target. Then the camera pans over to the main house, zooming in on a second-floor window, revealing the prey—a man in his office, swallowing some suspicious-looking pills.

Afrim Përmeti.

Elira's face turns ghostly pale, her grip on my phone white-knuckled as she struggles to breathe. "There's another video. Swipe left," I tell her, hating the way the fight drains out of her. I liked her fire, damn it.

She swipes. The next video mirrors the first but features a different target. Roan Përmeti sits on a quiet sidewalk outside of a small coffee shop that belongs to his uncle, completely unaware of the crosshair trained on him.

She turns a worrying shade of green, and her cheeks seem to swell as she drops the phone almost as quickly as she dropped the prenup.

I force myself to speak so she understands what the video is about. "So you see, Elira. You'll marry me, or my man will blow your father's head off his stubborn neck, and your brother will follow him."

She bolts from her chair, fleeing towards the bedroom at the back of the jet. Against my better judgment, worry gnaws at me as I get up to follow her. For fuck's sake, I shouldn't care how she's taking this. She's my enemy.

But I follow her anyway, right into the jet's bedroom. The ensuite door is wide open, and I find her on her knees in front of the toilet bowl, emptying her stomach. My chest tightens at the sight. And as I stand there watching her, I can't ignore the sharp stab of guilt winding its way through me.

I did that to her.

10

ELIRA

The suffocating sensation hits like a wave. It's like I'm underwater, drowning; something is weighing my legs down so I can't even swim up. The surface glimmers far above, unreachable, no rescue in sight. But the worst part? The bitter knowledge that I put myself in this position. I trusted someone I knew I shouldn't have, and now I'm not just in danger—I've dragged *Atë* and Roan into this nightmare too.

My fingers won't stop shaking as I grip the pen. Maximo's dark eyes drill into me, tracking every twitch and tremor as I sign the prenup. The man never stops watching. At first, those eyes used to make my skin tingle with excitement—still do, damn him straight to hell. Even after his awful betrayal shattered everything, my body betrays me with little sparks of heat, and I hate it. So I force myself to go numb instead. He won't get the satisfaction of seeing how he affects me.

I can't believe I willingly gave that bastard my first kiss.

My heart aches and hot tears threaten to spill over, but I blink them back fiercely. *He doesn't get to see my tears—not one single drop. He doesn't get anything from me anymore.* After I finish signing, he adds his own signature as well and tucks the paper into his jacket pocket like it's just another business deal. Maybe to him, it is.

As we exit his jet, followed by three of his men, he dares to place a possessive hand on my waist, and I stiffen instantly, increasing my pace so his hand falls away. *He doesn't get to touch me.*

I swallow hard, forcing down the bile that rises with each vivid replay of the sniper's scope fixed on *Atë* as he took his blood pressure pill, completely oblivious to the threat a heartbeat away. I'm the only one who knows about the doctor's warning, that he needs to take it easy after his blood pressure suddenly went through the roof last month. I was the one who nagged him to take those pills, and now... I'm the reason he has to.

The tears win their battle, spilling down my cheeks as I descend the jet's short stairs. Dammit. I grit my teeth, forcing my legs to keep moving, though each step feels like I'm sinking further under this weight. Toughen the fuck up, Elira!

I quickly wipe the tears away, dragging in deep breaths until the pressure in my chest eases. Tears won't solve anything. Tears won't save anyone.

Maximo falls into step next to me, pointing towards two hulking SUVs with the windows blacked out parked several feet away from the jet in the middle of the deserted airstrip.

As we near the vehicles, the setting sun dips lower, which makes no sense. It was still mid-morning when he drugged me. My heart jitters. Did I really lose all those hours? Or is this some twisted, time-zone trick? *Ugh, I don't even know what time zone we're in anymore.* Everything feels wrong, distorted.

A mountain of a man emerges from the first SUV's driver's side and opens the back door. I scramble inside, scooting so far up against the opposite door I can feel the handle digging into my side. Let him see exactly how far I want to be away from him. I don't care if it's childish.

Maximo's face is pulled into a scowl as he gets in next to me, but I keep my face turned to the window, shutting him out. The door closes behind him with a firm thud, and our driver hustles back to his seat, starting the engine and pulling away from the airstrip.

Outside, the desert stretches out, bathed in the fiery glow of the setting sun. It's breathtaking in a way, but I can't muster any awe for it. My mind is miles away, trapped in the cold realization that, in mere hours, I'll be married to this ruthless man next to me.

Why me?

He's still relatively young, filthy rich, and so annoyingly handsome. A man like him could snap his fingers and have a line of willing women at his feet.

The irony hits hard: if he'd just let me leave after what I stupidly thought was a magical date, he probably could have had me on his terms anyway. I'd have been curious enough, enticed enough to come back, again and again. And if he'd proposed a few months down the line, I might have been blissfully happy saying yes, drunk on the fantasy of him.

Heck, even learning his true identity might not have scared me off right away. That's how thoroughly he had bewitched me in just one day.

The silence in the SUV is oppressive and crackles with angry tension as we drive to who-knows-where. For a moment, I wonder what reason *he* has to be angry. I'm the victim here!

But I push it out of my head, because the anger creeping into my oasis of numbness only invites hurt along with it. I'd rather stay numb—feel nothing at all. It's the only thing keeping me sane.

The minutes drag until the city rises around us from the desert—towering skyscrapers, flashy hotels, and neon-bright casinos everywhere. In another life, I'd be pressing my nose to the window in wonder. But right now, I just stare, unfazed.

The SUV weaves past the gaudy heart of the strip, stopping at a smaller building with white bricks and imposing columns. My stomach drops as I recognize it—the *courthouse*. The place where my freedom ends.

Maximo extends his hand to help me out, but I ignore it completely. Instead, I fling my door open and jump out on my own.

When I glance at him, his hands are curled into fists as he stares at me with fire blazing in his onyx eyes. I round the SUV with my head held high, and with a trail of his men behind us, we climb up into the civic building.

In the lobby, Maximo stops me with a hand on my elbow, igniting a surge of heat that pierces right through my fog. The arousal hits hard, unwanted, and right on its heels is anger—at him, at my traitorous body that *still* responds to his touch. I yank my elbow out of his grip, meeting his sharp glare with one of my own.

"Here." He takes a small box out of his pocket and hands it to me. What now? I narrow my eyes, not ready to trust anything coming from him, but curiosity gets the better of me. The box feels kind of weighty as I take it, practically pulsing with bad omens.

What's inside? Something to reinforce the trap he's set? A USB loaded with another reminder that he owns my life—and my family's?

But when I flip it open, I forget how to breathe.

Nestled inside is a rose gold ring, scattered with tiny diamonds along the band, all leading up to a huge cushion-cut diamond at the center. The light catches every facet, sending tiny prisms of color dancing across my skin. *Wow.* It's so big, so brilliantly clear, it has to be at least fifteen carats, if not more.

But the awe fades as fast as it flared up, leaving only cold reality. My lips curve down. This isn't romance—this ring is nothing but a symbol of his threat over me, a reminder that this kidnapping and marriage shenanigan was premeditated by him. How else could he have something this elaborate ready so quickly?

He knew exactly what he wanted, even when he pretended to help me escape. When he spent the day with me, acting like he cared, like he actually wanted to show me the best view of the city. And I fell for it all. He must think I'm such a fool.

"Do you like it?" he asks, watching my face closely, almost like he's... hopeful. "It's your engagement ring. We can get another one if it's not your style."

"It's fine," I say, keeping my voice as flat as possible as I slip it on. Despite myself, a small tremor rolls down my spine when the heavy rock settles perfectly on my finger. *I love it,* damn him. And damn him for knowing my size. "It's not like this is a real marriage, so it doesn't matter," I add. It doesn't matter if I love it.

Ohh, he doesn't like that answer. His eyes flash with something that might be hurt before he masks it. Good. Let him hurt. Let him feel a fraction of what he's put me through. I curl my fingers, letting the heavy stone dig into my skin.

What did he expect anyway? That I'd squeal with delight, throw myself into his arms, declare my love of the ring, and *thank* him? If so, he's crazier than I thought and suffering from severe delusion.

"Ready to be my wife?" he asks, and my heart betrays me yet again with a treacherous skip.

"It's not like I can say no without signing my family's death warrant." The words land heavy, and yeah, he doesn't like that answer either. His jaw tightens, but he doesn't snap back. Just spins on his heel in silence, leaving me to trail after him into a small, nearly empty courtroom.

The only person waiting for us is the man behind the counter-thingy—the justice of peace? Magistrate? I don't know what he's called. All I know is he's here to make this twisted arrangement official.

We stop in front of him, and I fidget, feeling the heavy weight of Maximo's ring on my finger like a brand. The pretty jewelry nothing more than chains shackling me to him.

The ceremony passes in a blur, too fast to fully grasp. When the official asks if I'm here willingly, I almost laugh—*no, but my family's lives are excellent motivation*. A quick check of IDs, a few nods, and suddenly Maximo is saying "I do" In a deep, confident voice like he's been dreaming of this moment. And then it's my turn.

I lick my lips nervously and croak out my, "I do."

The words feel like they're coming from someone else, a thousand miles away. But apparently, it's enough for the official who gives a short nod and says, "I now pronounce you man and wife." And that quickly, the trajectory of my life changes.

The room spins, almost like it did when I drank that sedated water. Just as I'm about to lose my balance, Maximo's arms are around me, steadying me and pulling me closer than I want. Meanwhile, the official drones on, "You may kiss the bride."

My eyes go wide when Maximo leans down, aiming right for my lips. *No. Never again.* At the last second, I turn my head so his lips brush over my cheeks instead. His fingers dig into my back almost painfully before he releases me like I've just burned him.

We sign the marriage license, and before I even have a chance to process it, we're leaving the courthouse and getting back into the SUV.

"What was that in there?" he asks as he slides in next to me.

"What was what?" I ask tonelessly.

"You gave me your cheek," he grits out.

"Oh, *that*. Excuse me if I don't want to kiss the man threatening the lives of my loved ones. In case it's unclear, kisses are off the table, Maximo." *Along with everything else you thought you'd get from this sham marriage.*

His face hardens to granite, but without a word, he yanks out his phone and starts typing furiously, ignoring me entirely. Fine. I cross my arms, leaning against the window, watching the city blur as we speed away from the courthouse.

We drive back the way we came, and by the time the SUV descends into the underground garage of some luxury hotel skyscraper, my nerves are shot. Maximo leads me straight to the bank of elevators tucked to one side, pulling out a card from his jacket pocket to tap against the screen. The doors slide open silently, and he hits the button for the penthouse. I blow out a breath of relief. At least I won't have to play happy bride with a bunch of strangers.

As we ascend, I catch my reflection in the mirrored wall of the elevator and cringe at my disheveled appearance. I've never given much thought to what my marriage might be like, but I certainly wouldn't have imagined getting married in jeans and a plain top, with curls falling messily from my ponytail. I brush some hair off my face, only for the huge rock on my ring to jab me in the cheek, surprising me. Ugh, that will take some getting used to.

The elevator finally dings open into an elegant foyer, and Maximo storms out like he's in a rush.

"Maximo!" I call after him, and he stops, glancing back at me with a questioning brow. "I want my purse back. My phone is inside, and I need to call my father." I realized it was missing the moment I woke up, and I'm guessing he made sure it stayed that way—another piece of control stripped away by this man who thinks he owns me.

"No," he says and continues into the penthouse, leaving me gaping in disbelief.

"What do you mean *no*?" I ask incredulously, jogging to catch up. "My family is going to be worried sick! I need to let them know I'm alright." And I need to confirm that *they* are alright too. That they're still alive. *That this sacrifice actually means something.*

"Last I checked, 'no' has only one meaning. You won't be calling home, Elira." He starts to walk away again, but this time I grab his arm before I can think better of it. His gaze drops to the monstrous rock on my finger, and a possessive glint appears in his eyes as he meets my stare.

"Don't look at me like that. The fact that we're married doesn't change anything. Your father remains a worm trying to burrow into my territory. Finding out I married his daughter will only give him undue confidence. I want him to stew in his worry for a few more weeks. If it distracts him from his pathetic attempts to continue his criminal activities in my city, even better."

My grip goes slack with shock. I knew *Atë*'s work isn't legal and that I'm probably the only one who thinks of him as *nice* because I'm his daughter. But it's still a slap in the face to hear Maximo say it that way and to see the hate he has for him.

But what about him? He's no better than *Atë*. "So, what? You kidnapped and married me, all to settle some score with my dad?"

He snaps his fingers in my face like I'm a child who finally understood a simple lesson. "Bingo."

That's it. My fists clench at my sides as fury washes over me, effectively piercing through my numbness. This absolute bastard. This arrogant, motherfucking piece of—I'm not much of a curser, but suddenly, a torrent of Albanian curse words pour from my mouth, the kind of words I've only ever heard my brother's or my *atë*'s men mutter over the years. And now here I am, hurling them at him, each one feeling like a tiny slice of satisfaction. I swear I want to tear into him, make him bleed, make him hurt like I'm hurting, *fucking claw his handsome face out until it matches his ugly soul.* I'm half-shocked at the violent thoughts and urges running through my head, which only escalates when he starts slowly clapping, his lips curling up at the corners, winking his stupid dimples at me.

"Impressive, Elira."

I roll my eyes and stomp away into the first bedroom I see. I need to get away from him before I do something reckless like try to throttle him—which would only make things worse for my family.

Slamming the door behind me, I start pacing as the anger boils into adrenaline, making my whole body vibrate with rage. I have to find a way to burn it off somehow—that doesn't actually involve my bare hands on my new 'husband's' neck, no matter how tempting that sounds. Not that I could take him in a fight anyway. He probably has training I can't even imagine. The thought just adds to my frustration.

Then the door opens behind me, and I swirl around to see Maximo strolling in, calm as you please. *Of course. Privacy means nothing to him.* He shrugs off his suit jacket, letting it drop to the floor as he starts undoing his shirt buttons.

"What the hell are you doing?" I demand, refusing to believe the answer my brain supplied for me. He can't possibly expect—

"Getting ready to consummate this marriage. Take off your clothes, Elira, unless you'd rather I do it for you."

"You must have a death wish. Do you know how furious I am, right now? Touch me and I'll bite your head off!" I threaten, meaning it with every fiber of my being.

But he doesn't even pause; those arrogant fingers just keep going, popping each button until his shirt joins the jacket on the floor, exposing a broad expanse of tanned, muscular chest.

My eyes immediately go to the beautiful arrays of color on his left arm, climbing up from his wrist to his shoulder blade. My breath hitches, and I wrench my gaze away, fuming at myself.

Fuck him for being so infuriatingly attractive. I start scanning the room for anything I could use as a weapon—lamp, heavy book, chair?—until his next words knock the wind right out of my anger.

"You do realize that unless we consummate this marriage, it can easily be contested as illegal, right? I'm not taking the risk." He says it casually, as if he's explaining a minor technicality in a contract. "And if you need a reminder, it's all spelled out in the prenup you signed." He unbuckles his wristwatch and places it gently on top of his discarded clothes.

"No way. It's not." But uncertainty weakens my protest. I didn't exactly comb through the fine print before signing the damned thing. At the time, all I cared about was doing whatever would keep my family safe.

Maximo leaves the room without a word, and for a second, I dare hope. I blow out a tentative breath of relief. Is he actually giving up?

But no, not a chance. He's back just as fast, waving a paper up—the prenup. *Unbelievable.* I snatch it out of his hand, scanning frantically until I find it. My heart stops, then starts again double-time. Something heavy and molten pools low in my belly—a mix of rage and... something else. Something that sends heat between my thighs and self-loathing through my soul.

It's just biology, I snap to myself. Pure animal response to an attractive male. Nothing more.

The clause hides in smaller font, nearly invisible unless you search for it.

The marriage is to be consummated to make the union binding. And afterwards, the bride shall grant her groom access to her body if he so wishes, or he would be well within his rights to annul the marriage.

So that's it? He'll annul the marriage if I don't grant him access to my body? I'm *sooo* scared. "Fine. Bring the annulment papers, then. Do you think I care? Let's end this circus right now."

"You do know the only thing saving your precious father and brother from my bullet is..." He pauses to wave a hand between us. "...this marriage."

Of course.

More threats. His favorite weapon. Fury surges anew, and I tighten my grip on the prenup until it crumples in my fist.

"That's fine. You can tear it. It's not the original copy." His tone is almost kind, and it makes me want to scream. I shoot him a glare that could burn through steel as I hurl the crumpled paper at him.

"You think you're so smart, don't you?" I spit, each word brimming with venom. "Well, congrats, Maximo. You've got me well and truly trapped. Consummate away." I yank my top over my head and fling that at him too, loving that it smacks him right in his stupid face.

My jeans follow, tugging them off and kicking them aside until I'm in just my underwear. My pulse is roaring in my ears, and the furious adrenaline falters, just a bit, as cool air grazes my skin. But I grit my teeth and reach behind to unclasp my bra, letting it fall, then slip out of my panties, leaving nothing between me and his gaze.

A glimmer of discomfort zips down my spine as his eyes roam over me, assessing, drinking me in. And I hate the heat creeping up my cheeks, hate the way my heart races. I can't believe this is happening. Here I am, naked before a man for the first time, and it's *him*—the man who's made sure I have no way out.

11

MAXIMO

That fucking chin. She tilts it high, defiantly, those hazel eyes flashing with anger and, just beneath, a hint of unease she can't hide. She's wound up tight, her whole body stiff as a board. Red splotches burst across her cheeks, spread over her forehead—a telling sign of her inner turmoil. My gaze holds steady on her face as I close the distance between us, catching every splotch of that delicious redness. I need to see how far it goes.

When I finally let my eyes travel downward, I'm rewarded. That flush isn't just on her face—it spills down her neck, her sternum, and below her tits. My hand reaches out, wrapping around her throat, craving the warmth of her skin. The second I touch her, her breath hitches, lips parting slightly, and she releases this shaky exhale that gives away everything she tries to hide.

With my hand anchored around her neck, I take in the pale flesh of her perky tits crowned by strawberry-colored nipples. My mouth waters at the sight. I need to taste them, mark them.

I raise my left hand and move my thumb over one nipple, over and over, until the flesh tightens and puckers. Beneath my palm on her throat, her heartbeat picks up, hammering erratically. I glance up, curious if it's arousal or fear I'm sensing, and my lips curl into a smirk when I see it's definitely the former.

She might hate me, but her body certainly doesn't. Her eyes narrow on me, but she remains still—such a good girl, even in her defiance.

Reluctantly, I let go of her tit and trail my hand down the slight swell of her belly, teasingly dipping my thumb into her belly button. She jolts, letting out a soft squeak, so I do it again and again, until a shudder rolls through her. Satisfied I drift even lower, but just as my hand inches towards its destination, her thighs snap together, shutting me out.

My eyes flick up. The look on her face stops me cold. A shade of trepidation mingles with something deeper. *No fucking way*. "You're not a virgin, are you?" I ask, half-mockingly, expecting her to scoff, to deny it outright. But the color on her face deepens, and she tilts her head down, breaking eye contact. *That's answer enough*.

A fierce, primal roar fills my head as blood flows south in a dizzying rush until my semi-erect cock is rock hard. *Fuck me*. She's untouched. Pure. I'm the first to see her totally naked. The first to touch her like this. The first one who will sink between those thighs and lose himself in that sweet cunt of hers.

The only one who ever will.

Unconsciously, my hand tightens around her throat as an unholy possession consumes me. She's mine, mine, *mine*. Her panicked scrabbling at my wrist breaks through my haze. I ease up immediately, forcing myself to breathe as I close my eyes to wrestle my demons back into their cage. When I open my eyes again, her wary observation tells me she saw too much in that moment of lost control.

But fuck, I can't help myself. The hunger to taste her mouth is overwhelming. I move in, my lips barely brushing hers before she twists her head away. A flash of irritation snaps through me. How dare she try to deny me again? I tighten my grip on her neck and firmly guide her face back to mine.

"No." The word comes out breathless but firm when I try to forcefully kiss her. "No kissing."

"This again? What the hell, Elira. In case you don't remember, you've already kissed me once before. I'm looking at your naked body, and I'm going to fuck you before this night ends." The crude words reflect my growing anger. "You'll give me your mouth, goddamnit."

"No, Maximo. That kiss happened before you threatened to kill my family. I'll have sex with you to save them, but nowhere in your precious contract does it demand my kisses."

"You'll have sex with me because your body begs for it."

"My body's an idiot."

"Aren't they all."

I lean forward, ready to steal another kiss, when an odd sensation flickers inside me. Usually, I couldn't care less about kissing, but after that soft, tentative kiss she gave me at the museum, she's whetted my appetite. It took everything in me not to stare at her lips the whole flight here. Her refusal, infuriating as it is, only stokes my desire for her even more.

"No," she says, one more time.e

"Fine. Keep your kisses to yourself." The words scrape out through clenched teeth. "But I'll have everything else, you hear me? *Everything else*. Every. Fucking. Thing." I back her towards the bed, my hand firm at her throat. Then, with a strong flick of my wrist, I send her sprawling onto the mattress.

She scrambles up, trying to retreat, but I grab her ankle to pull her back. "Christ, Elira, I won't kiss you," I remind her, holding her gaze until she finally stills and just watches me carefully as I climb up her body.

"Tell me what I already know," I growl. "Tell me that you want this, me, and not just because of any threat."

"You are the threat..."

Then I bury my nose into her warm neck, enjoying the citrus and vanilla scent that wafts up my nostrils. My tongue flicks out, eager to consume her essence.

As I lick, bite, and suck at her neck, my right hand lands on her tit, palming the soft flesh and rolling it slowly between my fingers.

"Say it."

A low noise slips from her throat before she bites it back. Oh no, *dolcezza*. That won't do. It won't do at all. I want all your noises. Every raw reaction.

"I want you to fuck..."

"Fuck you?" I smirk, moving down her body, lifting her tit to my waiting mouth.

"To fuck off."

My eyes lock onto hers as I drag my tongue over the pale flesh, teasing and tasting. Her pupils dilate, and the back of her head digs into the mattress as her breath quivers. I lick it again, then give a gentle bite before soothing the sting with my tongue. By the time I graze her nipple, the flesh is already so stiff, I wonder if she's feeling that sweet ache as intensely as I want her to. I blow a warm breath over it and goosebumps ripple across her skin, her reaction a delicious reminder of how her body responds to me.

Then, I pull away–only for a teasing, mocking moment—but before I can get too far, her fingers are in my hair. Forming a tangled knot, she pulls me back down into her body.

Victory.

"For somebody who hates me so much, your body sure is responsive. Whether you like it or not, you want me," I say with satisfaction.

"Fuck you," she pants, the words barely audible. Her fingers snap back, releasing my head. But I don't give her any relief. Not this time.

"You're about to, *dolcezza*." I roll my tongue over her nipple, then take it fully into my mouth, suctioning. She goes wild underneath me, her back arching off the bed as a low keening sound escapes her lips. *Yes. Give me everything.*

The sound goes directly to my cock, making it throb painfully. But I ignore it. She needs to come first—at least twice—so her virgin cunt is wet and ready to ease my way inside.

My left hand kneads one tit while I suck the other, my free hand snaking down to the fiery red curls at the apex of her thighs. Her legs snap shut again, and when I glance up at her, she's staring at me, her gaze a complicated mixture of desire, misgiving, and a little bit of...*softness*?

Shit. Alarm bells ring in my head, reminding me why I always avoid virgins. That hint of softness is dangerous—more dangerous than any weapon she could wield against me. The last thing I need is for her to develop a tender spot for me, even if a small part of me wants that. But that's not what this is.

Her family and I are on opposite sides of a war. My threat to kill them was a bluff to force her into marrying me, but hell, there might come a time when I actually have to hurt or even kill them. So, no matter how much I want to, *I'm not taking her virginity with my cock.*

With slow intent, I trace my fingers along her inner thigh, feeling her shiver as I suck her nipple again. Her eyes flutter shut with a breathy cry, and her thighs part almost involuntarily. It's like magic, watching her resistance melt away beneath my touch, her body surrendering even if her mind is fighting. Not wasting a second, I wedge my leg between hers, making damn sure she doesn't attempt to close them again.

Then I glide my fingers through her wet folds, the first touch nearly undoing my careful control. When I find her swollen clit, I time my movements with a sharp bite to her nipple and a firm squeeze of her tit. And Christ, she detonates beneath me, almost bucking me off her as she arches off the bed with a wild scream. I keep the rhythm steady, my hands and mouth working in sync, drawing out her pleasure for as long as possible.

Only when she finally floats back down from her high do I release her tits and slide down her body, eager to drink up every drop of her arousal. I lift my glistening fingers and lick them clean as I watch her face. The way she blushes at the show, her eyes growing heavy-lidded—*perfection*.

"Delicious," I murmur, making her blush deepen into a charming tomato red. *Fuck.* I groan, shoving my hand into my pants to adjust my steel-hard cock, squeezing the head tight at the base in a desperate bid for control. I need to hold on just a little longer.

Settling down between her thighs, I hook one leg over my shoulder, which makes her gasp. My gaze hones in on the pretty pink flesh of her tiny hole, and I'm unable to resist running my nose through her wetness until I'm drowning in her tangy, citrus scent. The moment my mouth tastes her, she shudders beneath me, her whole body reacting to each lick as I feast on her sweet and tart cum.

A low, breathy groan spills from her lips, and when her hands dive back into my hair, my control nearly snaps—the rush of victory leaves me dizzy with arousal. Holy hell, she's touching me. *Participating.* I swirl my tongue around her clit, taking my time, teasing her just right. Then, I lash at the bundle of nerves, again and again, until I'm rewarded with another full-body shudder. I want more—more of her reactions, more of that delicious sound she makes when pleasure overtakes her.

"This might hurt a little," I warn as I sink my index finger into her tight sheath. Her gasp is music to my ears, and the way her grip tightens on my hair almost makes me lose my damn mind right there. She's too hot, *too* tight.

Another dizzy rush washes over me as I imagine her strangling my cock. Pre-cum gushes out of me, and I grind my hip against the bed for a little relief as I stir my fingers inside her until I feel it—that thin barrier that marks her as untouched.

"This needs to go." My voice is thicker than ever as I roll the tip of my finger against her hymen. Another finger slides in alongside the first, and with a forceful thrust, I break through.

"Maximo!" she yells, clamping her legs around my head like a vise. "Ouch, that hurts, that hurts. Stop. Please stop."

"Shhh," I soothe, pressing her back down with a steadying hand on her belly. "It will only hurt for a few moments, relax." I return my attention to her clit, using my tongue to distract from the discomfort as I work my fingers in and out, gradually stretching her virgin tightness.

Slowly, her tensed thighs relax, and she loosens her grip on my hair. "Better?" I murmur, glancing up at her. She hesitates, then nods, and I smirk. "It's better my fingers than my cock. That would have hurt way worse."

My gaze drifts back between her thighs, and I lick my lips at the sight of her virgin blood slowly dripping out. She tenses again when I lean in. "Maximo, no. You can't do that, the blood—" Her horrified protests fizzle out into a moan as I lap her up, enjoying the metallic taste of her blood mixed with her sweet cum.

Fucking hell. I need to be inside her. *Now.*

But I force myself to remain still, fighting the insistent urge riding me.

She needs to come again. She's still too tight. I lap at her cunt until all traces of her virgin blood are gone before I thrust two fingers inside her while nibbling on her clit like I'm starved. When she starts rocking her hips against me, meeting my thrusts—*fuck.*

That's it. That's fucking it.

I shift back slightly to see her expression, rubbing my thumb on her clit as I curl the fingers inside her upward, moving around slowly, seeking the subtly ridged nerves of her g-spot.

When I find it, I tap it gently—once, twice—until it swells against my fingers, just like her clit did. Then I drag my fingers over it, tickling it.

"*MAXIMO!*" She screams my name to the ceiling. Her eyes roll back, and her pretty face scrunches up in ecstasy as her cunt tightens around me, gushing out her orgasm.

My chest swells with pride as I lean down to drink up her nectar, still working that g-spot to prolong her pleasure. I'm lost in her, in the moment, in everything she gives me.

One final shudder rips through her before her hands drop from my hair and she collapses limply into the bed, *spent and glowing*.

I get up from the bed, quickly toeing off my shoes, my body buzzing with anticipation. Just as I'm about to undo my belt buckle, a loud ringing pierces the heated atmosphere. It's my phone. I freeze, heart pounding as I watch her spread out on the bed for me like a delectable offering. An offering no one is going to distract me from having.

I take the phone out of my pocket, ready to silence it—but Rafael's name stops me cold. *For fuck's sake*. It has to be important as hell if he's calling me right now.

Squeezing my eyes shut with pain and frustration warring in my chest, I answer the call. "What?!"

12

ELIRA

Something bad must have happened back home, because Maximo's whole demeanor changes after that phone call. I've never seen anyone switch from passionate to deadly so fast. Before I can process the change, I'm being rushed off the bed into my clothes, then bundled out of the hotel suite and straight towards the elevators. When we hit the basement garage, the SUVs are running and his men are already inside.

Throughout the ride to the airport, Maximo is glued to his phone, firing off rapid-fire Italian that sounds like a storm of thunder. I don't understand Italian, so I just rest my head against the window and watch the city blur into a kaleidoscope of colors as we race back through the desert to the airstrip.

But just as I start to lose myself in the scenery, a slight shift shoots a throb of awareness through my core, and suddenly I'm drowning in memories of his hands, his mouth, the way he—

Stop it. I cross my legs tightly, as if I can physically contain the rush of heat those thoughts bring. *We almost had sex.*

Almost.

Heat creeps up my cheeks. I'm not a virgin anymore, not

really—not after what he did. The worst part is, once the pain faded, *I loved it*. Every single second.

What kind of person does that make me? Getting turned on by the man who ruthlessly threatened my family to force me into marriage, who demanded I have sex with him? My stomach twists with guilt as I remember how I moved against him. I'd told myself I'd lie as still as possible, not show him any reaction. But his touch had burned away all my resistance, and I lost myself completely in pleasure. *Too much pleasure.*

Ugh... why couldn't I hold it together? The memory of those shameless little moans makes me want to sink through the car floor.

I peek at him from under my lashes. He's still yelling on the phone. The thunderous expression on his face promises hell for whoever's on the other end. Just watching him makes my pulse quicken—and not entirely from fear. And that, that's what makes him truly dangerous. More dangerous than I thought.

We reach the airstrip in record time. The jet engines are already roaring, fans whirring, as we pile out of the SUV. The drivers stay behind and wave us off as we board, and within moments of strapping in, the plane is speeding down the runway and into the sky.

Once we're airborne, Maximo disappears into the meeting room, leaving me to my own devices. I retreat to the back cabin bedroom—same one I woke up in just a few hours ago. Hours... Has it only been hours? So much has changed since then, I feel like a different person.

In a way, I *am* a different person.

The old Elira died somewhere between "I do" and Maximo's hands on her body.

I need to escape this memory. The ensuite bathroom calls to me, so I make my way there to take a quick shower. Under the hot spray, I wash my shoulders, then my arms, and let the water cascade over my chest and stomach before scrubbing my soapy hands between my thighs, but I'm relatively clean there. My face heats as I recall exactly how it got this way after all the bodily fluids expended. His tongue... *No. Stop.* I scrub harder, as if I can rinse him out of my very skin.

Post-shower presents a wardrobe crisis. Wear my old, now dirty clothes again or the clean ones that clearly belong to Maximo that I find in the small closet. After a mental debate that feels endless, I take out a dark shirt and dress pants. I sniff them first. No scent of him—just soap, so at least I won't have to smell him on me.

Okay. I can pretend I'm not wearing my enemy's clothes.

Swallowing my pride, I slip the shirt on without my bra. It swallows me whole, hanging to mid-thigh but thick enough to hide my nipples. I fold my bra and ruined panties together, stuffing them under my sweatshirt and jeans, then pull the dress pants on. I have to get creative with one of his ties through the belt loops for them to stay up, but eventually, I make it work.

Finally, I tackle my hair—which is a matted mess. With no products available, I wage war against the tangles with my fingers until I can wrangle it into another ponytail.

All set...

But I stall, dreading going back out there and facing him again. The searing anger might have faded—for now—but the heat of resentment still simmers. I'm still here against my will. And he *did* threaten to—to—I can't even think about it without getting riled up, so I push it out of my head. What's the point of getting angry when I'm so helpless? I'll just bide my time and wait.

A sharp knock on the door pulls me out of my musing, and my eyes narrow on it. What now? It can't be Maximo. He's arrogant enough to barge right in, no checking if I'm dressed or not.

Sure enough, a voice that's not his comes through from the other side. "Mrs. Leonotti, are you in there?"

My heart jolts as the realization that *I'm* Mrs. Leonotti now sinks in, and I gape at the door like it just revealed a terrible secret. When the knock sounds again, I finally pull myself together and go to answer.

Bodyguard 1 from the park stands there, holding a tray of food and water. He raises the tray with a hesitant look in his eyes. "The boss asked me to bring this to you. Said you must be starving."

Oh, so now he's worried I'll what? Starve to death before the plane lands? I glance over Bodyguard 1's shoulder, but I can't see past the hallway to the door of the meeting room.

What's his deal?

He can't exactly have sex with you if you starve to death. The bitter thought creeps through my head and brings me sharply back to reality. I scowl as I step back. I can't believe for an instant I thought he might actually be worried about me. How laughable.

I need to remember who my new husband really is. Maximo Leonotti, Don of the Queens *Cosa Nostra,* isn't feared for his thoughtfulness but for his ruthlessness.

He crushes anyone he sees as an enemy without hesitation, showing no mercy. And right now, that enemy is my family—and by extension, *me*.

So yeah, no matter what title I wear now, this marriage means nothing. Even if I'm not just a tool for him to use against my father, the reality that he kidnapped and threatened me to marry him is more than enough strikes against him. Fool me once, and all that.

"Mrs. Leonotti?"

I blink at the man still standing in front of me. "You can tell the *boss* that I'm not hungry," I say coolly, just as my stomach decides to betray me with an audible growl. Mortified, I slam the door in his face before he can respond. Damn traitorous stomach. *Traitorous body*. It keeps betraying me today in new and humiliating ways.

I crawl into the big bed, curling into myself as my stomach protests again. Besides, I can't trust whatever food he offers me. What if it's laced with more sedatives? Not that he needs to drug me anymore. He already got what he wanted. Marriage, submission, my vir—

The door crashes open with enough force to make me jump. Maximo fills the doorway like an angry storm cloud, food tray in hand.

Yup. Arrogant asshole. "Can't knock?" I snap, gaze fixed on him as he approaches the bed.

He doesn't say a word as he places the tray on the night-stand next to me, just scowls at me as if I somehow forced him to come here. Then he stalks back out, slamming the door behind him. I stare at the closed door in confusion. What the hell was that about? What does he care if I reject the food or not?

I'm not going to eat it, I think stubbornly, turning my back to the nightstand.

I won't. I absolutely won't.

But in less than thirty minutes, I find myself dragging the food tray into my lap and practically inhaling the food. As I gulp down the water, I remember I haven't eaten anything since breakfast—was that even today or yesterday? I have no idea what time it is, or even what day we're in.

Shit, *Atë* must be going crazy with worry by now.

A heavy sigh escapes my lips as I flop back down on the bed. When we get to wherever we're going, I'll try to convince Maximo again to let me call him. Just to let him know I'm fine. He doesn't have to know where I am or who I'm with.

Exhaustion hits suddenly, and I burrow under the blankets, the events of this long-ass day finally catching up to me.

I'll just lie back and close my eyes for a bit...

I wake up to a strange sense of weightlessness, like I'm floating. My arms flail out, searching for something to grab onto until they clamp down on warm, muscular flesh. My eyes snap open, and the first thing I see is Maximo's hard jaw above me, barking out an order to one of his men as he carries me down the jet's stairs. He adjusts me in his arms, cradling me closer, and my hands instinctively tighten around his neck.

So, we're finally here. Wherever here is.

"Are we back in New York?" My voice comes out scratchy from sleep, and I have to clear my throat.

"Yes." His response is curt, distracted, as his sharp gaze scans our surroundings, like he's expecting someone to leap from the shadows to attack at any moment. He carries me towards one SUV and slides inside with me still in his arms. For a fleeting moment, I let myself sink into his warmth.

Then the memories flood back in, and I scramble out of his hold, almost falling on my ass in the process. His sardonic brow lift only fuels my embarrassment, but he's already back to his phone, dismissing me as easily as breathing.

"When will I get my purse back?" I ask him for what feels like the umpteenth time, but really, it's only the second. "My phone and other stuff are in there."

"When I'm sure you won't reach out to your father as soon as you get it," he answers without hesitation.

"But I could just call him once to let him know I'm alright! I don't mind doing it in your presence if you're worried I might spill something. Please, Maximo." I can't shake the nagging feeling that the longer *Atë* goes without news from me, the higher the chances of his blood pressure going up.

He glances up from his phone to give me a weird look that

makes me shift self-consciously. After a long, loaded moment, he returns to his screen. "I'll think about it."

It's not a yes, but it's not a no either. I'll take it. For now. But the first chance I get, I'm contacting my father—with or without his permission.

As the last remnants of sleep clear, I gaze out at the city whizzing by. A wave of nostalgia washes over me, bringing back the thrill of my birthday just a few days ago. I just turned twenty–one, but right now, I feel so much older.

13

ELIRA

My spine crackles with tension as we take a turn onto what looks like a main street, cruising past a canyon of towering buildings before finally pulling to a stop in front of a stark white condominium.

Maximo, ever the 'gentleman', extends his hand to help me out. I deliberately slide out from my side instead, pretending not to notice his outstretched fingers. The concrete is cool under my bare feet—another indignity of this forced marriage. No shoes, no phone, no freedom.

"You have to stop doing that," he grits out as he leads me into the lavishly decorated lobby.

Oh, I plan to keep doing that. There's no way in hell I'm ever holding hands with him again. It's bad enough that I have to fulfill marital obligations to the person threatening me—and that he can make me enjoy the damn thing. I draw the line at holding hands and other intimate things.

"In case you haven't noticed Maximo, I can walk perfectly fine without your assistance, so I'm going to keep ignoring your hand," I say as I follow him towards the elevators.

He jabs the call button hard enough to crack it, and I bite back a smirk. *At least something's getting under his skin.*

The elevator arrives with a soft ding that seems too cheerful for my current situation. As we step inside, I notice his usual shadow squad isn't following. "What about the others?" The question slips out before I can stop it, and I internally curse my curiosity.

"I have to leave soon to deal with something urgent that's come up, so they're waiting for me in the car. I'm just going to drop you at home and introduce you to the guys."

The guys? I frown. If his operation is anything like *Atë*'s, we're talking about a small army.

We're silent the whole ride up to the penthouse. He seems to have an obsession with penthouses. What is it with this man and being above everyone else? Some kind of god complex? I guess my read on him back at the park was spot on, after all.

The elevator opens into a large, airy hallway filled with about six men who look like they bench press cars for fun—two standing guard by an oversized set of double doors, and four patrolling up and down.

As soon as they spot us, they all snap into position, and it's almost reflex when I shuffle behind Maximo, not all comfortable with the sudden wave of attention. How is that for irony—hiding behind my kidnapper from his own men. What has my life become?

Maximo's not having it. His hand finds my arm, and suddenly I'm being yanked forward until I'm standing next to him. "You're my wife now, Elira. Your place is beside me, not behind me." His voice is firm, but before I can retort, he's turning to his men and speaking to them in Italian.

Frustration bubbles up inside me. I hate not being able to understand what he's saying, so I lean into him and pinch his arm to grab his attention. "It's rude speaking Italian when I'm standing right here."

He gives me a thoughtful look, but then, surprisingly, he switches to English. "This is my wife, Mrs. Leonotti. Your queen."

The men, who were already throwing me curious glances, now stare at me directly, studying me like I'm some rare specimen in a zoo. I fight the urge to shrink back, painfully aware that I'm still in Maximo's oversized clothes—probably looking more like a kid playing dress-up than any kind of queen. But no way I'm letting them see my discomfort. Instead, I lift my chin, channeling the confidence of the queen he's just dubbed me. *You want a queen? I'll give you a queen.*

"You'll treat her with the same reverence and respect you give me... or else." Maximo's words catch me off guard. I half-expected him to unleash some tyrannical lecture, but this isn't bad at all.

Well, well. Maybe being the 'queen' has some perks after all.

My mind immediately starts calculating how I might use this to my advantage—maybe get access to one of their phones?

The men nod, and one by one, they parade forward for introductions. I try to memorize their names and faces, but after the first three, everyone just jumbles up together.

Marco, Giuseppe, Antonio... or was it Angelo? I give up trying to track them and just nod regally at each one.

Once the introductions wrap up, Maximo opens the door and leads me through a beautiful foyer into a spacious open-concept living area that flows seamlessly into the kitchen and dining room, with only fancy sliding glass doors separating each space.

My gaze is immediately drawn to the kitchen, where marble and navy countertops gleam, and a big industrial-grade oven has my eyes popping and salivation pooling in my mouth. *So pretty!* I can already picture myself baking all sorts of delicious treats in there. Maybe some *shëndetlie*, layered with some creamy yogurt and topped with crushed nuts, or *trileç* with—

"Come on." Maximo says, and I scurry after him, almost tripping over my own feet to keep up with his brisk pace. We go up the stairs to the first floor, which opens into a hallway similar to the one outside, except this one has some stunning artwork on the wall that deserves a second look. But no time for that now—I'm too busy trying not to lose him.

He opens one of the doors and gestures inside. "This will be your room."

I slowly walk inside to take it in the space that's meant to be my new 'home'. It's... annoyingly beautiful, actually. Beige walls that somehow manage to look elegant instead of boring, an electric fireplace that casts a warm glow across the double bed. And then there's a small vanity mirror, loaded with beauty products. My feet carry me to the vanity, fingers trailing over unfamiliar bottles and compacts. *Did they rob a makeup counter or something?*

"I don't know what you use, so Marco just bought a bunch of items. Make a list of whatever you'll need, and he'll get them for you." I glance back to catch Maximo checking his watch, looking every bit as impatient as he sounds. "I really have to go now. When I'm back, I'll give you a tour if you want. I'll have someone wait for you downstairs."

And with that, he's gone, leaving me alone in a room that feels as much a gift as a cage.

I eye the makeup collection with all the enthusiasm of a cat being offered a salad, then turn my attention to the two mysterious doors in the room. I push open door number one, half-expecting a bathroom fit for royalty, maybe even a golden toilet just to drive the point home. Instead, I'm met with... well, just a bathroom. Nice, sure, but considering the grandeur of everything else in this place, this feels almost disappointing.

A single sink, a small glass shower, an equally compact bathtub, and a normal toilet. That's it. Not even a heated towel rack or one of those fancy rain showers. I bite back a laugh.

Here I am, practically expecting a spa when I should just be thankful to have the basics.

Inside the shower, though—*that's* where things get interesting. It's stocked with enough products to fill a small boutique. I brush my fingers over a plush white robe hanging next to the door, the tag still on it. Then I start opening bottles, one after another, letting the scents swirl around me—lavender, citrus, something that's probably way too floral but still nice. My favorites go back into the shower, and the rejects end up in a pile on the bed. I'll take them to the men outside when I'm done exploring—no point in wasting expensive products I'll never use.

Finally, I turn to the second door. When I reach for the handle, my hand actually hesitates on the knob. Please don't be a Red Room of Pain. I push it open and... *Oh.*

It's a closet. No, scratch that—it's what my closet dreams to be when it grows up. Rows upon rows of female clothes. I hesitate, wondering if someone used to occupy this room, but as I go inside and finger the first cashmere coat, my gaze snags on the tag. All the clothes are still tagged, all horrifyingly expensive, all... *exactly my size*? A chill runs down my spine.

How did he so accurately guess my size?

Most of the clothes are dresses and skirts with only a few slacks and sweatpants, no jeans. But they all scream designer. Just as I'm about to leave, my eyes zone in on the rows of items on the side shelf, looking suspiciously like the gift bags Maximo had on my birthday.

"No freaking way," I whisper as I creep towards them like they might suddenly spring up and attack me. One peek inside the first bag confirms it—a set of lingerie I remember all too well. I snap it shut and back out, then spin around to leave, closing the door behind me with a decisive clink. Out of sight, out of mind.

But my brain, won't let me forget about Maximo's rushed

exit. Why was he in such a hurry? What if my father had somehow found out he kidnapped me and he's now trying to retaliate?

Worry settles at the base of my spine.

I hope *Atë* doesn't get hurt if that's the case. *Please, please don't let them kill each other.* My father, despite his many flaws, is a very principled man, and I know until he's sure I'm safe he won't do anything drastic. But Maximo... he's a whole other story. I barely know the guy, and from what I *do* know, he can be a heartless bastard when he wants to be.

Take, for example, his little 'no family contact' rule. Just because he likes the idea of them being worried about me.

My brain keeps going. What if *Atë* called Roan back to Queens so they could look for me together? My heart pounds at the thought. My brother's fuse is even shorter than mine, and he's almost as overprotective as *Atë*, if not worse. If they somehow suspect I'm with Maximo... there's no telling what he might do.

Another flicker of worry rises in my chest, and I ruthlessly push it down as soon as it appears. If Roan hurts Maximo, he has it coming.

"I'm only worried about him because I doubt I'll be allowed to leave here without his order," I mutter to myself, as if saying it out loud will help push away the nagging thoughts. But they don't budge.

I glance around the room again, filled with angst for my father and brother. They're the only family I have left. I can't lose them. Heck, I married Maximo because I can't lose them.

Maximo got what he wanted. But what if he goes back on our deal? He went back on his word once. Shit, shit, shit. I should have made him sign something too, but I didn't think this far ahead.

Panic starts clawing up my throat, legs jiggling as my brain goes wild with different scenarios of my husband killing my family. What if—

No. Stop.

I need a distraction before I drive myself crazy.

The Kitchen. Yes. Baking will get my mind off things for now.

I leave the bedroom in a hurry, but as I walk down the hallway, my legs pull to a stop, drawn to the last painting on the wall just before the stairway—a beautiful oil portrait of a lush Lily of the Valley.

It reminds me of his restaurant's sign, where the very same flower is painted next to *Mughetto*—even the name literally means 'lily of the valley' in Italian. It also reminds me of his tattoo.

I only got a brief glimpse of it before he distracted me, but I remember seeing the flower inked on his arm amidst the array of other flowers. Why that flower? What's the story there? For a man like Maximo, it feels out of place...

I quickly shake my head. "I don't care, I don't care." I don't give a shit about him or his story. I'm not going to be curious.

Downstairs, true to Maximo's words, a man is waiting. He leaps off the sofa when he sees me, watching me carefully. He has curly dark hair cropped on the sides of his head, brown eyes, and a crooked nose. What's his name again? I remember meeting him in the hallway earlier, but for the life of me, I can't recall.

As I walk into the room, I clear my throat, unsure if I should address him or not. Instead, I wave him down like I really am a queen and make my way towards the kitchen area. The glass doors are already open, so I just glide inside, feeling my babysitter's eyes drilling a hole into my shoulder blades as I throw open cabinet after cabinet. Empty. Empty. Empty.

Are you kidding me?

I frown, glancing around the beautiful kitchen in utter disbelief. How can everything be empty? I march over to the fridge, practically gasping when I fling it open. Just a few bottles of water and some beers glares back at me. This is a kitchen? More like a desert island.

"Is something the matter?" my babysitter asks, getting to his feet and walking towards me.

I turn to face him, hand on my hip. "What do you guys eat?"

He shrugs, looking a bit sheepish. "We're rarely inside the apartment, so we just order in or take turns eating at a restaurant. Are you hungry, ma'am?"

I'm so distraught, I let him calling me 'ma'am' slide. "No. But I need a lot of stuff in here. Groceries, baking supplies—"

Maximo's words come back to me. *Make a list of what you need and Marco will get them.*

"Get me Marco," I command, feeling rather pleased with myself.

The man's brows furrow. "*I* am Marco."

Oh. Heat creeps up my neck, but I barrel on. "Right. Of course, you are. I need a pen and paper so I can write you the list of what to get. Maximo said you bought the makeup products in my room?"

The tips of his ears go red, like he's embarrassed about that, as he nods. "Yes. But we'll have to wait for the boss to give his permission before I can go get anything else, and he's given us instructions not to call him unless it's very important."

Something in me snaps. All the fear, the worry, the helplessness of the day crystalizes into pure, crystalline rage. *What, I can't even bake if I want to?* "Who am I, Marco? The boss's wife." Even though I'm an unwilling wife, I'm still his wife, damn it. "And who do you think will be in charge here when the boss isn't around? *Me.* What did Maximo say? Treat me like you would treat him?"

The transformation is immediate. Marco straightens like someone attached strings to his spine, whipping out a phone jotter faster than I can blink. "Type what you want in there."

I accept the phone with narrowed eyes, still a little pissed from his earlier resistance.

If Maximo has a problem with his wife sending his men to buy groceries with his money, he can take it up with me when he gets back home. My fingers attack the keypad with savage satisfaction. Let's see just how much damage I can do to his credit card while he's gone.

After all, a queen needs her kitchen properly stocked, doesn't she?

14

MAXIMO

"What do you mean, the rerouting was approved? Approved by who?"

My fist connects with the desk, making the pathetic excuse for a man behind it jump like I just set off a bomb, eyes blown wide behind his glasses. Good. He should be scared. He should be very, *very* scared, because my anger is on a precipice right now, and it will only take a single wrong word to trigger it.

"I–I—" His glasses slip down his nose as he stammers, his hands now shaking violently. "I don't have—I–I don't—"

"Stop stammering and tell me already!" The roar tears from my throat, and he squeaks—actually squeaks—like a toy being stepped on.

"Maximo." Dante's quiet voice behind me slices through the red haze of my rage. One word, loaded with meaning. *Control yourself. This isn't the way.* I curse in disgust as I glance back at him. He just shakes his head slightly.

He's right, damn him. It isn't this man's fault that the shipment we're expecting got rerouted and is now on its way to Serangoon Harbor in fucking Singapore instead of my dock. But I still need some fucking answers.

I rake a hand through my hair, feeling each strand pull against my scalp as I try to rein in the storm brewing inside me. "Answer me—" My eyes shoot to his nametag, "—Paul. Who approved the rerouting?"

"I don't have the access to see who approved it, sir." His lips quake as he speaks, voice trembling. "I–I called as soon as I was alerted."

Yes, he fucking did. Called and called and called, while my phone sat silenced to unknown numbers because I was too busy playing husband with my new bride. So he had to go through Rafael to reach me.

Fuck, this is all such a mess.

I storm out of the warehouse, fists clenched. Outside, the wharf sprawls before me, lined with various ships. Even at this ungodly hour, workers scurry about unloading cargo. My ship should have docked right there one month from now. Instead, several millions worth of firearms are headed to the wrong fucking continent, and I can't do a damn thing about it.

"Do you think the Albanians did this?" Dante asks as we weave between containers. "Do they know we have their daughter?"

I almost laugh at that. "No. They don't have nearly enough power to execute something this clean, even with the Russians as their ally. And I doubt even they would fuck with that shipment without making contact first."

Because the cargo on that ship wasn't just mine. It was a collaboration between Rafael, Michael, Romero, and me. And what our enemies fear more than each one of us alone, is all four of us united. And fucking with our business is practically a declaration of war against not just us, but the entire *Cosa Nostra*.

They wouldn't dare.

My phone buzzes, and I take it out of my pocket to see an

incoming group meeting with my brothers. Fuck me. I don't have an answer for them yet, but they aren't going to wait.

I slide into the car's backseat as I accept the call. One by one, my brothers' faces pop up on screen like a gallery of barely contained rage. They don't waste time.

"Any update?" Rafael asks.

I meet each of their gazes, hating the answer I have to give. "No. Nothing yet. I've tried to reach out to the nav officers and crew, but they've gone dark. According to my intel, when they got the order to switch route to Singapore, they were warned about potential sabotage and told to cut off their communications with our city's port." Their radios are off too.

I refuse to believe they were gullible enough to have done that without touching base with me first. Someone with relative power must have given them the go-ahead. But I keep that suspicion to myself for now. No need to add fuel to this particular fire until I'm certain.

Romero and Rafael curse colorfully. With the ship's comms down, no one will be able to get in contact with them until they arrive at Serangoon Harbor weeks from now, meaning the shipment will be delayed for two more months. In our world, that's a fucking eternity.

"I'll try to hack into the system, force a backdoor message, see if I can turn them the fuck around," Michael says, though a flicker of doubt crosses his face. After all, he created that system with the sole purpose of being unhackable, in case anyone got the wild idea to get back at us by sabotaging our shipments.

I don't know all the intricacies, but I remember when he created the system years ago—he was so proud when he tried to hack it and even *he* couldn't get in. We were confident the only way to sabotage us was by hacking the system. Hell, the culprit probably *tried* that first before getting cocky enough to reroute the whole damn shipment.

"I'm having my guy trace the comms chain between the

man who gave the order and the ship, but it might take a while," I add.

Romero sighs, rubbing a tired hand over his face. "Sounds like there's nothing to do but wait for now."

"I also tried to trace that line as soon as I found out. You know I hate waiting." Michael's frustration bleeds through. "But It only led to a dead end. I couldn't find shit. Whoever we're dealing with isn't just some random player. It's either the Bratva, the Albanians, the Irish—or..."

"The Greeks," Rafael says, picking up the thought.

Michael nods, grim. "Maybe even all of them, somehow united, pooling their power to take us down. You know, the enemy of my enemy and all that bullshit, which I seriously doubt because the Greeks are our staunch ally." He pauses, his jaw tightening as he lets the thought settle. "Or... it's a higher power. Like Uncle Sam."

I inhale sharply. The thought had brushed my mind, but I waved it off. Now, though? If even Michael—who once hacked NASA for shits and giggles—can't find out who sent that order, it's definitely either government-level interference or every underworld power we know banding together against us like he said. Neither scenario is one I want to entertain.

"We're just making assumptions right now," Romero, ever the voice of reason, interjects. "We have no solid evidence to back anything up. Let's cool off—relax—and I'll have one of my contacts dig into it, see if Uncle Sam truly is interested in meddling in civilian activities."

"When isn't the government meddling?" Rafael's bitter question grabs our attention, and when we give him questioning glances, he just waves a hand. "I mean, we're no longer just some civilians. We're on their radar, and we have been for years now."

"How do you know that?" Michael's question mirrors my own thoughts.

Rafael shrugs, but there's something in his eyes I can't quite read. "Just don't be surprised if it's them. They're like fucking sea ticks—cling to you when you go into the ocean and refuse to let go. Parasites."

I frown at him. Sea ticks? Parasites? What the hell is he talking about?

"Anyways, it's late. Try get some sleep if you can. We have a long day tomorrow." Without waiting for any replies, Rafael abruptly ends the call.

The rest of us sit in silence for a beat, then Michael and Romero both raise their brows at me.

I throw my hands up. "Don't look at me. I have no idea what that was about." I pause, grimacing. "I'll look into things some more in the morning and let you know what I find." *If* I find anything, I add silently, exiting the meeting as well.

Dante, who just finished a call while I was in the meeting, slides into the driver's seat. "Ready to go home?"

"Yes." The word carries the weight of this endless fucking day as I recline my head back in the seat, tired as hell.

From tripping the fire alarms in Përmeti's compound, to following Elira to the park, spending the day with her there, then stealing her away to Vegas and marrying her, nearly having her... and now this entire shipment mess blowing up in my face. It's been twenty-four hours that feels like a goddamn lifetime.

"Who was on the phone?" I ask through closed eyes, more out of habit than interest.

"Marco. Mrs. Leonotti seems to be settling into her new home nicely." Something in his tone—*is that amusement?*—makes me crack one eye open. There's a smirk playing at the corners of his mouth that I don't like one bit.

"What's that supposed to mean?"

"Let's just say you have a surprise waiting for you at the

penthouse," he answers cryptically, pulling out of the port's parking lot.

Before I can demand clarification, my phone pings with a text from Romero.

ROMERO:

I'm going to reach out to the DA in my city, feel her up and try to see if she knows anything or knows someone who might. You should do the same. I've told Michael and Rafael as well.

ME:

Yeah, that wouldn't hurt. I'll pay him a visit in the morning.

I exit the texting app to find my inbox flooded with new emails. As I start firing off replies one after the other, Dante's weird behavior gets pushed to the back of my mind, and before I know it, we're pulling up in front of my apartment building.

We exit the car together and make our way into the lobby, taking the elevator up to the penthouse. The moment the doors slide open into the hallway that leads to my front door, my brows pull together in confusion. "Where are the men?"

The usual security detail is conspicuously absent, and the hair on the back of my neck stands up like it always does when something's not right.

Dante *snickers* next to me, and the sound is so foreign coming from him that I actually do a double-take. In the nine years since I've known the man, I don't think I've heard that sound pass his lips. Something is definitely up here.

My frown deepens as I lengthen my strides down the hallway and yank the door open, bracing myself for whatever chaos lies within. *I swear, if I find my men cozying up to my wife, there will be hell to pay.*

I hear the voices first—deep husky tones that unmistakably belong to my men, mingling with a softer, more feminine one that can only be my wife. My hands form fists at my sides as possibilities flash through my mind. I'm already prepared to be thoroughly displeased when I pass through the foyer's glass doors, and I'm not disappointed.

The scene that greets me makes my blood pressure spike to dangerous levels.

My wife—*my wife*—is sitting cross-legged on the floor in front of the large screen TV, and behind her, my men are crowded on and around the large sofa like teenagers at a sleep-over. Some are even leaning over the shoulders of others, all attention focused on whatever's happening on the screen.

"No!" Elira exclaims, hunching forward with the kind of fierce concentration I've only seen her direct at me, her thumbs flying over the game controller in her hands.

"You're dead meat," Perro says with unholy glee, leaning down from the couch to punch her shoulder playfully, and I see *red*.

She's completely dressed, still wearing my shirt and dress pants from the plane ride. But it doesn't fucking matter.

How *dare* he put his filthy hand on *my* wife?

"What the fuck is going on in here?" I bellow, making my men jump up from the couch like they've been electrocuted. The ones leaning over the back straighten up so fast I'm surprised I don't hear spines cracking, and they all turn to face me with expressions ranging from deer-in-headlights to oh-shit-we're dead.

Elira glances back at me, and a light of disdain fills her hazel eyes as she slowly gets to her feet with all the grace of a queen addressing a peasant. "Maximo, relax. We were just playing a game."

Her words, probably meant to bank the fire of my anger, only stoke it higher. I sweep my gaze over my men, each look promising future retribution as I say as calmly as I can, "Get out. All of you."

Like they've only been waiting for my permission to flee, they scramble out of the penthouse, the front door slamming behind them.

And then it's just Elira and me.

"Of course. Here comes the wild dragon of the West, ruining the fun. You're like a black cloud who only knows how to do one thing—be angry." She rolls her eyes and spins around to leave.

Her words strike hard, and before I know what I'm doing, I'm moving. Two long strides and I'm right behind her, grabbing her arm with enough force to make her gasp. "Not you, wife. You, stay."

She glares back at me with pure impertinence. "Unfortunately, I do *not* want to stay. I've spent more than enough time with you to make me sick."

My eyes narrow to slits, the thread of my control fraying rapidly. "Shut the fuck up, Elira." Every single word that leaves those perfect lips only seems to make the frustrations of the day coalesce into something dangerous, something primal.

"Or what?" she demands, and anticipation, anger, arousal—all slam into me in dizzying waves. I tighten my grip on her and forcefully drag her to the dining area, towards the tall dining table.

It's high time I teach my little wife exactly what happens when you challenge a dragon.

15

ELIRA

"What the hell do you think you're doing?" The words burst from my lips, pulse pounding in my ears as he leads me to the dining table. "What—"

The rest of my protest dies in my throat as he releases my arm to press firmly on my lower back. The pressure is inexorable, bending me until my belly folds across the table's edge and my upper body sprawls over the cool surface. "Maximo..."

I manage to twist my neck to glance back at him as he arranges my limbs on the table as he wants. But the expression I find on his face nearly stops my heart. There's a fierce fire burning in those dark eyes, filled with something wild that sends a strange heat through me.

Then his hands are sneaking around my waist, fingers finding the makeshift belt—his tie—holding the borrowed dress pants in place. With a smooth pull, the fabric gives away and slides down my legs unceremoniously. A cool rush of air brushes against my buttocks and bare pussy, making me shiver and press my thighs together to shield myself from the sudden chill.

He's angry—that much is clear from the tension radiating off him in waves.

But I'm not sure whether his anger stems from finding me with his men or from wherever he disappeared to earlier. What I do know with bone-deep certainty is that he's about to take it out on me, and my heart triples its rhythm, skipping into my throat as he spreads a proprietary palm over my ass, caressing and squeezing it gently until my core contracts with shameful pleasure.

I should hate this, damn it. Every fiber of my being should revolt. Instead, my treacherous body only coils tighter with anticipation.

When he glances up at me, his eyes are as dark as the midnight sky, and there's an unholy glint in them that only sends my desire spiraling higher. *What's he planning?* Is this it? Is he going to finish what he started in Vegas before we were so rudely interrupted?

But instead of removing his slacks, he leans over me to grab the arms I'm using to balance myself on the table and twists them behind my back, securing my wrists in one strong palm.

Shock jolts through me as my upper body hits the table and my cheek presses against the cool wood. "What are you—"

"You sat down on my living room floor surrounded by my men," he growls darkly, leaving me genuinely struggling to understand his warped logic. I try to turn my head as best I can, hoping to catch some hint in his expression, but all I see is him raising his free hand. "You let Perro *touch* you."

"What? Nobody touched—" My protest ends in a yelp when he brings his hand down on my ass with a loud smack. "Ow, shit, Maximo!" Hot fire fills the spot, and I'm stunned to the core. *I've never been hit before in my life.*

His palm smooths over my ass cheek soothingly, and for a moment I think maybe that's the extent of my punishment. But oh no, he isn't done. Far from it.

He raises his hand again and another sharp smack lands on that same spot. My body rocks against the table, trying instinctively to squirm away from him, but he's got me trapped firmly beneath him.

"What the hell do you think you're doing?" I demand angrily, voice breathless as I rear my head up to glare at him.

"Punishing you for running your mouth at me. Spending time with my men. Giving them your time and attention. Letting them touch you." Each offense is punctuated by the increasingly familiar sound of his palm meeting my flesh.

"Nobody touched me, Maximo!" I protest vehemently. What Perro did was a playful, completely platonic shove. What the hell is wrong with him?

He growls at me. *Growls* like some kind of wild animal. A sound that practically gives life to his dragon nickname.

"You're still running your mouth because you haven't learned your lesson." His hand lifts again, and what follows is a symphony of sharp spanks and soothing caresses that turns my world into a kaleidoscope of sensation. He alternates between cheeks, each impact sending shockwaves through my body, each gentle stroke afterward like a benediction.

I grit my teeth, trying desperately to swallow down the sounds building in my throat as fire spreads from my ass all over my body, igniting every nerve ending his hand touches.

With each spank, he eases the sting with gentle circles, almost as if he's apologizing, before starting the cycle again. My mind empties with every hit, until the universe narrows to just this moment—just the two of us. His hard body behind me, the heat of his calloused palm searing my ass cheeks, the strangely tender way he rubs the skin.

This goes on and on until both ass cheeks burn white-hot and something warm and squirmy settles in my lower belly, spreading down to my core, sending a wave of arousal seeping out. Until I'm all flushed and jittery and dripping with anticipation.

I'm so turned on, and I have to wonder—*what the hell is wrong with me?*

Finally, he stops, and I squeeze my eyes shut, cheek pressed to the table as I drag in ragged breaths. Just when I think I might get a moment to gather myself, Maximo leans over me, his clothes rustling as his chest meets my back. "You good?" His hot breath fans the shell of my ear, and despite my best efforts to hold it in, a low, shuddering moan slips out. Unfiltered. Uninvited. Goosebumps prickle up my arms and all over my skin as if my own reaction has somehow taken *me* by surprise.

Oh, God, did he hear that?

Maximo goes still behind me, and I squeeze my eyes tighter, mortification flooding me. *Please just go away. Leave me here to die of shame.* But no, the man is glued to me, close enough to feel every heartbeat racing through me, taking his damn time to process whatever's going on in that twisted mind of his.

I swear, if I could melt into the wood right now, I would. But he's just lingering, quiet, either figuring out his next move, or worse—relishing every bit of my embarrassment. *The asshole.*

At last, he pulls away from me, releasing his grip on my wrists, only for both of his hands now to return, tracing soothing circles over my burning flesh, drifting lower until his fingers graze the curve of my hip. I suck in a sharp breath when he cups my drenched center from behind, and my body jerks against the table, drawing a string of curses from his lips.

"Ahh, *dolcezza mia*. You enjoyed that, didn't you?" His brogue is thick as he runs his fingers through my wet folds, and before I even think, my thighs go slack, parting for him. "Hmm, that's it. Such a good girl. *Good wife*. You're drenched for me."

His words wash over me, silky and enticing, making me lightheaded as the ache between my legs pulses stronger, drawing more wetness out of me. He continues the teasing, his fingers gliding through my folds while his other hand grips my ass, squeezing the tender flesh as he inserts one finger into me. The dual sensation shoots equal measures of pain and pleasure through my body, intensifying until it's almost too much.

And then I shatter.

A raw, unfiltered cry breaks from my lips, echoing off the walls as white light bursts behind my eyes and my core tightens around his finger. Somewhere in my haze, I hear him curse, and I get the feeling he wasn't expecting that. But by then, I'm gone. All thoughts scatter, leaving nothing but a rush of pure, dizzying pleasure as I soar high to the ceiling.

When I finally drift back down, my ears are ringing, and I realize it's my heart roaring in my eardrums. I try to regulate my breathing, but one glance back steals whatever oxygen I've managed to gather. Maximo is unzipping his pants and taking out his cock. *His huge cock.*

Holy hell.

I gulp, my eyes going wide as I stare—utterly transfixed—at the angry, swollen, purplish crown seeping white liquid, then down the thick, veiny length to the root where a string of dark hair curls onto his pelvis. My face heats up as he strokes it, making more liquid gush out.

"Is that—is that cum?" I ask curiously, even as my core contracts. *Will he even fit in?*

"It's called pre-cum, *dolcezza,*" he answers, all calm and matter-of-fact, as he steps into me. His hands fall to my hips and spread my thighs impossibly wide. My eyes flick up to his face as he drags his cock through my slippery folds.

His gaze is laser-focused between my thighs, brows pulled together tightly. Then he notches himself at my entrance and another flicker of worry rushes through me. What if he truly can't fit? The crown alone looks like it could break me—what about the rest? *How is this even going to work?*

But there's no time to overthink. He doesn't stop. I bite my lip hard as he starts to push in, inch by agonizing inch. It's a slow stretch that feels both foreign and intense. I gasp as it starts to burn, and that burning spreads into more pain—more discomfort—yet he *still* isn't fully in. As I hiss out a breath, tensing around him, Maximo's eyes fly to mine.

"*Shhh.*" His fingers slip into my hair, tangling into my curls and sending my hair tie flying out. He massages my scalp gently with one hand while the other toys with my clit. Both sensations feed the fire building inside me, igniting a frenzy that has my eyes rolling back and my lips parting on a soundless cry.

"That's it, love. That's it, you're doing so good for me. Taking your husband so well." His words trail off into husky Italian, and even though I can no longer understand what he's saying, the sultry tone remains the same. It's so sexy, *so hot*. I shiver, caught between the sensation and the heat radiating from him. The building pressure snaps and I'm coming again, my release aiding the fluid movement of his hips. He curses and tightens his grip on me.

"See? I'm all in now. That wasn't so bad, was it?" he murmurs a few moments later.

My eyes open sleepily at his question, and I glance back to confirm his claim—sure enough, he's completely sheathed within me. His pelvis presses flush against my stinging ass, his cock stretching me to my very limit. The fullness is so intense, so overwhelming, I swear I can feel his cock throbbing inside me. My body responds instinctively, and my inner walls flutter helplessly around his impressive length, struggling to adjust to the impossible stretch.

His eyes go heavy-lidded, mouth parting as he rumbles out a groan. So I do it again, testing, and he answers with a rough squeeze to my hip and scalp.

Then he slowly, carefully, rolls his hips, and I cry out as intense pleasure rushes through me, too sharp, too much. Fuck, maybe it's because I've already come twice, but I'm suddenly hypersensitive.

I register *everything*—the table's hard edge digging painfully into my belly, promising bruises. The pad of his fingers on my scalp, his calloused palm on my still stinging ass. Every nerve ending is alive and only intensifies my hunger for more.

"Good girl." His praise accompanies a slow withdrawal followed by a measured thrust. My toes curl against the cool hardwood floor, grounding me as I chase the delicious ache building deep in my core.

Leaning over my back, he drags his nose along my throat while murmuring sweet nothings in thick Italian that envelop me like a warm blanket. His hips shoot forward and backward between my thighs, sending our pleasures soaring.

My fingers scrabble helplessly against the dining table, uncontrollable moans breaking free as his thrusts become harder, faster, stealing my breath until I'm gasping, barely able to pull enough air into my lungs.

Then he uses his grip on my hair to yank my head up, and I catch him staring at my mouth with such intense longing. I can't help it; my own gaze drops to his parted lips, remembering how sweet he tasted. *Geez, why did I ever deny myself his kisses?*

My mouth waters, and I try to recall why I ever thought a no-kissing rule made sense. But with him looking at me like that, every reason slips away, and I start to lean in, drawn to the taste of him like a moth to a flame. His mouth, his scent, everything pulls me in until—"Absolutely not," he bites out, forcing my head back down. "If you're going to break your little rule, you're going to do it when you're not fuck-drunk." Anger edges his voice as he says that, and as he withdraws his cock, he surges back into me harder than ever, and I know he *is* angry.

The pleasure borders on pain, drawing a shocked cry from

me. My fingers claw at the table again, desperate for something to hold on to. The hand on my hip slips to my clit, then he rolls the sensitive nub between his thumb and index finger as he pistons into me with punishing force.

"So fucking tight," he grunts. "You're strangling my cock, *dolcezza.*"

As he works my body, sweet pleasure starts to settle at the base of my spine, gathering, gathering until it finally spills over in a rush that steals my breath again. My mouth parts in a soundless scream, vision going hazy, back arching into his chest, hard nipples dragging on the table through my shirt. I feel every single thing as I orgasm.

Behind me, Maximo's thrusts grow erratic, and his Italian tumbles out in a hoarse, almost frantic tone as his cock seems to swell inside my tightening cunt, then he orgasms as well, his hot heat bathing my inside as he empties himself.

For a long, hazy minute, I lie limply on the table, my legs losing sensation until he wraps his arm around my waist, holding me to him. It stops what would be a graceless descent to the floor as he rests his chest against my back, his heart drumming a fast, fierce rhythm that almost matches my own thundering pulse.

We stay like that, wrapped together, his arms loose yet secure around me. Then a few breathless moments later, he pulls back, withdrawing from me. My core spasms around the sudden gaping emptiness after having his huge cock inside me.

He helps me to my feet, keeping a steadying hand on my arm. "You okay?" he asks huskily. My cheeks suddenly heat up with embarrassment as the reality of what we've done sinks in, and I just nod quietly.

"Come on, I'll run a bath for you." He says it like he's doing me a favor, like this is the natural next step after—well, whatever *that* just was. He starts leading me towards the stairs, but the haze is lifting, the shock of what we just did settling in now that the pleasure has cleared. I need space, not another second drowning in his overpowering, hypnotizing presence.

I shrug out of his grip and take a step back. His face shifts, his brows knitting with concern, as if he cares.

"It's alright. I'm fine," I say, clearing my throat, though my voice sounds anything but. "I can run the bath myself. Just... stay here or something." I don't wait for his response. I turn, then walk away on shaky legs, up the stairs.

Once inside my room, I close the door behind me and lock it, feeling like it's my one line of defense. I lean against it for a moment, just breathing. Then the realization slams into me all over again.

I just had sex for the first time.

Not just any sex—mind-blowing, earth-shaking sex.

With my enemy.

And worse, I almost kissed him in the middle of it, not caring about breaking my own rule. If he hadn't pushed my head back down, I would have done it, Hell, I know it. And from the look in his eyes, he wanted it just as badly, maybe even more.

But he stopped me. *Why did he stop me?*

I shake the thought out of my head and something wet trickles down my thigh. My cum. My thigh feels sticky with it as I make my way to the ensuite. I give the bathtub a longing glance, but I'm too wrung out to even think about running it. So I just slip into the glass shower instead, cranking the water up as hot as I can stand it.

As I shower, I rub between my thighs to wash the cum off, but more keeps dripping out. My hand stills as I stare at it in confusion for a moment before the horrifying realization dawns. It's not just my cum. *That bastard came inside me!*

And I'm not on birth control.

Panic follows that realization, obliterating every last trace of the lingering haze. *No, no, no. Did he do it on purpose?* Is this some sick way to trap me? Get me pregnant so I can never leave?

My throat closes up as my heart threatens to burst. The room seems to close in, darkening at the edges as the full weight of it hits me. No, this can't be happening. One thought penetrates the panic: *I need to get out of here.*

I turn off the shower and run out of the bathroom, dripping water everywhere as I make my way to the walk-in closet. Inside, I dry myself clean haphazardly with one of the clothes, then tug on a pair of panties and a bra, not caring that it's basically lingerie, before pulling on a gray cami top and slacks.

Fully dressed, my panic abates a little and rationality attempts to return, at least enough for a plan to form. From what I can tell, there's only one entrance into this place—the elevator outside.

But when we came in together earlier this evening, his men were guarding it. And even though we bonded a little over pastries and a couple rounds of video games, I doubt that's enough to get me a free pass out.

But I need to try.

I haven't forgotten his threat to my family, but my plan isn't to escape from him—I'm not stupid. I fully intend to come back, because I know damn well he'll make good on those threats if he thinks I've broken my end of our deal. But right now, I desperately need to reach a pharmacy, or a hospital, and get the morning-after pill. *Fast.*

I can't afford to get pregnant.

Getting pregnant by him is not an option, no matter how mind-blowing the sex is.

Steeling myself, I slip out of my room, scanning the empty hallway. Are there cameras here? Is someone watching me right now? My face flames as I remember what happened between Maximo and I in the living room earlier.

Did someone watch that too?

I shake it off, forcing my mind to stay sharp as I walk down the stairs to the kitchen. There, I open the cabinet where I stashed the knives earlier and take one out. The steel gleams, cold and sharp, in my hand, and I tighten my grip on it.

My plan: Hold one of the men outside hostage with the knife to his throat so the others let me leave. Easy, right?

My heart pounds frantically as their faces fill my mind. Maybe before I ate and played games with them, I could have carried out my plan without thought, but now I feel sick to my stomach as I make my way to the front door.

Tucking the knife behind my back, I inhale sharply and turn the door's handle, half-expecting it not to open. Maximo might have locked it when he came in—*where even is he?* But the door swings open quietly.

Marco spots me first, and his face breaks into a warm smile. "Did you need something?" His smile catches the attention of the others, and they look over, their expressions showing varying shades of the same warmth. So different from their stone-cold indifference when Maximo first introduced me to them.

The knife feels heavier by the second.

I can't do this. Can't hurt them, even if it's for my own good.

I glance around at them, my hands shaking behind me, and start to hyperventilate as I slowly raise my hands and show them the knife. They all go still, their eyes going wide, and the shift in atmosphere is immediate. Enzo starts to walk towards me, his movements careful like he's approaching a spooked animal. In desperation, I lift the knife and place it at my own throat. I don't even know what I'm doing—only that I need them to understand how serious I am.

"I just... I need to go buy some personal things. I'll be back before you even know it, so just—just let me go, or I'll...I'll..." I trail off, not able to complete the threat. Behind Enzo, I catch

Perro discreetly typing out a text. And I know *exactly* who it's going to.

Damn it!

I slowly start to back away from them, and they watch me go, not doing anything. I gulp, afraid to take my eyes off them, to even blink, as I walk backwards to the elevator.

Then the penthouse door swings open and Maximo walks out.

Shit, shit.

He's in nothing but a pair of dark pants slung low on his hips, water dripping from his hair down his bare chest and tattooed arm like he just came out of the shower. He shoves an impatient hand through his wet hair, sending droplets scattering all over the hallway. The gesture would almost seem nervous if I didn't know better—if I didn't know him. His eyes are fixed on me with deadly intent as he starts approaching me.

The sight of him sends my survival instincts into overdrive. I spin around, sacrificing being able to see him in favor of getting to the elevator quickly.

My heart thunders in my chest as I frantically jab at the call button. Nothing. No welcoming ding, no illuminated numbers, not even a hint of life from the sleek metal doors. I press again and again, each futile attempt making my panic rise higher.

"It's not going to work unless you tap a clearance card there."

I jolt at how close Maximo's voice is and whip around to see him pointing to a small square security panel next to the elevator—a detail I'd overlooked in my desperate plan.

Stupid, stupid, stupid. Of course a man like Maximo would have layers of security. Of course escape wouldn't be as simple as pressing a button.

"What the fuck are you doing, Elira?" The question comes out calm but deadly—like the whisper of a blade being drawn. His gaze drops to the knife still trembling in my hand, and something dark and primal flashes across his face. Before I can even blink, the knife is twisted from my grip and thrown to the floor behind him.

And just like that, my brilliant escape plan disintegrates. I gape up at him, despair sinking in as he commands, "Follow me."

16

MAXIMO

She doesn't make a sound as I guide her back into the penthouse. Not a whimper. Not a word. My traitorous wife knows exactly what she's done. The tension radiating from her small frame could power half of New York.

I'd just stepped out of the shower, water still dripping down my neck, mind set on finally getting some damn sleep when Perro's text lit up my phone. And yet, as much as I should be raging, I'm not even angry. Not really. Despite my threat to her family, I expected her to try at least one escape attempt eventually. I just didn't think it would be tonight. Not after what we just did and the day we've had.

"You have to let me go, Maximo." Her voice breaks through the silence, trembling with raw terror. When I turn to look at her, she has a fiercely earnest look on her face. "I'll come back, I promise. I just need to go get something."

My eyes narrow on her. "Go get something? Is that code for slipping a message out to your family?"

"No! Of course not." The vehemence in her denial catches me off guard. Her brows pinch together in genuine distress, and damn it all if I can't read the truth written across her face plain as day. This isn't about her family at all.

"Then explain yourself. What could possibly be so fucking urgent you'd put a knife to your own throat?" My hands clench involuntarily as that image burns through my mind again—her with the blade pressed to her neck, looking half-crazed. It stirs something in me, an anger I'd rather ignore.

The fact that I'm angry about *that* instead of the escape attempt itself pisses me off even more. What's it to me if she stupidly tried to off herself in a desperate bid to get away? She's just a means to an end. Just a wife on paper.

She presses her lips together, gaze skittering away from mine. The stubborn set of her jaw tells me everything—she won't spill unless I force her hand. "Tell me, or you can say bye-bye to Daddy dearest," I snarl, irritated at myself because this time, I know I don't mean the threat. Her father is safe from me. At least for now.

Her eyes jump to mine, and for a second, she looks ready to spit fire. "Oh, so this is how it's gonna be? Anytime you want to get your way, it's 'do this, Elira, or I'll hurt your father'?" She deepens her voice in a mocking imitation of mine. "'Make me dinner, Elira'. And if I say no, you'll, what, just dangle that threat over me?"

I drag a hand down my face, too tired for this shit. *Is this damn day ever going to end?*

"Fine. Tell me what you wanted, so I can have my men fetch it for you. Or don't. I honestly don't care." I shrug, already turning away from her to go back to my room. I've had enough. Tomorrow starts early, and I need some sleep, damn it.

"I wanted to get the morning-after pills!" she calls after me, panic threading through each syllable.

I freeze mid-step, slowly pivoting back. "Morning-after pills?" I ask, slowly.

Her face flames scarlet. "You–you came inside me, and I'm not on birth control."

A curse tears from my throat—not at her, but at my own carelessness. Of course she isn't on birth control. She's a virgin, for Christ's sake. At least she was. I stalk away from her and down the hallway towards my study.

"Where the hell are you going?" she demands, footsteps quick behind me. "Did you even hear what I said?"

I ignore her, shouldering through my study door.

"I knew you did this on purpose! You planned this!" She follows me in, her voice rising almost incredulous. "Are you trying to get me pregnant? You asshole, do you—"

I raise a hand to silence her as I yank open my desk drawer and take out one of the numerous burner phones.

"Did you seriously just try to shush me?"

I scroll through the contacts until I find the number I need, then hit dial. It rings several times before a groggy voice answers. "Hello?"

"Ethan, this is Maximo. I need you here, right the fuck now."

"*Now*?" Sleep evaporates from his tone, replaced by disbelief. "It's 1 AM in the fucking morning."

"I expect you to be here in thirty minutes." I end the call on his protests and finally look up to meet Elira's confused stare. "That was a doctor. He'll be here soon."

Her lips purse. "Is he a gynecologist?"

I shrug. "He patches up my men and I when we need it. Works at one of the top hospitals. He knows his stuff."

"Right. But he's going to show up thinking someone needs to be patched up again and might not bring—" She waves her hand in the air between us, cheeks still flushed. "You know. What we actually need."

Damn it, she has a point. I fire off a text to Ethan spelling out exactly what I need him here for, and adding a not-so-gentle reminder that he has twenty-eight minutes now. He lives in East Flushing, which is just a thirteen-minute drive away if he hits every green light. Plenty of time.

When I finish, she sighs, shoulders dropping as some of the tension bleeds out of her, and something in my chest eases at seeing her relief. But now that the immediate crisis is handled, the full weight of what I did hits me.

I shove a hand through my hair as I spin away from her, then grip the edge of my desk until my knuckles turn white. I fucking fucked her without protection, Not only that—I came inside her and didn't even think twice about it.

If she hadn't brought up her concerns, I wouldn't have given it a second thought.

What the hell is she doing to me? I'm never this careless and messy. Protection is non-negotiable with my partners because the last thing I want is a bastard—and an opportunistic bitch who thinks she can use the brat to get to me.

Except... Elira isn't just another woman. She's my wife. If she got pregnant, it wouldn't be a bastard but my heir.

A sudden, vivid image fills my mind: Elira, swollen with my child—my heir. *Mine.* My cock stirs, hardening instantly at the possessive thoughts that surge through my veins.

"Fuck me," I mutter, dropping my head and breathing deep through my nose as I try to focus on something else. Gunshot wounds. Broken ribs. Blood. Pain. Anything to kill this sudden, overwhelming urge to text Ethan to turn his ass around and go back home.

My fingers dig harder into the desk.

What the fuck is wrong with me? I don't even want a kid. Not yet anyway. The timing's all wrong—bringing a child into this mess right now would be insanity. And Elira and I... we're nowhere near ready for that step. If we'll ever be.

"Are you clean?"

Her question breaks into my spiraling thoughts. I look up to find her gnawing on her fingernails as she watches me, toes tapping nervously against the floor. Makes sense. She doesn't trust me, rightfully so. And now that her fear of getting pregnant is settled, it's only natural for her mind to go to the other consequences of unprotected sex.

"Are you?" I throw back at her.

She rolls her eyes. "I was a virgin."

"That's immaterial. Virgins can get STIs too."

The clinical tone of my voice seems to irritate her further. Her eyes narrow to slits. "Fine. The doctor can run tests on both of us when he gets here!" She spins on her heel, storming towards the door.

"I'm clean!" I call after her, but she only slams the door in response, and I chuckle lightly. *Such temper.*

Twenty minutes later on the dot, Ethan arrives looking like he just rolled out of bed—which he probably did. His lips are pressed thin as I greet him in the foyer. His shirt's wrinkled to hell, dark hair sticking up in every direction.

"These middle-of-the-night house calls need to stop, Maximo. I have an early shift in the fucking morning and need as much sleep as I can get," he grumbles as he tries to tame his hair with one hand while holding his medical kit in the other.

"I already told you to quit your day job and work for me full-time," I remind him as I lead him up the stairs towards Elira's room.

Ethan snorts echoes on the stairwell. "Right. And do what? Twiddle my thumbs waiting for one of you idiots to get shot? I live for the chaos of the ER, not waiting on mob mishaps."

"Then stop whining about the late-night calls." I pause in front of Elira's room and knock softly. "The doctor's here."

"Come in." Her voice drifts through the door, and I crack it open first to make sure she's appropriately covered before stepping back to allow Ethan in.

Elira's brows climb towards her hairline as she takes in Ethan's youth. She was clearly expecting someone older, more traditionally doctorly.

"Elira, this is Ethan Lancaster, our doctor. Ethan, this is my wife—Mrs. Leonotti to you."

His blue eyes sparkle with amusement as he shakes her hand. "Nice to meet you, Mrs. Leonotti. And congratulations on the wedding. Not offended at all that I didn't get an invitation, by the way," he adds, giving me a pointed glance as he walks towards the bed and places his kit on the nightstand, hands already busy opening it. "Up on the bed please, Mrs. Leonotti. And I'll need you to remove your bottoms for the exam."

My heart rate spikes through the roof at his words. "What? Like hell. That's not happening. Do not take your pants off, Elira."

Ethan sighs, lifting his gaze towards me with an almost parental patience. "Maximo, I need to examine her cervix to determine if she could have gotten pregnant and to insert the contraceptive." He waves a thin instrument still in its sterile packaging at me.

His explanation makes perfect medical sense, but every instinct in me rebels. Logic be damned. "The only way you're going to examine her cervix is with your head blown off."

"Maximo!" Elira exclaims, but her shock doesn't faze me.

"It doesn't matter if she could have gotten pregnant or not. And put that damned thing—" I jab a finger at the contraceptive device he's holding, "—anywhere else but inside her." I know there are other options that don't require such intimate examination.

I'm the only man who's seen her pretty, tight cunt, who's been inside her, and that's how it's going to stay.

Ethan rolls his eyes, but his lips twitch with amusement.

The bastard was messing with me. "Okay, okay. Have a seat, Mrs. Leonotti."

"Please, call me Elira," my wife murmurs, perching on the edge of the bed, all polite and proper. I watch like a hawk, not missing a damn thing as he lifts her left arm and turns it this way and that, studying it from different angles with an annoying level of care.

"This is your non-dominant hand, right?" he asks her. When she nods, he gently helps her lie back on the bed and adjust her left arm, bending her elbow. I swallow the growl bubbling up in my throat at seeing another man's hands on her, even though it's clinical and I know Ethan is being professional.

He rummages through his kit and snaps on a pair of latex gloves before taking out a syringe filled with a yellowish fluid. "This is to numb the area so you won't feel pain as I insert the implant," he explains to Elira, who throws a nervous glance at me. That look she gives, like she's checking to make sure I'm still here—it pulls me in like a hook.

Before I can stop myself, I'm on the bed next to her, claiming her free hand in mine as Ethan gives her the injection. The needle goes in, and she flinches slightly, tightening her grip around my fingers.

Once the anesthetic's in, he trades the syringe for a long, thin applicator with a sharp needle at the tip. When he puts the implant into it and brings the needle towards Elira's arm, I find myself looking away, unable to see it being pushed into her arm.

Instead, I focus on brushing those wild curls off her forehead. "You're doing great," I murmur against her temple and press a kiss there. The small smile she gives me in return does something dangerous to my heart.

"All done," Ethan finally says, breaking the spell of the moment, and I glance at him to see him rolling a bandage over her arm. "You're covered for the next five years, Elira. If you decide you want kids sooner, just call me to take it out and you'll be all good." He throws her a wink that stains her cheeks pink. *How dare he.*

My glare could melt steel as I rise from the bed. "You may leave now, *Doctor*."

"Yeah, yeah. I'm going." He mutters it under his breath, stripping off his gloves and packing away his supplies like he's not all too happy about the dismissal.

I nod at Elira, who suddenly finds the floor fascinating, as I escort Ethan out. The door closes behind us, followed by the unmistakable sound of the lock clicking into place. Ethan and I exchange glances, and a glint appears in his eye.

"Not. One. Fucking. Word." I grit out, and he raises his free hand, acting all innocent and shit. But I can tell he's filing this away for future ammunition. Bastard.

17

MAXIMO

"What do you have for me?" I snap as I stalk into the basement, skin crawling with frustration. Three days. Three fucking days since I took my wife, and she's been a constant tick in my brain. I want more, *need* more, but Ethan said I'll have to wait three days for the implant to really kick in, so I've kept my distance; allowed her to avoid me.

But nothing distracts me from her. When I work, I'm wholly aware of her presence in my home, charming my men with her baked pastries—pastries I'm yet to try. By the time I get home, those idiots have inhaled every crumb.

I was supposed to go meet Carlisle, the Queens DA, but he's rescheduled on me again. That's twice now—which is worrying because now I realize he might be avoiding me. In my world, that's not just unprofessional, it's dangerous. And yet I can't stop my thoughts from drifting to Elira.

So, to distract myself from rushing home and fucking my pretty wife against the nearest surface, I'm down here.

Last night, our search led us to the port's former logistic and distribution manager, Heath Davis, who, according to new intel, was the one that approved the rerouting of my shipment before conveniently vanishing, leaving nothing but a resignation letter behind. By sheer luck, one of my men ran into him trying to sneak out of the country via boat.

I glance at Dante, who just shakes his head, confirming Davis hasn't talked. My eyes narrow on the sorry bastard strapped to the chair. His face is a masterpiece of violence—split lips, broken nose, skin painted in shades of purple and blue, courtesy of my men's...enthusiastic questioning.

"Well, Heath," I say casually as I stroll towards the table filled with various tools. "What's motivating you to keep quiet, huh? Is it money? Threat to your life? Maybe family?" My fingers trail over the cold steel until they settle on a pair of cutting pliers. I lift them slowly, letting him take a good, long look. "Because you know who I am, don't you? Whoever's got something on you, they're small fry compared to me—I'm the monster that haunts their nightmares. Whatever they've promised you, I'll return tenfold."

The man whimpers, eyes blown wide with terror as I close the distance, crouching down in front of him with the cutting pliers raised, letting him see their jagged edge. "You know these are actually quite sharp? Sharp enough to slice through industrial cable without a hitch." I scoot in, adjust the grip on his bound hand, then lift his ring finger up. "Want to test just how quickly they'll chew through bone?"

I don't wait for his answer before I clamp the pliers down at the root of his finger. His high-pitched scream grates against my nerves, and I throw him an annoyed glance as I press down harder and harder, feeling his phalanges give way under the pressure.

The pliers bite deep into his skin, and I twist back and forth, grinding through the joint until his finger finally pops out of the socket. For a moment, there's nothing but his scream reaching a new pitch—then a gush of warm blood spurts out, splattering across my cheek and clothes.

His scream fizzles out, and I barely step back in time as he doubles over, retching before promptly passing out.

Pathetic.

I scowl in disgust, flicking blood off my hands as I nod at one of my men. "You. Wrap up his finger." I don't want him dying from blood loss before he spills his secrets, after all. "And you," I glance at another, "bring me some icy water." Heath doesn't get to be unconscious for too long.

As my men scramble to follow my orders, Dante steps forward. "You have an urgent call."

I give him a look, tapping my finger against the pliers, barely holding back my annoyance. "I'm a little busy right now, Dante. If they can't speak to you, they can fuck right off."

"It's your father–in–law," he says, holding out the phone.

Now *that* gets my attention.

My eyes narrow on the device. Why is Afrim Përmeti suddenly calling me? Did he finally figure out that I have his precious daughter in my clutches? No... If he knew, he wouldn't be this calm. He'd be kicking down my door with an army.

I snatch the phone and unmute it. "To what do I owe this pleasure?"

"I want to see you. At a neutral ground," Afrim says without preamble. "I'll text you the address."

"Neutral ground?" I growl. "Nowhere in my city is neutral ground, Përmeti. That's where you're mistaken. Every inch belongs to me."

"I'll text you the address," he repeats, then cuts the call.

The phone creaks in my grip. He dares to hang up on me? To call anywhere in my city neutral ground? His life is literally in the palm of my hands, and the only reason I haven't ended his existence is because he hasn't crossed a line yet.

"What is it?" Dante asks, frowning at my expression.

"Get the SUV ready. We're meeting my father-in-law."

As we cruise down the clean, quiet streets of Old Howard Beach, I look around, half-irritated, half-amused. *This* is the 'neutral ground' Afrim picked? A small, tucked-away waterfront neighborhood where the Italians, Irish, and a few other ethnic groups have flocked to over the years.

A tight-knit community filled with mostly old, retired folks who like the slow pace, and married couples with young children who prefer to avoid apartment life.

I suppose that's why Afrim thought it would be neutral. With so many old-timers and children, I've mostly stayed away, and my men don't have much presence here.

One code my brothers and I stick to that the old families never gave a damn about is sparing women, the very old, and the very young.

I keep a loose pulse on the ground, making sure the town remains relatively crime-free, but beyond that, Old Howard Beach is a mostly forgotten spot.

A scoff escapes me as Dante steers us along the waterfront, where a handful of fishermen are busy cleaning up their boats and inspecting their day's haul. Does Afrim really think he'll be safe here? If he tries something, he thinks I won't retaliate? I already have three men stationed in strategic spots around the coffee shop he wants to meet. He's not as clever as he thinks.

As we get closer to our destination, we garner some attention. Some people recognize me; others just look baffled by a Cadillac SUV rolling into this sleepy corner of the city.

Dante finally squeezes us into a cramped space by the docks —a shitty excuse for parking, but it'll have to do—and cuts the ignition. Perro is already out, opening my door like clockwork. I adjust my lapels as I get out, and a punch of salty air immediately hits my nostrils, sharp with the scent of fish, sweat, and brine. Not exactly my ideal meeting ground.

My gaze sweeps the surroundings, cataloging everything before settling on my target. The coffee shop sits there all pretty and quaint, with umbrellas and chairs dotting the waterside. All empty except for one, where my father-in-law lounges with three armed men at his back trying to look intimidating as we approach. *Adorable.*

Afrim doesn't even bother standing when I'm in front of him. Fine, I'll play this his way. I sink into the opposite chair, raising a brow as if to say, 'This how we're doing it?'.

For a man in his late sixties, he carries himself well—solid looking, more dark hair than silver, and sharp green eyes that could probably still make most men squirm. My wife gets her red hair from her mother; the steel, though, that came from him.

Neither of us speaks, and I'm not about to break the silence first. So I just settle back, crossing my ankle over my knee and studying the bored barista in the coffee shop who's pretending not to watch the potential bloodbath brewing on her patio.

Finally, Afrim clears his throat, lifting his coffee cup. He takes a fortifying sip before speaking. "You might know why I'm here," he begins. "My daughter has gone missing. Someone stole her from my compound."

My brows fly up as I study the old man. "Didn't she walk out on her own?"

The tips of his ears go red, and he tightens his grip on the coffee mug. "That may be so. But she was... cajoled. She's a young, impressionable girl, my Elira, and quite fascinated by the world beyond our walls. I'm afraid someone must have found out and used that to lure her out—and then kidnapped her."

So, it's a guessing game. Either he genuinely has no clue she's with me and is hoping I'll 'help' track her down, or he knows exactly where she is and is trying to feel me out. Either way, I don't have time for this. I have more pressing things to deal with.

"And what does this have to do with me?" I ask impatiently.

"I suspect one of your people took her. It was her birthday a few days before she went missing, and my men told me she chose a restaurant of yours to celebrate the happy occasion." He tilts his head, studying my reaction.

Ah, so he's trying to bait me. He *knows* I was at the restaurant and that I offered her gifts. He probably suspects I have her but doesn't want to outright accuse me in case he's wrong. Still being so diplomatic.

I smirk, as I tell him with relish. "Let me save you the trouble, Afrim. *I* took her. She was ripe for the plucking and fell right into my clutches. If you didn't want to lose her, you should have kept a closer watch on her, locked her tighter in her cage. Elira Leonotti is my wife now, and I suggest you stop looking for her."

For a moment, his face goes utterly still, then a deep red flush spreads up his neck to his cheeks as he explodes to his feet. "You asshole!" Behind him, his men whip out their weapons, pointing them dead at me. My own men shift, angsty, but they know the plan.

"You have a hell of a nerve showing up here and admitting you took my daughter—forced her to marry you?" His fists are clenched, shaking with barely-contained rage. "If you've touched her..."

I chuckle darkly. "She's my wife, Afrim. What do you mean 'if'? I don't need your permission to do that. Or do you not understand how marriage works?"

The old man's practically choking on his rage now, eyes bulging as he stares at me in astonished fury, the redness of his face deepening. "You'll regret this," he spits and spins towards his men. As he speaks to them in low Albanian, I lift my right hand and snap my fingers.

A soft whooshing sound pierces the air in three quick successions, and one by one, his men crumple to the ground. One even topples backwards into the water with a loud splash, sending water spilling onto the pavement.

Stunned silence holds for a heartbeat before the street bursts with panicked cries as the fishermen and waterfront workers all abandon their stations and hightail it out of the street. But I pay them no mind.

"You don't threaten me, Afrim. Contrary to what you may believe, I have absolute control over my territory, and the only reason you're still alive is because it's not your time—yet. You can thank my wife for that."

His lips twist when I mention Elira, but he keeps his mouth shut.

"Don't tempt me, or one of my bullets might catch you one of these days. Stop looking for my wife, and I might consider letting you keep the slice of my territory you stole." I drop my ankle from my knee and unfold myself from the chair.

"I hope we have no reason to meet like this again." I adjust my cufflinks, turn my back on him, and walk back to the car, feeling his hate-filled gaze bore into me the entire way.

Half-expecting him to make a last, stupid move, I glance back as I shut the car door. But he's sunk back into his seat, looking bewildered, shaken. Weak.

He really should toughen up if he wants to continue dealing with me.

"Where to? Back to the warehouse?" Dante asks, catching my eye in the rearview mirror as he revs the engine.

The warehouse, where Heath Davis is still being taken care of by my men. I should probably go there to make sure he gives us the answers we need. But meeting with Afrim suddenly has me spoiling for my wife.

"No. Take me home."

18

ELIRA

The sweet scent of custard fills the air as I carefully extract the huge tray of *Galaktoboureko* out of the oven. My muscles tense with the weight—this custard pie is no joke. The moment it touches the countertop, Marco—who I've come to learn is my assigned bodyguard—practically levitates from his chair, rubbing his hands together like a kid on Christmas morning. Behind him, the other two men in the room snap to attention just as eagerly.

I chuckle at their reactions. They remind me so much of Dren. The thought of my old bodyguard sends a sharp ache through my chest, and I quickly shove the feeling down into that box of emotions I've been avoiding. I've already learned that thinking about home is a fast track to sadness, and since I've been dodging Maximo these past few days, I haven't had the chance to remind him about my phone call home.

And after what happened that night when I tried sneaking out to the pharmacy... well, let's just say I'm not about to bring it up to the men. Sure, they've warmed up to me considerably since I started turning this place into an impromptu bakery. But

I'm not stupid. Those pleased smiles and friendly chatter don't change the fact that their loyalty belongs to one person only, and it isn't the girl stress-baking her way through captivity.

"Is it ready to eat?" Marco asks, leaning over the counter to admire the custard pie.

Before I can answer, the front door's decisive click freezes us all mid-motion. Marco immediately backpedals so fast he nearly trips over his own feet, and suddenly the kitchen feels electric, charged with an energy that makes my skin prickle. Maximo sweeps in, his dark eyes scanning the room before landing on me. There's something in those dark depths that has my heart racing, but I force my face into what I hope is a neutral expression.

One thing Marco and the other men have teased me mercilessly about the past few days is how easy I am to read, and I'm trying to change that. I'd be mortified if Maximo knew just how much he affects me.

He walks deeper into the kitchen area while Marco retreats further. Then he leans against the glass door. "What's with you and baking? The whole house always smells like a bakery." His voice and face are neutral, which makes my stomach tighten. Is he annoyed? Amused? Impressed? I can't tell.

I shrug as I pick up a knife from the rack and carefully cut into the *Galaktoboureko*. "Since you've left me here to be a part of your decoration, I need to do the only thing I'm good at to keep my sanity, and that's baking."

My mind drifts to those endless hours at sixteen, hunched over my phone, watching baking video after baking video. Besart never baked, so if I wanted to eat the desserts I wanted, I had to learn to bake them myself. I grew to love it over time, and it became the one thing I could lose myself in when I was overwhelmed.

"Hmm." The low hum in his voice has me glancing up,

knife halfway through the pie, and *holy moly*—the predatory heat in his gaze sucks all the air from my lungs as he shrugs off his jacket and folds it neatly on the stool in front of the island.

Wait... when did he move away from the door?

My mouth goes desert-dry as he starts working on his cuff-links, then his shirt buttons, one slow button at a time. The shirt slips off his shoulders, exposing the beautiful golden expanse of his chest, and I feel heat creep up my neck. "What are you doing?" I hiss in a scandalized whisper, my gaze darting to the men in the living room trying their hardest to blend into the furniture.

He follows my gaze. "You may go," he dismisses them, and I swear they teleport out of there.

"Maximo." It's meant as a protest, but it comes out more as a plea.

He prowls towards me and checks the oven. Satisfied that it's off, he turns to face me. "It's been three days."

My brain short-circuits for a moment before catching up. *Oh.* Three days since the implant, since Ethan's instructions to wait. Three days of avoiding this very moment, pretending I wasn't counting down the hours myself.

I swallow, my heart thudding in my ears at the possessive hunger in his eyes as he advances. I skirt around the counter and raise my hands. "Wait, wait, I—*eep*!" A squeal tears from my throat as he lunges, and suddenly I'm dashing through the living room like some panicked little creature. Which is ridiculous because I *want* this. These past days, I've done nothing but replay our first time, cursing myself out for how much I enjoyed it—and how much I crave more.

His fingertips graze my lower back, and I jump away with a breathless giggle, but then those strong arms band around my waist, reeling me back into his chest. "Gotcha," he growls into my ear and runs his tongue over the shell, sending shivers cascading through my body.

Then, something silky dangles in front of my face. I blink, trying to focus on it, until I realize what it is. *His tie.* He hands it to me. "Wrap it around your eyes," he commands softly.

I lick my lips and study it for a moment. He... he wants me blindfolded. "I don't know..." I start reluctantly.

"Trust me, *dolcezza*, you'll enjoy it. Losing your vision will heighten every other sensation."

That husky, seductive tone has my heart skipping, and I take the tie with shaky hands. His words echo in my mind: *Trust me.* And that's the crazy thing—I do. I really *really* shouldn't, but in this moment, I do. I lift the silk to my eyes, the material cool and smooth against my skin, and Maximo grabs the ends from me and ties it firmly. I test my vision, but there's nothing beyond inky darkness and vague shadows dancing at the edges. It's disorienting, like being untethered, but... it's true. Every other sensation feels magnified—the whisper of air against my skin, the faint scent of his cologne, the warmth radiating from his body.

His hands capture my waist, and suddenly I'm airborne. My fingers find his arm, and I gasp. Beneath the smooth skin, I feel some unexpected bumps. Old scars, maybe? I start tracing them with curious fingers, but he catches my hand and guides it up around his neck instead. Questions lodge in my throat, but I swallow them down, knowing he won't answer me. Besides, some mysteries about Maximo, I'm learning, are better left unexplored. At least for now.

We move, and I cling to him, my disoriented brain struggling to track his steps. Then a door clicks, and my back meets something cool and very soft that feels like clouds—a bed?

I didn't even feel him walking up the stairs.

Good lord. My heart thumps harder at the realization that he carried me up all the way without his breathing changing. Without a single tremor in his muscles. *Such strength.*

I'm still catching my breath when he speaks. "Take off your

clothes without losing the blindfold and lie back on the bed." His footsteps retreat, leaving me floating in darkness.

I sit up, feeling around clumsily as I peel off my clothes, hyper-aware of every tiny motion. I fumble with my shirt, and of course, it gets caught on my hair, so now I'm awkwardly tugging at it, hoping I don't look like a complete idiot. My slacks are next, and without the help of sight, I practically have to shimmy out of them, biting back a laugh. This would be so much easier if I could actually see what I was doing.

Then, I pause, fingers hooked in the waistband of my underwear, my heart giving a little nervous flutter. Should I... take them off too? I mean, he didn't exactly say, but I know where this is headed. A wave of self-consciousness hits, and suddenly, the idea of sitting here, bare and blindfolded, has my stomach flipping.

Before I can think about it too much, his voice cuts through the silence. "As cute as you look in that lingerie, it needs to go."

My cheeks burn, but I comply, sliding off my underwear. Then I lie back down, nerves sparking to life as I hear him moving around, the faint rustling stoking my anticipation and killing my curiosity.

What's he doing?

The bed dips on one side, and I inhale sharply as his warm weight presses down over me. A living, breathing blanket I can't help but arch into.

He doesn't say a word as he caresses his palm along my neck, down my sternum, ghosting over my nipples, and *oh*—without sight, every feather-light touch feels supercharged, like he's playing my nerve endings like strings on a violin. I'm almost embarrassed by how my body responds, helplessly eager. Every shift and slide of his palm sends pleasure rushing through my veins in languid waves, making arousal coat my inner thighs as my core contracts needily.

He rubs his palm against my skin to create warm friction

until I'm writhing beneath him. Then he leans in and sucks my neck, moving his hot mouth down the path his hands took, and I hold my breath in anticipation as he moves towards my breasts, but the asshole only licks around them, deliberately avoiding my needy nipples.

I whimper and reach up blindly to wrap around his neck and direct him to where I want him, but he dodges my touch, and then he's gone, leaving me hanging in the air. My breath catches—*does he really think he can leave me like this?*

But before I can even open my mouth to protest, he's back, and then an incredibly cool liquid drips onto my nipple.

Holy—! The flesh contracts sharply, every muscle tightening as a ripple of goosebumps erupts down my skin. My body jerks in shock, and the coolness floods me with a sharp, delicious sensation that has me moaning, half in surprise, half in bliss. I can barely think straight when his mouth, chilled from whatever he has just poured, closes over the sensitized peak.

The contrast is unreal—his cool lips paired with the warmth of his hand, his mouth nibbling and sucking one nipple while his fingers roll and tease the other, sparking shivers that zips down my spine. My body reacts on instinct, writhing, arching up against him, feeling all kinds of tingling sensations attack my body all at once. Heat, cold, pleasure—it's like he's flipping switches inside me, and I'm helpless against it.

Just when I think I'm about to lose it, he rolls his tongue over my nipple one last time, then retreats. I wait breathlessly for his attention to shift to my second tit. But instead, something cool and solid—a rectangle?—lands on my belly button, wetness pooling even more between my thighs as my stomach coils tight and my hips buck up, each nerve ending lit with shock, arousal, and overstimulation.

Maximo pushes me back down with a firm hand on my sternum and takes the cool rectangle off my skin before dragging the hot, flat of his tongue over the flesh. I can almost hear the circuits of my brain fizzling out as my body goes slack, my thoughts dissolving completely until all that's left are the sensations flooding me.

It's too much. Too much. Too much.

"*Maximo,*" I gasp, my whole body alive with a trembling I can't control as I reach for him, needing an anchor in this whirlwind of sensation. He catches my hand, entwining our fingers together, and I grip it tightly, holding on for dear life as he begins a torturously slow crawl down my body, each inch closer driving me wild with anticipation.

Then I feel it.

The first stroke of his cool tongue through my damp folds sends a shockwave through me that has my eyes rolling under the blindfold and my head trashing frantically around on the bed as I clamp my thighs around him, holding him hostage.

With a quiet, primal groan—the vibration only adding another delicious layer of sensation—he places a cool, calloused palm on my inner thigh, pushing it apart without any resistance. My trembling ramps up as I feel the tsunami of pleasure building and building, almost scaring me with its intensity.

"Maximo," I whimper, trying to warn him, but he chooses that moment to insert one finger inside me, and my whole world nearly explodes. I jerk violently, tightening my grip on his hand and digging my free hand into the bedcovers as cold and white-hot heat rushes through my veins.

It's such a mind-fuckery feeling—this collision of two extremes—I can't even figure out which sensation is real anymore. My body doesn't seem to know how to deal with both at once, and the trembling only increases until I'm shaking like a leaf, not sure if I'll break from the cold or burn up in the heat.

"You're fine, *dolcezza,*" he murmurs, his voice low and probably meant to be reassuring, but the way he blows a hot breath on my cunt—*dear lord.*

Then, his finger moves—rubbing, teasing, pressing on that spot inside me and I'm gone. The world whites out as heart-stopping pleasure slams into me, making me buck and jostle beneath him, helpless against the sensation after sensation wracking my body.

I let out a long, shuddering groan, pretty sure I'm almost cracking his fingers with how hard I'm holding onto them as I ride out the most intense orgasm of my life.

But even when the pleasure begins to ebb, I can't stop shuddering as bone-deep chills slither through me and settle in my spine. "Ma–Maximo," I stutter, suddenly scared at having no control over my body. I don't know what's happening to me. It's like I'm short-circuiting. Not cold, exactly—this... it's something else. More like little aftershocks tingling up and down my nerve endings, making my muscles contract and relax in a constant, madding cycle, and I can't escape it. I can't even remember how to breathe.

Maximo curses softly and immediately climbs over me, wrapping me in his arms as he drapes the blanket over us, cocooning us. His skin is blazing hot against mine, and *ohh*—he's naked. The realization hits me when his hard cock drags over my hip, leaving a trail of hot precum that makes me shiver for entirely different reasons.

He runs his hands over my body in long, warming strokes as he murmurs gentle praises against my skin. The words spin through my head like honey, and gradually, deliciously, sexual tension begins rebuilding. Then he reaches behind my head and carefully removes the blindfold.

The room is dimly lit, but it still makes me squint after the total darkness. When my eyes finally adjust, I blink, taking in the deeply masculine space surrounding us with dawning realization—*he brought me into his room.*

"Are you okay?" His voice is soft, laced with a concern that reaches right into my chest. I move my gaze to him, inhaling sharply when his handsome face comes into focus, and my heartbeat triples.

"I'm fine," I murmur, trying to keep my voice steady. He threads his fingers gently through the tangled mess of my curls. When he grabs a curl, stretching it out, I feel a tug deep in my stomach—like he's playing with something more than just my hair. He releases it, watching as it springs back into its natural coil, and a fascinated gleam lights up his dark eyes.

My gaze wanders down his body, at least as much as I can see above the blanket covering us, and hones in on his right arm where the tattoo sleeve snakes along his skin. The entire tattoo forms one large thorny flower garden in black ink, with the stems, leaves, and thorns of different flowers surrounding each. As I stare, I realize that while it might look from afar like just one continuous vine climbing up his arm, up close, it's obvious the flowers are unique.

The centerpiece catches my attention first—a bunch of drooping Lilies that stand out in vibrant color against the monochrome background. But I tear my gaze away. *I want to see the whole thing.*

Curious, I study the inkwork surreptitiously, worried he might cover up if he notices me staring.

The tattoos start around his wrist with wide, funnel-shaped, and somewhat two-lipped petals I recognize as azaleas in black, circling his wrist and climbing halfway to his elbow. From there, the stems intertwine with those of the next flower in the hierarchy: tulips. The erect bulbs and broad, veined leaves are surrounded by dark, thick thorns that are so meticulously detailed they look almost real.

As the tulips go up to his inner elbow, the tattoo takes a fascinating turn. The stems intertwine with those of the Lily of the Valley, and I lean in slightly, captivated by the part where black ink meets the colored green stem.

The Lily of the Valley is the focal point: the white, bell-shaped flower droops dramatically towards the azaleas and tulips below, creating a huge contrast against the black and white surroundings. Little purplish thorns poke out from the green stem, adding an edge of danger to its delicate beauty.

The thorny stem climbs higher, curling around his bicep, then shifts back to black and white, introducing another flower. Although it's not colored, I know it's an iris, with its flattened, open-branched petals. It winds up his arm and ends sharply at the top of his shoulder, where more thorns jut up to his clavicle.

Finally, I return to the Lily of the Valley, drawn once more to the vibrant color. Before I can stop myself, my hand goes straight to the flower, and as I run the tips of my fingers over the beautiful design, I feel it—the raised bumps from earlier. *Scarred flesh.*

He flinches away and grabs my wrist before I can explore more. His expression shutters closed, and I can almost see the walls slamming back into place.

"What—what happened there?" It's probably useless, but I can't stop the curious question.

"Nothing," he answers tonelessly, then sensually runs his own fingertips up my arm, sending delicious tingles through my body. *He's trying to distract me.*

But I can't let it go.

"What do the flowers mean?" I press. I know they mean something. He doesn't strike me as a man who just tattoos a bunch of random flowers on his arm. And since I now know the tattoos cover up some kind of scars, it *definitely* means something.

"You're fine now," he murmurs, and I frown at him, not getting what he means, until he pulls away the blanket from our bodies and turns me around on the bed, face down, effectively ending the conversation as he runs a long finger down my spine.

One day, I think as desire begins to cloud my thoughts again, *I'll understand all your mysteries, Maximo.*

But for now, as his touch becomes more purposeful, I let myself fall into the moment, into the pleasure he offers. The flowers and their secrets can wait.

19

ELIRA

Maximo arranges my limbs on the bed until I'm on my hands and knees, and runs his hand down my ass with an appreciative murmur. The flesh tingles with the memory of his spanking from a few days ago, and I catch myself holding my breath, half-expecting him to spank me again—maybe even harder this time since I was asking probing questions—but he only caresses it softly, almost maddingly so.

His hand drifts lower between my cheeks, and I nearly jump out of my skin when his thumb circles that forbidden entrance. I bite my lip as I dare a glance over my shoulder, and *oh*—the intense look in his dark eyes makes me gasp. It's like being caught in the gaze of a predator, one who knows exactly what he wants to do with his prey. Oh no.

Then he shifts off the bed and takes some items off the nightstand. I track his every move, my pulse spiking as I see what he has picked up. The lube. And... a small cone-ish device with a wide, flat end. I blink, feeling heat flare up my face as realization sinks in. Oh. Oh no. I may be inexperienced, but I know exactly what he plans to do with it. "I'm—I'm not sure if this is such a good idea."

He chuckles. "I've yet to do something you don't like—or have I?"

I shake my head slowly, because it's true—everything he's introduced me to has unlocked pleasures I never imagined possible. *Damn him for being right.*

"Good, then trust me on this." He snaps open the bottle of lube and pours the cool liquid generously on my ass. Then his fingers begin a slow, circling massage that has my toes curling. He works the rim with careful attention until the skin heats up under his touch and a warm languid pleasure flows through me.

I try to swallow my moan but it escapes anyway, my pussy fluttering as he continues with his massage. More lube squirts onto my flesh and a shudder tingles down my spine as he holds me steady with one hand on my hip and return to making circles through the lube. Once, twice, he circles his index finger around my rim, and my body responds embarrassingly eagerly, the hole contracting and relaxing with each pass. Then he puts the tip of his finger at my entrance and—

I jolt forward instinctively as he pushes his finger in, but he holds me in place. "Shh, stay still."

The slow slide of his finger makes my head drop with a gasp as the strangest pleasure radiates through me. *What the—*

My pulse pounds in my ears as he withdraws, adds more lube, then circles back again, the movements now achingly familiar but still electric. Each careful thrust, each glide of his finger, sends waves of dazed pleasure through my body until I'm breathless and practically melting into the mattress.

When he switches to his thumb, I tense at the slightly thicker intrusion, but force myself to remain still, trusting him—and I can't believe I'm thinking this—not to do anything that would hurt me too much.

With the excessive lube and his earlier attention, it's an easier stretch than I expect, and the sound that escapes my lips is definitely not protest. I moan, arching my back, thrusting my ass back at him, and he chuckles. "Feels good, doesn't it?"

I nod breathlessly. He withdraws from me, and I glance back to see him coating the device with lube. "What's that?"

He holds it up so I can get a closer look, like he knows exactly how curious—anxious—I am. "It's called a butt plug. Having this in first for a few days will loosen you up a little and make it easier for you to take my cock."

Oh God. I bite my lip with trepidation as I move my gaze to the huge cock jutting out of his pelvis and weeping with precum. It's one thing to be able to take a finger, a thumb, or even the butt plug in my ass... but that monstrous thing? I swallow, nerves flaring up all over again. "I—I don't know Maximo."

"It's okay, love. You don't have to worry about my cock for a few more days."

That doesn't make me feel any better.

But then he's back behind me, and after another brief massage, he begins to work the plug inside. I gasp at the initial stretch, pleasure warring with discomfort as tears spring to my eyes. The feeling of fullness is overwhelming, my ass clenching around the intrusion as arousal drips down my pussy.

"That's it. You're my good girl. Look at you taking it so well. *So damn pretty,*" he murmurs softly, making my head spin with his addicting praise.

I suddenly would do anything to keep him calling me his good girl in that voice.

He pats my ass appreciatively, and when I look back, his eyes are transfixed to the plug now fully inserted, his expression so hotly possessive that I moan as I push my ass at him, not understanding what I'm doing or why—but he seems to like it. He circles my ass with his palm before rising, and I watch through heavy-lidded eyes as he pulls out a couple of wet wipes from the pack on the nightstand and cleans his hands. Then he's climbing back behind me, and with a strong hand on my spine, pushes my back down until my ass is raised shamelessly high towards the ceiling and my pussy is right in his face.

He rumbles out a pleased groan as he runs a hand through my soaked folds. "Look how pretty you are. So pink. So wet. All for me. All *mine*." Each word is punctuated with a light slap to my pussy that makes the plug shift in my ass, sending electricity jolting through me.

"I'm–I'm not a possession you can own," I gasp out.

He laughs darkly, thrusting his fingers into my tight flesh, making my eyes roll with pleasure. "Wrong, Elira. You *are* a possession I already own."

Did he just— Before I can summon proper outrage, he's rubbing that spot inside me that turns my brain to mush, and I'm crying out his name while bucking back against him like a cat in heat, ire forgotten.

"You're my wife. Your entire being belongs to me." His voice is gravel and sin as he removes his fingers and notches himself at my entrance. "*Mine,*" he growls, and with one savage thrust, he claims me.

I scream his name again as pleasure slams into me, but even lost in the sensation, I cling to one thought: *My body might be yours, Maximo, but that's all you get. Not my whole being. And especially not my heart.*

20

MAXIMO

"It's goddamn infuriating just how good this person is. It's like chasing shadows—there one second, gone the next. How are things on your end? Did you find anything? Maximo?"

My name jolts me out of my heated daydreams about my wife walking around the penthouse with my plug nestled in her ass. How is she taking it? I'm tempted as hell to call it a day and rush home to find her.

Will she be wet and needy for me, just like she's been the past few days while the plug's been in?

"Maximo."

I blink, snapping back to reality, and focus on my computer screen. There's my brother, eyes narrowed, waiting. A week has somehow passed so quickly, and we're back for our weekly meeting.

"Sorry, Michael. Missed that question. Run it by me again?."

He huffs impatiently, crossing his arms over his shoulder. "What the hell's gotten into you? You've been floating in space this whole damn meeting."

"Yeah, seriously, that's not like you, Maximo." Romero perks up, the bored expression that's usually on his face during these meetings vanishing as he studies me. "What gives?"

Before I can fabricate something better than 'I'm thinking about fucking my wife senseless', Rafael cuts in.

"Word on the street is our Maximo here got himself hitched. As in, he got *married,*" he deadpans.

My eyes narrow to slits. Of course he knows. Then I glance at Michael and Romero, who both give nonchalant shrugs like it isn't news to them.

"Yeah, I heard he nabbed Përmeti's daughter but couldn't believe he actually went through with the tying the knot part," Michael grouches.

"Well—" The word barely leaves my mouth before Michael steamrolls over me.

"You couldn't even invite us to the wedding? You didn't think we'd want to go to Vegas too?"

"Speak for yourself, Michael," Romero yawns, looking unaffected. "If accounts are true, I don't think I would have wanted to witness that dreadful ceremony." Dreadful? Did he just call my wedding *dreadful*?

I scowl at him. "Watch your fucking mouth. I'd like to see how dreadful *your* wedding is when the time comes."

"Oh, please. I'm never getting married."

"That's exactly what Maximo used to spew. Look at him now. You're next in line," Michael says with glee, clearly itching to rile Romero up.

"Guys," Rafael says before they can dissolve into their usual bickering. "Enough of that." Michael raises his hand, making him sigh. "What, Michael?"

He stares right at me. "Just wanted to remind Maximo to make sure to invite us to his *next* wedding."

His words are harmless enough, but the mere suggestion that my marriage to Elira might be temporary makes me want to reach through the screen and throttle him. "What are you trying to imply?" I growl.

He frowns at me, genuine confusion crossing his features. "Come on. Obviously you're only with the girl to get back at her father. I say enjoy her and dump her. There's no point in drawing out this ugly business."

Ugly business? My fist slams the desk hard enough to rattle my monitor. "The *girl* is my wife, and you'll refer to her with respect or lose your damn tongue, Michael."

"What the hell did you just say to me?" His blue eyes go menacingly cold as he leans towards the computer screen.

"Order in the meeting room!" Romero calls out with a chuckle. *The bastard.* There's nothing amusing about this shit.

I keep my glare on Michael, refusing to back down. The nerve—how dare he disrespect my wife? *My wife?* "Apologize. Right now."

He lets out a scoff, rolling his eyes. "You've known her for what, barely a week? And you're asking me to apologize for saying what we were all thinking? Does she mean something to you already? Is that it?"

His questions hit like bullets. She *should* mean nothing to me. So why am I so pissed at Michael for disrespecting her and trying to imply she's nothing more than some sex toy?

"She does." Michael's jaw goes slack and his eyes widen with shock. "Holy fuck, Rafael, Maximo is falling in love with Përmeti's daughter."

"That's quite enough," Rafael answers and tilts his head at me in question.

But fuck, I have no idea what's happening to me either. All I know is that every day this past week, I've been counting down the hours to get home to her. She's in my head more often than not, and I find myself doing stupid things in a bid just to make her smile at me.

Heck, I hate deserts, but last night I tried one of her pastries—a fucking *flija*—and I loved it. Then, not ten minutes later, I ate her out and fucked her on the dining table.

Fucking hell. I might *actually* be falling for my wife.

I don't say any of this out loud, but Rafael slowly shakes his head and lets out a curse that sounds like he's figured it out anyway. "Dinner at my place tomorrow. Bring your... *wife*." He says her title with cool disdain, and fuck if I don't narrow my eyes at him, not liking his tone at all.

"This should be interesting. Are we invited too?"

"Michael," Romero warns.

"Yes, you're all invited," Rafael says, shifting his gaze away from mine. "Anything else I should know? Anyone else suddenly coveting their rival's daughter?" The dig burns, and I have to grind my teeth to keep from snapping back. Elira is so much more than just a rival's daughter, and this thing I feel for her is more than just the thrill of the forbidden fruit.

Romero barks out a laugh. "When did you become a comedian, Rafael?" My glare swings his way, but he simply raises his hands innocently.

"Since this meeting is over, I need to go," I grit out.

"We'll see you and your wife tomorrow night." Rafael's steel gray eyes settle on mine like he's daring me to object.

"Yes. Yes, you will," I answer quietly and leave the call. Then clear off everything on my desk with a roar, my computer hitting the floor with a clatter.

My office door swings open and Dante bursts in, brows raised. "I take it the meeting didn't go well?"

"Get Fergio on the line," I tell him, running a hand through my hair, fighting to keep my cool.

"Fergio?" His brows climb higher. "You want to buy some more stuff for Elira?"

"We have dinner tomorrow night. With the *Capo di tutti i capi*."

His sharp inhale says it all. "I'll call him right away."

Dante is right to be worried. Hell, *I'm* worried. Rafael might be like a brother to me, and I trust him with my life, but he doesn't take lightly to anything he perceives as a threat to his empire. And thanks to this clusterfuck of a meeting, he might see Elira as exactly that—a threat. If he concludes that I'm falling in love with her like Michael accused.

Damn it all to hell.

My office line buzzes, and I snatch up the receiver. "Yes?"

"It's Fergio, Mr. Leonotti. I heard you needed me?"

Fergio's boutique is the crown jewel of luxury fashion in the city, and he's been a loyal associate for years, hence why I trusted him with Elira's birthday presents and her new wardrobe. The man has an eye for detail and discretion that's worth its weight in gold. Plus, he already knows her sizes—one less headache to deal with.

The call is brief but productive. I need Elira to look perfect tomorrow night—not just beautiful, but untouchable. A queen among queens. Let them try to dismiss her then.

I grab my jacket after my conversation with Fergio and drape it over my arm as I stalk out of my office. Dante rises, but I wave him down. "Stay here and handle anything important that comes up."

He doesn't argue; just sinks back into his seat with a grunt.

I make my way to the elevators, down to the basement level where my car is waiting. Three of my men take shifts patrolling the garage, and they stand at attention when I emerge.

I acknowledge them with a curt nod as I walk towards my Cadillac.

One of them steps forward. "Need a driver, sir?"

"I've got it." I wave him away as I slide into the driver's seat and turn the ignition. The Cadillac comes alive with a deep purr, and I relax back into the leather seat, then pull out of the garage.

The short drive home becomes a blur of traffic lights and inner turmoil. I need to handle the dinner tomorrow carefully. I don't know what I feel for my wife, but I certainly feel something. Regardless of what it is, I need to shove it down to the pits of hell by tomorrow evening. That's the only way our marriage will get the stamp of approval from Rafael.

Not that it matters whether he gives his approval or not. Elira and I are already married, and nobody can do or say anything to change that. Still, having his approval will make my life and marriage easier.

I pull up in front of my building just as a limo slides into the spot next to me. Fergio gets out with two girls I assume work with him. His attention snaps to me the moment I exit the Cadillac, and he quickly bows his head, his attendants following suit.

But my mind's already upstairs with Elira. What is she doing right now? Is she baking something new? Waiting for me? Still wearing the plug?

When did I start caring about these things?

21

ELIRA

The moment I hear the front door open, my heart does this ridiculous little flutter and my feet start moving of their own accord. I make it halfway to the doorway before my brain catches up with my body.

What. The. Heck? Since when do I jump like an eager puppy when he walks through that door?

Hello? Earth to brain: He's the *enemy*.

Marco shoots me a questioning frown as I pivot mid-stride and force myself to walk—*don't run, don't bounce, just walk*—back to the couch with as much dignity as I can muster. Sitting down requires a delicate maneuver thanks to the plug in my ass that's been my constant companion—and tormentor—these past days.

Footsteps echo louder, and damn it, my traitorous heart speeds up again. I glance at the doorway with anticipation.

Maximo appears, but he's not alone. The parade behind him makes my brows climb towards my hairline. There's a vaguely familiar older man, followed by two girls who look about my age, wheeling in a tall cloth rack bursting with designer dresses. And—*good grief*—half of Maximo's men trail in with another cloth rack, a gleaming full-length mirror on wheels, and their arms strained under mountains of shopping bags.

"What in the world is all this?" I ask Maximo, rising slowly from the couch, proud that my voice comes out steady despite the circus unfolding in front of me.

"A sudden dinner event came up for tomorrow evening, so we need to get you some appropriate attire," he answers as he walks into the living room with the crowd of people close at his heels.

"But I already have more than enough clothes in the closet." *The closet that you filled without asking*, I want to add, but bite my tongue. We still haven't had that conversation about him just buying clothes for me and dropping those extravagant gifts from my birthday in the closet. We should have talked about it, damn it. Maybe it would have curbed this fashion invasion.

Once the racks and mirror are wheeled into the room and the shopping bags carefully placed next to them, Maximo's men make a swift exit. Marco gives me a small nod that somehow manages to convey both sympathy and amusement before following them out, leaving me alone with Maximo, the older man, and the two models-slash-assistants.

"This is a special occasion that requires a very special dress. Come on." Maximo places a hand on the small of my back and guides me to the sofa, helping me sit before dropping down next to me.

The older man selects two dresses from the rack and hands them to the girls. I watch in confusion as they accept them with nervous glances in my direction. "Where can we change, ma'am?"

Ma'am? The title jars me for a second. They look about my age—or maybe even a little older? "Change?" I ask dumbly.

With an air of rehearsed elegance, the older man steps forward. "Hello, Mrs. Leonotti, I'm Fergio Dupont, owner of

Dupont's boutique down at East Flushing. These are Meghan and Paige. They're here to try out the dresses for you, so you may choose one you like without the hassle of changing into them yourself. And don't worry, they're your exact size."

I stare at Mr. Dupont, then at the girls. They're going to model the dresses? For me? What alternate universe have I stumbled into?

"There's a guest bathroom over there." Maximo points to the powder room by the stairs, and the girls scurry off, clutching the dresses like they're on some high-stakes fashion mission.

My jaw drops as I look between Maximo, Mr. Dupont, the dress racks, and the shopping bags. "This is too much, Maximo." Sure, my father is rich, but this? This is next-level extravagance. I'd always ordered new clothes online and dealt with alterations through shipping labels if needed.

I didn't realize designer stores go to clients' houses and model their items for them in a private runway show. *Is this how the top 1% lives?*

I'm still trying to process it all, when the girls strut back out, twirling to give me a full view of the dresses. Both dresses—one midnight black and the other a dusty pink—are beautiful but have a distinctly corporate feel. Maximo vetoes them before I can even form an opinion.

As the girls prepare for round two, Maximo gets up from the couch with a murmured excuse. I frown as I watch him go, then eye the bags.

"What are in those bags, Mr. Dupont? More dresses?"

"Please, call me Fergio, ma'am." His grin sparkles as he lifts one bag and brings it towards me. "And these aren't more dresses—they're accessories." He opens it and I gasp at the pretty pair of silver Jimmy Choos. With a conspiratorial wink, he waves at the rest of the bags. "*All accessories.*"

My mind spins at the sheer excess. Maximo really thought

of everything—except telling me where we're going for the dinner and what it's all about. That would be too easy, wouldn't it?

The girls return in new gowns just as Maximo makes his way into the living room holding a bottle of wine by the neck. He gives them one glance and shakes his head.

"What? Why? They look really nice!" I push myself up from the couch, ignoring the delicious reminder between my legs as I follow him to the kitchen. His frown deepens as he works the wine bottle open, and I brush past him to take out the wine glasses, rinsing them before handing them over.

He pours the red liquid generously, then turns to Fergio. "Care for some?"

The store owner declines with a polite shake of his head.

Maximo hands me my glass and studies me critically. "This is not going to work."

"If you had told me before bringing Fergio and company all the way here, I could have told you that myself," I point out, gesturing upstairs. "There are literally dozens of dresses in my closet I can wear."

"Not that." He shoots a look back at the girls as they parade back in. "You may all leave. You too, Fergio. No, leave everything here. We'll choose on our own."

I gape at him. "What? What are you talking about?"

"You need to wear them yourself so we can see the full vision," he tells me as Fergio and his staff make their exit, leaving their fashion arsenal behind.

I roll my eyes at him, even as my stomach flips. "So, what? You want me to model the dresses for you?"

He snaps his fingers. "Exactly." Then he's in my space, thumb grazing my cheek, sending my heart pounding and core clenching. "Finish your wine."

He grabs his glass and the bottle, taking them back into the living area with him. There, he sets everything down on the coffee table before moving to the racks with a serious, almost intimidating focus, like he's planning a tactical operation instead of choosing a dress.

With a sigh, I join him in inspecting the dresses. Because what else can I do? "Maybe if you tell me who we're meeting with and where, I can get an idea of what to go for. I mean, believe it or not, I've been dressing myself for over a decade now."

He glances at me briefly but turns back to the rack, shifting materials around as he answers absently, "Rafael has invited us to dinner. I know you'll impress him naturally, but he needs to respect you the moment he sees you and—"

The rest of his words fade into static. "What?" I ask, tightening my grip on my wine glass. He wants me to meet the king of New York City?

He tosses me another brief glance, as if that little detail is no big deal. "It's fine, it's not just us. My brothers will be there too."

Oh, right, because adding his two equally intimidating brothers to the dinner somehow makes it better. He might have said that in an attempt to calm me down, but it only makes my anxiety worse. Not only am I meeting the most feared man in the NYC's underground, but I'm getting the full collection of nightmares. A regular family dinner with the three most dangerous men in the city? *Fantastic.*

"You're taking me to meet the Nightshades?" My voice comes out flat, fear strangling any inflection.

That gets his full attention. He stops and looks at me, his expression softening as he takes in whatever he sees on my face. "Hey, you're going to be fine. You're married to one of them, after all, and you've held your own with me."

"But that's different. *You're* different," I blurt out without thinking, and something dark flashes in his eyes as he gives me a slow, knowing smile, his dimples winking at me.

Oh no. *Why did I say that?*

"Oh, am I?" His voice drops to a silky murmur, and suddenly he's there, in my space again, his fingers fisting in my hair, tilting my head back. "Tell me more about how I'm different."

My heart hammers at the predatory look in his eyes as he leans forward and nibbles my chin. "Tell me everything."

I gasp when he licks down my neck. Then I'm spun around until my back is pressed to his chest and I'm facing our reflection in the mirror. His hand snakes up to collar my throat, possessive but gentle. "Drink your wine before you spill it on the floor, *dolcezza*."

I meet his gaze in the mirror as I lift my glass, my pulse racing wildly under his palm. As I swallow, his hand follows the movement along my throat, and his eyes go impossibly darker. "Such a siren. You tempt me beyond measure." His words ghost against my ear before his lips claim the shell of it.

I can't hold it together anymore. My body goes limp against him. His grip loosens, just enough to let his lips wander lower, tracing the curve of my neck. And then—*oh hell*—he bites. A sharp, searing bite right on the sensitive flesh. Electricity surges through me, and the wine glass slips from my suddenly useless fingers as I arch back into him with a shameless moan.

The glass shatters on the floor, but I barely register it.

Maximo lifts his head, smirking at me in the mirror as he steps back. "We can continue this later. For now, you need to pick a dress."

Then he walks away like nothing happened, leaving me standing here, gasping, trying to catch my breath and settle my heartbeat. How does he do that? How can he be so unaffected? My eyes fall to the broken glass dazedly.

"Why are you just standing there? Choose a dress."

I glance back to see him return with a broom and dustpan. "Move along so the shards don't hurt you," he says as he carefully sweeps up the evidence of my weakness. Then he goes to dispose of it in the trash and return the cleaning tools.

When he walks back in, he finds me running my fingers over the delicate, expensive fabrics of the stunning evening gowns.

"You've not decided yet? Choose one, wife, or I'll be forced to make the choice for you."

"Don't rush me," I murmur, but my protest loses its bite when his arm drapes possessively over my shoulder. A dangerous idea forms in my mind, and before I can stop myself, I'm speaking. "Actually, tell l you what, husband. You can pick whatever you like, and I'll wear it. After all, it's basically accessorizing your property. *Me.*"

Oh. The way his arm tightens around me and the sudden darkness in his eyes—I've struck a nerve. A good one. His voice comes out rough when he asks, "And what would you want in return?"

Clever man. "I didn't say I want anything," I tease, but suddenly I'm too nervous to tell him what I want. What if he says no and I end up ruining the lightheartedness of the moment? He simply raises a brow, clearly waiting for me to spill.

I sigh and take the plunge. "Fine. I want to call my father. I can use any of your burner phones, and I won't tell him where I am. I just need him to know I'm okay," I add in a rush.

He studies me silently, long enough for my heart to sink. *He'll say no, huh.* But then he surprises me—he drops his hand from my shoulder and takes out his phone, unlocks it, and hands it over to me.

"Really?" I ask, lips parting in shocked disbelief. He gives me a soft, almost tender smile, taps the screen, and then puts it on speaker. I can hardly breathe as I accept the phone from his hand.

My pulse pounds in my ears through each ring. Three times, then—

"What is it?" My father's familiar voice fills the room.

"*Atë*?"

And just like that, I'm not Mrs. Leonotti anymore. I'm not the woman who just tried to seduce her captor-turned-husband with promises of submission. I'm just a daughter who misses her father, standing in a room full of designer dresses, trying not to cry.

22

ELIRA

Even though I try to reassure my father that I'm alright, he bulldozes right over my words, demanding I give the phone to 'that bastard'. I guess he's figured out I'm with Maximo.

"It's fine, *Atë*. I'm fine, I promise. I just wanted to let you know not to worry."

"It's been two weeks, Elira." His voice cracks with emotion that makes my chest ache. "Two weeks. Did he hurt you? I swear to God I'm going to kill him, I'm—"

My eyes fly wide, and I take the phone off speaker so fast I nearly drop it. Maximo's dark eyes dance with amusement as I spin away from him, pressing the phone close to my ear. "No, you won't, *Atë*. Maximo is my husband now. He's..." I swallow, surprising myself when I realize I mean what I'm about to say. "He's family."

When did my shotgun husband begin to mean something to me?

"I don't want to hear that bullshit from you, you hear me? He kidnapped you! And then he killed my men."

I throw a questioning glance at Maximo. That's news to me.

I didn't realize he'd met my father. "I'm sure he had reason to do that. Did you threaten him?"

"What did you just say to me, Elira?! My God!" He explodes into Albanian, cursing and ranting. I bite my lip. This is bad. My father rarely curses in my presence; he's always been careful about that. He must be out of his mind with worry about me.

"*Atë*, your blood pressure," I whisper. "You need to take it easy." I wince when he continues his tirade in rapid Albanian, his voice rising to drown out my attempts to speak. Maximo taps my shoulder, and I give him an apologetic look.

"Listen, I have to go. I'll—I'll try to call you again soon. I love you." I quickly end the call before he can protest and hand Maximo back his phone. My chest aches like someone's squeezing my heart, and tears burn behind my eyes. I stare at my hands, blinking furiously. *Don't cry. Don't you dare cry.*

"Thank you," I murmur.

"He knows I have you already." Maxim shrugs. "Now, come on. I'm going to choose your dress now, and don't even try to back out of our deal."

I smile faintly. "Never."

Monica, the hair stylist-slash-makeup artist who showed up about two hours ago, steps back with a satisfied smile and spins my chair to face the mirror. "What do you think?"

My breath catches as I take in my reflection. *Is this really me?* I carefully reach up to touch the tips of my transformed hair, half-expecting my fingers to pass through an illusion.

She's worked some kind of magic on my usually unruly curls. Instead of the tight ringlets I'm used to, they cascade down in loose, fat locks. A neat middle part now divides my hair, with the red curls styled in a half-up, half-down look, some falling over my right shoulder, settling just above my breasts.

"Wow," I breathe, turning my head this way and that to admire my hair and the subtle yet sultry makeup she's applied to my face. I don't know what she did with the colors, but somehow, they make the green in my hazel eyes pop like emeralds.

"You like it?" she asks, and I can hear the hint of anxiety in her voice.

"I love it!" I return with a grin. "Thank you so much."

Her relieved exhale makes me smile wider. "Awesome."

Together, we turn our attention to the dark green, shimmery evening dress laid out on the bed—*the* dress, the one Maximo chose last night with that predatory gleam in his eyes that still makes my stomach flip just thinking about it. I get up from the chair, sighing with pleasure as she helps me into it.

The satin flows over my skin like water—a long, sexy V-neck with off-shoulder sleeves and a shimmer that catches the light with every small movement. The built-in cups hug my breasts perfectly, the fabric clinging from there to my upper waist where a thin band holds it in place before flaring out into a ball skirt that falls in dramatic folds to my ankles.

A daring slit climbs from the right ankle up to my upper thigh, and—best of all—*hidden pockets*. Nestled so seamlessly into the sides that they're invisible but deep enough to be useful. Whoever designed this dress deserves a place in fashion heaven.

Once I'm zipped into the dress, Monica helps me back into the makeup chair, spinning it to face away from the mirror as she opens the mystery jewelry box next to her. Maximo took it from one of the numerous bags Fergio brought yesterday and wouldn't let me peek inside because it's supposed to be a surprise. But now... I sneak a look and inhale sharply at all the bling.

She lifts out a stunning necklace first—a delicate silver

chain adorned with a big round, brilliant-cut diamond pendant that settles just above my cleavage. Next come the matching earrings: long, elegant, with a cascade of diamonds that dangle gracefully near my neckline.

I think perhaps that might be all, but no, there's more. A diamond tennis bracelet is wrapped around my left wrist, competing with my wedding ring for the title of most dazzling. And on my right wrist, she fastens a slim, silver Rolex that makes me feel like I'm ticking with power.

As I'm about to stand—because surely that *has* to be it now, right?—Monica stops me. "Hold on, one last thing." She takes out what looks like the world's longest tennis bracelet. I'm about to ask where on earth that's supposed to go when she starts weaving it in through my curls. Ah, not a bracelet after all, but some sort of hair accessory.

"All done now!" She gives me a delighted grin as she moves back to scoop up the silver Jimmy Choo heels and their matching clutch from the bed and kneels to help me slip on the shoes. Then I get up from her chair for the last time and take a deep breath before turning to face the mirror again.

My lips part in awe. The long tennis bracelet winds twice around my head at the end of my middle part, making it look like a headpiece. *A sparkly little circlet.* I twirl slowly, eyes wide with wonder, watching as my jewelry and dress shimmer like something out of a dream. A delighted giggle escapes me, and I spin again, completely caught up in the magic of it all.

I look like royalty. *Regal. Cool.*

"Well?" Monica asks, hands on her hips, grinning like a proud artist.

I grin back. "I can't wait to see my husband's reaction."

Though, maybe that's not such a good idea...

If he looks at me the way he did yesterday during the fitting, we might not make it to this dinner at all. My cheeks heat at the memory, and a tiny spark of nervous excitement twists in my belly.

Carefully, I follow Monica out of Maximo's bedroom—which has somehow become *our* room—and down the stairs. The heels slow me down at first; it's been years since I had any reason to wear them. Clutching the railing like my life depends on it, I descend step by step, already catching the deep rumble of Maximo's voice coming from the living room.

When we enter, his back is to us, and he appears deep in conversation with Dante, who sees me first.

His reaction is priceless. He does a double take that nearly snaps his neck, his eyes bulging so wide I can't hold back a giggle. The sound makes Maximo turn around in what feels like slow motion, and then he sees me.

Time. Stops.

Good lord. He's wearing a tux with a cute dark green bow tie that matches my dress perfectly, and he looks good enough to eat. The way those pants fit his muscular thighs and the stretch of the jacket over his broad shoulders should be classified as a deadly weapon. I let out an embarrassingly dreamy sigh as he also takes me in and slowly approaches.

"*Dolcezza*, you take my breath away," he murmurs, raising my left hand to press a lingering kiss on the inside of my palm. A delicious tingle jolts up my arm and spreads through my body. "Absolutely stunning." His dark eyes are wolfish as he rises from my hand, making my knees weak with the promises they hold.

"You don't look too shabby yourself," I compliment through my racing heart. He chuckles, and those darned dimples appear like twin invitations to sin. I hold my clutch tighter so I don't do something silly like try to trace those cute dips with my fingers.

"Come on, we should leave now if we want to make it on

time." He drops his hand to the small of my back and leads me to the elevator, with Marco and Dante on our heels.

At the basement level, a procession of four cars is already waiting for us, each flanked by fully armed men. Maximo opens the backdoor for me, and I slide in, scooting over for him —but he only shuts the door.

My jaw drops as I watch him walk away through the window and get into another car. "What's going on?" I ask Marco, who's climbing into the passenger seat.

"It's a safety measure. In case we're attacked on the way, you two won't make easy targets for our enemy."

Well, that's reassuring. Exactly what a girl wants to hear when she's dressed up like a queen—the possibility of getting shot at.

I glance back at Maximo's car, my chest tightening with a mix of unease and... trust? It's strange, but I already know he'll do whatever it takes to keep me safe.

The cars pull out of the garage in perfect synchronization, and I rest my head against the window, careful not to ruin Monica's masterpiece. "But it doesn't really matter, does it? If we're attacked, they're not just going to pick random cars to shoot at, right?"

"No, but they won't know which car you're in," Marco says. "And if you're–you're carrying an heir, we can quickly squire you to safety."

An heir. My heart does a long pitter, and I drop a hand on my belly as I think about possibly getting pregnant, even though there's no chance of that—thanks to the implant. But still, what he's saying makes sense in a way. With this sort of precaution, the whole bloodline won't get wiped out in one single incident.

And then another nervous punch hits me in the belly. One of those potential attackers could be my own father. His anger over the phone last night still feels fresh in my mind. I sigh, watching the scenery blur past as our cars pick up speed. *What a mess.* I'll have to convince Maximo to let me call him again. Try to calm him down before he does something reckless.

The rest of the drive passes in heavy silence, and I try to talk myself out of my nervousness, but it doesn't help. Without Maximo in the car with me, I feel so alone. Crap, when did I start depending on his presence?

All too soon, we're going down another underground garage—this one even more secure. Armed men check us in like we're entering a high-security vault, and I half expect them to demand retinal scans. The moment we're parked, Maximo is out of his car and yanking my door open. His eyes search mine. "You good?" he asks as he helps me out.

I swallow, gripping his hand tightly. "I'm not sure."

"You'll be fine," he assures, squeezing my hand once before his palm finds its home at the small of my back again.

We approach the elevator, flanked by two men holding assault rifles angled towards the ceiling. They dip their heads respectfully as Maximo pulls what looks like a key card from his jacket. He gives a curt nod and taps it on a panel, prompting the elevator doors to slide open with a soft *ping*. We walk in alone.

"What about the men?" I ask as the doors slide shut and the elevator begins its rapid ascent without us even selecting a floor.

"They'll stay downstairs on alert with my brothers' men." His casual tone does nothing to settle the butterfly convention in my stomach. They're all here already? I rub my slippery palms down the back of my dress and resist the urge to shove my hands into those glorious hidden pockets without looking ridiculous.

"You'll be fine," Maximo repeats, noting my nervousness and rubbing my back soothingly. But before I can draw comfort from his touch, the elevator stops and the doors open into what can only be described as the anteroom to heaven—or hell, depending on how this night goes.

We step out directly into a great room that is a striking mix of grandeur and simplicity. Soaring ceilings and pristine white walls give it the feel of an art gallery, while the large drooping gold chandelier, sparking with countless crystals, screams old-world opulence. The beige marble floors gleam like mirrors, making me grateful for Monica's hour of heel-walking practice.

What catches my eye, though, are the paintings. Four massive flowers—an Iris, Lily of the Valley, Azaleas, and Tulips—burst from their frames in a vivid explosion of colors, breathing life into this stark monochromatic paradise. They're mesmerizing, yet somehow threatening at the same time, like poisonous blooms in a deadly garden.

"Come on." Maximo's hand gently urges me forward.

We twist around the corner into the living room, and I forget how to breathe. My eyes are immediately drawn to the enormous brass arch windows spanning an entire wall, forming the illusion of Manhattan being right outside, bathed in the soft, golden hues of a setting sun. Without thinking, I step away from Maximo and float towards the windows, and for a moment I forget my nerves, forget where I am, forget everything except the breathtaking panorama.

"Stunning, right?"

It takes all my self-control not to jump at the deep, strange voice. My body goes rigid for a split second, then I turn slowly, my heart doing a frantic drumroll against my ribs, and find myself pinned by a pair of icy blue eyes that could freeze Hell itself.

The man is lounging on the oversized couch that fits the oversized room—explaining why I didn't see him from behind it—legs crossed over each other. But his relaxed pose is deceptive, because his eyes are razor-sharp, alert, and I can practically feel the tension coiling through his muscles.

There's no question in my mind that he could be on his feet and neutralizing any threat before I even have time to gasp. It's like he's made of calm on the surface and pure danger underneath.

He's wearing a gray tuxedo, but it doesn't make him any less scary. Dark ink claws up from beneath his collar, climbing to either side of his shaved scalp and framing a mop of short, dirty blonde hair that falls over his brows—his *pierced* brows. Small dark earrings circle his earlobe, and as he raises a hand to push his hair back with mild annoyance, I catch even more tattoos creeping across his knuckles and peeking out from his sleeve.

"Elira Përmeti. You're a fine little thing," he smirks as his eyes slowly peruse me. "Ravishing."

Heat blooms across my cheeks, but it's not the flattering kind. It's irritation, mixed with a dash of discomfort. But before I can say a word, Maximo is suddenly there, his arm snaking possessively around my waist. "*Michael,*" he growls. "And it's Elira *Leonotti*."

Michael chuckles, completely unbothered by Maximo's territorial display, and cracks his knuckles—loud, deliberate, and so disrespectful. "Whatever man." His hand dips into his pocket and pulls out an expensive-looking cigarette case. From it, he extracts one thick cigarette, slides it lazily between his lips, and flicks open a lighter that gleams gold in the light. The cigarette glows bright red as he takes a slow drag and exhales a perfect smoke ring towards us. I watch him, fascinated despite myself.

Michael Hart.

So this is the CEO of HartSphere, a tech titan whose brilliance has shaped the modern world. He started out with video games, and once he broke into the market, branched out into everything tech—messaging apps, a social media platform, phones, tablets. Heck, I own a Celtro Ultra, one of the latest generations of smartphones from his company.

He's rich as sin, the stereotypical bad boy, and absolutely mad as a hatter. At least, according to Roan. He called Michael unhinged—the wildcard of the Nightshades, the one no one can predict. But watching him now, lounging like he owns the air in the room, I wonder if 'unhinged' even covers it. Though, he does look normal. Aside from the tattoos and piercings.

"No smoking inside the apartment, Michael, for Christ's sake." The irritated voice comes from a man strolling into the living room through a pair of open glass doors. I recognize him instantly—Romero Lombardi. Famous criminal lawyer.

Famous for helping criminals escape the wrath of the law, that is—nothing noble, mind you. This is a Nightshade we're talking about. His face is constantly splashed in one article or the other about his brilliance manipulating the law, or in gossip rags chronicling his escapades with women. He's the notorious womanizer of the group, never seen with the same woman twice. They say he hooks up once, then sends them a bouquet and a *fuck off* note. No bubbly. No apologies. Ruthless in and outside the courtroom.

His steps don't even hitch when he spots us by the windows. In fact, his lips curve into a smile so disarming, so utterly beguiling, that I find myself smiling back at him. *Damn*… that's probably exactly what convinced countless women to ignore all the warnings about him.

"Hell, have I gone and gotten myself killed, or is there an angel standing in the middle of Rafael's boring living room?"

"Romero," Maximo grits out, tightening his grip on my waist.

"What a vision for sore eyes you are. Finally, a dash of estrogen to tone down the ugliness of these fuckers," he continues as if Maximo hadn't spoken, his charm dialed up to eleven. My smile widens as he glides forward with the grace of a dance, taking my hands like we're old friends and pressing kisses to both cheeks.

"That's enough, you smooth-tongued devil." Maximo pushes his friend back with a hand and steps in front of me. *Steps in front of me.*

I can't help it; I peek around his shoulder, giggling as Romero winks at me, his green eyes filled with mischief.

But suddenly, the warmth in the room vanishes and a chill settles in my spine as the last member of the group walks in. *The leader.*

Rafael Moretti.

Those metallic chrome eyes of his make Michael's icy blues seem downright friendly, and the heavy silence that falls is suffocating, as if the room itself holds its breath. He flicks a disinterested gaze at Michael. "Put out the fucking cigarette."

Michael's response is to take a slow, deliberate drag and puff the smoky air at Rafael, almost challenging him. Another drag follows, and I brace myself for the explosion, but Rafael just shakes his head, looking like he's resisting a strong urge to smack him. My lips twitch briefly, but any form of amusement is wiped off my face when he turns his attention to me.

Oh shit.

Don't fidget. Don't look away. Don't show fear.

I repeat the mantra in my head as my heart skitters nervously in my chest and a swarm of angry horses stamp in my belly.

"Step back and let me see her," he tells Maximo, voice a deep timbre.

My husband hesitates for a fraction of a second, then offers me a reassuring smile before complying, leaving me exposed to that unyielding gaze. I lift my chin, channeling every ounce of courage I can muster. *I will not be intimidated in my own borrowed ballgown.* A ghost of a smile appears on his face so flitting that it's gone before I can register it.

Then he's standing in front of me, pinching my chin between his thumb and index finger, turning my head this way and that, studying me with cool, almost disinterested regard. I keep my expression neutral, though my lungs seem to have forgotten how to work properly.

When he releases me and turns to Maximo, I nearly sag with relief.

"She'll do, I suppose," he says to my husband, and my fear is pierced by a tendril of anger.

Excuse me? I'll do? He came in here like a bad cloud, studying me like I'm some trinket his brother picked up at a garage sale, and he's saying I'll *do*? What am I—a piece of furniture to round out his collection?

My glare burns into his back as he walks away, and before I can stop myself, I take an angry step forward, ready to give him a piece of my mind. My mouth is already forming words that will no doubt land me in trouble when Maximo catches my arm and shakes his head at me subtly. I scowl up at him, but his warning is clear. Not now.

Rafael glances back at me like he knows exactly what almost happened, then turns away. "Now that everybody's here, shall we go to dinner?"

Michael finally stubs out his cigarette in the ashtray on the coffee table and unravels himself from the couch, barely sparing me a glance as he follows Rafael. We all troop through the glass doors Romero came in from earlier into—

A second living room?

I blink, my brain struggling to process the sheer absurdity of it.

Who needs a second living room? This guy, apparently. Does he host simultaneous parties that can't mix or something?

This one is even more over-the-top than the last. In the middle of the room, behind a C-shaped white couch, is a sculptural wrap-around glass staircase with tall white railings. Rafael leads us past it, through the impressive apartment that I realize is basically a huge statement-piece castle in the sky, to an oversized dining room. I mean, everything in this place is oversized, so I'm not even surprised.

A gold pedestal glass table dominates this space, surrounded by ornate cream-and-gold chairs. But the chair at the head of the table—the throne, because what else would you call it?—demands all the attention. It's massive, easily three times the size of the others, with thick, elaborate carvings spiraling up the back.

When Rafael lowers himself into it, he glances around the room arrogantly—king of all he surveys. And somehow, the chair doesn't dwarf him like it would anyone else. If anything, he makes the thing look small, like the throne bends to his presence. How does someone pull that off? Is it the confidence, the raw authority, or just the sheer audacity? Probably all of it. Still, it takes a special power to achieve that.

As I slide into my seat, I can't help but study the carvings on his chair again. Those spirals... They're almost the exact same design as the tattoo on Maximo's arm. A detail so specific has to mean something. But what? Some secret code? A family crest? Or maybe just a fancy design they both liked? Yeah, right. Nothing in this world is ever just aesthetic.

My thoughts whirl as Maximo settles beside me at Rafael's right hand, close enough that the faint scent of his cologne grounds me. But even with him so near, my mind keeps circling back to the strange connection between the carvings and his ink. I glance at him, considering whether to ask, but the sharp glint in Rafael's gaze makes me swallow the thought.

Romero slides into the seat across from me, Michael next to him. As I admire the dining room with its vaulted ceilings and the same brass wall-length windows that seem to be everywhere in this place, my eyes land on the chair at the opposite end of the table.

Another throne. Smaller than Rafael's, but with the same

intricate carvings. Clearly designed for someone important. Designed for a woman?

A throne for a queen?

I surreptitiously glance at Rafael's ring finger, but it's bare. That doesn't mean much in this world, though, does it?

My gaze drifts back to the smaller throne. He has to have a woman. I mean, why else would he have a throne for a queen in his home?

And if he does... where is she? Hidden away? Gone? Or maybe she's just late for dinner. The last thought feels ridiculous, but I can't shake it.

23

MAXIMO

The dinner goes smoothly, better than I expected, and after a while, even Elira starts to loosen up, laughing at Romero's stupid jokes. *The rogue.* Of course he's pouring it on thick. I should be jealous, but instead, I'm just relieved to see her more at ease. At least she's not wearing that frozen, tense look anymore, and for once, I'm glad Romero's being his charming self.

After dessert—which, no offense to the chef, but Elira's creations put these to shame—Rafael's staff clears the table and cracks open a bottle of wine, and the vibe settles into something almost... normal. Mundane topics float around the room, and I find myself sipping along, half-listening, right about to let myself relax.

Then Rafael gets up from his chair, commanding the room's attention like he always does. "Maximo, see me in my study."

The hell?

I shoot him a frown as he walks away, then turn back to Elira. Her smile is gentle, understanding. "It's fine. Go."

I press a kiss to her cheek before standing, but not before locking eyes with Michael and Romero. "No funny business," I warn them, my voice carrying every ounce of promise of what will happen if they step out of line.

Romero winks, and Michael just rolls his eyes. Typical.

Reluctantly, I leave the table, stealing one last look at Elira. She's safe here—she has to be. Still, the thought of leaving her, even for a minute, grates at me. My feet drag as I pass the staircase and approach the thick white oak doors that lead to Rafael's study.

Inside, I find him already seated, leaning back in his chair, fingers steepled. The weight of whatever he needs to discuss already settles on my shoulders as I drop into the seat across from him.

We rarely hold separate meetings from the rest of our brothers. If it's important, we all hear it. So this must be personal. "What's up?"

"Afrim." The single word makes my jaw clench. "Snatching Elira from under his nose and marrying her without his permission has him out for blood. He's livid—at you, *us*." His voice doesn't hold judgment, just cold facts. "My sources say he's been reaching out to every Albanian family in all five boroughs. Something big is brewing, Maximo. Afrim won't just bring a fight to your doorstep—he might spark an uprising against all of us."

A knot twists in my gut as his words sink in. "That can't happen." The city is finally starting to stabilize. The last thing we need is Afrim tearing everything apart over wounded pride. The question is—how the hell do I stop him?

"Exactly," Rafael replies. "So keep your in-laws happy and in check. The Përmeti name carries weight in the Albanian circle, especially now that Kadri Përmeti has most of Long Island in his pocket. Having them on our side wouldn't suck."

Kadri Përmeti is Elira's uncle. He and Afrim used to rule Long Island together before their split and the latter came to Queens.

Keep my in-laws happy? Like it's that fucking simple. Maybe another call from Elira could buy us some time, but it's not a long-term fix. I need to call a meeting with Afrim.

The thought makes me sick, but Rafael is right. Having the Përmetis as our allies won't suck. I've made Elira mine, and nothing in this world will ever make me let her go, so I might as well forge a truce with her family. And if that softens her up towards me? Even better.

We shift to talking business—the legal side—for a few more minutes before Rafael gets up, effectively ending the discussion. As I rise to my feet, my gaze drifts to the framed picture of Rafael, Michael, Romero, and me on the wall. The same picture that's in my study at home, as well as Michael's and Romero's. It always reminds me of the missing piece of our puzzle—where there were once five, but now there are four.

"Rafael, about Emilia," I start cautiously. "It's been a decade and—"

"Don't," he cuts me off, his face going cold like it always does anytime I try to bring her up. "I don't want to talk about her."

"Have you thought about looking for her?" I push anyway, because I'm either brave or just too fucking stubborn for my own good. "I can lead the search if you give me the go-ahead." Fuck, Michael has been talking about it for a while now too.

Rafael's gaze turns arctic. "I never lost her, Maximo. So no, you won't be leading any fucking search party." He adjusts his cufflinks and starts walking towards his study door. "Let her spread her wings and climb up that ladder. It will be more fun to cut her wings off when she's at the highest point of her life."

What the fuck?

I frown at his back, unsettled by the sinister note in his voice. He knows where she is and is just... waiting to pounce? He's been plotting all this time? What the hell happened between them ten years ago? The man who wanted to make her his queen, who dreamed of ruling beside her, now speaks of destroying her with such cold satisfaction?

My heart grows heavy as I follow him back to the dining room. Could I really stand by and watch him destroy a woman I consider family? My *sorellina*? Could the other guys?

Thoughts of Emily slip out of my head the second we enter the living room. Romero, that smooth-talking bastard, has somehow migrated to sit entirely too close to my wife. "Romero Lombardi." I snap and quicken my stride, grabbing Elira's arm to pull her up from the chair. "Stay away from my fucking wife."

He throws his hands up, all innocence, but he's not fooling me. The guy's fucked his way through half the city, and while I know deep down he wouldn't betray me by going after my wife, it still makes my blood boil seeing him that close to her.

"Maximo," Elira chastises and gives Romero an apologetic smile. "Excuse him, please."

"That's alright, *carina*. Anything for you." The fucker grins, and a growl builds in my chest.

"That's it, we're leaving." I barely spare my brothers a glance as I wrap my arm around my wife's waist and bundle her out of the living room and through Rafael's sprawling apartment towards the elevator. As the doors close, my hands slide down her back to rest on her luscious ass.

"Did you take out the plug?"

Her cheeks pinken sweetly, and she lowers her head in that shy way that drives me wild as she whispers, "No. You told me not to."

Pride surges through me, clashing with a raw, relentless lust. She's been so obedient, letting me remove it every night, then easing it back in before I go to work in the morning, watching her face as her body slowly accepts the intrusion. The quiet gasps she makes, the way her fingers grip the sheets... *Christ*, just thinking about it makes my cock throb.

"Good girl," I murmur in approval, threading my fingers through the silky strands of her curls. It's been torture keeping my hands off her since she walked into my living room looking good enough to eat. But I know if I touched her then, I wouldn't have been able to stop and we would've missed Rafael's dinner. Not that I'd have given a shit, but he would've made us pay.

Now that I have her alone, my hunger is reaching feral levels. And nothing's holding me back. Except...

My gaze drops to the tempting swell of her pink lips and my mouth waters. Damn her for holding back her kisses. I should have just let her kiss me that first night we had together and gotten it over with, but I knew she would resent me once the pleasure wore off. For some reason, I couldn't bear that thought. I still can't.

The corner of her mouth beckons like a siren song, and before I can stop myself, I'm pressing a chaste kiss there, watching her carefully as her sweet taste explodes on my tongue. *More, more.* The need for more rides me savagely, but I won't force it. When we finally kiss properly, it has to be her choice.

Her lashes flutter, and just as I think she's leaning in, she slowly turns her cheek, denying me her lips once again. My restraint snaps. I tighten my grip on her and tug her head to the side to attack her sweet throat with angry hunger that's equal parts punishment and pleasure. *Mine, mine, mine,* each kiss seems to say. I'll take every other part of her.

The elevator chimes our arrival, and the doors slide open to reveal my men snapping to attention.

Reluctantly, I release her hair, then guide her to her car with my hand pressed possessively against her lower back. But as she gets in and scoots to the other side, instead of closing the door behind her, I follow her inside.

She stares at me, eyes wide. "What are you doing? Aren't we supposed to ride in different cars? For safety and all?"

"Fuck that," I growl, yanking the bowtie off my neck as I hit the button to bring up the privacy partition. The memory of the drive here, watching her car ahead of mine, knowing she was so close yet untouchable—it was its own special kind of hell. I almost stopped the cars a dozen times. I'm not about to go through that shit again. Never fucking again.

"From now on, you ride with me. We'll beef up security instead." Her lips part as if to protest, but I'm already sliding closer, closing the space between us. "Now come here. I need you."

I lift her into my lap, back to my chest, and spread her thighs easily thanks to the slit on the side of her dress. My palm glides over her panty-covered cunt, and her warm heat greets me, sending blood rushing to my cock until I go from semi to fully erect.

"Maximo..." she breathes, her voice trembling as I rub her gently, teasing her. She squirms, and the friction against my aching erection is almost too much.

"Don't. Move." I command, nipping at her throat as my right hand dives down the neckline of her dress, greedily claiming her tits just as my other hand slips into her panties. She moans and leans back into me, her head dropping onto my shoulder like she can't hold herself up.

Her sounds of pleasure as I slowly stroke her damp folds are fucking beautiful. When I finally find her clit and roll it under my thumb, she reaches up to grip the back of my head, her nails scraping my scalp in a way that makes me want to lose control. *Fuck.*

I toy with her clit until her low moans climb higher and higher, then slide my middle finger into her wet sheath, keeping my thumb right where she needs it. The cry that tears from her throat is absolutely filthy, and her head presses harder against my shoulder, mouth parted, eyes squeezed shut in bliss.

My gaze hones onto her mouth again and a fierce hunger

overwhelms me, but I force myself to look away, trailing soft kisses up and down the side of her neck instead as I fuck her hot cunt with my finger, adding a second digit when she starts making those breathy please-please-please sounds. Then I curl both up to her g-spot and flick her clit at the same time.

She shudders so violently I have to lock my arm around her waist to anchor her on my lap.

I rub her clit harder and thrust in and out of her, making sure each stroke drags over the swollen spot until she lets out this broken sound, her cunt clenching tightly around me as she climaxes.

My heart thunders in my chest, my cock throbbing painfully and leaking precum as she unravels in my arms. I focus on breathing slowly through my nose—this is about her, not me—and keep my fingers working, drawing out her pleasure for as long as possible.

Only when her breathing slowly returns to normal do I move my hands to her hips and drag her panties down her thighs. Bunching up her dress, I press it into her hands. "Hold it."

24

ELIRA

Heart pounding a hard staccato, I clutch my dress, fingers twisting in the expensive fabric while Maximo slowly lifts me off his lap, carefully arranging me on the wide SUV seat. I bite my lip as I glance nervously at the closed partition.

What if they can hear us?

A rustling behind me has me glancing back and—*holy hell*—the worry promptly fades when I see Maximo's eyes go heavy-lidded as he frees his cock and strokes the hard length. "Do you trust me?" he asks.

Yes.

The answer springs into my mind without hesitation, and my lips part in shock at my own certainty. Damn it, I *do* trust him—at least with this, with my body. I nod mutely, and his face fills with raw satisfaction as he kneels behind me.

His palm caresses my bare ass, his touch slow, teasing. Then he tugs at the plug, pulling it halfway out before thrusting it back in. A strangled moan escapes my throat, my core clenching as waves of sharp, electric pleasure dance up my spine.

"Always so wet for me," he murmurs, his voice dripping

with pride as his fingers dip lower, spreading my slick folds. "What a good wife you are."

Before I can comment, he notches himself at my entrance and drives into me with one brutal thrust. I gasp and let the hem of my dress fall, scrambling to grab the door handle for balance as my whole body jolts forward.

"Fuck." Maximo's deep, guttural groan rumbles through me, making every nerve light up. He doesn't rush. Oh no, he moves with maddening control, each deliberate stroke slow enough to drive me insane, his pace more a promise than a release.

Then his hand finds the plug again, and *oh lord*—he times it perfectly, withdrawing it and thrusting it back in rhythm with his cock until I'm seeing stars.

"*Ugghh.*" My eyes flutter shut as sensations rack through me. Pleasure like nothing I've ever felt before and a sensation of weightlessness fills my body. My senses become overwhelmed, my world narrowing down to just this: the stretch, the fullness, the building pressure that threatens to tear me apart.

Moans bubbling up in my throat are too loud, shameless, so I bite down hard on my lip, tasting blood as I fight to keep them in. But it's useless—he's relentless, maintaining his assault on both holes until I clench so tightly around him he spits out a curse.

And then I lose myself entirely. I'm floating, untethered, consumed by pleasure so intense it borders on spiritual. My entire body burns like I'm on fire, and everything is so dark, for a moment, I worry I might have lost my vision from the sheer force of the ecstasy ripping through me.

But then, as the wave of pleasure subsides just enough, my sight returns in a blur, and everything sharpens again. My heart thunders heavily, ringing in my ears as I struggle to catch my breath. I barely register him removing the plug, only aware of the cool liquid he squirts over my gaping hole. Twisting back, I whimper when he pulls his cock out of my pussy, leaving both my holes fluttering emptily.

The emptiness doesn't last long, though.

His cock glistens with my arousal, and I lick my lips hungrily as he spreads my ass cheeks and notches himself at my back hole. His thick head is big—way bigger than the butt plug—and I take a deep breath, willing my muscles to relax as he pushes inside me.

At first, the penetration goes smoothly thanks to the preparation, but once the thick head pops through my rim, my ass sphincter clenches around him instinctively as tiny pinpricks of pain start to bloom outward.

"Relax, *dolcezza*. You can take me." His voice is strained, but he lifts one hand from my hip, tracing upwards to caress my face gently, his touch a whisper of comfort amidst the ache.

I swallow, leaning my cheek into his warm palm in an attempt to center myself. Another determined deep breath, and I force my muscles to yield, to open, to submit. He advances slowly, inch by inch, pushing past the tight ring, filling and stretching me out to the point of unbearable pain.

Tears spring to my eyes, and I start clawing at the door handle in desperation. Just when I think I can't take anymore, when I'm about to beg him to stop and take it out, he seems to bottom out, his pelvis kissing my ass.

"*Good girl.*" His praise washes over me like warm honey, fingers briefly grazing my cheek, before sliding the hand on my hip lower to my starved cunt. He remains perfectly still inside me, my ass clenched around him and fluttering, letting me adjust to him while he works my sensitive clit.

A low purring sound vibrates in my throat, and suddenly I'm nuzzling my face against his hand like the cat who got the canary, licking and kissing his palm while he murmurs filthy Italian endearments. It's ridiculous, shameless even, but I don't care—he's turned me into this needy, desperate thing.

His first experimental movement sends me spiraling. I drop my head to the seat, pushing my ass up to him as sparks of electricity jolt through my skin, making my head spin.

I feel every inch, every ridge of his cock inside my ass, stretching me wide with just a tiny bite of pain accompanying the insane pleasure. I'm overwhelmed, so full, and when he presses down on my clit while slowly fucking my ass, coherent thought becomes impossible.

"Jesus fucking Christ." The words burst from him. "You're so fucking tight. Determined to strangle my cock, *dolcezza*? Want my cum before I'm ready to give it to you?"

Incoherent sounds spill from my lips as he thrusts back into me. Stars explode behind my eyes, pleasure hitting me so hard it feels like I'm being torn apart. His cock moving in and out is all-consuming, *too intense*.

He groans, his hand slipping from my face to sink into my hair, tugging me back as he starts to fuck me even harder. My brain fizzles, nearly blacking out by the intensity. My nerve endings light up like fireworks, and I can't keep track of where I end and he begins.

Every sensation muddles together—pain and pleasure, reality and fantasy—as the storm inside me builds. Then through the haze, there's a flick of clarity: I won't be able to contain my screams when I come.

He rubs my clit harder with his thumb, then thrusts a finger into my cunt, twisting deep, and that's it—I'm gone. My stomach tightens, and I scream his name over and over as my orgasm boils over. And then I'm babbling, words I don't even understand. Could be gibberish. Could be prayers. Could even be expressing my love. I have no idea.

The loss of control over my words, my body is so encompassing, so heated, so intense, I couldn't stop myself even if I wanted to.

Everything inside me fizzes and overflows like champagne

uncorked too quickly, and suddenly I'm floating again somewhere beyond my body; maybe I've floated right off the damn earth. Tears stream down my face, my head tight with lack of oxygen—I can't gulp in air fast enough as the orgasm goes on and on like it will never end.

Distantly, I catch Maximo shouting my name, feel the heat of his release flooding my ass. But it barely registers. I'm too consumed by my own orgasm, my heart thundering, my breaths wheezing out in ragged gasps, and I worry I might lose consciousness right here in his arms.

And maybe I do.

Everything goes dark.

When I come to, I'm cradled in Maximo's arms, his lips pressing tender kisses to my temple as he murmurs sweet Italian nothings into my ear. The car has stopped—we're home.

But even though the orgasm is clearly over, I'm still floating in that dreamy, hazy space, unable to fully come back to my senses. My body feels hot, tired, and utterly limp.

I shift in his arms, suddenly needing to be closer to him, and wrap myself around his waist, burying my face in his chest. His steady heartbeat is like a lullaby, and his scent surrounds me in a blanket of bliss.

His Italian endearments continue as he adjusts me in his arms and opens the car door. I clamp my eyes shut, not wanting to see anybody, and cling on tightly as he carries me out.

The warmth of his voice is a gentle anchor, pulling me through the haze as he walks us towards the elevator. "Are you okay?" he asks, and I blink my eyes open. We're alone. I nod into his chest, too drained to do anything else, and he presses a kiss to the top of my head.

"You did so good, baby."

His praise seeps into my bones, and I cuddle deeper into his body as he carries me into the apartment, up the stairs, down the hallway, and into his bedroom. He breezes through the room into the ensuite where he carefully deposits me on the double countertop.

I watch through heavy-lidded eyes as he draws the bath.

He tests the water temperature with his hand, nods to himself, then returns to me. Slowly, he undresses me like I'm a delicate antique that might break if he touches me wrong. After, he scoops me up again and gently lowers me into the warm water.

A contented sigh escapes me, head lolling back in satisfaction. When I open my eyes, he's shedding his own clothes, and my heart expands. Words of affection bubble at the back of my throat, but I swallow them down. *It's just the afterglow talking.*

There's something almost spiritual about the sexual act, like you're connecting on a soul level, and nothing else matters but the two of you and the pleasure you share. I don't know how people can have sex with one person for so long without catching feelings. They must have a heart of steel.

Maximo slides in behind me, and I scoot forward to make space for him. Once he's settled, he pulls me back against his chest and picks up a washcloth. With slow, gentle strokes, he glides it over my skin.

The only sounds are the gentle swish of water and my soft breaths as he bathes me. He parts my thighs with care, washing my pussy, then lifts each leg to the edge of the tub to clean my ass too. Every motion feels deliberate, almost intimate. When he's done, he tosses the washcloth aside, but I snatch it up and move away from him.

"Where are you going?" he protests, grabbing my arm.

"Your turn," I say, grinning, as I settle on his thighs. Almost immediately, his cock twitches to life and slaps at my leg. I glance down warily. "You've wiped me out, Maximo. I don't think I can go again."

He chuckles and runs a tender hand down my cheek. "Don't

worry about me. I'll be fine." His gaze drops to my lips, and I feel a flutter deep in my stomach.

Is he... no, surely not? As he starts to lean in, I inhale sharply. *He's going to kiss me.*

I want it, I do. *I really do.* But at the last moment, I turn my cheek, heart racing.

His eyes narrow on me. "Still not going to let me kiss you?"

"Will—" I lick my lips nervously. "Will you let me see my father?"

The change is instant. His eyes flash, and he sits up abruptly, sending water splashing to the floor. My heart sinks as he gets out of the bath. "Are you done?" he asks.

I look down at the washcloth in my hand, my earlier intention to wash him now ruined. *I* ruined it. But just as I can't turn off these growing feelings for him, I can't silence my love for my family. *I can't.*

Even though things are relatively calm right now, I know *Atë* and Roan won't rest until they see me. Until they know I'm fine and that I'm here willingly.

My heart clenches, and I gasp.

I *am* here willingly now. I never want to leave Maximo's side again—not anymore.

"Elira?"

I glance up to see Maximo watching me, his brows knit. I swallow hard and drop the washcloth, standing shakily. He helps me out and takes a towel, rubbing it over my body to gently dry me up. Then he scoops me in his arms bridal style and carries me back to the bedroom. Something fragile blooms in me, a tiny spark of hope that maybe things aren't broken between us.

But when he sets me down on the bed and pulls the covers up, he doesn't climb in beside me. Instead, he turns away. Panic spikes through me, and before I can stop myself, I grab his wrist—his tattooed wrist—and I feel more of that mysterious scarred bump. He goes rigid but doesn't try to snatch his hand from me.

"Where are you going?"

"I have some work to attend to," he answers coolly, his gaze averted.

"But–but—" My voice fizzles out, too embarrassed to tell him I wanted to cuddle.

When he finally looks at me, the coldness in his eyes makes my blood run cold. He's never looked at me like this before. "I'm not cuddling with you, Elira. You keep your kisses to yourself, and I'll keep my cuddles."

He gently disengages my hand and disappears into the walk-in closet. Moments later, he reappears dressed casually in sweats and a tank top, then whizzes out of the bedroom. The soft click of the door closing hits me like a gunshot to the heart.

25

MAXIMO

The insistent ringing of my phone jolts me awake, and I blink blearily around the guest bedroom as my hand automatically snags the device from the nightstand, muscle memory taking over before my mind fully surfaces. "What?"

The frantic voice on the other end snaps me fully awake. My pulse kicks up as I process the information, already rolling off the bed. "Alright. I'm on my way."

I end the call and make my way to my bedroom, opening the door as quietly as possible so I don't wake Elira. The urge to barrel through is strong, but I tread lightly, slipping into the closet to swap my sweats for something more presentable. My fingers rake through my hair—messy as hell, but there's no time to fix it now.

As I walk back out through the bedroom, my gaze drifts to the sleeping figure on the bed, and despite the urgency thrumming in my veins, I find myself drawn closer. She's sprawled on her stomach, the blanket half off her body, revealing the soft rise and fall of her back as she breathes.

Something in my chest constricts painfully as I recall the hurt in her eyes when I walked out earlier. God, I hated that look. My fingers move on their own, gently pulling the blanket back up to her shoulders. I brush those unruly curls off her face, tucking them behind her ear, and for a moment, I let myself simply watch her.

She's so beautiful.

Even like this—or perhaps especially like this—relaxed in sleep, lips slightly parted as she snores softly. She's beautiful. Peaceful. Completely untouched by the storm brewing outside this room.

I shake my head and force myself to turn away before I can do something stupid like climb in beside her. It kills me to leave her, but there's no choice. Easing the door shut behind me, I jog down the hallway, down the stairs where Dante is pacing as he waits for me.

We share a loaded look and quietly make our way towards the elevator. "How bad is it?" I ask once the doors seal us in.

"Pretty bad. Two of our warehouses are completely incinerated. The third is barely standing."

My hands curl into fists at my side, jaw clenching until it aches. Fucking Përmeti. I don't have proof yet, but my gut says he's behind this, and I fucking trust my gut. "Any casualties?"

"So far, four men dead, six badly injured, and three with only minor wounds."

Each number lands like a punch to the gut. These are my men. My responsibility.

Why now, though?

The timing nags at me, following me from the elevator to the lobby and all the way to the waiting car, where Perro is already behind the wheel, the engine purring.

I understand setting bombs on my warehouses as retaliation. But Afrim's had plenty of opportunities to strike back since I kidnapped—married—his daughter. Since the mess at old Howard Beach a week ago—even though that was his fault.

I wouldn't have had to kill any of his men if he hadn't been acting suspicious. Why wait till now? What changed?

I stare out the window, fingers drumming on my knee, as the city blurs past in streaks of neon and shadows.

After my conversation with Rafael last night, I've been on high alert and planned to reach out to the damn man in the morning to find some sort of middle ground. After all, his daughter is now my wife and will remain my wife. Fucking impatient bastard couldn't wait a few more hours?

We pull up to the first warehouse, and the sight sets my teeth on edge. The worst of the fire is out, but the aftermath is a fucking warzone—blackened beams, melted steel, and piles of charred rubble. I shove the car door open before Perro can, the acrid scent of burnt wood and chemicals hitting me instantly. "Any problems with the cops?" I ask Dante as he follows me out.

"Just one overzealous detective, but he's been handled. The rest know better than to get involved."

Good. I don't funnel millions into their department every month for them to stick their noses where they shouldn't.

My men are all slouched on the ground, ash clinging to their faces and clothes, mixing with sweat and blood. They look like hell. When they see me, a few scramble to stand, but I wave them back down. "Be at ease, soldiers." They've been through enough tonight.

I assess them, one by one. The critical cases are already at our pocket hospital, too severe for Ethan to handle alone. The rest stayed behind to try and salvage what they could from the wreckage.

Helpless rage burns in my gut as I take in their haunted expressions. Every fiber of my being screams to retaliate, to rain hell down on whoever did this. It won't bring the dead back or erase the trauma from the survivors' eyes, but it would taste like justice.

Usually, this would be simple. Someone hit us, we hit back harder.

But now... I can't even do that. Because it's Afrim Përmeti. My wife's father.

Elira and I are finally moving in a good direction, and even though I'm still fucking pissed at her, I know hitting her father where it would really hurt him—like killing his precious son and heir—would destroy our relationship *and* her.

Fucking hell, since when did I give a fuck about all that?

I acknowledge each man with a nod that feels wholly inadequate before moving to inspect the ashy remains of my warehouse, frowning at the damage.

"What do you think?"

I direct my frown at Dante. "What do I think?"

"About the bombing of the warehouses. It's too coordinated. Feels like a distraction."

Lead fills my gut, because now that I think about it, it clicks into place. The reason Afrim waited this long to retaliate. This *is* a distraction. But from what?

What is my father-in-law up to?

My gaze snags Perro's, who's still standing by the side of the car. He shakes his head grimly before jogging over. "Sir, you need to see this." He hands me his phone, where a video is playing. "It's a live feed from the port. I just got a call from one of the men stationed there."

The footage turns that lead in my gut to a solid mass of tungsten. A little over a dozen heavily armed men in black tactical gear and masks are herding a bunch of frightened-looking girls off one of the cargo ships towards a black, nondescript van. As I watch, understanding dawns with sickening clarity.

Human trafficking. On my turf.

"Fuck, we won't make it to them in time to stop them."

Dante's curse echoes my thoughts as he watches over my shoulder.

"Have Giorgio run a check on the license plate. And find out where the hell that boat came from, what time it docked at my port, and who approved their docking," I order Perro, returning him the phone. He nods, his fingers already flying across the screen when I turn to face Dante. "How many men do we have at the port? Enough to intervene?"

His wince tells me everything. "Just two. Everyone else was redirected to help at the bombed warehouses when we got the news."

"Of course," I mutter under my breath. "So, the bombing was a distraction after all." I feel the anger bubbling inside me, shifting from simmering frustration to full-blown rage. A distraction—just so they could smuggle those girls into my city without a hitch. Without my fucking interference.

The truth sits bitter on my tongue: we've been played.

There's no way in hell we can make it to the port in time. It's too far, and without our usual security presence stationed there, there's nothing anyone can do to stop them now.

"I didn't realize the Albanians now dabble in the fucking skin trade." I barely hold myself together as I issue orders. "We need a copy of that feed. And tell one of the men at the port to discreetly follow the van." At least if we can't stop them at the port, we can ambush them later and put a goddamn end to it.

My voice cracks despite my effort to steady it. What kind of scum of the earth traffic humans? Especially girls, teenagers. The absolute bottom of the fucking barrel. "We need to know where they're going," I continue. "Who they're meeting, every contact they make."

I brush an impatient hand through my hair as I try to think what else we can do. There has to be another way to get ahead of this. "What about Heath? He still hasn't cracked?" It's been a little over a week since we got the distribution manager in our clutches. Dante's regretful headshake makes my teeth grind. "That's it. Perhaps it's time I go remind him who the fuck he's dealing with."

The drive to the office in East Flushing passes in a blur of barely contained violence, and we arrive in record time. Perro and Dante trail behind me as I storm towards the elevator and take it down to the basement level.

My men stationed outside the interrogation room stiffen as we approach. Incompetent fucks couldn't even break a civilian. I'll deal with them later.

Matteo, the only brave one amongst the others, steps forward. "Boss, we heard about the attack on the warehouses and—"

"What about our guest?" I interrupt him.

Matteo hesitates. "We had to let him rest today… so he doesn't pass out or die too quickly."

Disgust twists my face as I push past him. Rest? For him? One of the men quickly gets the door for me, and as I enter the dim room, the stench hits me—blood, sweat, piss, terror. My eyes adjust slowly to the dimness, finding Heath's slumped form hanging from his chains.

Matteo speaks again, quieter now. "Boss, I think whoever we're looking for has threatened someone Heath cares about. He's been holding on for too long; I doubt we can keep him alive much longer."

Heath stirs at the words, and his head lifts slowly, terror flooding his dark eyes as I approach. Good. He's not completely broken yet. "Mr. Leonotti, I—"

My fist smashes into his face, cutting off whatever pathetic plea he had planned. His scream echoes off the walls as he swings back on the chains holding his hand up. When momentum brings him back, I meet him with another punch, then another, his head snapping sideways, body swinging with each impact.

When I step back, shaking out my fist, Heath is gasping, a mixture of blood and saliva dripping down his mouth.

"Get me the cutting pliers. It's time Mr. Davis lost the rest of his fingers," I order Matteo, my gaze narrowing on the mutilated stump where Heath's ring finger used to be. The man whimpers pathetically, more fluid escaping his mouth as he tries to squirm away from me.

I grab his shirt and yank him closer, forcing his glassy, terrified eyes to meet mine. His breath reeks of copper and desperation, and it makes my nose curl. "Do you have any idea what kind of inconvenience you and whoever you're working for have caused me?" My voice is conversational—almost mocking. "First it was fucking with my shipment and now bombing my storage warehouses? Weapons, drugs, millions in product reduced to ashes, just like that." I snap my fingers for emphasis, then roll up my sleeves and accept the pliers from Matteo.

"Cut him down and tie him to the chair."

Matteo has to go call two of the men outside to help him cut down Heath, who struggles weakly as he's cuffed to the metal chair. I crouch down in front of him, holding the pliers up so he can see them clearly. "One of two things is going to happen tonight, Heath; you tell me what I want to know, and I'll end your misery quickly. Or..." I let the pliers snap threateningly. "I start cutting off the rest of the fingers on your pathetic hands. Slowly. While keeping you alive so you can feel every single ounce of pain. And once I'm done with you, I'll run the prints; use those filthy fingers to find every person you're protecting. *Then*, I'll bring them here and give them exactly the same 'care' you've been enjoying."

The color drains from his face as I lean in closer. "By the time I'm done with them, they'll curse your name, Heath. And you'll hear their dying screams as a lullaby."

He shakes his head wildly, then leans forward gagging pathetically like he's going to vomit, but nothing comes out.

"So, what's it going to be, Heath? Your choice." I snap the pliers in the air for good measure. "Tick tock."

Tears spill down his swollen, bruised cheeks as he starts to sob miserably. "I'll–I'll tell you what you want, but please... my daughter. She's only six. I was told if I ever said anything to anyone, she'd be killed." His voice cracks, the fear in it almost pitiful. Almost.

I glance back at Dante. He arches a brow but doesn't comment, his silent approval enough for me. Turning my attention back to Heath, I allow a sliver of softness to slip into my tone. Just enough to give him hope. "What's your daughter's name? Where is she? We'll make sure she's protected."

He whimpers her name and her location through his tears, and I nod at Dante, who's already pulling out his phone to reach out to some of our men to go get the girl. "Now, tell me everything."

"I don't really know much. I never met the woman who ordered me to reroute the shipment," he starts, and I frown at him. *Woman?* "She was very careful when she reached out to me. Called once to grab my attention, then sent a link to chat with her on the dark web. After that, she called again to warn me my identity may be compromised and to leave the country with my daughter. And if I told you or anyone else the little I know..." He trails off, swallowing hard. "She swore my daughter and I would suffer... slowly."

"Did she tell you why she wanted the shipment rerouted to Singapore?" I ask.

He shakes his head. "No. She said it was better if I didn't know why and to just do what I was told like 'a good boy'. But..." Fear and hesitation wrestle in his eyes. "She did make a slip. She muttered something in Italian. I don't think she realized I could understand."

So, she's Italian? My frown deepens as I try to connect the dots. "What did she say?"

Heath's voice drops to a whisper. "'I'm going to make him pay.' She sounded... furious. Like she really meant it."

Make *him* pay? The words bounce around my head. Who the hell is him? Me? Michael? Rafael? Romero? I swear to God if this is some chick with a vendetta against Romero for breaking her heart, I'm going to kill him myself.

I slowly start to get up from my crouch, but Heath's frantic words halt me. "Wait! I—I have more. Please, listen!"

I pause, letting my silence speak.

He swallows hard, licking his bloody lips. "I know you said you're going to kill me, but—but what if I have other information you need to know?"

A dry laugh escapes me. "Trying to trade information for your life? Bold. Let's hear it."

"Will... will you let me live?"

My lips curl up as I answer, "*No*. But your daughter could be adopted by a loving, wealthy family and not have to go through any struggle in her life again. I'll personally make sure nothing happens to her," I vow.

His face crumbles up at the reminder of his imminent death and pathetic tears roll down his cheeks. I let out an impatient sigh and start to get up again when he blurts out, "The 9th of August!"

That's today's date. I narrow my eyes on him. "Yes? Go on."

"The day after I approved rerouting your shipment, I got a call about a cargo ship coming in on the 9th of August and was offered a million dollars to look the other way during unloading."

My heart races as I realize it's probably the man who orchestrated the trafficking of those girls. "Oh?"

"I can give you the ship's information so you can check through it when it arrives. I'm sure you'll find something incriminating, even though I don't know what that might be."

"Today is the ninth, Heath. If you had opened your mouth

earlier, we could have saved the people on that ship, but alas." I shrug carelessly as I get to my feet. "Unless you have more information?"

His Adam's apple bobs as he gulps. "The man who called—he had a strong accent. Not New York. Definitely not Italian or Russian or Irish—I know those." He rushes the words, sensing my impatience. "It could be... southeastern Europe maybe? But I've never heard it before."

I take out my phone and scroll through the audio files until I find the one I want. An old conversation between an Albanian rat and I. One of the first few who came into my city and lost his life thereafter.

I click play and increase the volume. Heath's head snaps up, eyes widening. "Yes! That's the accent."

So it's confirmed. Albanians. My suspicions solidify, and molten rage floods my veins. Përmeti. What the hell is he playing at? Human trafficking doesn't fit his profile. Did I misjudge him? I stop the audio and tuck my phone into my pocket.

As I leave the room, Heath's broken plea chases after me. "Please... protect my girl."

I pause to give him a reassuring nod. "Do what must be done," I tell Matteo as I walk out.

The moment I'm in the hallway, I spot Perro pacing feverishly, his phone clutched so tightly his knuckles are bone-white. His head snaps up at the sight of me, his face lined with something close to panic as he waves the device frantically. I reach for it, but before I can, my own phone starts ringing. With a quick nod, I gesture for him to hand it to Dante instead while I pull out mine.

My heart clenches when I see who's calling.

Marco.

And I just *know*. I know it's bad.

I answer to chaos. "*We're under ambush!* I repeat, *we're under ambush!*" Marco's voice roars through the connection, nearly drowned out by the deafening crack of gunfire.

My blood runs cold for a split second before the adrenaline kicks in. I spin around wordlessly and start running towards the elevator, my long strides eating up the distance, Dante and Perro right behind me.

"Elira?" I ask as I get into the elevator. That's the only thing that matters right now. If anything—*anything*—fucking happens to her, I'll scorch the earth. Turn this goddamned city into rubble and make Afrim regret trying to distract me with this bullshit scheme of his.

"I'm on my way to lead Mrs. Leonotti to the safe room and—"

"She's still in the *bedroom,* and you're wasting time on the phone with me?! Fucking hell, Marco. Get off the line and go to her! Move!"

I hang up just as the elevator doors slide open, and I'm off again, sprinting to the car. When I reach it, I practically throw myself into the driver's seat. Perro falters, halfway to the door, but I've already slammed it shut and started the engine. Dante barely gets the passenger door open before I'm peeling out of the garage.

The tires shriek in protest as I whip the car onto the road, the backend fishtailing slightly before I wrestle it under control. My foot stays glued to the accelerator, the engine roaring and my horn blaring as I force my way through the sluggish traffic. Red lights streak by, but none of it registers. Nothing matters. Not laws. Not rules. Not even collateral damage. Only *her*.

"Do you think it's Afrim?" Dante asks.

God, I hope it's Afrim. What better time to attempt a rescue of his daughter than now, with my men spread thin, putting out fires all over the city, and me away from home? If it's him, at least I know he wouldn't hurt his own daughter. But if we're dealing with some unknown force—*fuck*—that would mean Elira is in grave danger.

Dante curses harshly as I yank the wheel, the car lurching into a sharp turn towards the apartment block. His hand shoots up, gripping the overhead handle like it'll save him from my driving. "You trying to kill us before we get there?" he snaps, voice half-wobbling.

I don't answer. My mind is locked onto a single, unrelenting truth:

I can't lose her.

26

ELIRA

I wake up to Marco shaking me like my life depends on it—and judging by the tension radiating off him, it probably does.

"What is it?" I grumble, groggy and irritated as I sit up, wiping at my eyes.

"I need to get you to safety. Follow me." There's something in Marco's voice I've never heard before—a tightness that sends ice water through my veins. The man who usually maintains perfect composure sounds like he's barely holding it together.

I swing my legs off the bed, forcing my body to move despite the lingering heaviness of interrupted sleep.

"What's going on?" I ask, watching as his eyes keep darting to the bedroom door like he's expecting it to burst open any second. Something is very, very wrong.

"We're under attack." The words are barely more than a mutter, but they fall like lead weights in my stomach. My heart does a violent somersault, and suddenly I'm wide awake.

"What? By who?" *Please don't let it be who I think it is. Please, please, please.*

"We need to get you to safety," he repeats the words mechanically, deliberately ignoring my question as he turns his back to me. I expect him to lead me out of the room, but he makes a beeline for the double doors I've discovered are Maximo's walk-in closet. *What is he doing?* I think, following him with confused, stumbling steps. *Shouldn't we be heading for the exit?*

The closet lights flicker on automatically as we enter, casting a soft glow over Maximo's obscenely expensive wardrobe. While I'm still trying to process why we're playing dress-up during an attack, Marco moves with purpose towards the large glass display where all of Maximo's ties are laid out in a neat row. I watch baffled, as he starts pulling them out one by one. *Has he lost his mind?*

One tie, two ties, three... As he reaches for the fourth, the material snags, something holding it back. A metallic click breaks the silence, and I nearly jump out of my skin as the wall begins to move. The actual wall. Moving.

Holy shit, this is some Batman-level secret passage stuff.

I stand there gaping like an idiot while Marco shoves the ties back haphazardly and grabs my arm, practically dragging me through the opening.

As soon as we're inside the dark, secret room, motion sensors trigger overhead lights, brightening the space.

"Stay here. Do not come out until I come to get you," Marco orders urgently as he lets go of my arm. He waits until I nod my acquiescence before he walks out of the room, the doors sliding shut quietly behind him.

Now alone, my curiosity gets the better of my fear. I glance around the room in fascination.

I know what a panic room is—we have one back at *Atë*'s compound, and I used to go through drills every few months to learn how to get there in case of an emergency when my guards couldn't reach me. But where *Atë*'s panic room was an old, musty space in our basement, this one is modern and, despite the lack of windows, feels surprisingly airy.

The walls and floor are dark and tastefully decorated. A swanky, cream L-shaped couch rests against the wall, accompanied by a gleaming glass side table and an art deco lamp. Above it all, a large gold-framed black and white Lily of the Valley print hangs against the wall.

As I walk down the small steps into the room itself, my fingers trail along the seamless walls. When my hand catches on a barely-there handle, my heart skips. Another secret? I pull it open and—*whoa.*

It is! Another hidden door slides open.

Inside looks like an armory.

Guns of every size and shape imaginable line the walls. Rifles. Pistols, you name it. Even hand grenades, along with enough tactical gear to outfit a small army. I shut that door quickly, positive I wasn't meant to discover that.

My gaze darts around the room again, landing on a large standing fridge on the other side, but I ignore it. Now that I know there are hidden doors, I can't help but look for more. It's better than sitting here wondering if people are dying outside. So, I slide my hand along the walls again until—there! Another handle. Another door. *I was right.*

This time, the door opens to reveal a room lined with computers. The screens are facing the other way so I can only see the back and the wires running around on the floor. I enter the room and circle around until I can see the dark screens.

My heart pounds as I stare at them, curiosity and dread filling me. This is probably a monitor room and the computers are most likely connected to the cameras in the apartment. *I shouldn't*, I think, even as my hand reaches for the power button. *I really shouldn't*. But I do.

The screens spring to life, and sure enough, immediately open to multiple camera feeds from around the apartment. No password required. Because who's going to break into a secret room hidden in another secret room, all concealed behind a billionaire's tie collection? Well, except for me.

A bright light catches my eye from the corner of one of the screens. It's the hallway outside the apartment where the elevator is located. It quickly becomes clear that the bright light was from a gunshot. Multiple gunshots follow.

I gulp as I lean forward and try to zoom in on that screen. The hallway outside is a war zone. Gunfire flashes, bodies hitting the floor on both sides of a brutal firefight. Maximo's men are desperately defending the apartment door, but the attackers are relentless, slowly gaining ground with every shot fired.

I watch in horror as more of Maximo's men collapse. These aren't just faceless soldiers—they're men I've baked for, played games with, laughed with... and now they're falling one by one, their lives snuffed out right in front of me.

Shit, shit, shit.

The gravity of the situation hits me as I take it all in. My heart sinks with dread, and I raise my hand to gnaw at my nails —an old nervous habit I thought I'd outgrown. Now I understand why Marco ushered me into this panic room so quickly. This isn't just an attack. It's an outright slaughter.

I drag my hand away from my mouth and press it flat against my thigh, forcing myself to think. Marco said to stay put, but how the hell am I supposed to do that knowing what's happening out there?

What if they somehow get in here?

What if...

No. I can't think like that. I have to stay calm. I have to—

Then I see him.

The man in the middle. On the enemy side. He's wearing dark tactical gear, his head and face covered by a balaclava mask, but something about the way he moves and shoots his gun strikes a nerve. A horrible, gut-deep familiarity. As he glances back at another man—a broader, thicker-set man—the edge of his balaclava shifts, revealing a glint of red hair. *Red Hair*. My breath catches. *No, it can't be.* He yanks the mask back in place, but it's too late—I've already caught sight of the tiny dark ink on the inside of his wrist.

"Jesus, no," I whisper, horrified as my brain tries to compute what I'm seeing. *Roan*. Oh no. Oh no. My brother is out there killing Maximo's men. Which means...

I'm running before I can finish the thought, bursting out of the panic room, through the closet, down the hallway. My bare feet slap against the floor as I take the stairs two at a time. I have to stop him. I *need* to stop him before even more people die needlessly.

The scene that greets me when I burst through the front door is absolute mayhem. My ears ring from the deafening gunfire ricocheting in the small, enclosed area, and my nose wrinkles at the choking stench of gunpowder, sweat, and blood. Marco's eyes find mine, and the look of pure terror on his face would be almost funny if this wasn't so deadly serious.

"Go back in," he mouths desperately, careful not to draw attention to me as he subtly tries to shoo me back into the house. But I ignore him. My focus locks on the enemy line ahead.

"Stop shooting!" I shout, but my voice is lost over the loud gunshots.

A bullet whizzes past me, so close it ruffles my hair, and my heart leaps into my throat. Time seems to slow as I watch it pierce through Marco's stomach. "No. Marco!" He staggers back into the wall, clutching at the blooming red stain spreading beneath his shirt, but even then, his grip on the gun stays firm. Gritting his teeth, he steadies himself and continues shooting.

Determination surges through me like wildfire, burning away the shock. Pressing myself against the wall, I inch along its surface to the other side as I scream Roan's name at the top of my lungs. "Roan! Roan!" Over and over, until my throat hurts.

Nothing.

As I walk, my toes connect with something—a discarded pistol. *Yes*. Careful to keep out of the line of fire, I go down to pick it up. My fingers tremble as I check the chamber. One bullet left. *Please let this work.*

I aim at the ceiling and fire. The shot rings out like a thunderclap in the enclosed space, drawing every eye in the room. And finally, *finally*, Roan turns. Our eyes meet across the battlefield, and I see the exact moment he recognizes me. His body freezes, his gun faltering mid-aim. But it's too late. His trigger finger is already squeezing, his body operating on pure muscle memory.

The bullet pierces through my arm, and the pistol slips out of my hand, clattering to the floor as I slam back into the wall. I gasp, tears stinging my eyes as indescribable pain explodes through my body in white-hot waves. Blood—my blood—is everywhere, soaking through my sleeve, running down my arm in sticky rivers. So much blood. Too much blood.

"Lira!" Roan's anguished roar seems to come from very far away, and everything suddenly quiets down as the room collectively takes a deep breath. Through vision that's starting to blur at the edges, I see another figure running towards me, pulling off his balaclava mask. *Atë*. And he looks like he might have a heart attack.

His blood pressure... he shouldn't be here... he can't handle this kind of stress...

My knees buckle, and as I start to slide down the wall, Roan catches me, pulling me into him with one hand and ripping off his own mask with the other. I wince as the movement jostles me, sending more pain through me.

"Lira, fuck. I'm so sorry. I'm so sorry. I'm so sorry," he chants over and over, pressing his mask hard against my wound to stem the bleeding. *Atë* falls to his knees beside us, his face almost as pale as mine must be, and I wince again.

"Ca–careful... *Atë,*" I manage to rasp. I want to say more—to tell him to calm down, to breathe, to watch his heart—but the words won't come.

Then, everything changes.

The air suddenly grows heavy, charged with a new kind of tension, and my gaze shifts beyond my father, beyond his men, to the elevator sliding open and Maximo stepping out, looking murderous as hell.

Oh no.

27

MAXIMO

It doesn't take a genius to piece together what happened as I step out of the elevator. I dispassionately catalog every detail: the bodies and shell casings littering my hallway, the acrid stink of gunpowder hanging in the air. But everything else fades to background noise when I see her—my Elira—bleeding in the arms of another redhead I recognize as her brother. Roan fucking Përmeti.

Blinding, white-hot rage tears through my veins, so violently, it scorches every rational thought to ash, and before I even register reaching for it, my gun is out of its holster, aimed squarely at the back of his skull. "What the fuck did you do to my wife?"

The bastard doesn't even acknowledge me, just keeps murmuring in Albanian while pressing on Elira's wound. *Like he has any right to touch her after what just happened.*

Behind me, Dante curses, and I hear him get on the phone with Ethan, but it's muffled, distant. All I see is Roan, all I feel is the blood boiling under my skin.

I keep my gun trained on Roan as my strides eat up the distance between us. Then I swing the grip into the side of his temple with a satisfying crack. His head snaps to the right, and blood immediately wells up where the skin splits.

A soft gasp drags my attention down to Elira, my beautiful wife struggling to sit up. "Maximo, no. Please, no. Don't." Her hazel eyes overflow with fear—so much fear that I might hurt her precious brother.

Beside me, Afrim makes a sound somewhere between a growl and a warning, but I couldn't care less about his opinions right now. I toss my gun to the floor and shove Roan away from her. He tries to stay his ground, the stubborn fuck, so I fix him with an arctic stare. "Do not fucking test me right now, Përmeti."

"Roan, it's okay," Elira's soft assurance is the only thing that makes him move away. The moment he's clear, I'm shrugging off my jacket and tying it around her upper arm tightly. My hands don't shake—they never shake—but something inside me trembles as I lift her into my arms. She feels too light, too fragile. The thought that I could have lost her tonight makes me want to tear the city apart with my bare hands.

"It's okay, Maximo," she murmurs soothingly, like she's trying to calm a wild animal. Maybe she is. "It was a graze, an accident, I'm fine and—" She cuts off with a gasp as I deliberately ram my shoulder into Roan on my way past, the impact jostling her.

"Fuck. Sorry." I wince at her pain and adjust my hold, careful not to jostle her again. One of my men scrambles to get the door, practically tripping over himself, and I toss a quick glance at Dante, who's right on my heels. "Ethan?"

"He'll be here in five minutes. He understands the urgency." Dante's eyes flick to the Përmetis. "What do I do about the... intruders?"

My gaze drops to Elira, who's already staring up at me with those wide, doe-like eyes. *Christ, this woman will be the death of me.* "Take them to my study. They can wait for me there." I'd prefer the basement, personally, but something tells me that wouldn't go over well. "Have three men stationed there with them. I don't fucking trust them."

Dante nods and disappears to execute my orders.

"Thank you," my wife says sweetly, the tone far too innocent for someone dripping blood all over my shirt.

I narrow my eyes on her. "What the hell were you doing out there? Marco didn't show you to the safe room?" Fucking Marco. *If that incompetent fuck survives his wounds, I'll kill him myself.*

As if reading the murder in my thoughts, she reaches up with her uninjured arm to my neck, turning my face down to hers as I climb the stairs. "It wasn't Marco's fault."

I snort. "His job was to protect you in my absence. He failed." *Spectacularly.*

"He didn't fail, Maximo," she insists, those hazel eyes holding mine with unflinching determination. "He took me to the safe room, I swear. I walked out on my own after he left."

I nearly miss a step. "You *willingly* joined the fucking mayhem? Why the fuck would you do that?" I snap, making her wince. Carefully adjusting her weight, I shoulder open my bedroom door. Then I lay her on the bed with exaggerated care, tucking the blanket over her pajama-clad body. Despite the fury coursing through me, my hands remember how to be gentle.

"I found the monitor room inside the safe room," she admits, and I mentally curse myself for not better securing that area. "When I saw the CCTV feed, I recognized them. I couldn't just sit there and watch my brother and father shoot at your men."

Of all the stupid, reckless— "So your brilliant solution was to run out there, throw yourself into the middle of a firefight and, what? Try to heroically stop it?" Foolish woman. "Have you no sense of danger?"

Before I can rip into her some more, there's a soft knock on the door. "Come in!" I bark, still glaring at my impossibly stubborn wife.

The door opens and Ethan walks in, holding his medical kit as usual. "Mrs. Leonotti. Not exactly how I hoped we'd meet again." There's a hint of dry humor in his voice as he approaches the bed.

I take a step back to give him room to work, but every cell in my body rebels against the distance. Like a caged beast, I pace behind him, tracking every movement as he opens his kit and carefully unties my ruined jacket from her arm. His low whistle does nothing for my nerves. "Wow, that's a mean one. Luckily, it went through the flesh, so you won't have to go through the pain of me trying to root the bullet out. It needs some stitches, though. I'll try to leave as small a scar as possible."

He speaks to her gently as he works, offering painkillers and distracting her with calm chatter while cleaning and stitching the wound. All the while, I pace, unable to shake the burning urge to storm downstairs and make the Përmetis pay for daring to attack my warehouses and my home in an attempt to kidnap my wife. But there's no way in hell I'm leaving Elira until Ethan's done with her—until I know she's okay.

And then there's the question of how to deal with my fucking in-laws.

If it were anyone else, it would be a no-brainer how I would retaliate. Instead of sitting comfortably in my study, they'd already be in my office basement getting acquainted with my more... creative side. The same side Heath Davis got to know intimately before he took his last breath. But fuck, Elira. I can't do anything to them *because* of her.

What a fucking mess.

I don't miss the nervous glances she keeps throwing my way, her eyes darting away whenever I catch her looking. It's easy to see she's worried about what I'll do to them. She knows me too well already.

Ethan finishes in record time, and as he packs up his things, I'm already adjusting my sleeves and turning to leave the bedroom.

"Wait!" Elira's scrambling out of the bed before I can reach the door, and my vision goes red.

"What the hell do you think you're doing? Get back on the fucking bed, or I'll handcuff you to it."

She juts her chin out stubbornly. "No. You're going to see my father and brother, and I demand you take me with you."

"You *demand?*" I repeat softly as I take a threatening step towards her. But she holds her ground, chin tipping impossibly higher until her nose is practically scraping the ceiling.

"She suffered significant blood loss, Maximo," Ethan interjects, closing his kit with an irritatingly calm *snick*. "She needs as much rest as possible to recuperate."

"Tell *her* that. She's the one who just jumped out of the bed like it's on fucking fire," I snarl.

"And I *will* rest. After we see Roan and *Atë*. Unless you follow through on that handcuff threat, Maximo, I'm coming with you. And let me warn you, if you handcuff me, I'll struggle and try to break out of the damn cuffs until every single one of these stitches pops and I bleed out all over your thousand-dollar sheets."

My temper fucking snaps. "You're threatening me? You—"

"Maximo." Ethan quickly steps between us, and I growl before punching him square in the face. He staggers back as Elira gasps in dismay.

"What the hell is wrong with you?" she screams, moving to check on him.

"Fucking step away from him if you don't want me to rearrange his face permanently." Nobody gets between me and my wife. *Nobody.*

Elira shoots me a look that could strip paint but quickly steps away when she realizes I mean it. Then she's in front of me, her injured hand on my chest, the other on my cheek, forcing me to look at her. The gesture is so intimate, so naturally commanding, that it catches me off guard.

"You need to calm the fuck down, Maximo," she says softly, eyes flashing, and something about this tiny, injured woman cursing and trying to sound tough sends an unexpected tendril of tenderness through me, tinged with amusement. My lips twitch. "Are you fucking *smiling* right now?" The disbelief in her voice only makes it harder not to laugh.

"Don't curse," I tell her as the door closes behind Ethan's hasty escape.

"Oh, so you can curse, but I can't?" She rolls her eyes, dropping her hand from my face as she takes a step back. I grab her wrist quickly and press a kiss into her palm.

"I'm not going to hurt your brother or father." No matter how much I want to. "Stay in bed and get some sleep, Elira."

But she shakes her head, stubborn as ever. "I need to talk to them too. They need to see that I'm alright—and that I'm here willingly. Otherwise, they'll try something stupid again. Like attempting another rescue."

Fuck. She has a point, as much as I hate to admit it. I sigh, giving in. "Alright."

After a quick assessment of her condition, I sweep her up into my arms, earning a surprised squeal as she instinctively loops her arms around my neck for balance. Then she flinches—no doubt pulling at her stitches—and I carefully readjust her injured arm to rest on her stomach.

The warmth of her head on my chest as I walk towards my study fills me with more tenderness than I've ever felt in my life, and I'm not quite sure what to do with it. I've never been this tangled up over a woman before, never felt this... protective. Possessive, sure. Lustful, definitely. But this? This is dangerous territory.

Roan and Afrim get to their feet when I step into the study, their gazes immediately honing in on my precious cargo. "Elira is fine. No thanks to either of you." I glance at my men, and with a tilt of my head, they scurry out.

"Maximo." Elira's gentle admonishment comes with a hand pressed to my chest, and just like that, the last dregs of my anger evaporate. *Damn it.* Still, I narrow my eyes at her family as I settle on the sofa, keeping her carefully arranged in my lap.

Her fucking brother remains on his feet, his face pulled tight. "Lira, you're coming home with us."

"She's fucking home already." I tighten my grip possessively, but then Elira's pushing away from me, and I frown as I reluctantly let her go. She gets to her feet and carefully makes her way to her *former* family. Because that's what they are now—former. *I'm* her family now. The sooner they get that through their thick skulls, the better.

"I'm completely happy here with Maximo. He's my husband and I'm staying with him." She holds up her ring finger, and the sight of my diamond catching the light fills me with a satisfaction so primitive it should be embarrassing. *That's my girl.* I lean back, enjoying the show.

"He kidnapped you," her father argues, throwing a glare at me. "Are you trying to say you fell for your abductor?"

Elira grabs the old man's hands, her expression soft but unyielding. "I wasn't kidnapped, *Atë*. I know you watched the CCTV footage. I walked out on my own and messaged Maximo to meet me at the Flushing Meadows Park. After a wonderful day together, he proposed to me and, well, I said yes."

What a little liar. My lips twitch with the urge to smirk.

"No way. That's a fucking lie, Lira," Roan interrupts her sweet speech, ruining my entertainment. "You might be impulsive sometimes, but even you know better than to jump into marriage with a man you just met."

She frowns, crossing her arms. "You don't believe in love at first sight, Roan?"

The man snorts, and I can't help but do the same, earning a cross look from my wife. I raise my hands innocently, the smirk still tugging at my lips.

"Listen, all of you." There's steel in her voice now, despite the obvious effects of the painkillers. "I've just been shot for the first time in my life—which, by the way, is not an experience I recommend—and I'm sleepy as hell from the drug the doctor gave me. So I'm only going to say this once: Maximo and I are married now. That makes every single person in this room family, whether you like it or not. I thought I made that clear to *Atë* when I called him the other day, but apparently not."

She fixes them with a stern look worthy of a schoolteacher. "No more rescue attempts... and no more killing each other's men." The last part comes with a particular pointed look at me. I shrug. After the havoc Afrim and his men wreaked tonight, I'd say we're even.

"Good, glad to have that out of the way." Her voice softens as she looks at her brother. "Nice to see you again after so long, Roan. What did you do to your hair?" The question ends in a yawn that she tries and fails to suppress.

I'm on my feet before she can wobble, watching as Roan self-consciously fusses with his ridiculous bun. "I grew it out," he answers simply as I reach Elira's side.

"Come on, sleeping beauty. That's enough family bonding. You need to rest." Her body slumps against me, exhaustion finally winning, and I lift her carefully. "Wait here," I order her brother and father before carrying her back upstairs.

She's already nodding off by the time I place her on my bed. Pure stubbornness must have kept her awake this long. I pull the covers up to her chin, tucking her in gently, and start to turn away when I feel her hand wrap around my wrist.

Her brows furrow adorably as she forces her eyes open. "Be nice."

I lean down to press a kiss on her temple. "I'm always nice."

"Liar." The accusation comes out slurred with sleep, drawing a low chuckle from me as I leave her side. But it wasn't a lie. Not really. She has no idea what I'm really capable of because I've been nice to her—at least since we got married. And now, for her sake, that niceness will extend to her family.

The smile fades from my face as the night's events catch up to me, and I crack my neck to shake off the fatigue. I suddenly want nothing else but to crawl into bed next to Elira and sleep like the fucking dead.

Later, I promise myself. There's business to handle first.

Back in the study, I get straight to the point. "So tonight. Blowing up three warehouses? Trafficking little girls? Was that all part of the grand distraction for your attempt to attack my house? Or do you have something else to confess?"

The two men exchange glances, then frown at me. "We don't know what you're talking about," Afrim says.

I narrow my eyes on both of them. "I don't believe you."

Roan shrugs. "Believe what you want. We have no reason to lie when you have Elira. And apparently, she's not coming home with us. You can do anything you want to her, so that's even more incentive to tell the truth."

Before I can rip his throat out for suggesting I'd hurt Elira, he continues, "We only blew up your drug den at Flushing Bay because it was farthest from here and drugs are nasty business. That's all we did. If two more of your warehouses got blown, you should probably look inwards. You've made more than your fair share of enemies over the years."

"And what's this about trafficking girls?" Affirm puts in, face pulling in disgust. "How preposterous."

I take a seat across from them and steeple my fingers as I take them in. *Well, fuck.* They're telling the truth. They really don't know anything about it all. Which means...

"Then you must have a rat on your side of the fence. Someone who knew about your plan to attack me tonight and used it to make you take the fall for everything, because I know for sure the trafficking op was led by an Albanian."

They inhale sharply and exchange another one of those loaded looks.

"You met with other Albanian leaders a couple of days ago," I press, recalling Rafael's warning. "Why?"

"You had Elira," Afrim explains. "We had to inform them of our rescue plans—in case you and the Nightshades retaliated after tonight. We'd need their backing."

So that means roughly five people knew their plans. And there's every chance those people blabbed to others, meaning our suspect could be anyone. Fuck.

Rolling my neck, I force myself to dispel the tension. "You don't have to worry about retaliation from me or my brothers. After all, as my wife said, we're one big, happy family now." I flash a smile that makes Roan's jaw clench. "Let's cooperate, shall we?"

28

ELIRA

I snuggle deeper into the comfortable bed, enjoying the subtle trace of my husband's scent clinging to the sheets. Stretching lazily, I let out a contented sigh, arms reaching overhead—until a sharp twinge of pain shoots down my left arm and yanks me out of my bliss.

"Ah, damn it," I hiss, carefully bringing my throbbing arm back down to cradle it against my stomach. My eyes drift to the curtains that are still drawn tight, leaving the room in that weird twilight that makes you question what century you're in, let alone what time it is. And then the events of last night all come rushing back in an overwhelming slow-motion replay.

Atë and Roan's failed rescue attempt. Me, stupidly getting shot while trying to stop the madness. The impromptu meeting in Maxim's study—that I can barely remember because I was high off the anesthetics Ethan gave me.

I groan and smoosh my face harder into the pillow.

Shit, what is wrong with me? I can't believe I had a chance —*the perfect chance*—to tell my family about Maximo's threat to their lives and go home with them. But no. I willingly chose not to. What's worse, it didn't even *occur* to me at the time that I could do that.

My stomach twists. This is bad. Really bad. I'm not just falling for him—I'm tumbling headfirst off a cliff with no bottom in sight. That manipulative, dangerous, maddeningly gorgeous—

The door's hinges give a tiny whine of protest, and I whip my head around only to have my brain short-circuit completely. Because there's Maximo in all his shirtless glory, carrying an overflowing tray of food.

His sweatpants ride low on his hips, and I drool as I follow the veined, muscular deep V below his abdomen that disappears into the waistband and down to the enticing bulge pressing against the cotton material.

Oh, geez. I'm convinced sweatpants are the male equivalent of slutty skirts. They leave absolutely nothing to the imagination.

"My eyes are up here, *dolcezza*." His voice is warm, teasing, and smug as hell.

My cheeks go nuclear. "I wasn't—ugh, shut up," I grumble, quickly looking away like that will erase the image now seared into my brain.

Maximo chuckles as he places the tray momentarily on the nightstand so he can crouch down next to me. "How's the arm?"

"It's screaming bloody murder, but I'll survive."

The heavenly aroma wafting from the tray makes my stomach growl embarrassingly loud. Steam rises from a plate of perfectly twirled spaghetti drowning in rich red sauce and meatballs. Another small plate holds extra sauce, and a side of buttery garlic bread so fresh it's also steaming.

My mouth waters. "Did you make all these?"

The shrug he gives me makes his biceps dance, and I have to physically restrain myself from reaching out to touch them. "I tried. The disaster I made is in the trashcan where no one will accidentally poison themselves. So no, Santino saved the day. Remember him? He cooked your birthday meal for you at the restaurant."

My heart warms as I think about Maximo muddling his way through the kitchen in an attempt to cook for me. "That's so sweet, thank you, *burri im*." The endearment slips out before I can stop it, and I quickly clamp my mouth shut.

"*Burri im*." He repeats the words slowly, eyeing me with playful suspicion. "Did you just curse at me?"

"No." I keep it short, praying he'll drop it, but of course he doesn't.

"Are you going to translate or leave me in suspense?"

"You should probably be at work by now." I make a show of checking the alarm clock, hoping to distract him, but genuine shock hits me. I gasp dramatically. "Wait. Seriously, Maximo, is that thing correct? It's 11 am?" I've never slept this late in my entire life.

His fingers capture my chin and turn my face back to him. "Tell me, *dolcezza*."

My pulse quickens, head swimming as I whisper, "*Burri im* means... my husband." My cheeks go hot when his grip tightens, his nostrils flaring, eyes darkening. Oh. I think he likes that. He likes it very much.

"You'll call me that from now on," he commands, and I chuckle. "Say it again."

"Please." I roll my eyes, trying to play it cool, but my heart is pounding a sweet staccato.

"I'm serious."

"And I'm starving," I fire back, nodding towards the tray. "So, unless you want me to eat you, hand over the food."

His lips curve into a slow, dangerous smile. "Careful, *dolcezza*. Offers like that might get you into trouble."

His thumb traces the corner of my mouth, and I swear I can feel that small touch all the way down to my toes. For a moment, desire flares in his eyes before he looks away, dropping his hand. But that spot his thumb touched tingles pleasantly with phantom sensation, and I find myself wishing he had attempted to kiss me again. I wouldn't have turned away. Not this time.

He helps me sit up, carefully arranging my left arm over two stacked pillows before setting the tray across my lap. Then, to my surprise, he's on the bed beside me, tearing off a piece of the hot garlic bread. My mouth waters as he dips it into the rich sauce and—wait, is he actually going to...?

He lifts the bread to my lips, and I raise a brow. "Are you really not going to work today?" I ask in all seriousness. Usually, he's long gone by the time I drag myself out of bed at eight, but here he is, lounging in those sinful sweats, and also... my gaze moves down his arm, to the dark and colorful burst of beautiful sleeve tattoos.

"Of course not," he scowls like I've insulted his honor. "You got shot last night. What kind of husband would I be if I just left you and went to work? I wouldn't be able to stop thinking and worrying about you anyway." The last bit comes out in an annoyed rumble as he pushes the bread towards my mouth.

Before I can overthink it, I part my lips, accepting the offering of bread. The moment it hits my tongue, my eyes flutter close and—*oh sweet mercy*—an embarrassingly obscene moan escapes me as the delicious flavors explode across my taste buds.

"Good?" Maximo asks huskily, and I open my eyes to see him staring at me through a hooded gaze, already tearing off another piece of bread.

I nod, though a little self-conscious about how I reacted. "It's incredible. Santino needs to give me the recipe, or better yet, just promote him to our personal chef."

"Done," he answers with such ease I almost miss it. I blink, smiling because, surely, he's kidding—right? But then he shifts and takes out his phone from his pocket. I gape at him as his thumbs fly furiously across the screen and quickly grab his arm.

"What are you doing?" *Please tell me he's not actually...*

"Informing Santino about his new duties," he replies with a *duh* tone, like it's the most obvious thing in the world.

I snatch the phone out of his hand, laughing through my shock as I erase the message. "I was just kidding, Maximo. No! Let the poor man be."

With a grumble, he pockets his phone, though the glint in his eyes tells me he'd do it in a heartbeat if I asked. Shaking my head, I watch as he picks up the fork and rolls a perfect swirl of spaghetti. He blows on it gently before bringing it up to my mouth.

It's just as delicious as the bread, but this time I'm hyper-aware of his gaze on me as I chew, my taste buds in spice heaven. He feeds me slowly, alternating between the spaghetti, meatballs, and bread until I'm stuffed.

"No more," I groan, turning my head away from another meatball. "My stomach will explode if I eat more."

He chuckles and then redirects the fork to his own mouth. I inhale sharply, my eyes fixed on the way his jaw works and his lips close around the tines. It shouldn't be hot watching a man eat a meatball, but somehow he makes it look like a scene that belongs behind a paywall.

The fork clinks against the plate as he sets it down to reach for the water bottle. He pours it carefully into a glass, and I watch the muscles in his forearm flex with the simple movement. Then he produces a bottle of pills from his pocket, and my post-food bliss evaporates instantly.

"No, thank you." I wrinkle my nose at the red and blue capsules he's holding out to me.

"They're your antibiotics. Not optional." He rolls his eyes—actually rolls them—and I'm stunned. Maximo. Rolling his eyes. That's like seeing a unicorn. "What?" he asks, lips twisting, like he's trying not to do it again.

"Nothing." I chuckle, stretching my hand out for the damn pills. He drops them into my palm, and I lean forward expectantly. "Water?"

He obliges, lifting the glass to my lips. I slip the pills onto my tongue and take a mouthful, cheeks puffing slightly as I hold the water in my mouth. Closing my eyes, I force myself to swallow, grimacing at how the capsules scrape their way down my throat.

"More," I croak, waving a hand, and he tilts the glass back to me.

I gulp the water down eagerly, but the unpleasant sensation lingers, making me shudder in disgust.

"So dramatic," he comments dryly, earning him a glare as I open my eyes.

"Sorry, we can't all be masochists who swallow pills dry." Another shudder runs through me at the thought. People who do that are psychopaths for real.

Maximo shakes his head, then picks up my abandoned plate, and I stare, mesmerized, as he practically inhales the leftover food. And, oh boy, the meatball from before was just the warm-up act; now, I'm getting the full show. *Is this how he felt when he watched me eat?* I lift my hand, pretending to fix my hair, but really I'm just checking the corner of my mouth to make sure I'm not drooling.

When he's done, he places the food tray on the nightstand and grabs the water bottle next. *Don't look*, I tell myself as he unscrews the cap. *Don't you dare look*. But of course, I do.

The way his Adam's apple bobs with each swallow is so hot, and suddenly my mouth is dry despite all the water I gulped down earlier. I lick my lips, then quickly tear my gaze away, fighting the heat pooling low in my belly. *This is ridiculous. You're losing it. Over a man drinking water.*

But damn him for being so maddeningly attractive.

I need a distraction.

My eyes snag on his tattoos, and without thinking, I lean forward, studying the details I've only glimpsed before. When he sets the water bottle down and catches my stare, he goes still and watches me through a narrowed gaze as I slowly—so slowly—stretch my uninjured hand towards his arm, giving him enough time to stop me like he has the last few times I've tried to touch them. But this time, he doesn't.

My fingertips make contact with the warm flesh just above his wrist, and I swear I feel him shiver—or was that me? I trace the patterns of inked stems and thorns up his arm. When I get to the inside of his elbow, the texture changes—smooth skin gives way to the flat, lumpy, and bumpy scarred skin. His sharp intake of breath makes me pause, and I move my gaze up to him to see his eyes are squeezed shut.

"Does it hurt?" I ask softly, afraid to break whatever spell has fallen over us.

His eyes crack open. "No. Not anymore."

It must have hurt like hell when it happened. I gasp when I trace the scar further up his elbow, surprised when I realize it extends all the way to his biceps. He must have lost a lot of blood from this injury. How did he survive it?

I study the beautiful ink that has another meaning to me now that I know what it covers. It tells a story about him. A story I desperately want to know about.

Following an impulse I don't quite understand, I lean forward and press a gentle kiss on the inside of his elbow. His hand twitches and I feel his pulse skitters beneath my lips. That tiny, involuntary reaction fills me with an odd sense of triumph, knowing I can affect him the way he does me.

I don't stop there. I let my lips linger on that spot for long moments, then slowly pepper kisses up his arm to the end of the scar and back down, each one saying what I can't put into words.

When I finally glance up, his eyes pin me in place. The tenderness in his gaze is staggering, like I've peeled back layers of armor without even trying. My head spins, my chest tightens, and the room suddenly feels too small, too charged. He murmurs something in Italian, raising a hand to caress my cheek. I catch one word—*dolcezza. Sweetness.* But the rest is lost to me. "What did you say?" I ask.

"You undo me. You're a dangerous witch."

My breath snags at the seriousness of his tone and face. I hold my breath as he leans down so close that his warm breath on my lips sends tingles down my spine, between my thighs, until my panties are damp. My heart pounds a desperate rhythm as my lips part, waiting, wanting... but he only places a chaste kiss on the bridge of my nose before pulling back.

I gulp. Shit, I really wanted him to kiss me. Should I just ask? Tell him I'm ready for his kisses?

But before I can gather even a shred of courage, he shifts to stand, and panic bubbles up. I grab his arm to stop him, but when those dark eyes fall on my face, I'm too chicken to say what I really want, so I ask something else I'm curious about. "Your tattoo—what do the flowers mean?"

I expect him to evade my question or ignore it entirely, but he sighs like he was waiting for me to ask. "It's a symbol of loyalty between my brothers and I. A reminder of the hell we escaped to become this powerful."

His brothers. He means the Nightshades. According to Roan, all four men have been friends for decades. My mind flashes to the four different flowers printed and framed on the wall in Rafael's great room. The same design of Maximo's tattoo on Rafael's dining chair and the smaller chair. The ink on Michael. Do they all have something similar tattooed on their bodies?

I can't imagine the uptight and cold Rafael with tattoos, but it would make sense if it really is a symbol to them. "The men at the dinner all looked very different." I think out loud.

"That's because we're not brothers by blood." Maximo's lips twitch into something almost wistful. "But even better. We're brothers by choice. By shared experiences and pain. That bond... It's stronger than anything else."

Brothers by choice. The weight in his words makes me think of battlefields and foxholes, the kind of bonds forged in fire.

I study his face, weighing my next words. *Push too hard and he'll shut down, but...* "I noticed something similar to your tattoo carved on the back of the chair Rafael sat on in his dining room —and the smaller chair across from him. Does that chair belong to someone connected to this shared pain you mentioned?"

And just like that, the shutters come down. His face closes off, and with a pang of regret, I know he's done answering me.

"You should get some rest," he says, grabbing the breakfast tray like a conversation-ender.

I swing my legs off the bed in annoyance. "I literally just woke up, so I think I've had more than enough rest. I need to check on Marco."

The second I stand, the room tilts dangerously. Maximo moves faster than should be humanly possible, shifting the tray to one hand and wrapping the other around my waist, pulling me against him until I'm steady on my feet. And suddenly, I'm very aware that he's still shirtless as my cheek meets warm skin and hard muscle. *Holy hell.*

Stubborn woman," he growls, but there's worry threading through his irritation. "The bullet might have gone straight through your flesh, but it pierced an artery and you lost quite a lot of blood. You. Need. Bed. Rest." Each word is punctuated by him carefully maneuvering me back onto the mattress like I'm made of spun glass.

"But—" I start to protest weakly but stop when he glares at me.

"The bastard is fine. But if you're that worried about him, I'll have Marco check in. Now stay put before you fall and crack that pretty head open. I'll be back soon."

I sigh dramatically as I sink back under the covers, lying flat on my back and glaring at the ceiling like it's to blame for my predicament. The thought of being trapped in bed all day makes me want to crawl out of my skin. Maybe I can convince Maximo to bring me a book. Or a TV. Or a circus—*anything*. At this point, I'd settle for juggling clowns just to avoid boredom.

The door opens again almost immediately, and Maximo returns with Marco limping in behind him. "That was fast."

Maximo frowns. "He was already waiting outside to see you."

I sit up as my bodyguard shuffles closer, guilt practically pouring off him. "I'm so sorry. I failed to protect you."

Oh, for heaven's sake. My glare shoots straight to Maximo, knowing instinctively he's the one who planted that nonsense in the man's head. Then I turn to Marco, my gaze dropping to where he's holding his side, the place he got shot. The sight makes my chest tighten uncomfortably. He took a bullet because of me, and here he is, apologizing?

"No, you didn't fail, Marco," I start, ignoring Maxim's growl as I pick up his free hand. "You woke me up and safely got me into the panic room. If I hadn't stumbled into the monitor room and recognized my brother in the chaos, I would have stayed in that room. But I couldn't just hide and let my father shoot at my family. I couldn't—"

Marco gives me a tentative smile. "Your family?"

I blink at him, confused. Then my own words come back to me. *Oh. Oh, crap. Did I just say that?* My eyes dart to Maximo, whose sharp gaze is suddenly trained on me like a wolf scenting something interesting. Heat climbs up my neck, and I quickly turn back to Marco. "Well, yes. I'm a Leonotti now after all." I give him a reassuring smile, my thumb rolling over the big rock on my ring finger, which I'm so used to now that it doesn't even feel that heavy anymore.

"I'm sorry we lost some men," I continue softly. "Sorry you and the others got hurt. If I'd known sooner..." A shiver runs through me as I let myself think about it. If I had stayed hidden and done nothing, my father or brother might've killed Marco. Or Maximo. Or worse... Marco or Maximo might've hurt them. I shake my head to dispel that horrifying thought. "So no, Marco, you didn't fail. I succeeded in diffusing what could have potentially ended in disaster."

I pat Marco's hand once more before sinking back into the pillows, suddenly exhausted. Maximo notices immediately—*does anything escape those dark eyes?*—and dismisses Marco with a look that could wilt flowers.

"Go get some bedrest as well," I call after him. "No point in guard duty when I've got my own personal watchdog." I shoot Maximo a teasing smile.

And what a watchdog he proves to be. The darned man stays glued to my side all day, helping me to the bathroom, bathing me, feeding me lunch.

I grumble and complain, telling him repeatedly to go to work, to give me space to breathe, to stop hovering like a particularly muscular mother hen. But secretly? Deep down where I barely admit it to myself...

It makes me feel all fuzzy and precious.

I love it.

29

MAXIMO

Those incompetent men at the port managed to lose track of the trafficked kids last week. I couldn't deal with it then—not with Afrim and Roan Përmeti's ambush on my penthouse that left Elira bleeding from a bullet wound. But now it's payback time.

An hour ago, we finally got our break—a tip about where they might be holding the girls. A whole goddamn week later. Seven fucking days of these kids being God knows where, enduring God knows what. The thought sits like acid in my stomach.

"This the place?" I ask through grinding teeth as Dante guides the SUV through the dirty backroads of the Queensbridge projects. The buildings here are desperate things, barely holding themselves together, spaced far enough apart that screams would echo into nothing. Perfect place to hide something you don't want found.

"Yeah." Dante turns right down towards the waterfront, where the old, abandoned houses are clustered together, and parks the SUV around a corner—a blind spot from the cameras in the area. Not that it matters; Giorgio's already scrambling the feeds. Still, I like to cover all bases. Being extra careful never hurts.

Dante and I climb out, and behind us, four of my men exit the second SUV. Together, we head towards the chain-link fence surrounding the abandoned property. I scan the quiet, deserted area while one of my men makes quick work of the padlock—old-school, almost laughably simple.

Within seconds, the lock clicks open, and we slip inside, moving silently towards the buildings.

"They're in apartment eight," Dante murmurs beside me. I nod, my eyes fixed on the skeletal structures ahead. Up close, they're even worse than they seemed from a distance—windows shattered, doors hanging off hinges, walls sagging under years of mold and neglect.

Hiding the girls here was disgustingly clever, really. The place is likely inhabited mostly by rodents and a bunch of homeless people. No one would think to look here. Hell, I wouldn't have.

"Over here," one of my men calls in a loud whisper, waving us towards the apartment building off to the left.

I follow, my gaze narrowing on the building's front door—or what passes for one. It's held in place by a shiny, high-tech lock panel that looks absurdly out of place on a structure this decrepit. They are definitely in there. But something feels off.

While Dante scans the lock and sends it to Giorgio, I glance around again.

Surely whoever is in charge of this operation didn't just leave the girls unguarded?

So where are his men? It's too quiet. Unease creeps up my spine, and I rub an impatient hand over the back of my neck.

Dante's phone beeps softly, and when I glance at him, he flashes me a thumbs up. "We have the code." He leans in, typing fast. The lock disengages with a faint *click*, far too smooth for my liking.

This is too fucking easy, damn it. This might be a trap.

As Dante tugs the door open, I pull my gun from its thigh holster, and my men follow suit. Trap or not, we're going in.

The interior is dark, and it takes a while for my eyes to adjust. When they do, Dante's low curse fills the air. "What the fuck..." I don't need to ask why.

Because there they are. Young girls—younger than I expected based on the feed we got from the port last week.

They're underaged.

Rage sears through my chest as I take in their flimsy skirts and crop tops that are more like costumes than clothing. They're all huddled together, likely trying to share what little body heat they can, their wide, terrified dark eyes locked on us like we're the monsters in this nightmare. And honestly, who could blame them? Drenched in shadows and armed to the teeth, we probably look just like the bastards who dragged them into this hell.

"They're not Americans," Dante states in Italian. No shit, Sherlock—my bet is they're Chinese or Japanese. "Fuck, Maximo, they're so young. *Too* young."

I step deeper into the dusty, crumbling lobby, and the girls flinch, shrinking back with soft, terrified whimpers. My eyes flick to the gun in my hand. Fuck. "Everyone, put your weapons away," I command as I slide my pistol back into its holster.

Then I raise my hands slowly in what I hope looks like a non-threatening gesture. "Shh, it's okay. We're not here to hurt you. Can any of you speak English? Do any of you understand me?"

I keep my voice low and harmless as I glance over them. "We need to get you out of here quickly before the bad men come back." The irony of me calling someone bad is not lost on me. If these girls knew half the things I've done, they'd run screaming. But I really am not going to hurt them. Even monsters have lines they won't cross.

Their fearful eyes stare back at me, unblinking. My jaw tightens. This has to move faster.

"If you can speak English and you understand me, you need to signify. *Now*." I infuse my voice with urgency as I glance back at the entrance. The unease crawls deeper up my spine with each passing second. Something is coming—I can feel it in my bones. I tilt my head at my men, silently ordering them to go outside and keep watch.

When I turn back to the girls, one has separated herself from the group. She looks so thin, I swear a gust of wind could knock her off her feet. Tangled dark hair falls in greasy waves down her back, and her bare arms are wrapped tightly around her trembling frame. She looks like she hasn't had a proper meal in days, let alone a shower, fresh clothes, or a good night's sleep. Hell, they all do.

"A–are you–are you really here to save us?" Her English comes out broken but clear enough, weighted with an accent and far too much fear.

I drop to my haunches, and she flinches back. Every muscle in my body goes still, like approaching a wounded animal. "Yes. We're here to rescue you and send you home safely. But we need to leave here as soon as possible."

Her eyes bore into mine, filled with a weariness that makes my stomach turn. No child should have eyes that old. I work to arrange my features into something trustworthy, something gentle—expressions that feel foreign on my face. What she sees must satisfy her because she finally nods and turns back to the group. Then she starts speaking in her native tongue, and I recognize it instantly. Japanese.

They're Japanese.

The tension bleeds out of the room as she speaks, and suddenly all their eyes are on me. Not with fear now, but with something dangerously close to hope.

"I'm Maximo, what's your name?" I ask the young girl when she turns back to me.

"I'm Sachiko."

"How old are you, Sachiko?"

"Twelve," she answers, biting her chapped lip.

Twelve. Twelve fucking years old. I swallow my burst of anger, trying not to let it show on my face. I'll unleash it later, when I find whoever's responsible for this.

"Okay, Sachiko. Is anyone here injured?" I wait for her response. When she shakes her head, I continue. "Good. We need to leave now. I want you all to follow me and walk as quickly as your legs can carry you. Can you explain that to them?" I nod at the girls behind her.

She turns back to the group, Japanese flowing faster now, ending on what must be a question because when she finishes, they all look at me and nod in unison.

Just then, Dante appears at my shoulder, phone in hand. "We just detected movement from the south entrance. About half a dozen men, laughing and talking loudly. I think they might be drunk."

Figures. A week of nothing happening made them sloppy. Fools. The unease in my spine eases slightly—better a straightforward fight than an ambush. "Can we take them?"

Dante nods. "I think so. But we need to get the girls away first so they're not caught in the crossfire. I have a motorhome arriving in about five minutes, so we should be able to get them out on time."

Good. I glance back at the girls and tell Sachiko. "It's time to go."

Dante stays behind with three men while I lead the girls towards the entrance. Perro brings up the rear, scanning the area like a hawk. As we walk through the chain-link door, a dirty RV that looks like it crawled out of a junkyard pulls up. But actually, it's the perfect cover. No one would look twice at rust and dented metal in this neighborhood.

The driver's window rolls down, and I recognize the man who peeps out as one of my own. He pales when he sees me, eyes widening, and quickly jumps out of the vehicle. "Boss, I didn't expect to see you, I—"

I raise a hand impatiently. "It's fine. We need to transport them to one of our safe houses." I motion to the girls behind me as I walk towards the RV's side door and pull it open. The inside looks surprisingly decent—roomy too. That'll do.

I turn to Sachiko again. "This man works for me. He's going to take you to one of my houses where a doctor and cook will be waiting for you. You'll all be safe there until I can take you back home."

Sachiko's little lips tremble, then she does something unexpected. She walks straight into me and wraps her tiny arms around my legs. "Thank you," she whispers while I just stand there frozen.

After what feels like a long moment, she joins the girls, and one by one, they all file into the RV. I give Sachiko one last look before closing the door behind them. "Follow the driver," I tell Perro, who nods and circles to the passenger side.

I wait until the RV is out of sight, then make my way back to the development area, my blood already heating for the fight. To my disappointment, it's already over by the time I return, and the drunk men are tied up.

"They're mercenaries," Dante tells me as I come to a stop in front of him. "Hired by someone they never met. Instructions came through a burner phone that's untraceable. They know nothing."

"Fuck." I curse, shoving a hand through my hair angrily. "Kill them and dispose of their bodies. Keep the burner.

Whoever's running this will try to make contact eventually. We'll have the bastard then."

We collect the phone and watch the executions before walking back to the entrance, leaving the men to handle the disposal. But I can't shake the feeling of being one step behind.

First it was the shipment a couple of weeks ago—still no leads—and now the trafficking of Japanese girls? The fucker pulling the strings is too smart, too damn evasive. Could both culprits be the same person?

Only one thing is certain at this moment: Someone is moving pieces on the board. Maybe more than one someone. And I hate not knowing who the fuck is playing the game.

On the drive back home, I dial the number of the *kumicho*, the head of the *ninkyō dantai*.

"Leonotti. What is it?" Yuto Hayashi asks dispassionately as he answers the phone. I lean back in my seat with a sigh.

We're not enemies, per se, but we're not allies either. Still, I calmly run him through the trafficking I witnessed last week and tonight's discovery that they're Japanese. "I have them in a safe house and will take care of them until they leave American soil." I finish.

Silence hums on the line, and I can practically feel Yuto grinding his teeth. "And the culprit?"

"Still working on it." I hate admitting it, but I hate loose ends even more. "We'll find out who's behind it soon."

His anger simmers for a moment, but when he speaks again, it's quieter. "See that you do. I'll arrange for a jet to retrieve the girls within the week. And Leonotti..."

"Yes?"

"I'm grateful for this. I owe you a favor."

The weight in his words isn't lost on me as the call ends. I didn't help the girls for his favor, of course, but it doesn't hurt having it.

"I'm wiped," Dante announces as he pulls up into my building's garage. He rubs a hand over his face, exhaustion clear in his eyes. "I think I'll skip heading up with you tonight."

"That's fine." We exit the car together, and I adjust my jacket as we head for the elevator together. I own the entire building, and Dante and my other men live on the different floors.

Having them stationed throughout it isn't just convenient—it's strategic. No outsiders snooping where they don't belong, no pesky questions regarding some of the activities we have to carry out here.

He gets off on the 15th floor, the one directly beneath my penthouse, and gives me a brief nod before the doors slide shut.

As I ascend alone, I roll my neck, leaning back on the railing, just as the elevator reaches my floor. I get out quickly—and stop. My eyes narrow at the sight of my men casually munching on some snacks on a plate. My jaw tightens. Fucking Elira.

"I told her to stay on the fucking bed," I growl under my breath, and the men shift awkwardly, avoiding my glare like guilty kids caught raiding the cookie jar. Dragging the front door open, I stride inside, my irritation already bubbling over.

I find my wife in the kitchen, moving something from the oven rack to the countertop, laughing at whatever bullshit Marco is saying to her.

My heart quickens as I stare at her glistening lips, curled up in a pleased smile. So fucking tempting. *So fucking out of reach.* All my anger and frustrations boil to a peak at the reminder that I can't kiss her.

"I thought I told you to stay in bed," I snap, and she jolts mid-laugh, staring up at me with the same guilty expression as my men.

"Maximo. You're home."

"Obviously." I stalk towards her, eyes locked on hers.

She quickly takes off her mittens and raises her hands defensively. "I can explain! I'm feeling better now, and it makes no sense to just lie back on the bed when that's what I've been doing all week—I'm not an invalid. My arm is almost healed, and I—" Whatever else she's saying turns into a startled squeal when I scoop her up, one arm under her knees and the other cradling her back.

Marco wisely avoids my gaze, chewing his snack silently as I carry my wife out of the kitchen.

30

ELIRA

Maximo's jaw is locked tight, and every step he takes up to his bedroom feels like it shakes the walls. His arms around me are unyielding, as if daring me to squirm free. I crane my neck to meet his eyes, frowning as I raise my uninjured hand to his face. "*Çfarë*? What is it? Are you really this mad because I didn't stay in bed like you ordered?"

But somehow, I know that's not it. No, he's angry at something else—maybe a mix of whatever happened outside and whatever he thinks I've done to wrong him.

He answers with nothing but a scowl as he shoulders open his bedroom door and places me on the bed. Before I can even process his next move, he yanks my shorts and panties off and buries his face between my legs with a primal groan that reverberates through my core. I cry out in surprise, head slamming back into the bed as lightning cracks through my veins.

His hands grip my inner thighs, firm but not rough, spreading them wider. My body yields to him without question, though my mind still scrambles to keep up. Then his right hand moves, and I hear the jingle of his belt. One-handed, he works the buckle. The sound of leather sliding, metal zipper lowering—each tiny noise builds anticipation until I'm trembling with it.

My gaze locks on him as he frees his cock, and I can't help the way my mouth falls open. It's hard, veined, the broad head glistening invitingly with precum. I lick my lips unconsciously.

The sound of his dark chuckle sends a shiver straight through me, and I glance up at him, dazed. "Christ, you're staring at my cock like it's the first meal you've seen in days. Tell me—have you sucked cock before?"

I shake my head wordlessly, and his lips curl up in a fierce smile. "Good. You may keep your kisses to yourself, but my cock will dominate that mouth just as it has dominated every inch of your body." He plants a kiss on my inner thigh, then drags the flat of his tongue upward, and somehow that's so hot it sends my brain fizzling out.

When he releases me and steps back, I frown at him. What's he doing now? My confusion only grows as he starts shifting me around, careful to avoid touching my injured arm while gently guiding me down until my head is hanging off the edge of the mattress. The position feels strange, vulnerable, but the intensity in his eyes as he gazes down at me sets me ablaze all over again.

My breath catches as he steps closer. From this angle, with the light casting shadows over him, he emanates pure dominance, looming like an avenging warrior about to lay claim to his spoils of the war. He takes another step closer, adjusting my head until it's positioned between his thick, muscled thighs, his heavy balls and hard cock mere inches from my face.

The musky, heady scent of him floods my senses, leaving my head spinning. He's too much—too close, too intense—yet I don't want him to stop. When he taps his cock against my lips, they part eagerly. But instead of pushing in, he drags the tip across them, smearing the bead of precum like lipstick.

My pussy clenches tightly as wetness gushes out. *That's so sexy*. I lick the cum quickly, moaning at the combination of sweet-salty flavor. He drags his cock over my lips again, once, twice, groaning each time my tongue flicks over him.

"Eager for more, *dolcezza*?"

I nod, beyond words.

"Then take it. Take all of me."

His hands cradle my neck, holding me steady as he slowly pushes his cock past my lips, feeding it to me.

My mouth clamps around his crown, sucking greedily, and a low growl escapes him. "So fucking eager." He thrusts deeper, making me whimper as my mouth stretches to accommodate his girth, drool dripping down the corner of my lips.

When the broad head touches the back of my throat, I tense. Gag reflex kicks in, and I jerk involuntarily.

"Shh." He slowly pulls out. "You can take me, *dolcezza*. Relax. *Relax*." He repeats when I don't comply right away and shifts his hand on my nape to rub his thumb down my cheek.

Our eyes meet, and my heart stutters. I release a shaky breath and let my muscles loosen, sinking fully into his control. "There you go. Good girl. You're doing so good." His thumb continues its soothing path as he eases back in. "Breathe."

He matches his movements to my breathing—pushing inside on my inhales, withdrawing on my exhales. Once, twice, until we fall into a rhythm. Each gentle thrust earns me murmured praises while his fingers trace appreciative patterns down my throat.

"Fuck, you're doing remarkably well for your first time, *dolcezza*," he groans, hands tightening on my nape. There's a hint of pride laced in his voice, and paired with his sweet praises and tender touches, it messes with my mind, stroking my arousal and affection for him even more.

I *like* pleasing him.

Eager to earn more of those sounds from him, I draw a

deeper breath as he thrusts in again. Then I let the flat of my tongue glide along the underside of his cock, and—*oh boy*—does he curse violently. So I do it again and again, watching his reaction as he slowly fucks my mouth, enjoying how his control slips with each thrust. Enjoying the fact that *I'm* the one doing that to him. *Undoing him.*

A wicked thought crosses my mind. I wonder how he'll react if I—

On his next thrust into me, I swallow as I inhale, feeling him slip past the barrier of my throat. My eyes widen when he sinks deeper, tears stinging as my gag reflex tries to kick in again. Above me, Maximo yells my name, his fingers digging into the flesh of my neck and cheek as a hot spurt of cum hits the back of my throat.

"Fucking hell, *dolcezza.*" His thrusts speed up. "Such a sweet, greedy girl. So perfect for me. Swallowing my cock like you were made for it. You want my cum, huh?"

I moan desperately, squeezing my thighs together to create the needed friction on my aching clit as I suck him down.

"Shit. I can feel those pretty moans vibrating right through my cock."

The memory of how his groans feel against my clit spurs me on. I moan again, swallowing him down. "*Dolcezza!*" he roars, his balls slapping my cheeks as his thrusts turn frantic.

I reach up with my uninjured hand to cup them, fingers fondling as I hum around his cock. I think my skin breaks with how much his fingers are digging into my neck, but I'm too caught up in his pleasure. The way he shouts my name to the ceiling, the way his head falls back, the way he pulses against my tongue as he empties himself down my throat. My eyes squeeze shut, and I press my legs tighter, mewling against him.

His release seems endless, his whole body shuddering with every pulse. Then slowly his hands ease, the punishing grip softening into something tender, *possessive*, until finally, he pulls out of my mouth. But I barely have time to suck in a ragged breath before he's lifting me up on the bed and flipping me around again.

He grabs one ankle, then the other, tossing my legs over his shoulders like I'm his personal feast. "Such a slut for me," he growls as he settles between my thighs. "Soaked through just from sucking my cock."

I'm too breathless to answer, and thankfully he isn't holding out for a response, just blows out a hot breath on my sensitive clit that makes me groan. My belly quivers as he swipes his tongue through my wet folds, once, twice, thrice.

On the third pass, he thrusts a finger into my opening, and I scream his name, body coiling off the bed as my climax explodes through me. My hands form fists on the sheets, and a twang of pain travels through my bandaged arm, but at this point even that pain only heightens my pleasure.

He keeps up his pressure. Licking and fingering me, dragging out my pleasure as my cunt clenches around his digits, contracting and pumping with each release of my juices. One orgasm rolls into another and another. Sensations barreling through my body sending my teeth chattering until the overstimulation becomes too much.

"Maximo, stop—" My hand flies to his hair, tugging hard to pull him away. The flesh is too raw, too sensitive, and every single pain is felt through my soul. He relents, but not before planting a last lazy kiss on my inner thigh, making me shiver.

Our breaths come in deep pants as we watch each other, and slowly I unclench my fingers from his hair and smooth them down his handsome sweat-dampened face. For a fleeting moment, he leans into my touch, his eyes falling shut as if savoring the connection.

But just as quickly, he pulls back, retreating into himself. He heads for the nightstand, retrieves some wet wipes, and returns to clean between my thighs. The soft, cool touch of the wipe against my folds draws a relieved sigh from me, soothing the oversensitive flesh. Then he gets up, cleans his hands, and tosses the used wipes into the trash can.

I push up on my good arm and pat the spot next to me invitingly. His brows furrow as he watches me, his gaze dropping to where I'm biting down on my bottom lip. I release the lip, but the hot desire in his gaze doesn't abate.

Instead, he scowls, dragging his pants up with a rough tug. The tension in the air thickens as he storms to the door and yanks it open without looking back. The slam that follows rattles the walls—and my chest.

That sound echoes in the silence. My breath hitches, eyes stinging as I fall back on the bed. *Damn it.* I rub a hand over my aching chest, willing the tightness to ease. He's mad at me. Really mad. And somehow that hurts worse than my injured arm. *I hate it.*

The restless ache in my chest pushes me to move. I swing my legs off the bed and make my way to the ensuite where I wash my face and my cunt. Once cleaned up, I shuffle to the closet and raid it for one of Maximo's shirts. As I button it up, I turn to the chest for underwear. The top drawer stops me cold—my underwear sits neatly folded next to his, as if they've always belonged there.

My chest tightens even harder. He hasn't let me return to my bedroom in over a week. I've been wearing his stuff when he's home, only retrieving my own things when he's gone. This casual claiming of space, this quiet assumption of permanence—it says more than any words could. Fighting back fresh tears, I take out a pair of cotton panties and slip them on before heading out.

Padding barefoot down the stairs, I find Marco lounging on

the sofa in the living room. He jumps up when he sees me, wincing as his hand drops to his side. I narrow my eyes on him. "If you don't stop moving like that, you're going to tear your stitches again," I scold, shaking my head at his sheepish expression. *Men.*

Just days ago, he had the foolhardy idea to spar with some of the other men, predictably busting his stitches in the process. Poor Ethan had to come back to re-stitch the wound.

"Where's Maximo?" I ask.

Marco hesitates. "The boss is in his study. He gave instructions not to be disturbed."

I roll my eyes at that as I walk around the stairs. His warning is pointless—I don't take orders from Maximo unless I feel like it. The door to the study looms ahead, and my heart does a little stutter-step, but I square my shoulders and march right in without knocking.

Maximo glances up from his computer with a scowl that softens just the tiniest bit when he sees me at the doorway. "What is it?" he asks, though I can't help but notice he's put on a shirt—which is a shame.

I close the office door gently behind me, just to be contrary, and approach his desk. His chair swivels to track my movement, and for a moment we're caught in an unspoken standoff. I study the hard lines of his handsome face, the tension in his jaw, the way his fingers drum against the armrest, then give in to the impulse to crawl into his lap.

He grunts, stiffening at first before his arms wrap around me, hands settling naturally on my ass. Such a man. I can't help but smile as I snuggle into his warm chest, loving how his scent surrounds my senses.

My fingers find the collar of his shirt, needing something to fidget with as I gather my courage. "At first, I wanted to take kisses off the table as a punishment for you threatening my family," I admit softly, tracing the edge of the fabric, letting my fingers brush against his collarbone. "Then I realized just how intimate the sex act itself was, and how kissing would have heightened everything, especially being my first time experiencing it all. And I thought... I thought I needed to protect something of myself from you."

Protect my heart, I don't say, though it hardly matters now. That ship has long since sailed.

Maximo's hands move up to my waist, and he gently pulls me back from his chest. When I meet his eyes, he's frowning at me with an expression I can't quite read.

"You think withholding kisses would protect your heart from me?" His lips curl up in a way that suggests he finds the very idea funny, and my heart skips traitorously. One large hand slides up my body to wrap around my nape, his thumb stroking my cheek in a gesture that feels almost unconscious. "You're wrong, wife. Your body fully belongs to me—mine to touch, to own, control, and use as I please. You think your heart is exempt from that? That's quite the delusion."

His thumb continues its hypnotic path across my cheek as he speaks, and his words swirl around me like silk, making me lightheaded as my heart thunders in my chest. Because he's right, damn him.

My gaze drops to his lips, and his fingers flex on my nape, his thumb stilling.

Then a shrill ring cuts through the tension, making me jump in his lap. Maximo curses, and his hand drops from my cheek as he spins his chair to face the desk where his phone is demanding attention. He keeps one hand firmly on my waist to keep me steady, then he leans forward to pick the device from the desk, but not before he gives me a sardonic smirk. "Unless you're going to kiss me, Elira, get out."

My heart leaps into my throat, and I let go of his shirt as I slip from his lap. I wrap my arms around myself as I walk out of his office, shaken by what he said earlier. Was withholding my kisses really such a useless endeavor?

Even without kissing him, I've already lost a piece of my heart to him.

And I'm not sure I'll ever get it back. I can't imagine a life without him ever again.

31

MAXIMO

Three days later...

"When are the girls getting transported back to Japan?" Rafael asks absently as he types something on his phone.

I glance briefly down at my own phone where Marco's text glares back at me:

> Elira's on her way to your office.

Great. I barely keep the grin off my face as I answer Rafael, "Yuto's jet is landing tomorrow evening." The words are barely out when the door bursts open.

And there she is—my wife, standing in the doorway with her arms crossed and a storm brewing in her pretty hazel eyes.

'You've been avoiding me," she announces, loud enough to draw every eye on the video conference to my face.

I can't help the smirk that plays across my lips as I wave her over. She narrows her eyes on me and stomps over, face scrunched up in an adorable scowl that makes her nose wrinkle. Christ, it shouldn't be this endearing.

I push my chair back, silently inviting her in, and just like she did three days ago, she easily slips into my lap. But this time I spin her around, positioning her back against my chest so she can face the screen. The startled gasp when she spots my brothers makes her whole body tense in my arms.

"Ahh, *bella*, good to see your pretty face amongst these ugly mugs." Romero leans forward in his seat, green eyes sparkling mischievously. Elira chuckles, a little of her tension slipping.

"Hi, Romero." She smiles at him, then nods at Michael and Rafael.

The latter's glare is a dagger aimed right at me, which I meet with one of my own, daring him to say something. "I think we've covered everything. I'll let you all know if I find any new clues. Goodbye." I exit the meeting before anyone can protest.

Elira bites her lip, glancing up nervously. "I didn't mean to interrupt. You should've told me to come back if you were busy."

I smile faintly. "It's fine. The meeting was already winding down before you came in." I turn her around on my lap so she's straddling me, her legs dangling on either side of me. "Now, what's this about, *dolcezza*?"

"You've been avoiding me... because of what happened the other day?" She drops her eyes to my throat and starts drawing lazy patterns on my chest with her finger. Shit. She's bothered by that.

"No, of course not. I've just been really busy," I say firmly, though it's only half true. Yes, I've been busy, but I've also been deliberately keeping my distance. The more we interact, the more I want to push past her boundaries and kiss the hell out of her until she forgets why she didn't even want me to in the first place.

The more I think about it, the more afraid I am that I'll just do it without her permission. One impulsive move like that might set me back on any progress I've made with her. She has finally stopped looking at me as her captor, and I don't want to jeopardize that.

"Prove it," she says, finally meeting my eyes. Her hazel eyes swirl with bronze and emerald. "Prove you're not avoiding me by spending time with me. Today. *Now*."

I chuckle. "What?" But my amusement fades as her chin juts out stubbornly. She's serious. Of course, she is. "Elira, I have mountains of work I need to get through. I don't have the time to frolic with you."

Hurt flashes in her eyes, and her hand drops from my chest. She starts to scramble off my lap, but I secure my arms around her waist, holding her to me. My heart constricts watching her turn her face away.

"Elira."

Her voice, when it comes, is like a knife to the gut—low, broken, and stripped of all defenses. "Am I going to be just another prisoner here?"

My jaw tightens, but I force myself to stay still, to let her keep going. Her gaze drifts somewhere over my shoulder. "I've been locked up in *Atë*'s compound since I was eleven, Maximo. That day... I begged Mama to take me to the beach playground. It was sunny, hot. Perfect. She loved the beach too much to say no to me."

Her voice cracks, but she pushes through. "We were laughing, playing, and then... they came. *Atë*'s enemies ambushed us. And my mom she–she—" She swallows, blinking rapidly, but a single tear falls down her face regardless.

"*Dolcezza*." I lift my hand, using my thumb to wipe that single tear away. A brick lodges itself in my lungs, my heart, making it painful to breathe as I watch the torment etched into her face. "It wasn't your fault."

"Wasn't it?" Those eyes lock onto mine again, glistening with unshed tears. "*Atë* didn't talk to me for over a week, and when he finally did, it was only to tell me I wasn't allowed to go out anymore. Ever. I accepted it as my punishment, and I also knew he did it to protect me. But it was suffocating. The longer the years went by without any change in sight, I felt like I was going crazy. Then on my 21st birthday, I'd had enough and was ready to get into a fight with my father to let me go out. But I didn't need to. I guess I have you to thank for that."

"Me?" I frown.

She smiles faintly, the tears thankfully drying in her eyes. "Yes, you. I overheard him talking with his right-hand man, and he was cursing your name. You must have done something to him because he was so distracted, he let me go out without argument."

My frown deepens as I think back. Then the memory clicks. "*Ahh.*" That was when I intercepted his weapon shipment. So that's what did it.

"Why am I even telling you all this?" Elira sighs and tries to get out of my arms again, but I don't let her.

"I don't know, Elira. Why *are* you telling me?"

She scowls down at me. "The point," she snaps, jabbing a finger at my chest, "is that I've been a prisoner all my life, and if this—" She waves her hand wildly between us, "—is going to be my new life, I *refuse* to spend it as a prisoner again. So I'm going out. Right now. With or without you. And don't you *dare* smile, Maximo!"

I school my face into place, but my chest warms with amusement. She's so adorable trying to threaten me. "I'm not smiling. Fine," I surrender. "Where do you want to go?"

The transformation is instant—her entire face lights up, so bright it steals the breath from my lungs. She grabs my neck, practically bouncing in my lap. "Really? Really, really?"

Christ. I chuckle, nuzzling her cheek. "Yes, really, really."

Standing, I hoist her up, and she squeals, clinging to me like an excited monkey.

I carry her out of the study, ignoring the shock on my men's faces as we walk past them up the stairs. Let them stare. Elira doesn't care, and neither do I.

"Wait!" she says, tugging on my shirt as we go down the hallway to our room. "Take me to my room first. My clothes are in there."

I narrow my eyes but quietly change course, already making a mental note to have Bianca, my housekeeper, move all the clothes in Elira's closet to mine. This separate room bull-shit has gone on long enough.

When I finally set her down, it takes all my restraint not to pull her back immediately. Not that I could—she bolts into her walk-in closet and quickly takes some clothes out like she's scared I might change my mind any second. I lean against the doorframe, watching her with an indulgent smile as she slips out of my shirt into a pair of form-fitting slacks and top. Effort-lessly stunning, as always.

"Do you have a specific place you'd like to go? Or should I surprise you?" I ask her as I take my phone out to text Macro that we're going out and to get the cars and the men ready.

"Actually..."

Her hesitation makes me glance up. "What?"

"I'd like to go to a gun range."

I freeze, my fingers pausing mid-text. Sweet, sunshine-smile Elira wants to what now? A *gun range*?

"It's just one of the things I've always wanted to do. Roan tried to teach me at home a few times—how to shoot and a bunch of other things that interested me—but we had to sneak around so *Atë* wouldn't find out, and it's been years since I really shot a gun," she blurts out in a rush.

Now it makes sense. I remember watching the footage of the night her father and brother attempted their foolish rescue, and the way she picked up that pistol from the floor without hesitation. That wasn't a fluke.

I walk up to her slowly and pull her into me. "Are you trying to refine your shooting skills as a warning to me?" I tease, slipping my hand beneath her top, enjoying the way her breath hitches.

"N–no. Of course not," she gasps, her head falling back when I palm her tits through her lace bra. I press a kiss to her throat, then step back abruptly, leaving her flushed and wide-eyed.

"Fine. Let's do it. But we're going to my gun range where the men practice. It's private, so we'll have more than enough privacy," I tell her, and she gives me a smile so wide, it warms my heart.

The drive down to the small enclosed park I own is short, but Elira spends it bouncing on her seat like an over-caffeinated kid on Christmas morning. I've never seen her so excited. Damn it, I should have done this sooner. A mistake I'll fix. I make a mental note to try to do stuff with her outside the house at least twice a week going forward.

The tall gates swing open as our car approaches, and Elira practically has her face pressed to the window. I chuckle, but it doesn't even faze her. Her awe is so genuine, that by the time we pull into the sprawling concrete parking lot behind the square main building, I'm already thinking of what else I can show her next.

Inside, the man at the front desk jumps up at the sight of me. "Mr Leonotti, I–"

I wave him down. "It's fine, I know my way around." Turning to Marco and the rest of the men who came with us, I nod towards the waiting area. "You guys can wait here."

Elira's vibrating as I guide her to the gear room. When she enters, her gasp of delight is everything. "This looks just like the room in your panic room," she says, eyes wide while taking in the arsenal, "except... bigger. And with *way* more weapons."

I smirk, pulling down a pair of earmuffs and handing them to her. She takes them with a frown. "What about you?"

"I'm good," I answer as I pick up the gloves none of my men use and hold them out.

She eyes them with suspicion. "Really?"

"You're going to gear up correctly, or this is not going to happen."

She scowls but drags them on with exaggerated annoyance. The goggles come next, and this time, she doesn't argue. I step back, giving her a quick once-over. Satisfied, I gesture towards the wall. "Alright, which one can you shoot?"

"Almost all of them," she answers without hesitation.

I watch, intrigued, as she scans the options before settling on a 9mm. A smart, reliable choice. But just as I'm nodding in approval, she returns it, and—oh, hell no—picks up one of the assault rifles.

An AK 47.

I gape at her. "Babe, I don't think you can handle that. Your first choice was perfect."

She throws me a look that could melt steel. "I handle *you* alright, don't I?"

Fuck, I can't even argue with that logic.

"Fine," I grumble, grabbing the 9mm she discarded, just in case. If she's dead set on trying, who am I to stop her? But I'm keeping backup close.

As we step outside, a surprised gasp cuts through the open air, the wonder in her expression impossible to miss as her eyes dance across the outdoor range with its scattered targets placed haphazardly at varying distances.

"Ready?" I ask, my own excitement building as I watch her.

Her grin is all teeth and fire. "I was born ready."

I'm floored when she walks forward, holding the gun up

against her shoulder like some expert mercenary, her hips swaying seductively. I swallow my groan as I adjust my hardening cock in my pants and follow her.

She kneels gracefully, then lies on her belly, squinting through the scope as she chooses a low target and aligns her rifle. My lips curl up in amusement as I take in her every movement.

The target she chose is farther away—a glass bottle blending almost perfectly with the grass—rather than the easier paper mannequins set up for beginners. I'm sure she'll miss it, but I leave her to do her thing.

Part of the fun, after all, is missing.

She fiddles with the weapon, glances back to give me a saucy wink, then focuses on the target again. My smirk grows. Cute.

The gunshot cracks through the air, startling a flock of birds from the nearby trees. When the smoke clears, my jaw drops.

The glass bottle is gone.

Shattered into a hundred glittering shards.

She turns to me, smug as hell, and winks again. "Didn't expect that, did you? My brother was thorough when he taught me things that would've given my father a heart attack if he'd found out."

My semi turns into a full-blown erection, and a growl rips from my throat as I stalk towards her. She jumps to her feet with a squeal, throwing her hands up as she backs away from me.

"I know that look, Maximo. Stop it—we're in public! And I'm not done yet. Don't try to distract me."

I narrow my eyes but force myself to stop, muttering a curse as I rearrange my cock again. This is going to be a long-ass day.

32

ELIRA

We spent hours on the shooting range, and I absolutely reveled in every single moment. Teasing Maximo was the cherry on top. I was surprised—no, thrilled—that seeing me shoot so expertly aroused him. And oh, did I milk that reaction.

Every perfectly placed shot came with a cheeky wink and a seductive sway of my hips as I strutted past him. I teased him mercilessly, pushed his patience to the limit, until he finally had enough, pounced on me, and carried me laughing and squealing to the bathroom where he screwed my brains out. By the time he was done, I was screaming his name to the rafters for his men to hear.

Now, walking beside him to the car, my body still hums with the aftermath.

"I'm starving," I complain as I get in through the door he's holding open for me. He turns to our driver and speaks to him in Italian before getting in with me. The driver follows suit and turns the ignition.

"We'll stop for some food on our way," Maximo tells me as we pull out of the parking lot, running a hand through his disheveled hair and making it look even more deliciously messy.

I chuckle, scooting closer to swat his hand away. "You're hopeless. Let me fix it."

He smiles at me indulgently as my fingers comb through those thick, silky strands, and suddenly I'm remembering how those same strands felt clutched in my fists as I came earlier.

"Interesting. What are you thinking about that's making your cheeks go so red?" Maximo's hand rubs over my hot cheek. "Are you thinking naughty thoughts?"

I roll my eyes to hide my embarrassment and push his head away playfully as I move back. He chuckles, and my gaze drops to his lips. We've been skating around actually kissing—stealing hungry glances at each other's lips, lingering too long—but he doesn't seem willing to make the first move.

Then a sudden realization hits me. He won't kiss me unless I explicitly ask for it or take the lead myself, because I was the one who originally took it off the table. So no matter how much he might want to kiss me, he's holding back in a bid to respect my wishes.

"Maximo, I–"

His phone ringing interrupts me, and he holds up a hand as he answers, "Yes? Deal with it, Dante, I'm busy right now." He pauses to listen, then checks his watch. "We should be home in about an hour. Yes." With that, he ends the call and shifts his attention back to me. "You were saying?"

My heart stutters, and just like that, I chicken out, shaking my head. "Nothing." His eyes narrow. He knows it's not nothing, but he chooses to let it go.

The car slows to a stop, and the driver announces, "We're here."

I glance out the window to see we're parked in front of a fancy-looking restaurant. But suddenly my excitement fizzles out. My body feels heavy, the kind of tired that seeps into your bones. I lean back with a sigh, tilting my head towards Maximo. "Can we just get the food to go?"

Maximo doesn't argue. He simply nods and asks me what I want. Armed with my order, our driver gets out to get the food and is back in record time.

After we get back on the road, I let my head loll against the window, staring at the passing scenery. The rhythmic hum of the tires against the pavement starts to lull me into a calmer state, but my thoughts betray me. My mind wanders, circling back to the one thing I keep trying to ignore—kissing. Or rather, the lack of it.

Why does it keep creeping into my head? I chew on my lip and tap my feet on the floor nervously as I try to focus on something else. But it's like a magnet.

I'll just blurt it out, I think. Or better yet, *just do it*. I risk a surreptitious glance at Maximo, only to find him already watching me. Crap.

He rolls up his sleeves, and my eyes fall to his bulging muscles and the tattoos on his arm. An idea takes root. "I want to make you a deal," I blurt out before I can change my mind again.

His brows lift in an amused arch, and he gestures grandly, like a king entertaining a subject. "Go on."

I blow out a nervous breath and continue. "Tell me about your tattoo. Why the flowers? Do they mean something? And what about you and the guys? What happened that made you so loyal to each other? You mentioned shared experiences and pain."

His entire demeanor shifts. His teasing face hardens, and his eyes cloud over. A fortress of old wounds slams shut. "You said it was a deal, so what do I get out of it?"

Here goes nothing. "A kiss."

That gets his attention. He watches me for a moment,

searching my face. "A kiss. You think I want your kiss that badly to tell you something so personal?"

My stomach knots. Shit, did I miscalculate? "I told you something personal earlier," I remind him.

"Fair point. Alright."

"Alright? As in, you'll tell me?"

He shrugs, feigning nonchalance. "I would've had to eventually, so I take your deal. But I want more than one kiss. I want the right to kiss you whenever I want. *Anytime.*"

Yesss. That's what I want too. Even if he hadn't taken the deal, I would have found another way to bring up the topic. But I keep that part to myself as I smile at him. "Done. Now tell me."

He chuckles. "It's a long story."

"Then it's a good thing we still have about thirty minutes left before we get home."

He gives me one last smile before his face becomes serious, his gaze shifting away from me as a faraway look settles on his face. "It's such a long story, I don't even know where to start."

I scoot closer until I'm right by his side and rest my head on his shoulder. "Start anywhere."

He sighs, a sound that feels heavy, as if he's reaching into a dark corner of himself. "Rafael, Michael, Romero, and I… we all grew up in Little Italy. Rafael and I were pretty close from birth since my father was his father's enforcer before he died. After that, his father didn't mind me sticking around, especially because I helped with the things I could."

"We became friends with Romero after his father joined the old Moretti syndicate when we were thirteen. A year later, we met Michael. His father was a corrupt senator who used Alfonso, Rafael's dad, to take out his perceived enemies in exchange for looking the other way at the crimes Alfonso committed—and occasionally bailing him out."

I nod against his shoulder. I already knew Rafael's father

was a don back in the day, and rumor has it Rafael killed his own father —which, to be honest, I don't find all that hard to believe. The man is pretty scary.

Maximo stretches his arm out behind me and wraps it around my shoulder. "Anyways, the guys and I were tight. Then, in senior year, we got a new student—a clever sixteen-year-old girl who skipped grades because of her big brain."

I hear the smile in his voice and glance up. A twinge of jealousy shoots through me at the obvious affection on his face for this new girl.

"The day she started at our high school, the guys and I were shit-talking about her, not knowing she was behind us, and she clapped back with some shit of her own. She was fearless. Rafael declared protection on her for reasons only he knew. Maybe because she was so small compared to the other students. Good thing he did, too, because she ended up being assigned as his tutor."

"His tutor?" I ask, trying to keep up.

"You see, back then, we were all so busy running errands for Don Moretti—things no teenager should have been doing—that we didn't have much time for school. So we were all falling behind, with the exception of Michael who was pretty smart back then. Still is, the fucker."

He chuckles, and I smile as I think about the tattooed man. If he wasn't the CEO of a top tech company, I might doubt that. At first glance, with his tattoos and piercings, I would've pegged Michael as just another rich, white man with a taste for criminal activities.

"Anyways, we all got a warning from the school, and Romero and I worked harder the following semester, but Rafael couldn't be bothered. So the principal intervened by assigning him a tutor. The new girl. Emilia Rossi."

Emilia. Even her name sounds pretty. I ignore the tightening in my throat and raise my hand to Maxim's chest, reminding myself *I'm* married to him, not this other girl.

"Well, Emily joined our table for lunch after that, and we all just took to her. She was smart, witty, and couldn't stand Rafael's arrogance, which was funny to watch. A week later, her father was killed. Turned out he was a detective investigating Rafael's father, and Alfonso had him murdered."

I gasp at the dark turn in the story, my fingers stilling on Maximo's chest as I glance up at him. His face tightens, brows furrowed, the lightness from earlier gone.

"It was all over the news, but like I said, Alfonso was well-connected. He not only had Michael's dad in his pockets but also other top politicians, so no arrests were made. Emily closed herself off from us. I mean, we were still essentially strangers. She must have been going through hell, especially since she'd lost her mother years earlier and was now an orphan."

My heart aches as I think about losing my *atë*. I can't fathom how I'd be able to cope alone if I didn't have Roan or Maximo. I blink back the tears stinging my eyes.

"Then she got the foolish notion of revenge and went to one of Alfonso's well-known warehouses with her father's gun. It didn't end well." He trails off, his fingers flexing on my shoulder.

"She got brutalized by the men, and they were going to—they wanted to *defile* her. But thankfully, the guys and I had an errand that day. So we were coming to the warehouse to submit our report and saw what was happening. Rafael went berserk."

He describes how Rafael pulled out his gun and shot the man trying to take off Emilia's clothes, and how he and the other guys also drew their guns to defend their friend. It was messy, but luckily the men weren't expecting resistance and were so caught off guard that the guys managed to kill them easily.

They helped Emilia to the hospital and dumped the bodies of the dead men in the river in an attempt to clean up. But they didn't realize there was a camera in the warehouse. Alfonso inevitably watched the feed and was pissed at them. *Shit.*

My stomach churns because I know something worse is coming.

"He said we should have let the men do whatever they wanted to her. She was just sixteen." His voice sounds stricken.

I shift on the leather chair, crawling into his lap until I'm straddling him. My face presses against his neck, and my fingers run down his arm, offering what little comfort I can.

"He was so mad at us. He tied us up and carved into my arm —as well as Romero's and Michael's—with his knife, making sure to cut through the arteries. He wanted us to bleed out and for Rafael to watch it happen so he'd learn a lesson about how to conduct himself in the future."

I swallow my gasp, closing my eyes as if that will stop the nausea assaulting me at the horrifying situation he's painting.

"He had one of his men bring Emily from the hospital where we'd taken her. His plan was to make her and Rafael watch Michael, Romero, and me die slowly. Then he'd do what his men couldn't do to Emily before killing her. All this to harden Rafael, who he couldn't kill because he considered him his legacy. His heir. The way he took so much pleasure talking about his sick plan..."

"He was a very sick man." I can't resist adding. I can't even fathom what Rafael must have gone through growing up with that psychopath. Maybe that's what shaped the man into the iceberg he is today.

"The one mistake Alfonso made was not tying Rafael up. He had beaten him to a pulp and thought he was too weak to do anything. But Rafael slowly got up, got his hand on a gun, and ended his father's life. That one singular action saved our lives."

Now I understand why all these strong men are so loyal to Rafael. Hell, he has my loyalty too now. Without him, I'd never have met Maximo because he wouldn't have survived.

I shudder at the thought of never meeting my husband. Never feeling what I feel for him now.

"After that, we ran away from the town, barely alive. Emily did a rough job patching up our arms since we were too scared to go to the hospital. Scared Alfonso's men would catch up to us. We found a tiny studio apartment in Hell's Kitchen and lived there for a while, stealing and doing other small crimes to survive."

"Exactly a year later, the guys and I decided to get tattoos to cover up the scarred flesh and celebrate escaping death. We wanted something similar as a way to declare our commitment and loyalty to one another."

Pulling away from his chest, I meet his eyes, then cup his face. "I'm so glad you made it out alive." I let go and bend down towards his arm.

Then I nuzzle the scarred flesh, feeling all the pain, all the history there, before slowly kissing every single mark and bump. "Why flowers?" I murmur against his arm.

"That was Emily's idea. Something beautiful to cover up something that was meant to be dark and ugly. Michael drew the line at roses and said if we were going with flowers, it should be deadly nightshades. But there were only so many nightshade flowers.

"So we each did our own research to find something that represented us. I chose Lily of the Valley because the drooping bell buds reminded me of pain, loss, and resilience in the face of adversity. It felt like a reflection of myself and my brothers. The others carefully chose their own too, which is why there are four different flowers."

I frown as I stare at the pretty ink that now seems alive with meaning. "Shouldn't there be *five* flowers? Emily didn't choose one for herself?"

"She chickened out when we got to the tattoo shop, the weakling." He chuckles, and I smile up at him.

"Now." His tone changes to something darker as he drops a hand to my face and lifts me from his arm. "Your turn to uphold your end of the bargain."

My heart stutters, then takes off like a racehorse, pounding wildly as I remember what started all this. His palm slides to the nape of my neck, his fingers pressing lightly, possessively, while his thumb grazes the sensitive skin there. A shiver ripples through me, goosebumps erupting in its wake, and when he leans closer, his warm breath fans my face, sending a teasing heat straight to my core..

My body reacts instinctively—my lips part, my eyes flutter shut, every nerve on high alert now. But he doesn't kiss me. No, the bastard brushes the corner of my lips, once, twice, then pulls away. My breath catches, and before I can recover, he moves to the other corner, repeating the maddening game.

Heat and frustration swirl in my veins, and a needly little sound slips out as I turn my head to chase his retreating lips. "*Maximo.*"

He chuckles darkly. "You've led me on a merry-go-round of want these past few weeks. If I want to torture you for a few seconds, you'll take it quietly like the good girl I know you are."

Good girl? Oh, *hell no.*

I whimper again, tightening my thighs around his hips and pressing my ass down on his now-hard cock in a silent rebellion against his taunts. But all he does is smirk, the cocky bastard, and as he finally leans down, a harsh knock on the window makes me jolt.

Whipping my head towards the sound, I spot Dante outside, waving his phone at Maximo impatiently. Wait. I glance around and realize the car is already parked in the underground garage of our apartment. *When did we even get here?*

"Fucking hell," my husband curses and releases me.

"No. Maximo." I grab his hand desperately; he can't just leave me like this—hot, needy, and spiraling towards frustration.

His intense gaze softens as he caresses my cheek, his thumb brushing my skin in that maddeningly tender way of his. "Hey, it's okay. We'll continue this later."

I groan as I reluctantly slide off his lap, my legs shaky with lingering tension. Maximo opens the car door and gets out, then helps me out.

"What is it?" he asks Dante.

Dante frowns at me briefly before turning back to Maximo. "We just got a call from the airport. The *kumicho*'s jet just arrived. It's a day earlier than expected, so the landing permit he has will expire in less than five hours."

Maximo mutters a low string of curses, then turns to me. "Go on in, *dolcezza*."

A slew of curse words flies around in my own head, but I swallow them down and rise onto my toes to press a quick kiss to his cheek. "Be careful," I tell him as I step away, then head towards the elevator, Marco close behind me. Heck, it feels like I spend more time with my bodyguard than my husband. Or maybe it's just my sexual frustration talking.

In the elevator, I slump against the railing, breathing in and out as I try to calm myself, though the sticky mess between my thighs isn't helping. Marco's presence beside me only makes it worse. There's something humiliating about standing next to a stone-face bodyguard while your body is buzzing from a makeout session that went nowhere.

By the time we reach the penthouse, my arousal has fizzled into a low simmer of irritation. I nod at the men in the hallway as I get out of the elevator and make a beeline straight to our bedroom. A cold shower is my only salvation at this point.

The icy water does its job, snuffing out the last remnants of heat and leaving me shivering but clear-headed. Afterwards, I pull my hair up into a tight ponytail and slip into my comfiest oversized shirt and pants.

Maybe it's for the best that Maximo had to leave so suddenly. Going from one extreme—the telling of his violent history—to another—the intensely charged kiss and arousal—would only soften my heart even more towards him, giving him the pass to wedge himself deeper than he already is. As if he isn't deep enough already. He's in my heart, my brain. When he's not with me, I'm thinking about him and wondering what he's doing.

Yes, this short reprieve is good. It will give me time to put things into perspective and compartmentalize. I nod to myself as I walk out of the bedroom and down the hallway, pausing to admire the artwork on the wall. Now that I know their meaning, I see them differently, appreciating the layers of thought and emotion behind them. But the hunger gnawing at my stomach leads me towards the stairs.

I was so distracted earlier, I forgot my takeout in the car with Maximo, so now I need to make something for myself.

Perhaps, I'll make some Italian cuisine and set up the dining area for dinner for two—a little mood-setting ahead of time. I could nibble on some of the leftover pastries I baked yesterday so Maximo and I can eat together. My lips twitch into a smile. Dinner for two. A warm meal, soft lighting... and then we'll see where the evening takes us.

My heart pounds in anticipation and my steps lighten as I practically float into the kitchen.

33

MAXIMO

"For fuck's sake, can this fucking thing move any slower?" I grouch, gripping the steering wheel tight as we follow the RV carrying the girls to the private airstrip where Yuto's jet is waiting to take them home. But at this pace, we might as well walk.

Dante's low chuckle beside me grates on my nerves. "Wow, I never thought I'd see the day when you're actually eager to go back home. Elira has you wrapped up around her finger."

I grunt, refusing to give him the satisfaction of a proper response. Instead, I check the time on my watch for the umpteenth time. There's no point denying what is so glaringly obvious—my little wife has me all twisted up inside for her. When this all started, could never have imagined her having an effect like this one me, but now... I wouldn't trade what we have for anything.

With a sharp exhale, I unlock my phone and call Perro, who's driving the sluggish RV. "Even a snail would leave you in the dust. Speed up."

"Yes sir." The vehicle lurches forward, and I can feel my muscles unclenching fractionally. *Good.*

Minutes later, we pull up onto the airstrip and drive down the tarmac, parking a few feet away from the medium-sized jet. As my men and I get out of our cars, Dante and a few others quickly guide the girls into a single file towards the jet's stairs.

Out of the corner of my eye, one of the girls breaks away from the others. It's Sachiko. She approaches me timidly, clutching something in her hands. I crouch to her level, meeting her wide, earnest eyes, and she wraps her arms around my neck in a quick hug.

"Thank you," she says sweetly, then holds out what looks like wilted green wool. "I made this for you."

I smile as I accept it, lifting it up into the lights for a better view, but I still can't make out what the green mess is supposed to be. "What exactly is this?"

"A four-leaf clover! For good luck. I knitted it myself." Her face lights up with pride. *Huh*. Now that she's said it, I can *kind of* see it—if I use my imagination.

"Wow, thank you, Sachiko. It's perfect," I pocket the improvised charm and offer a high five. Her tiny palm slaps mine, her infectious grin stretching impossibly wider.

But just as she turns to head for the jet—

CRACK.

A gunshot.

No time to think. Pure instinct takes over. I tackle Sachiko to the ground, my body a human shield, covering her completely as one gunshot turns to two, to three, and then multiple shots in rapid succession.

"Stay down!" I bark, the words practically torn from my throat. Around us, my men are shouting, firing back, or worse —falling. The thuds of bodies hitting the tarmac echo like a drumbeat of hell.

Fuck.

Sachiko's small body trembles beneath me. "W–what's

happening?" she whimpers, and I glance down at her tear-stricken face.

I keep my voice steady, even as adrenaline roars through my veins. "Nothing you need to worry about. We're getting you on that plane. You're going home. But you have to listen to me, okay?"

Her teary nod is the only answer I need. I scan the wide-open space. Whoever's shooting at us has the upper hand. Shots seem to be coming from everywhere, and we're just out here exposed—like fucking fish in a barrel.

We need to move. *Now.*

Slowly, I get onto all fours. "Get to your knees and crawl. Fast as you can. Stay low and don't stop," I command her.

She obeys instantly, and I crawl over her, guarding her from any stray bullets. My remaining men are trying their best to fight back, but we're losing ground fast, and I can't tell if we're hitting any of those fuckers shooting at us. These aren't random shots. This is coordinated. Planned.

Professional.

My mind races through potential threats. Who? Why now? Right when the girls are about to leave?

A bullet sparks off the ground inches from my head. I don't flinch. Can't afford to.

"Faster," I tell Sachiko, and she whimpers but picks up speed. Thankfully, the other girls are in the jet already, so I don't have to worry about them.

Halfway to the plane, the asphalt starts to tear at my knees and palms, but the pain barely registers. The screams of my men falling drown out everything else.

Shit, I hope she can make it.

Another bullet hits the ground we were just at, and I curse under my breath, snatching Sachiko up. No more subtle approach. We're targets now.

I shield her with my back and shoulders, pushing through

the searing pain in my knees as I run for the jet stairs. Then up we go, taking them two at a time.

Almost there. We're going to make it.

But just as I get to the top, a bullet hits my arm. *Fuck.* Pain tears through me, but I grit my teeth and keep moving, staggering into the jet with Sachiko still clutched to me.

I set her down. "Get in a seat and buckle up."

But she's frozen, her wide eyes locked on the blood pouring from my left arm. "B–blood..."

"Seat. *Now*!" I snap, and she finally scrambles to a seat.

Then I spin towards the pale flight attendant trembling near the cockpit. "Close the doors behind me and tell the pilot to take off immediately!" She nods, and I quickly take my gun out of the small of my back as I descend back down the stairs, my arm throbbing with every step.

The shooting has stopped and more than ten of my men are lying on the floor. Dead.

"Fuck." My curse is swallowed by the fans whirring to life—slowly at first, then gaining speed until the sound grows into a roar.

I move away from the jet as it begins to taxi down the runway. Good. At least the girls are safe. Staying on high alert, I make my way down the tarmac towards our cars, where the rest of my men are huddled, using them as cover.

As I stop in front of the first SUV, movement catches my eye—shadows emerging from the edge of the airport. Men with guns.

I stay still, watching as they approach us. My gaze locks on the woman leading the group. Something about her is so achingly familiar.

She steps into a sliver of light, and the breath is ripped from my lungs. *No. Fucking. Way.*

Brown hair pulled in a bun, and a face I know all too well.

She lifts a grenade, her fingers dancing over it with a calmness that makes my blood run cold, her light brown eyes cold as winter as they pin me in place. "Are you into the trading of humans now, Maximo? Little girls?"

"*Emily,*" I breathe, stunned.

She shakes her head slowly, clicking her tongue against her teeth. "When are you and the others going to stop? Drugs. Weapons. Murders. And now little girls?"

I don't bother to correct her. There's no time for words. I start striding towards her quickly, ignoring the sound of the men behind her cocking their guns at me. Let them shoot. She's going to hear me out, one way or another. But just before I reach her, she yanks the pin from the grenade and tosses it on the floor towards me.

My heart stops, my jaw dropping as I watch her hard face. Is this how I die? At the hands of a woman I consider my *sorellina*?

The grenade rolls past my feet, but instead of an explosion, it lets out an ominous hiss and white smoke spills out, curling and spreading fast. *Sedatives? No. Just normal smoke.*

Before I can react, three more grenades are hurled towards me and my men, releasing an avalanche of smoke. The haze wraps around me, suffocating, clinging, blinding. I can't see Emily. Hell, I can't even see my own damn hands.

Goddammit.

"Emily!" I shout, coughing as I push through the smoke. My steps are clumsy, the sting in my arm worsening with every move. I reach where she stood moments ago, but it's empty. Nothing but the ghost of her presence and a bitter chill in my chest.

She and her men are gone. What the hell? Why would Emily come to the city and shoot at me? Has she been in cahoots with the people messing with our business?

My arm throbs sharply, and I groan, taking off my jacket to tie it around my bleeding arm. The fabric darkens as blood seeps through, but it's not the worst of my concerns.

What the hell are you playing at, Emily? Have you really turned against us?

The shrill ring of my phone distracts me from my thoughts, and I take it out, frowning when I see the call is from my father-in-law. "Afrim."

"I heard a private jet landed from Japan this evening. Have you seen the girls off?" he asks and my frown deepens. How the fuck does he already know about the jet?

I clench my jaw. "I'm a little busy right now. We were ambushed trying to get them out. My men and I need time to regroup. I'll call you later."

"Wait!" Afrim's sharp tone stops me. "I found out who's the mastermind behind their kidnapping. It pains me to admit it, but it was Gjon, my very own second-in-command. He's been acting suspicious the past few days, and—" The words blur into background noise as my ears pop. Footsteps crunch on the tarmac behind me. I pivot, gun raised..

It's just Dante.

I lower the weapon with a slow exhale and signal for him to hold. "Listen, I'm glad you found the fucker, Afrim, and I trust you'll deal with him appropriately, but I have shit to deal with here." As I end the call with Afrim, my phone immediately starts ringing again.

Marco.

Ice fills my veins, and my spine stiffens with a bone-deep sense of dark déjà vu. Something is wrong. "Marco, what is—"

"Elira is missing!"

The world stops spinning. My heart stops beating. Everything narrows down to those three words. "What the fuck are you talking about?"

"She was in the kitchen making dinner when the fire alarm went off on the 9th and 12th floors. The men all ran to check it out, so I went out the door to stand guard. But then I noticed the stairwell door was open. When I went to investigate it, something hit me from behind, and I blacked out. When I woke up, I immediately ran into the apartment, but she was gone."

"Check the cameras. Who took her?" I ask calmly, even though I'm anything but calm. I need my wits about me if we're going to find her quickly.

"I already did. The feeds were tampered with; someone glitched the cameras to cover their tracks and—"

"Find her!" I roar, my nerves unraveling at the fact that we know nothing. "I don't give a fuck what you have to do. Find her. Now!"

This feels too goddamn familiar—a repeat of the missing shipment. Except this time, it's Elira. And I refuse to let her stay missing for longer than a few hours.

"If something happens to her—" My throat locks up, and I'm unable to complete the threat, but he gets my point.

I hang up and immediately hit the number two on my speed dial. I need reinforcement, and I'll call it all in if I have to.

"Well, well, to what do I–"

"*Michael*, someone hacked the cameras in my apartment and took my wife. I need you to get into those feeds and find out who it was and where they took her."

He's the best fucking hacker in the States, having hacked into NASA and several government systems like they were kids' puzzles. If anyone can recover the missing feeds, it's him.

"Fuck. What? Hold on." His tone becomes serious and clothes rustle on his end of the call as he moves around. A feminine voice says something I can't hear, and he responds with a cold, "Get the hell out of here. *Now*."

I start pacing impatiently, toes digging into my shoes as I walk. A door slams on his end, followed by the rapid click-clack of keys.

"I'm on it right now. I'm hacking into the cameras in your building and the public ones in the area. We'll find her, *fratello*."

I end the call, shove my hands into my hair, and let out an agonized roar.

Whoever took her better not touch a single curl on her head.

Because when I find them—and I will—I'm going to fucking peel the skin off their flesh, scoop out their eyes with a spoon, and make them choke on their own screams before cutting their doomed life short.

34

ELIRA

I step back from the fridge and close it, nearly jumping out of my skin when I see her—a young woman, who looks about my age, leaning casually against its side like she belongs here. Except I'm pretty sure she doesn't. She's shorter than me, her brown hair pulled back away from her face, highlighting her soft features. A button nose. Small pink lips. Pale brown eyes that glint with something unreadable.

She's stunning. And I hate that it's the first thing I notice.

My brows knit as I glance past her, scanning the kitchen and past the glass door to the living room, and even the shadows beyond, hoping Marco will storm in any second.

But he doesn't.

The fire alarm went off a few minutes earlier, and he had to run outside to guard the door while the men rushed downstairs to stop the fire from spreading. So I'm alone.

My pulse ticks faster. "Who are you? How did you get in?"

Her lips tilt up in a smirk, and she pushes away from the fridge. "So, Maximo really got himself a little Albanian wife. Interesting." The words drip with a bitter undertone that makes my skin prickle.

My frown deepens as I study her, not sure what to say to that. There's something off here.

I open my mouth to respond, maybe demand answers, but before I can string two words together, she moves.

Fast.

One second, she's near the fridge, and the next, she's right in front of me. My heart jolts as a healthy dose of fear settles in my spine.

No way she's an ordinary woman. That movement was smooth. *Too smooth.*

Instinct kicks in. I raise my fists, ready to take her in a fight, but she's faster. Her hand snatches my wrist, twisting it hard, and suddenly I'm spun around, her boobs pressed firmly to my back. "Mar—" I try to shout, but the sound barely escapes before something covers my nose—a pink bandana, sickly sweet and cloying.

Shit, not again, is all I can think as a wave of dizziness and fatigue crashes over me. My eyes roll back, vision fading as my limbs turn to jelly. Helpless, I sink into the darkness.

The soft vibration of an engine and the gentle sway of motion startle me awake. My head feels stuffed with cotton as I blink groggily at the back of the leather seat in front of me. Disoriented, I glance around.

I'm in a car. My gaze flicks to the window, squinting at the bright lights of the city whizzing past me.

A moving car.

What the heck?

The last thing I remember, I had just put the salad into the fridge and—I jerk upright as the rest of the memories rush through me. The sudden movement sends the car spinning in a dizzying haze, and a fierce headache erupts at the back of my skull.

"Ugh." Groaning miserably, I clutch my head, squeezing my eyes shut as I try to breathe through my nose and ground myself. Gradually, after what feels like an eternity, the spinning subsides, and the insistent throb at the back of my skull begins to ease.

When I finally dare to open my eyes, I lock onto the driver's seat. It's her. The woman from my kitchen is driving the car. The passenger seat is empty.

So, I'm alone in the car with her.

I glance out the window, straining to recognize the streets, but nothing looks familiar. Cold fear settles at the base of my spine. How long was I out? Where are we? *Are we even still in Queens?*

My voice cracks when I finally find it. "Who–who are you? Why did you—"

"Hi, Elira. I'm an old friend of Maximo's. Though he wasn't exactly thrilled to see me earlier." She shrugs carelessly, sparing me a brief glance through the rearview mirror. "I wish we could have met under better circumstances, but I doubted you'd follow me willingly."

An old friend of Maximo's? What does that even mean? "Follow you willingly? Follow you *where*? What do you want with me? Ransom money? Some—"

I'm cut short by her light laughter, and she stares at me through the rearview mirror again, brown eyes twinkling with mirth. "Ransom?" she echoes, like I've told a bad joke. "Please. I don't need yours or Maximo's blood money, Elira." Her laughter fades, and her expression shifts, softening into something almost... mournful.

"What I want," she says, voice quieter now, "is for your husband to stop." Her fingers tighten on the steering wheel, knuckles whitening. "To go back a couple of years and get my old friends back. I want them out of the clutches of that *fucker* and–"

Her breath catches on the last words, and her eyes darken with a rage so fierce it has me worried what she'll do if that anger is directed towards me. But then she exhales, shaking her head as if to banish the storm inside her. "What I want doesn't matter. It's impossible to get it anyway. But I *will* make them see the error of their ways."

Slow realization pierces my fog of confusion as I stare at the woman, and it all clicks into place. I *know* who she is—or at least, I know *of* her. "Where are you taking me, Emily?" If I hoped saying her name would rattle her, I'm in for some disappointment.

She simply gives me a cool, surveying glance through the rearview mirror, not even showing a flicker of surprise that I've figured out who she is. "I'm taking you somewhere you'll be safe," she answers. "I know all about how Maximo kidnapped you and threatened to kill your family if you didn't marry him. I'm saving you from him."

Somewhere I'll be safe? Away from *my husband*? My stomach twists violently at her words. "But I don't want to be saved from him," I say softly. She doesn't respond. Her silence, coupled with the unyielding determination on her face, squeezes my chest, making it hard to breathe.

She's not going to listen to me.

Panic claws its way through me, my body going ice-cold as I glance outside again. We must have taken a turn somewhere, because we're now driving through an old-looking area with cracked streets and little potholes that rattle the car, jostling me on my seat. Large, abandoned warehouses loom on either side of the road, their dark silhouettes casting an eerie shadow over the path ahead.

Shit. This is bad.

I can't let her do this to me. I won't be a victim again. *Never.* If she gets me to wherever it is she's planning to take me, I know instinctively that it will be over. I'll never be back in this city again. Never see my father or brother.

Never see my husband again.

The fear spreads through me, chilling me even further, and I shudder in horror. I want to remain with Maximo. It doesn't matter how we started, we've gotten to a better place now, and I love him and—I gasp, making Emily glance back at me with a furrow between her brows.

I love my husband.

Somehow, I've gone and fallen in love with the asshole, even though I tried my hardest not to, holding back my kisses like that would save my heart from him.

"Where is this 'safe' place you're taking me to?" I force the words out, trying to sound calm, even as my mind races through a dozen plans in a blur. I'm buying time, scrambling for anything to stop this. I refuse to be taken away from Maximo just when I've made the realization about my feelings for him.

No. I'm not some helpless girl, some damsel in distress. My brother made damn sure I wasn't going to be anyone's victim. It was bad enough that I let Maximo kidnap me, but back then, I was naïve, lost... vulnerable. No more. If there's anything I've learned from that incident, it's to never trust a stranger's motive, especially when they claim to be trying to help me—or in this case, trying to *save* me.

I glance around the car, searching for something I can use to make my escape, but the interior is squeaky clean and empty. Not even a bottle of water or a pen or used wrapper. But there has to be a way. There *has* to.

"You're going to Budapest," she answers, grabbing my full attention.

"Budapest?" I gape at her. That's like millions of miles away.

She nods. "That's the one place he won't think to look for you. A couple of documents are waiting for you on the plane. A brand new passport with your new name. You'll have to dye your hair—red is far too distinctive. Black or blonde will do. We'll change everything about you until even your father won't be able to recognize you. Tonight, Elira Përmeti—or rather, Elira Leonotti—will die."

I break out in a cold sweat, my heart roaring in my ears as I picture what she's saying. Erasing my identity? Changing everything that makes me *me*? "What—what if I don't want that?" I ask, not able to raise my voice past a shaky whisper under the weight of my fear.

Emily shakes her head, and for the first time, there's a flicker of something like regret in her eyes. But her voice remains firm. "I'm afraid that's not an option."

The car takes another turn, and suddenly, we're driving through a rusty gate into a wide sandy field where a small plane waits at the far end. And reality sets in. Unless I do something to change my fate, this is happening.

"What's the difference between what you are planning to do and what Maximo did to me?" The supposed kidnapping that she's attempting to rescue me from. Can she not see how horrible and demonic her plan is?

She glances at me as she slows the car down and turns off the engine, taking the key from the ignition. "I don't pretend to know Maximo's motive, but *I'm* saving you from him... and from yourself. This is for your own good."

My own good? What the hell is she talking about? My whole world is spinning, and she's acting like she's the hero here.

She rolls her neck, then—out of nowhere—pulls a gun and waves it at me. I immediately freeze as she speaks. "Now, I don't want to have to hurt you, Elira. So you must cooperate. Hold on, sit tight, and I'll be back before you know it."

She opens the door and slips out, slamming it shut behind her. Then her eyes fix on mine through the window, the gleam of the gun still in her hand as she lifts her key fob and locks the car with a soft *click*, trapping me inside.

35

MAXIMO

I tap my foot on the floor, my agitation growing with each passing second as the elevator slides up to my penthouse. My hands ache from being clenched so tight and the metallic taste of blood fills my mouth—I've been biting the inside of my cheek raw without realizing it.

"You need to remain calm, Maximo," Dante murmurs beside me and immediately takes a step away from me when I direct my glare at him.

"Calm?" The word comes out as a serpentine hiss. "My wife was stolen from under our fucking noses, inside my own home—where she should be the safest. This is as fucking calm as I'm going to get, Dante."

While we wait for Michael's intel on the scrambled feeds, I've decided to come back home. Though home feels like a mockery now, violated and empty.

The elevator doors slide open, and I storm out, Dante and Perro trailing behind me. My men are all lined up in the hallway, heads bowed in shame. They should be fucking ashamed. Fucking incompetent fools.

"Maximo, I–" Marco steps forward, but I don't let him

finish. My fist connects with his face before I even register moving. A satisfying crunch of cartilage is followed by a spray of blood as he grunts and staggers backwards.

The Glock materializes in my hand, trained between his eyes. The collective intake of breath from my men is almost musical. But Dante's there, his hand closing over mine. "Maximo." He shakes his head slowly.

I wrench away from his grip, holstering the weapon. "Pray," I spit at Marco, "that not a single fucking hair on her head is harmed." The threat hangs in the air as I shoulder past him into the penthouse.

I swallow around the lump in my throat when I walk into the kitchen and see the ingredients littered on the countertop. She was just cooking, damn it. Who the hell would do this?

My phone buzzes in my pocket. Michael. I answer instantly. "What did you find?"

He's silent for a moment, then he says thickly, "I've sent you the footage I recovered from the cameras. Check your email." He sounds shaken, but I don't have the time to worry about what might be going on with him.

I end the call and quickly scroll to my inbox. Two video files. My heart pounds as I hit download.

The first video shows the hallway outside the front door. I frown as I watch my men suddenly scramble for the elevator, likely when the fire alarm was tripped. Moments later, the emergency stairwell door swings open just as Marco walks out of the front door.

He glances down both sides of the hallway and does a double take when he notices the stairwell door ajar. As he starts walking towards it, I squint at the screen, catching movement above him. Pausing the video, I zoom in. One of the ceiling panels has been shifted, leaving a gaping hole.

When I press play again, someone dressed in all black silently drops down behind Marco and whips their gun at the back of his head, sending him sprawling to the floor, knocked out. The person tucks their gun into the small of their back and turns around, facing the camera.

I inhale sharply. *Emilia.*

What the fuck? How the hell did she get to my penthouse from the airstrip so quickly?

The video ends as she walks through the front door. Dread coils in my gut as I swipe to the second video.

In this one, I watch Elira closing the refrigerator after putting a bowl of salad inside and then jumps back when she sees Emilia standing right there. They exchange words, but I can't hear them. I had purposely disabled audio in my system to prevent sensitive information from being captured in case anyone hacked the feed.

My wife shifts back and raises her fists, ready to defend herself. She's brave, but no match against Emily's speed and expertise. My frown deepens as I analyze Emily's quick movements. She's good, too good. This isn't some random skill. She's been professionally trained.

She presses a pink cloth against Elira's nose, knocking her out, then slings her over her shoulder like she weighs nothing.

The camera pans to the hallway where Emily exits into the stairwell. She closes the door behind her just as the elevator doors slide open and my men pour out. They notice Marco's sprawled figure on the floor and rush to him, frantically trying to wake him up.

I close the video, fingers clenched tightly around my phone as I hit Michael's number again.

"I got into the camera on the eastern side of your building where that stairwell leads and was able to trace the path Emily's car took," Michael starts before I can say anything. "Sending you a picture of the car, plates, and the route now. I'll meet you there."

"Thank you, Michael," I tell him as I spin towards the living room where my men are waiting for me. They straighten the second they catch my expression, and for a moment, I imagine grabbing them by the collars and shaking some damn sense into them.

But I push past them, ignoring the insistent voice in my head saying even if we end up tracing Emily's location, it would be too late. She's too skilled for this to be her first time doing something like this.

"I—I had to tell the other guys about this new development, Maximo. Romero and his men are also coming to back us up."

"Good." I end the call and storm out of the house towards the garage, my men behind me.

Dante slides into the driver's side of my SUV, and I take the passenger seat, needing to be at the front of things. Around us, engines roar to life, and I tap my foot impatiently—a habit I didn't even realize I had—as the cars crawl out of the garage in a slow procession.

After the fifth car exits, Dante pulls out too, more vehicles following in line as we trace the route Michael sent us.

I study my map, frowning when I realize where Emily has taken Elira. An old industrial area, riddled with abandoned warehouses left to rot for who knows what reason.

I open the tracker app again and stare at it blankly, willing the tracker to come to life but no such luck. Whatever device Emily's using to hide their location is too damn good. My phone's screen dims and goes dark, and with a frustrated sigh, I drop it on my lap, glancing out the window impatiently.

"Can't we go any faster? Reach out to the lead car and tell them to floor it."

Dante nods and radios Perro. As the convoy picks up speed, my phone rings, and I frown at it. It's Rafael. "What?"

"Michael filled me in on what's going on. I'm sending some of my men to the location now. We'll find your wife, *fratello*."

My chest tightens, a lump forming in my fucking throat as

fierce emotion hits me. We *are* going to find her. We *have* to. "Thanks, brother."

"When you do, do not touch her."

I don't need to ask who the 'her' refers to. It's obviously not Elira, leaving only one other person—the woman I once considered a sister. "This is out of your jurisdiction, Rafael. It happened on my territory. She took my fucking wife."

There's a line you don't cross, and she fucking crossed it without a second thought. All bets are off.

"I know. And she will be punished. I'll make sure of that. But do not fucking touch her, Maximo. She's *mine*."

My jaw works furiously, but in the end, I just cut the call and slam my elbow against the window next to me, embracing the stinging pain that fills my being. Fuck Rafael. I decide what to do with the little shit. Little traitor.

Rafael might be the king of New York, but Queens is my fucking territory, and in this situation, my authority supersedes his.

Emily fucked around, and I'll make sure she fucking finds out. Family ties be damned.

36

ELIRA

As soon as Emily disappears from view, I scramble into the driver's seat and lean towards the glove compartment. I hold my breath as I tug it open, but thankfully it opens easily. She didn't lock it.

My trembling fingers sift through the mess of crumpled receipts, black face masks, and other useless junk, heart sinking into my stomach like lead as I realize why she didn't lock it. There's nothing here. Nothing I can use.

A sob escapes my lips, eyes stinging with tears as I teeter on the edge of giving up before I've even begun my escape attempt. But then—something sharp pricks my fingertips. I gasp and quickly close my hand around it. My chest tightens as I pull it out and hold it up like a lifeline.

An old, rusted screwdriver.

It *will* do.

Wiping my tears from my face, I glance out the windshield. Emily is standing next to the small plane, deep in conversation with two men. One of them is holding a thick hose attached to a nearby truck and seems to be attempting to connect it to the plane. They're fueling up.

That should keep them busy for a while. *I hope.*

I turn my attention to the dashboard, then the keyhole. My stomach twists into knots as doubt rears its ugly head. I don't know much about cars, and this one looks nothing like the old sedan Roan used to teach me how to hotwire. This setup looks more modern, more complex. The overwhelming helplessness creeps back in, whispering that I'll fail, that there's no way out. But I shove it down ruthlessly. *No.*

Come on, Elira. You can figure it out. So what if they're different cars? The same principle has to apply. Right? And I have to at least try. No time to second-guess myself.

With one last glance out the window to ensure they're still distracted, I grip the screwdriver tightly and get to work.

I squint, running my hand over the steering wheel, searching for the tiny screws holding the column in place. *There.* My heart skips with nervous excitement as I lean forward and try to undo the screws as quickly as possible.

Sweat dribbles down my back, and I keep darting glances out the windshield at close intervals. My fingers shake, slipping once, but adrenaline keeps me moving. First one screw. Then another. A third. Until all the screws are littered across the passenger seat. The panel comes off with a hard tug, and I toss it aside.

Exposed wires spill out like a tangled mess of colored snakes. For a moment, I just stare, the panic threatening to crawl back.

Be calm and try to figure out which wires are connected to the battery and which ones are connected to the ignition system. Roan's voice is cool and collected in my head and helps me compartmentalize.

The battery wires are usually red. The ignition wires, brown. Starter wires, yellow.

Roan's warning surfaces next. Be careful. Messing with the wrong wires might get you electrocuted.

A shaky, almost hysterical laugh escapes me at his wry warning, and a little tear rolls down my cheek. I have two choices: sit here, meekly waiting for Emily to smuggle me to Budapest, never to see Maximo or any of my family again... or risk being electrocuted and possibly escaping.

Decision made, I grab the red battery wires and dig my nails into the insulation plastic until I peel off about an inch. *At least I hope it's an inch.* Then I twist the exposed wires together. The dash lights flicker on, and I gulp, glancing up through the windshield, but thankfully Emily and her goons have their backs turned to the car as they fuel the plane, so none of them notices the faint glow of the dashboard.

I turn back to the car. Now for the most dangerous part. My heart thuds in my throat, and my hands shake as I wipe the sweat down my pants. I need dry hands for this. Stripping an inch off the brown starter wire, I hold it carefully in my right hand.

With my left hand, I pick up the twisted battery wires and pray to every god in the universe as I touch the exposed ends of the different wires together.

A spark bursts like tiny fireworks. My teeth clench, but I don't pull back. The wires meet again. Another spark. And again. Then, on the fourth try, the engine coughs to life with a low rumble.

Yes!

I carefully shift in my seat, pressing myself against the driver's door, as far away from the wires as possible. Dying from electrocution isn't on the agenda—not now that I've tasted victory.

The gearshift groans under my death grip as I yank it into reverse just as Emily's head snaps around. And then she's running, her eyes wide with realization, but it's too late. I floor the gas pedal, and tires scream in protest as I roll the steering wheel, sending the car into a sharp, reckless spin.

Her hand slaps against the car's trunk—too slow. I don't even flinch. I gift her my middle finger through the rear window, a final act of defiance as I slam the accelerator down with everything I've got and drive away from her, leaving her in a cloud of dust.

The car barrels towards one of the gates on my way out of the abandoned old airport and—*crack*—there goes the side mirror, snapping off like a cheap plastic toy and ricocheting across the ground. A maniac laugh bursts out of my throat, part adrenaline, part holy-crap-I'm-actually-doing-this hysteria. "Perfect!" I whoop.

But sweet victory doesn't last long. As I drive down the pothole-ridden road, uncertainty starts to creep in. I pass several turns, unsure which to take. I have no idea where I am. I could be *anywhere*. My heart pounds as I keep going straight, praying to break out of this forgotten neighborhood and into the city.

A curve comes up ahead, and I bite my lip as I lean into the left turn. The road stretches on until I reach a crossroad. My legs bounce nervously, my head swiveling between the options —right, left, right again—what the hell do I do?

Which turn? Which turn?

I tighten my hand on the steering wheel and decide on a right turn, figuring another left might just lead me back to where I'm coming from, and that's not a risk I'm taking.

The universe must be throwing me a bone for once, because suddenly my windshield fills with a constellation of harsh headlights from a convoy of expensive SUVs, and as I drive past the lead vehicle, my heart performs an Olympic vault straight to my throat. I *know* that car. Never been inside, sure, but I've seen it enough times in Maximo's garage to recognize it instantly.

Heart in my throat, I wrench the wheel hard, veering into the other lane, and slam on the brakes to block the next car in the procession. Tires screech as the convoy grinds to a halt. Several doors swing open, and heavily armed men spill out, pointing their weapons at the car. But I'm not scared. Not of them, at least.

With shaky hands, I unlock the car, able to override the lock mechanism because the engine is running. Then I shove the door open and stumble out.

Arms raised like a surrender flag, I backpedal away from both my car and the SUVs, putting as much distance as I can until I'm on the edge of the road. My eyes frantically scan the men for the one face I need to see. My husband's. And thank whatever deity is watching this madness...

"Elira?"

As I turn my head towards the sound of Perro's voice, relief floods my system for half a second before the world goes supernova. The car I just escaped explodes, a fiery blast of heat scorching my back as the force propels me forward. The ground rushes up to meet me and darkness follows close behind.

37

MAXIMO

As we turn into the industrial area, my car jerks to a sudden stop. "What the hell is this?" I snap, blood pressure spiking at the unexpected roadblock.

Dante doesn't answer. He's already out of the vehicle, snapping a quick photo before sliding back in. My men, fully armed, pour out of their cars and advance towards the front to check out the threat.

I accept Dante's phone and frown at the dirty vehicle that's now sandwiched between my cars. It looks familiar and—my heart damn near stops. "That's Emily's car." The picture of the vehicle and its plates that Michael had sent are burned into my memory.

Dante curses, his gun materializing in his hand as he throws the door open and jumps out again. I follow suit, my own weapon heavy in my hand. Each step tightens the knot in my gut until the scene unfolds into clear view.

The car door slides open, and out she comes—a tangle of red curls and shaky legs. Her hands shoot up, palms out, as she stumbles away from the car and my men. The world tilts and a roar fills my ears, drowning out everything else. *Elira.*

"Drop your fucking weapons!" My voice tears through the night like thunder, and thank Christ, Perro's already in the thick of it all, orchestrating the stand-down.

As I start to stride towards my wife, who's still backing away from my men, Dante grabs my upper arm. "Maximo, wait. This is too easy. What if it's a trap?"

I rip away from him, fury blazing through my veins. "Do I look like I fucking care?"

The words are barely out of my mouth when it happens.

Boom.

The explosion comes like judgment day—a flash of hell-bright orange that catapults Emily's car off the fucking ground and swallows it whole. My gaze hones in on my wife just as the force of the blast catches her, launching her small frame through the air like a broken doll until she crashes to the ground face-first with a sickening thud.

"Elira!" I shout from my soul as I charge towards her. Around me, my men scatter in a chaotic frenzy to dodge the hungry flames, but not everyone is lucky. Agonized screams cut through the crackling flames. Screams my mind blocks out, because my universe has narrowed to a single point: reaching the still form of my wife on the ground.

I hit the pavement hard enough to tear my pants, my hands already reaching for her when a bullet whizzes past my ear. "Goddammit." I gather her limp body against my chest, my heart threatening to explode when I feel her breath. She's unconscious, but breathing—thank fuck, she's breathing. And someone's shooting at us again for the second time this fucking night. Except now I know who it is.

Dante and Perro step in front of me, and the remaining men quickly form a protective shield around Elira and me as I carry her to my bulletproof SUV. I yank open the back door and slide inside with her in my arms. Once we're safely inside, the men move away to return fire, but Dante stays, slipping into the driver's seat.

"Is she okay?" he asks.

My chest tightens as I examine her scrapped face and neck. "Elira. Wake up, *dolcezza,*" I whisper, shaking her gently. Her pupils dance behind her closed lids, and I shake her violently now, scared out of my mind. "Please, *please*, *dolcezza*, open your eyes."

When her lashes flutter and those hazel eyes finally focus on me, the relief nearly breaks me. "Ma–maximo..."

"I've got you," I breathe, pulling her against me like she might vanish if I let go. "You're fine. You're fine." My voice cracks, the words tumbling out in a frantic mantra as I rock her, burying my face in her hair. The smell of smoke and ash clings to her, but she's here—she's alive. The crippling realization of how close I was to losing her has me unraveling. One minute later, or even one second...

"Maximo," she sobs into my shirt and hugs me back.

"Shh, it's okay, *amore*. I've got you. You're safe, you're safe. I'm never letting anyone hurt you. Never again. I swear it."

She nods into my chest as she cries. My eyes flick to the window, catching my men driving the attackers back while the flames from the burning car slowly die down.

Then suddenly, a sleek red sports car rolls past my SUV with a low rumble, pulling to a stop behind my men. My stomach knots until I recognize it—Michael.

The door lifts, and the bastard emerges like he's strutting onto a runway, rocking a pair of fucking sunglasses and a black leather jacket. His inked scalp gleams in the firelight, the ring on his thumb catching the glow as he runs a hand over his head. Completely unfazed by the chaos, of course.

Adjusting Elira in my arms, I roll down the tinted window so he can see me. He raises a pierced brow when our gazes connect, but his face softens a little when he spots Elira.

"There are you," he says, striding closer. "Is my *sorellina* okay?"

"She'll survive."

Elira stirs against me and lifts her tear-streaked face to glance at Michael.. He offers her a faint smile, though it looks more like a grimace, then shifts his focus back to me.

"Romero and his men are pulling up on the other side of the road to trap those fuckers. Get her the hell out of here. We'll end this."

I nod at him gratefully and roll my window back up as he returns to his car, takes out an M16, and lifts it with a wide grin before diving straight into the thick of it. I shake my head as I watch him go. Crazy motherfucker. He has a few loose screws, that one.

"Take us home," I tell Dante, who promptly starts the car. I pull up the privacy partition, and when I glance down, Elira's hazel eyes are already locked on mine, her expression a mix of exhaustion and... something deeper. Her trembling fingers trace over my jaw before her hands cup my face. Then she pulls me in, pressing her lips to mine—sweetly, yet carrying the weight of everything we've been through.

My heart swells, expanding almost painfully as I kiss her back as tenderly as I can with all the emotions running through me, my hands rubbing up and down her back, needing to feel her warmth, to remind myself she's really here—alive.

She breaks away with a shaky breath. "I thought I might never get the chance to do that again. Thought I'd never see you again. Never get to—"

"No. No matter where you go, I'll always find you. *Always*," I promise savagely, pressing my head against hers. "You're my life now, Elira. My everything. I would kill anyone who dares stand between us."

Her lips tremble as she smiles at me. "I love you, Maximo. You're a fucking thief—you stole my heart."

My eyes fucking sting, and I inhale sharply. "Fucking hell, Elira. I love you. *Sono innamorato di te.*"

Her watery laugh is the sweetest sound I've ever heard as she burrows her head into my chest, her wild curls tickling my chin. Behind us, gunfire continues to paint the night in muzzle flashes, but here, with her in my arms, I've found my peace in the chaos.

I shift her carefully, taking my phone out of my pocket to text Ethan to meet us back at the penthouse. Time to get my queen back where she belongs.

"We really need to stop meeting like this, Mrs. Leonotti," Ethan teases, though I can see the concern in his eyes as I walk into the living room with Elira in my arms. She's straddled to my chest like a koala because when I tried to carry her bridal style, she let out a scream. Guess the heat from the explosion seared her back. Damn it.

"I know, right? I seem to be getting into one scrap or another whether I want to or not," she responds dryly.

I take her up the stairs to our bedroom and carefully place her on the edge of the bed so she's sitting. When she peels off her shirt and twists her back at Ethan, the sight makes my blood run cold. Angry red blisters mar her skin, each one screaming at me for failing to protect her. But I shove down the guilt.

Thankfully, it's not as bad as it could have been. My mind betrays me with flashes of a worse scenario—her trapped in that metal coffin as it burst into flames. I shudder and promptly push the thought out of my head, uninterested in entertaining it.

Her small hand finds mine, anchoring me to the present. Those hazel eyes, still bright despite everything, look up at me with such trust it makes my chest ache. I sink down beside her, holding her hand tightly. I'm never letting her out of my sight again.

The room is filled with a heavy silence as Ethan carefully tends to her back, my wife occasionally wincing from the pain. When he finishes, he turns her around to inspect her face, frowning at the scrapes before cleaning them and sticking a plaster over her left brow.

"Well, I'm happy to announce that you'll live," Ethan says, stepping back from her with a smirk that doesn't quite hide his relief.

My wife chuckles, but it quickly turns into a pained wince. "Glad to hear that. I was starting to worry."

After Ethan leaves, I help Elira take off the rest of her clothes and gently carry her to the bathroom. I run a warm bath for her and ease her into it, careful not to get the gauze on her back wet. "We're moving out of here," I say while running a washcloth down her arm. "To somewhere more remote and secure."

Her brows knit together as she watches me. "I love this place."

"Well, I don't. I think I might build a compound like your father's and lock you up tight so nobody can ever get to you."

"I hope that's a joke, Maximo. I'm not going to be a prisoner." She lifts her chin stubbornly, and I smile faintly as I flick some water on her face.

"You're not going to be a prisoner. But I'd feel better knowing no one could ever get in, no matter how good they are. I hate seeing you hurt."

"I'm no damsel in distress, Maximo. I think I did a great job rescuing myself." She nudges my arm playfully. "If you hadn't been halfway to my rescue, I might have just turned up here on my own."

True. I'm beginning to learn just how capable my wife is. "How did you even get away from her?"

She launches into the story, her voice animated as she tells me about hotwiring the car after Emily got out to talk with some men fueling a plane, my heart stuttering when she mentions the wires sparking. God, she's incredible.

My brave girl.

I lean forward and kiss her temple. "Remind me to send Roan some flowers or something for teaching you how to hotwire a car."

"Forget Roan. How about you give *me* some flowers for hotwiring the car successfully." Her hand falls on my arm, and her fingers start tracing over my tattoo. "I'm thinking... a Lily of the Valley or two."

I study her face, trying to gauge her seriousness. "You want a tattoo?"

"Not just any tattoo. Yours. This one." She taps my lily of the valley tattoo, and my heart fucking spills up to my throat.

"I love you so fucking much," I murmur as I lean down to kiss her on the lips this time.

I don't deserve her, but I'll spend the rest of my life treating her like the queen she is.

EPILOGUE

ELIRA

A week later...

"Are you ready?" Maximo's voice is dark honey, his eyes gleaming with that predatory anticipation that makes my insides liquify. I bite my lip as I nod, ignoring the hard pounding of my pulse.

His answering smirk is pure sin as he leans forward to press those wicked lips onto the tight skin of my upper arm. The motion shifts his powerful thighs beneath me, and when his cock grinds against my core, an involuntary moan escapes from my throat. My fingers dig into his arm for stability—or maybe just sanity.

He wiggles his brow as he leans back from me. Then his hand drops to my ass, rearranging me until the insistent hardness of his cock throbs exactly where it drives me wild, sending little shocks of pleasure through me. The distraction nearly works while he cleans the area around my upper arm where the scar from the gunshot sits. I shiver when the cool alcohol touches the shaved area, and I try to stay still, but it's harder than expected.

Then he grabs the stencil sheet on the table next to him and carefully holds up the tattoo design against the spot I've chosen —directly around my scar. The flesh tingles, becoming a little ticklish, and I giggle helplessly as he fumbles with it until he's satisfied. When he finally lifts the moisture stick, the sensation fades, and I blow out a shaky breath.

"Ticklish?" he teases.

"Just hurry up," I mutter, heat blooming in my cheeks.

But instead of grabbing the tattoo gun, his hand slips to my nape and pulls me into a wowzer of a kiss. I clench my thighs around him, gripping his arm harder as he thrusts his tongue into my mouth with domineering force. My head falls back listlessly, my panties becoming damp as he deepens the kiss, sucking my tongue into his mouth.

I'm breathless by the time he breaks the kiss.

"I love you," he murmurs against my lips. "Thank you for trusting me to do this."

All I can do is stare at him through lust-hazed eyes, completely drunk on him. He chuckles, brushing his thumb over my chin before picking up the tattoo gun. That clears the fog of lust, and I tense in his arms.

"Relax, *amore mio*." His voice is soothing, but still I whimper as the machine buzzes to life, squeezing my eyes shut when he brings the needle close to my skin—I can't watch.

I inhale sharply, holding my breath as tiny pinpricks, like a thousand bee stings, attack my flesh. My nails dig crescents into Maximo's arm, while the pain drags on for agonizing minutes. Tears spill uncontrollably down my cheeks, and I sniff, biting down on my lip until I taste the metallic tang of blood.

"You're doing so good for me, *dolcezza*," Maximo praises. "Breathe for me."

Breathe? Oh yeah, air. I part my lips, blowing out the breath

I've been holding, and the intense pain slowly melts into a faint burning sensation. Then I dare open my eyes and peek down at Maximo's focused expression as he traces the design.

For the next several minutes, I just watch him, the soft buzzing of the tattoo gun and his occasional words of reassurance the only sounds in the room. Maybe it's the endorphins, or maybe it's just my husband's particular brand of pain and pleasure that I've grown addicted to, because soon the stinging from the needles gradually morphs into white-hot, aching heat that spreads through my body, pooling low and insistent.

I squirm on his lap restlessly, trying to drag my clit against his cock through his pants.

"Stay still," he commands quietly, but the warning in his tone makes me whimper. My arousal builds steadily with every glide of the tattoo gun across my arm until I can't stay still anymore. *Damn the consequences.* I start to writhe in his lap, just as he lifts the tattoo gun from my arm.

"Great job, *dolcezza.*" He glances up at me and goes still at whatever he sees on my face. "Elira?" His gaze searches mine, a bolt of lust entering his onyx eyes. Holding his stare, I deliberately grind my core against him.

He groans, his hands dropping down to my ass, kneading the flesh and holding me still. "Maximo," I whine, twisting against his hold, but his grip is unrelenting.

"Fuck," he curses, releasing me slightly. I take advantage of my freedom and roll my hips again, this time pressing down on him so I can feel every single ridge of his erection. The friction is perfect, sparking an electric jolt that has me gasping and shivering all over.

"Elira, wait, hold on–" His voice cracks, and I almost smirk at the strain in it, but then he clamps down harder on my hips. "Shh, it's okay, sweet. I'll give you what you want. But we need to finish your tattoo first."

I swallow the dramatic cry that builds at the back of my

throat and drop my face into his neck quietly. Sensing that I'm yielding to him for now, he releases me and caresses my ass in slow, soothing strokes. "I know, sweetness. Just a few more minutes."

He picks up another tool and works gently over my arm. The precision in every turn of his wrist should not be as arousing as it is. But dammit, I can't stop watching him. The flex of his forearms, the slight furrow of concentration in his brow—it's all too much.

Everything feels so overwhelmingly stimulating, and my skin is so hot, I feel like if he doesn't touch me, I might just burst out of my skin, and if he *does,* I might detonate—and—

"Done," he finally says, shifting back, grinning proudly at his handwork as he drops the tool and carefully applies a layer of ointment over the flesh. "You should look at it before I cover it with the bandage."

I drag my gaze from his stupidly handsome face down to my arm and gasp. "Maximo, it's *stunning.*"

I told him I wanted a Lily of the Valley covering the scar that formed where Roan's bullet hit me, and that's what he's inked into my skin.

Pretty green stems with drooping white bulb wrap around my upper arm like a cuff, sloping down to just above my elbow. It blends so seamlessly, I can't even make out the scar I know is there. In place of the thorns in his own tattoo, he's inked tiny ornamental dots that remind me of baby's breath, tying up the design beautifully.

He grins and presses a small kiss on the inside of my elbow just below the tattoo, then carefully covers my arm with a bandage and pats it cutely.

"Now, where were we?" His hand snakes around my front, cupping my right tit possessively. He squeezes gently, rubbing his thumb over my nipple until it puckers, tightening painfully, sending a jolt of pleasure rushing through me. My clit throbs in response as my dormant arousal makes itself known.

He moves his hips just the slightest bit until the broad head of his cock snags on my clit through our clothing, rubbing that needy bud deliciously. My head tips back as I moan throatily, catapulted closer to my orgasm.

Then he bucks his hips hard, jolting me in his arms, and I cry out as sweet pleasure assaults me. I clutch his shirt to hold myself steady in his arms as he does it again, and again, each thrust obliterating whatever control I thought I had left. My eyes roll to the back of my head, and for a moment, I swear I can almost taste the heady orgasm hanging just out of reach.

But it's not enough. *I need more.* My gaze drops to his lips and my mouth waters. Leaning down, I capture his mouth with mine, greedily claiming him. His lips part willingly, and my entire body shudders as fireworks ignite under my skin. I deepen the kiss, swallowing his groan, losing myself in the loud roaring filling my ears until it's all I can hear.

I quicken the movements of my hip across his lap, desperate for my orgasm, wanting more, needing to—

"*No!*" I wail, clutching him tighter as he breaks the kiss and stills his hips beneath mine. "Maximo, please darling, get me to the finish line, and I'll love you forever."

His brows furrow, and he raises a hand to my cheek. "In English, *dolcezza*. I have no idea what you just said."

I frown at him, my brain buzzing. Then I realize I just spoke in Albanian. Before I can repeat myself, the loud roaring in my ears starts up again. But then I hear it more clearly—it's coming from his computer. I twist slightly to see the screen flashing with an incoming conference call.

No. Actual tears sting my eyes because I know who's on the other side of that call, and that it means the end of this interlude.

Maximo sighs, presses a quick kiss to my cheek, then joins

the call. The hard faces of Michael, Rafael, and Romero fill the screen, and I stiffen in Maximo's arms.

Romero notices first, and his sharp gaze warms into a smile. "Hello, *sorellina*. How are you today?"

I now know *sorellina* means little sister, and it's kind of sweet, though I'm too flustered to enjoy it. I burrow into Maximo's chest to hide my hard nipples as I murmur a hello. The others greet me as well, and I notice their faces seem to soften a little when they address me. It makes my heart light, knowing they're beginning to accept me.

I start to slide off Maximo's lap to give them privacy for their meeting, but his arm tightens around my waist. "Stay," he murmurs in my ear. "I'll try to discharge them quickly so we can get back to what we were doing."

My cheeks heat up, and I'm sure I'm as red as a tomato, so I hide my face in his chest.

The guys dive into business talk, and I zone out, bored by what they're saying, until Michael brings up Emily.

"I finally tracked the rerouted shipment order. It leads back to Emily. Took me weeks to crack the system—way too sophisticated for her to pull off without help. I don't think she's working alone."

Maximo stiffens. "I *know* she's not working alone. Someone's backing her. Someone powerful."

There's a tense pause, then Rafael chimes in. "She's working within the system. She's in a government agency."

Romero leans forward. "What government agency?" he demands.

Rafael shrugs slightly. "Just know that someone high up isn't happy with the amount of power we've accumulated, and they're trying to sabotage us. They won't get anywhere, of course. They might give us minor setbacks, but they'll never take away the power we worked so hard to achieve."

"I'm going to look into whatever this government agency is.

The CIA? FBI? DIA? Not that it matters, they can't just fuck with our business," Michael growls. "I'll crack their system and destroy everything."

"Where does Emily stand in all of this? Is she just a tool that's being leveraged against us, or does she have her own game?" Romero asks quietly. "We need to know that before we can move forward."

Even though the question isn't directed at me, I push away from Maximo's chest and answer. "She seemed angry. Like, very angry. It felt personal—like she's after revenge. But..." I hesitate, feeling their eyes pin me in place, and I stifle the urge to cower. "I'm not sure. It's just what I got from the little time I spent with her and her cryptic words. She wants revenge, but I think she also still cares about you guys. She mentioned something about wanting her old friends back."

"Too fucking late," Maximo snaps. "She should have thought it through before she kidnapped you and attempted to ship you out of the country, away from me."

"She didn't hurt me," I remind him, but he just growls. "In fact, she seemed to be under the impression that she was saving me from you. Just like she wants to save you and the guys."

"Save us?" Michael snorts. "Save us from what?"

"Her exact words were: 'I want them out of the clutches of that fucker'. But I don't know who." I shrug as I speak, but I catch a subtle shift in Rafael's expression. It's so faint that if my gaze hadn't landed on him, I wouldn't have noticed. I frown, wondering if he knows more than he's letting on.

"I'm afraid I don't care to find out what Emily's motives might have been," Maximo says. "I care about her, as I'm sure everyone else in this meeting does, but she not only fucked with our business—she also fucked with my wife. *My wife*," he repeats, his tone hardening, and I have to place a soothing hand over his chest.

"She tried to take Elira from me," he continues. "And that's one thing I'll never forgive. She better pray I never find her."

Before anyone can respond, he ends the call, chest heaving with barely contained rage. I know that look. He's not ready to hear any defense of Emily's actions. So I'll bring the subject up again later.

I let it hang for a beat before I nuzzle against him and slowly raise my hand to his face, threading my fingers into his hair as I suck his neck. "I think," I whisper, my lips brushing his skin, "we were right about *here*." I roll my fingertips over his nipple, feeling his sharp inhale.

He chuckles gruffly and tugs at my shirt. "Right here, indeed," he says as he pushes his head between my breasts.

BONUS EPILOGUE

EMILY

Two weeks later...

I rub my sweaty palms down the front of my pants, parting my lips slightly as I time my exhales to the pounding staccato of my heart and the low footsteps that have been tailing me relentlessly—three blocks now without a single tactical error.

Thump, thump, thump. Exhale.

Thump, thump, thump. Exhale.

Thump, thump, thump. Exhale.

Who the hell could it be? This isn't one of Maximo's men—they have never managed to track me this cleanly. No, whoever this bastard is, he's in a different league.

Doesn't matter who, though. He picked the wrong target tonight. This cat-and-mouse game ends now.

12th Street stretches out in front of me, and I purposely slow my pace just enough so my stalker doesn't suspect anything as I turn the next corner. Once I'm safely out of sight, I dash over to a narrow gap between two tall buildings and flatten myself into the shadows, my heartbeat racing as I wait for him to take the bait.

He doesn't disappoint.

Right on cue, I catch a glimpse of movement. He slows and scans the empty alley. All I can make out is the shadow of a very tall, very muscled man, his face hidden beneath a dark baseball cap. Damn it, who the hell is this guy? No way this is some random stalker who spotted me on the streets of New York. I grit my teeth. If I wasn't a highly trained U.S. agent, I might never have realized he was there at all.

I watch, waiting as he surveys the area. Then, just for a split second, he angles his body a few degrees away from me. That's all I need. It's go time.

With my weight balanced on the balls of my feet, I sneak up behind him, gun drawn and ready.

The instant I close the gap, I jam the muzzle right against the back of his skull and flick off the safety. "Who are you? Why are you following me?"

The stalker slowly raises both hands, but he stays maddeningly silent. Frustrated, I dig the gun harder into his head. "You don't seem like one of Maximo's underlings. Who do you work for?" Nothing. Deafening silence. I want to scream. And I do. "Tell me who sent you!"

Ever since I kidnapped Elira two weeks ago, Maximo has been sending his men after me nonstop. A pointless, desperate waste of manpower in his misguided attempt to hurt me because of what I did.

Evading those fools has been child's play.

So why is this guy—

In a burst of movement almost too quick to process, he whirls around, reaching for my gun. *Oh no you don't!* I leap back, aiming a brutal kick at his calf while simultaneously swinging my arm to knock away his hand.

But it's like he saw it all coming. He twists effortlessly out of the way and somehow manages to punch the gun clean from my grip. Damn it! The weapon clatters to the ground and skids away into the darkness. But I don't waste time crying over it.

Feigning retreat, I take a step back, only to spin around and drive my foot into his chest with every ounce of power I have. The impact sends him staggering several feet, arms windmilling as he fights to keep his balance. While he's distracted, my eyes dart, searching frantically for my lost gun.

There!

He seems to spot it the same time I do, and we both lunge for the weapon. But I'm faster. I hurl myself forward, reaching, grasping. My fingers close around the handle, relief surging through me—

A quiet snick pierces the air, and cool metal kisses my throat. I glance down and see a knife poised right over my jugular.

"I wouldn't do that if I were you, *piccola.* Why are you still in my city?"

The world stops spinning.

That voice. Those words. *It can't be...*

My fingers tighten around my gun reflexively as my throat closes up for a moment. "Rafael?"

"It's rude to answer a question with a question. But then again, you've always been a little impudent."

It *is* him.

I swallow hard against the knife still pressed firmly to my throat. "What do you want? Are you here to kill me?" Now that I know who it is, adrenaline rushes through me, and my finger slips to the trigger. If I'm dying tonight, I'll make damn sure I take him with me.

"I wasn't planning on it," he starts with a scoff. "But now, I'm rather tempted to do so."

I take that as a no, so I slowly reach up to push his knife away, my palm getting slightly nicked in the process. *What a wickedly sharp knife.* I wipe my hand down my pants to clean off the blood as I slowly get to my feet. His knife stays pointed at me, so I raise my gun, aiming dead center at his chest.

I squint, trying to make out his face, but the shadows from his cap and the glare of the distant street lights hide his features. So damn frustrating. I need to see his eyes. I need to know what he's thinking.

"Holster your gun so we can talk," he orders, giving the knife a little wave for emphasis. Is he kidding me?

"How about you sheathe your knife first, then we'll see about talking?" I return sharply. His lips quirk up in that familiar, infuriating smirk, and my blood boils.

"Let's both lower our weapons together. On two. Ready?" He pauses, waiting until I give a tight nod. "One... two."

Neither of us so much as twitches. Weapons still out, still aimed.

"Why are you following me, Rafael?"

"Elira. Two weeks ago," he says flatly. "What the actual fuck, Emilia? She could have lost her life."

Even though his voice stays level, I can feel the pure, seething rage roiling off him. He spits out a curse and lowers the knife. With a deft flick of his wrist, the weapon vanishes up his sleeve.

But I don't lower my gun. I keep it trained on him, finger dancing along the trigger. *This is it*—my chance to kill him. Despite my betrayal all those years ago, he still has a measure of trust in me, huh? Enough to let his guard down.

He's wide open. Defenseless. I can end this, end *him*, once and for all. End the man who murdered my father.

Do it! Pull the trigger!

I glare at him, my finger twitching. Every instinct screams at me to do it, but I... I can't. Maybe it's because of his darned near constant interference in my life over these past few years. I feel like I owe him. The bastard has saved me from a tight pinch more than once.

This is why I hate owing people.

"*Emilia.*" His voice holds a maddening calm, his posture relaxed, like he just doesn't give a fuck if I decide to shoot him or not. *Fuck him, and fuck me too for being too principled to just pull the damn trigger.* Like he can read the decision in my gaze, he says, "I know you're not going to shoot me. Drop the fucking gun and explain what the hell you were thinking kidnapping Elira."

My glare fades, and with a sharp exhale, I slowly holster my gun, shoving aside the biting guilt that's been on my heels since the incident two weeks ago. "It wasn't supposed to go that far. You guys made it escalate, not me," I try to say flippantly.

"What?" he snarls. He reaches up and rips off his cap in a burst of fury, fingers tearing through that dark hair I used to love to touch, and my lungs forget how to work. "You fucking broke into Maximo's house and *kidnapped his wife*. This after shooting at him at the fucking airstrip, almost costing him his life and the lives of the kids with him!" His voice rises at the last notes, practically a shout.

"I saw the last child get on board before my men and I opened fire." Despite telling myself not to care what he thinks of me, defensiveness wraps around me like armor. "I didn't know there was still one more with him."

The memory flashes in my mind. When I got the intel that Maximo and the *Nightshades*—those bastards with their ridiculous nickname—had gotten their hands on over a dozen little girls, my mind just blanked out. I didn't think. I couldn't think. I abandoned my post in Chicago, mobilized a few of my colleagues, and went after them even before getting approval from my supervisor. All I could see was what happened nine years ago playing out all over again.

The reminder of what happened nearly a decade ago fans my anger, burning away any lingering guilt and defensiveness —for now. "I wanted to rescue the girls, not kill them. And we used low-caliber bullets that wouldn't pierce the plane's hull."

"So why did you leave so quickly when you couldn't rescue them?" There's a note of derision in his voice, but it doesn't cut through the fog of my emotions, and there's a host of them battling inside me. "Shouldn't you have stayed until you got them out?"

I don't miss the contempt in his steel-grey eyes or the flicker of something hotter—an anger tinged with desire that echoes my own internal war when it comes to Rafael Moretti. He's a monster. What he did nine years ago... there aren't words. He did worse than traffic girls. That's why I was so reckless with the shooting two weeks ago, why I couldn't let history repeat itself. And yet, that's not even the worst of his crimes.

So what does it fucking say about me that I still care about his monstrous hide?

My hands curl into fists at my sides, my arms shaking with the conflicting urges assaulting me. I want to punch him, claw his damn eyes out with my nails, sink my teeth into his ears and tear and tear until he screams. But God help me, at the same time... I want to kiss him. I want him to hold me and tell me I'm not alone. *Not alone.*

Except I *am* alone.

Because of him.

I spin around, taking one unsteady step, then another. I have to get the hell away from him. I have to clear my head before I do something reckless again.

After the incident, I've been put on a month-long 'break' from work. Some fucking vacation. And why? Because I made a damn fool of myself. It turns out Maximo and the guys weren't trafficking the girls at all, but saving them. Yes, *saving* them.

And Elira, well, she never needed me to rescue her from Maximo.

I fucked up. I fucked it all up. Almost lost my colleagues[C1] their jobs too. Hell, I'm lucky I still have mine. I can't risk another disaster now. Not after this. If I screw up again, I'll definitely lose my job. And I can't, I can't, I can't.

It's the only thing I have now.

A rough, warm hand clamps around my upper arm, sending sparks through my body as I'm wrenched back around to face him. I gasp, my eyes widening up at Rafael. He's so close I can see the flecks of light blue dancing in his silvery gaze.

"I'm still talking to you, damn it. You think this is like last time?" His voice is a low growl, demanding, but when his eyes search mine, I see a little bit of his anger drain away.

"And what time is that?" I ask, grateful I don't sound breathless, because I *am*. God, I am. I can barely draw in air without getting a mouthful of his drugging cologne. And he's so close, so close—too close.

I can't get my eyes off his lips, from the perfect curves and planes of his gorgeous face. Damn him. He fucking hurt me so deeply, I should hate him. *Hate him, hate him, hate him*. I *do* hate him. So why can't I crush the rest of the foolish emotions that mix with the hate every damn time I see him?

Even so, hatred isn't supposed to make you ache like this, isn't supposed to make you want to taste and touch and—

"What time, Rafael?" I repeat, getting a little angry now. Anger is safer than desire. Anger I know how to handle. "The time you gave me that disgusting 'gift'? Or when you–"

"That time I found out you still have that 'disgusting' gift," he taunts with a ghost of a smile that sends a fresh wave of anger and maddening lust through me. "That you keep it close..."

"It's evidence," I bite off, trying to pull my arm free from his grip. But he only tightens his hold, trapping me against him. Damn him, I can't breathe, I can't think. I'm on the verge of doing something reckless.

His smirk widens. "Evidence you say, then why—"

I surge up on my toes and crush my mouth to his, cutting off his words. I only mean to shut him up. I need him to stop taunting me, just for a second, so I can *think*. And try to breathe.

It's supposed to be just a light peck to put him in his place. But the moment our lips meet, it's like he's been waiting—expecting me to cave. His grip on my arm tightens even further, his free hand sinking into my hair as he kisses me back with fervent hunger. No, he *devours* me.

Electricity crackles in my brain, sending bright sparks behind my closed lids, and the rest of my thoughts fizzle out until I can only feel. And oh, what glorious feelings. It's like coming home, like finding the missing piece of myself.

Like I'm drowning and he's air.

His tongue forces my lips apart, and I gladly let him in, moaning when he gains access, my arms lifting to wind around his neck. I thrust my tongue up to meet his, letting it glide against the rough ridges of his mouth. A deep groan vibrates in his chest, echoing through my body, and my core contracts, leaking wetness as if on command.

My fingers dig into the corded muscles of his neck as he deepens the kiss further. He eats out my mouth, drawing my tongue between his lips and sucking hard enough to make my knees buckle. The sound that escapes me is barely human as I claw at him, pressing my body closer until I feel his cock, hard as steel against my stomach.

I gasp at the contact, breaking the kiss briefly as I release one hand from his neck to caress down his body and cup the rigid heat straining through his pants. *Mine.* The primitive thought scares me, almost jolting me out of my lustful haze. But Rafael's fingers tangle in my hair, massaging my scalp, and the fear fades into a needy moan.

Oh God. I want it. I want him inside me.

My fingers tighten on his cock as I start to rub him up and down through the fabric, earning a hiss from his lips. His hands slide down to my ass, gripping firmly, and with no warning, I'm lifted off the ground as though I weigh nothing. I gasp again, instinctively wrapping my arms around his neck.

For an endless, aching moment, we just stare at each other breathlessly, chests heaving. Then he leans in and claims my mouth again. But this time, his eyes stay locked on mine.

And for the first time in years, I feel that familiar pressure building in my head, my brain crawling as I stare into someone's eyes.

Come back to me.

I snap my eyes shut against the sudden, crystal-clear thought and push at his chest, trying to drown out the deep ache blooming in my heart.

He breaks the kiss with a wet pop. "Emilia? Are you okay?"

The hand on his chest closes into a fist, and suddenly I'm hitting him as tears I can't stop slip down my cheek. "Hey, *piccola*, what is it?" His voice is so soft, so tender, it almost breaks me. My eyes remain stubbornly shut as I try to gain control of my emotions and the unbearable ache.

"Let me down," I murmur. A plea. I hate how small and broken I sound. His hands tighten around me instead. The contradictory asshole. "Please, Rafael. Just... let me go."

He hesitates. For a terrible, airless moment, I think he won't. That he'll keep holding me, caging me against him. But then, slowly, he lowers my feet back to the ground. His hands stay on my hips, though, burning through my clothes.

I force my eyes open, risking a glance up at him, and nearly drown in the well of concern and hurt on his face. It's so much, I almost fool myself into believing he's the man I fell for so long ago. The man who asked, no, demanded I become his wife. But he's also the same man who did what he did, knowing how much it would destroy me.

"I can't do this with you." I can't. I can't. I can't.

I turn away from him as self-loathing hits me. *Whore. Slut. What is wrong with you, shagging up with the enemy. Are you that hard up for it? That lonely? Fucking–*

"Emilia." Rafael's voice stops the voices in my head, and I glance at him one last time.

"I'm sorry Elira got caught between us, and I…" My voice catches, because I know that if they didn't hate me before, the other guys surely do now. I hate myself for what I did through my thoughtlessness. I hate that my hatred for Rafael means I have to lose out on a relationship with them.

Some hatred, my mind mocks. *You were just sucking tongues with the devil.*

I drag in a shuddering breath. "I'm sorry," I rasp again, forcing the words out past the jagged lump in my throat. "I really am."

Then I run.

I bolt down the alley as fast as my shaking legs will carry me. I don't look back. I can't. Because if I do, if I see his face, I'll break. I'll shatter into a million pieces right there on the filthy concrete.

So I run. I run until my lungs burn and my muscles scream. I run until the sobs finally break free, tearing out of me in great, wrenching heaves. I run from him, from the memory of his hands, his mouth, his eyes.

But most importantly… I run before I give in to one of my most compulsive desires.

Fucking him.
Or killing him.

NEXT IN THE SERIES

The next book in the series is Devil's Tulip!

Devil's Tulip Amazon Page - click here.

ALSO BY SASHA LEONE

Soulless Empire

King of Ruin

Lord of Wrath

God of Lies

Crown of Hate

Ruthless Dynasty

Ruthless Heir

Lethal King

Sinful Lord

Unholy Tsar

Brutal Reign

Merciless Prince

Brutal Savior

Cruel Knight

Wicked Master

Twisted Lover

Savage Don

Nightshades

Wicked Mistletoe

Devil's Lily

Devil's Tulip

Devil's Azalea

Printed in Great Britain
by Amazon